Praise for

Real Vampires Have More to Love

"The Glory St. Clair series is, for me, fresh, fun and light-hearted. I'll keep reading 'em as long as Gerry Bartlett keeps writing 'em."
—*Romance Reviews Today*

"Each book is like coming home and catching up with old friends. These books are keepers."
—*Night Owl Reviews* (top pick)

"If you are a fan of the paranormal genre and you like your vampire stories with healthy, heaping doses of humor and spice, I cannot recommend *Real Vampires Have More to Love* enough."
—*TwoLips Reviews*

Real Vampires Hate Their Thighs

"Laugh-out-loud fun . . . the story that sets up several interesting prospects for future Glory adventures. *Real Vampires Hate Their Thighs* has a reserved spot on my keeper shelf!"
—*Fresh Fiction*

"The chemistry between Glory and Jerry is explosive. But when you add in the secondary characters, the result is non-stop laughter! Gerry Bartlett brings Glory to life and deals with the problems we all face. There is a little something for every reader in this story: sex, laughter, romance and a surprise ending that leaves you wanting more."
—*The Romance Readers Connection*

continued . . .

Real Vampires Don't Diet

"Fun and fast moving with lots of action." —*Romantic Times*

"An engaging urban fantasy filled with action and amusing chick-lit asides. Glory is terrific." —*Midwest Book Review*

"Provides the adventure and surprises fans have come to expect from this fun series, with more turmoil and temptation than ever." —*Darque Reviews*

"Another must-have. In her trademark witty voice, Gerry Bartlett adds another chapter to her highly entertaining series. What I love about these books is the lighter tone and humorous play on vampiric lore. *Real Vampires Don't Diet* is honestly a tasty treat that's sure to please even the most discerning palates." —*Romance Reviews Today*

Real Vampires Get Lucky

"Let's just say, if you know what's good for you, then you'll check out *Real Vampires Get Lucky*." —*Romance Reviews Today*

"Gerry Bartlett delivers another winner . . . Ms. Bartlett's gift for humor, the bawdier the better, is evident throughout, and the different story lines are interwoven seamlessly to give the reader a thoroughly entertaining read. Fans, rejoice—this one's a keeper!" —*Fresh Fiction*

"A laugh-out-loud series. Ms. Bartlett puts a different spin on the vampire romance. Fast-paced with appealing characters you can fall in love with. It's like visiting old friends." —*Night Owl Romance*

Real Vampires Live Large

"Fans of lighthearted paranormal romps will enjoy Gerry Bartlett's fun tale starring a heroine who has never forgiven Blade for biting her when she was bloated."
—*Midwest Book Review*

"Gerry Bartlett has created a laugh-out-loud book that I couldn't put down. *Real Vampires Live Large* is a winner."
—*The Romance Readers Connection*

"Glory gives girl power a whole new meaning, especially in the undead way. What a fun read!"   —*All About Romance*

Real Vampires Have Curves

"A sharp, sassy, sexy read. Gerry Bartlett creates a vampire to die for in this sizzling new series."
—Kimberly Raye, *USA Today* bestselling author of *Sucker for Love*

"Hot and hilarious. Glory is Everywoman with fangs."
—Nina Bangs, *New York Times* bestselling author of *Eternal Prey*

"Full-figured vampire Glory bursts from the page in this lively, fun and engaging spin on the vampire mythology."
—Julie Kenner, *USA Today* bestselling author of *Turned*

"A sexy, smart and lively contemporary paranormal romance . . . The plot is engaging, the characters are stimulating (not to mention, so is the sex) and the writing is sharp. Glory St. Clair is . . . a breath of fresh air."   —*Romance Reader at Heart*

"If you love Betsy from MaryJanice Davidson's Undead series or Sookie from Charlaine Harris's [Sookie Stackhouse novels], you're gonna love *Real Vampires Have Curves*."
—*A Romance Review*

Real Vampires
Don't Wear Size Six

GERRY BARTLETT

B

BERKLEY BOOKS, NEW YORK

THE BERKLEY PUBLISHING GROUP
Published by the Penguin Group
Penguin Group (USA) Inc.
375 Hudson Street, New York, New York 10014, USA
Penguin Group (Canada), 90 Eglinton Avenue East, Suite 700, Toronto, Ontario M4P 2Y3, Canada
(a division of Pearson Penguin Canada Inc.)
Penguin Books Ltd., 80 Strand, London WC2R 0RL, England
Penguin Group Ireland, 25 St. Stephen's Green, Dublin 2, Ireland (a division of Penguin Books Ltd.)
Penguin Group (Australia), 250 Camberwell Road, Camberwell, Victoria 3124, Australia
(a division of Pearson Australia Group Pty. Ltd.)
Penguin Books India Pvt. Ltd., 11 Community Centre, Panchsheel Park, New Delhi—110 017, India
Penguin Group (NZ), 67 Apollo Drive, Rosedale, Auckland 0632, New Zealand
(a division of Pearson New Zealand Ltd.)
Penguin Books (South Africa) (Pty.) Ltd., 24 Sturdee Avenue, Rosebank, Johannesburg 2196,
South Africa

Penguin Books Ltd., Registered Offices: 80 Strand, London WC2R 0RL, England

This is an original publication of The Berkley Publishing Group.

PRINTING HISTORY
Berkley trade paperback edition / August 2011

Library of Congress Cataloging-in-Publication Data

Bartlett, Gerry.
    Real vampires don't wear size six / Gerry Bartlett.—Berkley trade pbk. ed.
        p. cm.
    ISBN 978-0-425-24135-6
    1. Saint Clair, Glory (Fictitious character)—Fiction. 2. Vampires—Fiction. I. Title.
    PS3602.A83945R424   2011
    813'.6—dc22   2011014491

PRINTED IN THE UNITED STATES OF AMERICA

10   9   8   7   6   5   4   3   2   1

For Oliver and Pauline Bartlett.
Thanks for your love and support.
And Christian, of course!

Acknowledgments

It's wonderful to have so many members on the Gerry Bartlett "team." First, I have to thank my pitcher, my fab agent, Kimberly Whalen of Trident Media Group, who believed in this series from the beginning. Kim, you rock! My editor, Kate Seaver, is certainly an all-star. She and the fantastic crew at Berkley make sure that Glory St. Clair and her gang always hit a home run. From the great covers to the copyedits and Kate's tweaks, I never worry that we missed something that will make my story the best it can be.

Then there is the coaching staff: As always, my buds Nina Bangs and Donna Maloy are present every week to make sure I don't let my story wander off into left field. Thanks, ladies, for making sure I stay on task and almost on time. I also have to thank Romance Writers of America and my two fabulous home chapters, Houston Bay Area and West Houston. The members are always there in the bleachers, cheering me on with support and encouragement.

Last, but never least, are the fantastic readers who pick up my books and take the time to e-mail me. I love to hear from you on Facebook or at gerrybartlett.com. If I can make you laugh or even shed a tear, it has made the hours at the computer worth it. You can't know how hearing from you lifts me. It makes me feel like I've won the World Series. Thanks so much for supporting Glory and her crew.

One

"The vampire council is all for running you out of town, Glory." Damian frowned at me, for once not bothering to put on his sexy vibe.

"No! Austin is my home now. I have friends, my business." Could I be at any more of a disadvantage? I'd just stepped out of the shower when I'd heard that knock on the door. I'd hoped it was Blade, my boyfriend, who'd been sulking since we'd almost broken up recently. So I'd thrown on a robe and dashed to the door. Now I tightened the sash on my admittedly ratty robe and jerked off my shower cap.

"That business is part of the problem, Glory. Vintage Vamp's Emporium. You know we like for vampires to stay under the radar here, and then you name your little store something like that." Damian Sabatini always made moves on a woman, even one without makeup and with bed head. The fact that he looked serious and was pacing around me like I was a piece of furniture worried me.

"Vamps are also Roaring Twenties hotties, you know that. What's up with these council members? Where's their sense of humor?" I grabbed Damian's sleeve. "Help me out here, Damian."

"I know what vamps are. I got lucky with quite a few, back in the day." Damian smiled and suddenly snapped to the fact that I was naked under my robe. "And I did go to bat for you. Explained that my sister had painted that mural of a vampire on your wall as a joke."

"Flo *did*." His sister, Florence da Vinci, is my best friend. She had spent a long lifetime admiring artists up close and personally. Her mural had caused a burst of publicity that had brought me business, but also some vampire rumors.

Damian's eyes gleamed in a way that reminded me his nickname was Casanova. Okay, I could use that. I locked the door and gestured to the couch. "Sit, talk to me. Tell me what I can do to fix this. You want a bottle of something?" I drink synthetic blood. I happened to have several different brands on hand for a change.

"No, thanks." Damian patted the seat next to him. "You flashed red eyes at Florence's wedding. Several council members saw them. We all know what that means and it's what really got the get-rid-of-Glory thing moving. We don't tolerate demons in Austin."

"Yes, well, I *was* possessed. Past tense. And my temper got the best of me that night." I collapsed next to Damian. He *was* a friend. We'd figured out a long time ago that we weren't going to have a love connection. Or at least *I'd* figured that out. I plucked his hand off my knee where my robe had parted and smiled. "As I was saying, I *had* a demon on board, but she's gone now. My friends arranged an intervention and Alesa went screaming back to hell. I'm all better now. Good as gold."

"I'm happy for you. But I'm not sure everyone on the council will be reassured. The best way to prove your goodness to the members would be an act of contrition. Do a favor, perhaps." Damian leaned back and I realized he was trying to scope out my cleavage. They didn't call him Casanova for nothing.

There was a thump in the hall and I jumped up. "What

was that? Is there someone out there?" I looked for a weapon and came up with my hot pink umbrella. Lame, but better than nothing. At least it had a point on it.

"Relax. I have other tenants in this building, don't I?" Damian put his hand on my shoulder and took the umbrella, leaning it against the wall. "You're still on edge, I think. That brush with the demon obviously upset you."

"Of course it did! I was on the fast track to hell." I sighed and plopped into the chair across from the couch. "How am I supposed to make the council happy? I *am* demon-free. Ask your sister. Flo and Richard came back from their honeymoon for just one night. They're the ones who did the ceremony that got that demon out of me."

"That's good, that you have reliable witnesses." Damian sat and leaned forward.

"Blade was here too. And Valdez." I sighed. It had been quite a night. Everyone I loved. Who loved me. Jeremy Blade—Jerry—was the boyfriend and my sire, the vampire who'd turned me. Rafael Valdez was the shape-shifter who'd been my bodyguard until recently. I loved him too and we'd gotten close, too close for it not to hurt my relationship with Blade.

"Glory, is Valdez still living here with you?" Damian looked around, like maybe Rafe would pop out of the back bedroom.

"Quit reading my mind. And, no, he has his own place now." I'd asked him to move out in hopes that would prove to Jerry that I was serious about making our relationship work again.

"Then you have an extra bedroom and are living here all alone." Damian stood and I jumped up.

"Yes, but I don't know what that has to do with you. You have a castle on a hill for crying out loud." I freaked for a moment. I'd never been afraid of Damian but he was an ancient vampire and could overpower me without breaking a sweat. Of course he was usually a lover, not a fighter. He

4

looked at me and smiled. Oops, should have blocked my thoughts. He was still reading them and liked what he'd heard.

"Relax, Glory. I have a proposition for you, but it's to help you get in good with the council. Nothing to do with love-making. Though if you want to pursue that thought . . ." He was close in a heartbeat and had his hand on my shoulder. "You smell fresh from your shower and full of that Bulgarian synthetic." He smiled and showed fang. "Did you know it's made with real blood?"

"No. Make that a double no." I straight-armed him, my hand on his broad chest. "What's the proposition, Damian? The one not headed to my bedroom."

"Ah, Glory. Someday." He backed off and lounged on the couch so casually that I was convinced he'd never meant me to take the pass seriously. "I have a young vampire, a fledgling. She was turned by a vamp who has been disciplined and is no longer with us." Damian's face grew hard and I was reminded that he could be a fighter when he wanted to be. "Anyway, she's stuck now and not happy about it. I need to find a mentor for her and you've proved you can handle that job. Like you did for Israel Caine."

Another new vampire. I sat back in my chair. Yes, I'd mentored Ray—Israel Caine. But he'd been a rock star, my crush, and he still held a place in my heart. To take on some poor girl who'd been turned against her will . . . Well, it would definitely prove to the council that Glory was a good person, willing to sacrifice. Because new vamps could be a pain in the butt. I sure didn't want to leave Austin though.

I had a thriving business where I sold antiques and vintage clothing. And I had friends who'd turned into the kind of extended family I'd always craved. Of course Jerry was here too. I had to stay to work on getting our relationship back on track.

"I'll do it. When do I meet her?"

Damian grinned. "I knew you wouldn't fail me. She's right

outside. I'm sure she made that noise you heard." He got up, unlocked my door and opened it. "Come in, Penny."

I took one look at the scowling girl who strode into my apartment and knew I had my work cut out for me.

"Glory, meet Penny Patterson."

"Hello, Penny."

Penny glared at me but I kept smiling, deciding anyone who'd been through what she had this week was entitled to a little attitude. Still, my sad-sack robe and wild hair were an aberration for me. I pride myself on never facing the public looking less than my best. This girl? She looked like she was the one who'd just rolled out of bed. Her bad makeup was worse than no makeup at all. And her hair needed a decent cut and a wash. Clearly some of this look was pre-fangs.

Then there were the clothes. Penny and I have some of the same figure issues. Demon thing aside, had Damian brought her here to me because she carried too many pounds for her five-foot-tall frame? I sent him a glaring mental message but he put out his hands and added an innocent face, the picture of denial. Anyway, Penny was a little round. Okay, a lot round and she'd done the unthinkable—she'd worn horizontal stripes. Please. Even zebras knew to keep their stripes vertical.

This girl needed me. And not just because she was now a vampire. She needed a wardrobe intervention and a makeover, stat. I turned to say something to Damian but the man had slipped out while my back was turned and quietly closed the door.

"Well, Penny, looks like you're stuck with me." I smiled and gestured at her bulging backpack. "Is that all your stuff? Want me to show you to your bedroom?"

"Forget that." Penny stepped close to me, a rookie mistake, and grabbed the lapels of my robe. "There's only one thing I want from you."

"Whoa, girlfriend." I jerked her hands off my robe. "Rule number one. Back off the intensity." I tried to read her mind.

What the hell? How had this fledgling already learned to block her thoughts?

She smiled a creepy smile, and looked me over. "You'll learn that I'm a quick study. I'm nineteen and I've already got three degrees from UT."

"Three college degrees? At nineteen?" I knew UT was the University of Texas here in Austin. I was turned vampire in 1604. Back when I'd been school age, I'd been lucky to learn basic letters. I'd had to teach myself what I knew today, which was practical stuff and wouldn't have earned me a degree anywhere.

"Yeah. I'm a geek and a freak. Big whoop." Her smile had changed from creepy to a sad little twist.

I realized that this girl would be pretty if she'd let me guide her. She had nice auburn hair and skin that would be golden if she didn't mask it with pale makeup. She sure didn't need the black lipstick she'd obviously decided went with her new vampire status.

"Hey, being a brain *is* a big whoop. And lay off the freak thing. Being a vampire isn't all bad. Trust me on that." I sat on the couch. "Now what is it you want from me? I'm going to be your mentor. I'll do what I can to help you adjust to your new life." I smiled and gestured at the chair across from me.

Penny sat, then leaned forward. Her eyes were a golden brown and they shone with an intelligence that saw too much. I put up a block. If Penny had already figured out how to block her thoughts, she was probably already reading other's too.

"There's just one thing that will make me happy right now, Glory. Damian said that's your name, right?"

"Yes, it's Gloriana St. Clair. I'm a four-hundred-plus-year-old vampire, Penny. I've had a few centuries to learn the ropes. So if there's something you need, something you want to learn, I'm your gal." I kept smiling, feeling all motherly, even though to look at me, I'm only twenty-two to Penny's nineteen. Mortals would think we were sisters. Maybe I'd even introduce her in the shop as my sister from out of town. Yes, that would work. I realized Penny was waiting for me to focus on her, to give her my full attention. I finally did.

"Okay, Penny, what do you need?"

"Help me kill my sister."

TWO

"Excuse me?" I hadn't heard correctly. Couldn't have.

"I said you have to help me kill my sister. I have a twin." Penny jumped up and pulled a picture from the side pocket of her backpack. "This is Jenny."

"Whoa. Never would have guessed—" I shut up. Penny had probably grown up hating to be compared to the blond angel in the cheerleading outfit who smiled into the camera.

"We're fraternal twins. Obviously." Penny smiled down at the picture. "I got the brains, she got the beauty."

I waited for the snark. Teenagers. Sisters, at that. I'd watched those reality shows on TV. There was bound to be some sibling rivalry, bitterness.

"So now you want to break in your fangs by *killing* her? Isn't that a little radical?" I was ready for the explosion. Some kind of meltdown. What I got was Penny looking at me with a shimmer of tears.

"No, you don't get it. Look at her. She's beautiful, perfect. She's smart too, just not the phenom I was. How can I let her grow old when I never will? We can turn her, Glory, and she'll be like that forever." Penny rushed me and grabbed my hands. "You've got to help me do this. Jenny's my best friend. I can't just leave her to be human when I'm"—big sniff—"not."

"Are you kidding me? Did you hear what Damian was saying when you were standing in the hall?" I knew she had vamp hearing and was sure she'd eavesdropped. Who wouldn't?

"He was persuading you to take me on. Obviously he got the job done." Penny sat on the couch. She laid the picture on my cluttered coffee table, right on top of my copy of *InStyle* magazine. I bet it was Jenny's bible. Penny probably used it as a coaster.

"Yes, he talked me into it, because I'm about to be kicked out of Austin. I'm hanging by a thread here." I sat across from her. "You also heard him say the guy who made you vampire isn't around anymore. You know what he meant by that?"

"Guess he was asked to leave too. That bastard deserved to have his nuts cracked." Penny heaved a sigh and stared at her sister's picture again. "I didn't ask for this, though the living forever thing has me stoked."

I leaped over the table and landed beside her. That finally got her full attention. "Listen to me, Penny. That bastard may have gotten his nuts cracked, but it was right before he got a stake through his heart. He's dead, girl, dead for what he did to you. The Austin council doesn't want anyone turned vampire around here. It's rogue behavior. Only tolerated when it's done to save a mortal's life. A last-ditch effort."

"They *killed* him?" Penny bit her bottom lip and I glimpsed her new fangs. "Wow. That's so Gothic."

"Yeah, well, vampires like to keep a low profile, not easy with all the vamp books, movies and TV shows out there now. People pay attention when weird things happen."

"Would it be so bad for vampires to come out of the closet? I think this is kind of cool. So will Jenny." Penny was fixated on the picture of her sister again and I wanted to shake her.

"Really? Will Jenny like missing cheerleading practice in the mornings? Or hitting the drive-thru at McDonald's?"

Penny frowned. "The cheerleading, sure. But she gave up Big Macs years ago. Way too busy counting calories. Not like me." Her eyes filled. "No more of those fries? Ever?" She bit her lip again, then gasped when her new fangs popped through her skin. "Ouch!"

"At least you got to taste one." I made a face. "I drive by those places, inhale, and just fantasize." We both sighed. "Anyway, face facts, Penny. And for every vamp groupie, there will be a vamp hunter who sees you as a demon from hell and is eager to exterminate you." I shook my head. Was I getting through to her? Didn't think so. She was obviously still figuring out how to convince her sister that the trade-offs for immortality were worth it.

"Maybe we could arrange some kind of accident." Penny smiled at me. "Then we would *have* to turn Jenny. The council couldn't object to that."

"You think they wouldn't see through that? The council is fairly new and trying to establish control. To prove that zero tolerance means exactly that. It's bad enough that Austin has a Bat Festival every year and puts 'Keep Austin Weird' on T-shirts. We don't need to become known as the vampire capital of Texas." I put my hand on hers. "I'm sorry about your sister, but running her over with your car might not be her idea of a good time." I squeezed her fingers. "You haven't told her what happened to you, have you?"

"No, not yet. I wasn't sure how." Penny's eyes filled again. "Jenny's just a sophomore, in a sorority and doing all the normal college things that I never did." Penny sighed. "I figured my news would just bring her down."

I let her go. "Yes, finding out your twin's a vampire might put a damper on date night."

Penny frowned at me. "You don't get it, Glory. I think it's great that Jenny's having fun. I was always too busy studying, being the whiz kid, to do the things Jen does. So I'm getting a vicarious thrill from her life now." She glanced down. "And then there's the way I look. I'm not exactly cheerleading material."

"Don't put yourself down. I've seen those competitions on TV. Cheerleaders come in all shapes and sizes. With the right hair, makeup and wardrobe, you could fit in with that crowd, pre-fangs of course. And the way those people hop around, you would have trimmed down in no time." I wondered why Jenny hadn't helped her sister do just that.

"It's no big deal. Jen and I don't compete." Penny still blocked her thoughts and I wondered if her relationship with her sister was as easy as she claimed.

"Obviously, who could with your three degrees? I guess you proved that whiz kid thing." I patted her shoulder.

"Yeah, well. I enjoy the academic stuff." She shrugged. "Sue me, I'm an unrepentant egghead. That's what Jen calls me." A tear ran down her cheek. "God, how can I just show her my f-f-fangs and tell her what happened? She's so happy now. She just made the cheerleading squad for next fall and even has a new boyfriend. This will just bring her down."

"You're a good sister." I was getting a little misty-eyed myself. I don't know if I could have been so generous. Screw vicarious. There's no substitute for doing things yourself. I made up my mind then and there that Penny would have a great start as a vampire. Adventures. Rafe could help me there. I wished for my buddy Florence too. How long before she got back from her honeymoon?

"Jen and I don't always agree on things. In fact, we had a giant fight the night I ended up a vampire." Penny grimaced. "Turns out I should have listened to her. But just once I wanted to see . . . Never mind." She tried for a shrug but I could see her hands plucking nervously at her gray sweatpants. "I've texted her a few times since then. Let her know I was okay, just snowed under with school stuff. But I bet she's wondering what's up. We usually talk or see each other at least once a day." Penny sniffled. "We'll never do the morning coffee-and-donut run again now, will we?"

I pulled her against me when she finally broke down and sobbed. Who wouldn't? The realization that you can never eat or drink like a human again is hard to take. Hey, I still mourned my hot chocolate and the Cheetos I'd impulsively tasted once, to my regret. I gulped back sympathetic tears.

"Enough of this." Penny pulled back and dug a tissue out of her pocket. "What now, Glory?"

"You can't tell your sister you're a vampire." There, I'd said it and I got the reaction I knew I would. Penny was up and at the door in a blur.

"Try to stop me. We don't keep secrets from each other." She snarled at me—me!—showing fangs when I grabbed her shoulders. "Damn it, Glory, I *have* to tell her. I'll put a positive spin on it."

"Chill and put your fangs away, fledgling. A positive spin?" I leaned against the door, making damned sure Penny wasn't getting past me. "I can hear that conversation now. 'Hey, sis, I was killed the other night but, not to worry, a vampire gave me my own pair of fangs and now I'm here to take you down too. Say bye-bye, pom-poms, and hello, blood bank.'"

Penny huffed and puffed and even did a few moves that looked like martial arts. I wanted to trot out that cliché and growl, "Go ahead and make my day." But in the end she slouched back to the couch without making a serious move.

"I've got to tell her sometime. She can read me too well. Even without the vampire tricks." Penny sighed when I sat across from her again. "She'll know something's off with me."

"Then avoid her. Text, tweet, e-mail—whatever the hell you two do—but let her know you're too busy to meet. You're not telling her, Penny. Not yet anyway." I hardened my heart when it looked like she was going to tear up again. Why me? Even a rock star had been easier to handle than this. No crying from Ray; he'd been more about colorful adjectives and mourning his Black Label Scotch.

"For how long? And when we do get together, am I supposed to just arrange to see her at night and hide my fangs?" Penny kicked her backpack. "Which I realize I'm not exactly in control of yet."

"No, you're not. Glad you've figured that out." I reached down and slid the backpack out of range. "Concentrate. Mind over matter. But be aware that your emotions affect your fangs. You're upset and down they came."

"Yeah, well, this whole thing has me crazed." Penny's eyes widened. "Seriously, controlling any of this seems impossible right now. I was around a human at Damian's. Just the smell of that blood, pumping through her veins, and I wanted to jump all over her and take a bite. Which is skeezy. You know?"

"Not skeezy at all. It's your new nature. It'll settle down after you've done this awhile." I leaned forward. "But, whoa. Mortals at Damian's? Are you telling me he has pets there? I thought the council didn't like that kind of action."

Penny frowned. "Maybe I wasn't supposed to say anything. I never saw a vampire bite anyone." She sagged, like she was tired of the whole thing. "Which is weird. But Damian is hot, don't you think? The women were all over him. My guess is he could do whatever he wanted with them, once they were in his bedroom."

"Forget Damian and think about how you reacted to being around those mortals, Penny." I waited until she looked up at me. "To the blood. You craved it. Couldn't think of much else when you heard that sound. The pumping. Smelled that fresh-in-the-pipes juice. That's bloodlust, fledgling. And you've got about as much control over it as you did when you used to drive past McDonald's and smelled those fries."

"Which means zero." Penny looked at me in horror. "So you mean that, while she's still human, I could be a danger to Jenny? My own sister?"

"True enough." I nodded. At least this would buy me some time to work with Penny and keep her from spreading the word that, hey, vampires were in town.

"You're right. What if I go postal when I smell Jenny's blood and attack her?" Penny clapped her hand over her mouth, smearing her black lipstick.

"Entirely possible." I watched her tear up again and searched for reassurances. Facts were, though, fledglings were notoriously hard to control when they were thirsty. I walked into the kitchen and grabbed a bottle of synthetic out of the fridge.

"Drink this. When you're well fed, you're less likely to get out of control when you're around a mortal—we call them mortals, Penny." I smiled and patted her shoulder. "Come on. I still consider myself a human, don't you?"

"Y-y-yes, I guess. When I can think at all." She twisted off the cap and took a swallow, made a face, then looked at the label. "This isn't as good as what Damian gave me. Must be cheaper. And I don't think I'm crazy about A positive."

"Sorry. We'll figure out your faves later and make sure the council springs for it." I opened a bottle for myself.

Penny took a deep swallow. "Any other tips about being around mortals besides filling up first?"

"Not yet, but you don't go see Jenny without me. I can always intervene if it looks like you're losing control." I smiled. "I know you're smart and think you can figure all this out for yourself." Penny flushed and I knew I had her. "But give me credit for having been there, done that, a time or two. Okay?"

"I get that you're ancient." Penny looked me over. "Incredible to imagine. That you've been around since before airplanes, telephones"—she tipped her cold bottle at me—"microwaves!"

"Yes, a lot's changed. But some things never do." I gave her a stern look. "New vampires need guidance. And primal urges are what get you in trouble. Things you can't rationalize, Einstein."

Penny at least looked thoughtful as she sipped her synthetic. "Still, I can't imagine attacking my own sister. I haven't even tried taking blood from a, uh, mortal yet, just been drinking the bottled stuff. Wouldn't have a clue how to even go about feeding, as Damian called it, except for what I've seen on TV or movies and that looks pretty messy. What do *you* do about your blood supply?"

"I stick to the bottled stuff. That's why I have a fridge full. And I drink it cold because I spent a few years in Las Vegas and decided I liked it cold on a hot day. Plenty of those in Texas too." I smiled. "Feel free to nuke yours if that floats your boat. And help yourself whenever you feel the slightest bit hungry. Promise me that."

"Sure. But obviously not all vampires stick to the bottle." She brushed her neck. "The guy who took me down used me for his breakfast, lunch and dinner."

"I'm wondering why he didn't just drain you and leave you for dead. Turning you vampire is serious stuff. A responsibility for the sire and obviously a mistake in Austin." I leaned forward. "Did Damian tell you anything about that?" Gossip, I loved it. What can I say? It's one of my minor vices.

"He said this guy was starting his own little family. I remember the man, he said his name was Vince, calling me 'Daughter' when he dragged me to the shack where that other vampire found me." Penny shuddered and drained her bottle of synthetic. "He was deranged, dirty and touched me in a way that my dad would never . . ." Penny shuddered again. "Sick bastard. Anyway, Damian said the council didn't tolerate that kind of thing, the turning part. Guess I know now it earned him the death penalty. Earned me one too." She set down the bottle on my magazine and wiped her wet cheeks.

I wanted to hug her again, but I could see she had decided to try to move on. I had to admire her for that.

"And immortality, Penny. Like you said before, that's the cool part." I sighed when I saw her dig into her bag and pull out a compact.

"Damn, I keep forgetting, we really can't see our reflection. Jenny will hate that." She snapped the compact shut with a frown.

I gritted my teeth against the urge to argue about Jenny again. "We all hate it. But I have a computer setup in my bedroom that works like a mirror. Help yourself. You've got mascara and lipstick everywhere." I wondered what this sudden urge to tidy up was about. Was she still thinking to make a break for it? Just because she felt full of synthetic . . . I'd definitely keep a close eye on her.

"Seriously?" Penny darted into my bedroom and came out with the white laptop with the mini-cam. "This is neat."

"It was a gift from Ian MacDonald. He's a California vampire and a techno-genius. He invented it and a lot more cool things to help make the vamp lifestyle more livable. You'd love him. He's a very clever guy."

"Sounds interesting." Penny quickly fixed her face, which unfortunately included adding a new coat of black lipstick, then closed the computer. "Makes me think, though. I need my stuff. From my apartment. How do I explain to my family and Jenny that I'm moving *here*?" She swept her gaze around my admittedly tired-looking digs.

"What's wrong with here?" I'm not much for housekeeping and spend most of my time downstairs in my shop, but the mix of secondhand treasures and Ikea bookshelves wasn't that bad. Especially when compared to dorm rooms and college apartments.

"Nothing, really. I like the location. Sixth Street is cool, though a little farther from campus than where I'm living now. Guess we can make this work. It's near the end of a semester. Logical time to move, if I'd been thinking about it." Penny sighed. "Didn't mean to come off as critical. This place is nice, much nicer than my digs. Blame my attitude on the vampire thing. I'm still reeling. Who knew you guys even existed?"

"That's because we're careful, Penny. Your sire's behavior could have put a spotlight on us." I had been through quite a few near misses in my time. Rogues made life uncomfortable for all of us. "It sounds harsh, but the council did the right thing, taking him out."

"Yeah, would hate to think he was still running loose out there, making more daughters." Penny shuddered. "So I'll move in here, learn the drill. But I need my stuff—research books, my big-ass computer and my cat. Damian said he arranged for someone to feed him every day, but I have to go get Booger."

"You named your cat Booger?" I shuddered. "That's cruel and unusual."

Penny smiled for a moment. "What can I say? He's fifteen and Jen and I have had him since he was a kitten. We liked the sound of the word and my mom hated it. So of course we kept saying it." Her lips trembled. "My parents! God, I can't just let them get old and die when I could turn them too. And Gram!" She grabbed me again.

"Oh, no, we are not turning your entire family into vampires, Penny. Just get that idea right out of your enormous brain. Sit, I mean it." I could actually see her mind working this out as she slouched over to the couch again. Thinking about how the process might work. Hell, by the time an unleashed Penny got through, there would be a whole colony of vampires populated by her family, friends of her family, anyone her family thought deserved to live forever. It was worse than a freaking cell phone network. Dozens, hundreds, thousands of vampires could be made from this one brainiac teenaged vamp.

I sat on the sofa, tempted to pick up my own cell phone. It would be nice to call for help. No, that was the old Glory. I was going to handle this by myself. I'd just decided that when there was a knock on the door. I jumped up and ran my fingers through my hair. Why now? I knew who'd dropped by, and wished for a few minutes with my makeup bag and, good grief, a hairbrush.

"What's up, Glory? You're freaking." Penny looked interested as there was another, louder knock.

"My boyfriend. Well, maybe we're on break. Not sure. Anyway, he's also my sire." I glanced down at my well-worn robe. "Look at me."

Penny grinned. "He's not going away."

"Gloriana, I can hear you in there. Open up before I knock this door down. I need to talk to you."

"I'm coming, Jerry." I sighed and opened the door. "I'm not dressed and I have company." I gestured for him to come in.

"I certainly have no problem seeing you undressed." He grinned, then came to a halt as he saw my visitor on the couch. "Who's this?"

"Penny, this is Jeremy Blade, my sire. He turned me vampire in 1604."

"Seriously?" Penny gazed at Jerry with a look I recognized. Yep, the girl was checking him out and liking what she saw. Who wouldn't? Jerry was forever tanned and forever hard bodied with the broad shoulders and lean waist of a warrior who'd earned his physique in battle. He smiled with a slash of white teeth and stepped forward to offer his hand.

"Seriously. Jerry, Penny Patterson, a fledgling that I'm mentoring for the council."

Penny had snapped out of her initial lust fog to jump to her feet. Jerry did that to people, made them come to attention. He was good at intimidating, though this time it wasn't intentional.

"Hi." Penny took his outstretched hand and shook it. "Glory just got stuck with me tonight. We're still working out our arrangements."

"Will you be living here or is Valdez still here?" Jerry turned to me.

"Oh, Rafe's gone. Has his own place. Penny will be staying in the extra bedroom." I sounded desperate to explain. Not cool. I made myself stroll to the couch and sit, pulling Penny down beside me like I didn't care what Jerry thought. "Anyway, Penny was recently turned against her will. She'll need a lot of guidance to work through the transition."

"Of course she will." Jerry sat in a chair. "Penny, I wonder if you'd mind giving Glory and me a few minutes alone together. Some personal business we need to discuss." He gave her one of his charming smiles and Penny grinned back.

"No problem. I was about to go out anyway." She glanced at me. "To pick up some of my stuff." She grabbed her purse and tried to look innocent.

"Forget it. Go unpack. Your bedroom is at the end of the hall." I grabbed her arm, marched her past her backpack and thrust it into her arms, then guided her toward her new room. "We'll arrange to get your things soon. I'll talk to Damian about it." I leaned down to hiss in her ear. "You think I'm an idiot? You'd run straight to your sister because you feel full of synthetic, am I right?"

Penny flashed me a defiant look. "I *am* full. I could handle it. I'm not a child."

"In this world you're an infant. We'll finish discussing your sister later." I was sure she was going to nag me about it endlessly. I kept my gaze stern.

"Geez, get physical, why don't you?" Penny rubbed her arm. "All right, I'll unpack. Nice to meet you, Mr. Blade."

"Call me Jeremy." Jerry was on his feet, ever the gentleman.

"Jeremy. So you're Glory's sire. Does that give you the power to tell her what to do?" Penny glared at me. "Glory didn't sire me, but she seems to think she did."

"I'd listen to her, if I were you." Jerry turned to look at me. "Gloriana's advice will help you survive." His eyes darkened as he studied me. "Our relationship is complicated. Much more than sire and fledgling. Gloriana can tell you about it if she wishes, but I've given up trying to tell her what to do."

"Interesting." Penny looked from Jerry to me and back again. "Well, guess I'll put on my iPod and earphones, otherwise it seems my new supersonic hearing picks up everything within a hundred yards." With a wave, she headed down the hall.

Jerry looked so yummy I wondered if I could drag him to my bedroom for that "private word" he wanted. He patted the seat beside him on the couch. Guess not.

"What's going on, Jerry?" I sat beside him, not worried when my robe opened over my knees.

"I've got to go back to Florida for business." He reached over and closed my robe. Closed it! *Now* I was worried.

"Still having management problems?" I scooted away to

lean against the corner, putting several inches between us. He wanted to be distant? I could play that game.

"Yes, the new manager I hired needs training and I should have stayed longer when I was there before." Jerry stared at me. "The last time I left town, things happened here that I haven't forgotten."

Uh-oh. Those "things" had been my being unfaithful to Jerry with my former bodyguard. Jerry's thoughts were blocked, no surprise there. I sat up straight, trying to decide if I should grovel or not.

"You can trust me, Jerry. Rafe and I are just friends now." I didn't block my thoughts and let him see the truth there.

"I know you two are friends. But Valdez wants more than friendship. And once a man has been with you, Gloriana, you're damned hard to forget." Jerry eased closer, his gaze hot.

"I think I heard a compliment in there." I put my hand on his knee. "Jerry, I can't keep apologizing and I won't beg you to forgive me again. If you need more time . . ."

"I guess I do." He stared at my hand until I pulled it back into my lap. "I've been thinking about our relationship."

When a man admits he's been thinking about stuff like that, it can't be good. And I'd cheated. I was pretty sure having a demon inside me had made me weak enough to give into the urges I'd been feeling for my dear friend Rafe, but the urges had been there before the demon had come along and Jerry had figured that out. Well, actually, I'd burst out that info in a big confession. The whole fiasco had killed Jerry's pride, his trust in me and maybe his love. No wonder he'd been "thinking."

"Okay, spit it out, Jer. What's on your mind?" I was strangling on my breath, on my knotted insides that had worked their way up into my throat. I couldn't stand what he might say, but my imagination conjured up such horrible things, I hoped his words would be easier to take.

"I'm not over what you did. I keep seeing you and Valdez

together." Jerry thumped his forehead hard with his fists and I gasped.

"I'm sorry. I don't know what else I can say." I wanted to reach out to him, but there was a wall between us as surely as if it had been bricks and mortar.

"I know. I heard your words, saw your tears. I know you love me." This time he squeezed his head between his hands until I was afraid his skull would crack. Jerry was being really hard on himself, trying to erase that image from his mind. If only that would work.

"I do love you. I have for over four hundred years." I couldn't stand it. I grasped his hand and pulled it away from his head.

"You and I have a pattern. This on-again, off-again love affair of ours. It ends when you become frustrated with my high-handed ways, as you call them, and you usually cut and run." Jerry opened his fist and gripped my hand. "You'd think I'd learn or you'd learn. That one of us would figure this thing out." He pulled my fingers to his lips, his tongue touching my knuckles lightly before he let them go. "But we never have."

"Yes, I run. I admit it. But we always agree that it's time for a break first." He blurred when my eyes filled with tears. "This time I stayed but . . ."

"Broke faith." The words were clipped, cold.

Had I finally pushed him too far? Wounded him too deeply for healing? I reached out to him, wanting to feel his arms around me. Needing his strength. He dragged me against him and laid my head against his chest.

"I'm so, so sorry, Jeremiah. What can I do to make this right?"

Jerry took a breath and I heard the slow beat of his heart. "What's done is done. If I can't get that picture of you and Valdez together out of my head?" His arms tightened almost painfully around me. "Then I suppose that's my problem."

"God." I held on to him, afraid to move or say another

word. What *could* I say? He was right. This was for him to decide. I couldn't erase the past.

"Killing him might help."

I jerked out of his arms. "Don't even joke about such a thing!"

"Who's joking? Sending that demon dog to hell would go a long way to making me feel better."

I jumped up. "Well, it's not an option. Not if you're interested in ever getting together with me again."

He stood and faced me. "You're not helping matters, Gloriana, by defending him." He yanked me into his arms. "Forget him, damn it."

He kissed me then, the kind of soul-stirring kiss that never failed to weaken my knees and remind me of who'd made me. This time? I had his words ringing in my ears, damning Rafe. A man I did love. But Jerry? I grabbed his hair and felt his fangs scrape my tongue as he kept kissing me. I kissed him back, pushing my body against his.

He finally raised his head, his eyes narrowed. "Trying too hard, Gloriana. Yes, I still want you, stupid to deny it." He pushed his hips against me and it wasn't news that he was hard. "But I've always been a fool for you. I even thought we would be together forever."

"So did I." I brushed his cheek, wanting that. Why did I even hesitate? Was it because I still felt his disapproval? And why had I ever been tempted by Rafe? Was it because my relationship with Jerry didn't satisfy me on some level? Too many questions to just brush past this and pretend things were okay between us.

"I need to cool off." He frowned and put some space between us. "And you need to be sure you're ready to let go of Valdez as a lover."

"I am. I have. Rafe understands that we're done, Jerry!" I flushed and stared at his shirt, not wanting him to see how hard that decision had been for me. "The demon influenced me before or I never—"

"So you say." Jerry shook his head. "But you and Valdez

are close. You share secrets and keep them from me. And you love each other. You've said that more than once."

"Yes, but as friends." I met his gaze this time, though it wasn't easy. Could I just be friends with a man I'd made love with? A man who could still make my heart race when his hungry eyes met mine? I'd have to, if I wanted to be with Jerry.

"Enough. We need to take a break." Jerry turned and walked to the door.

"Jerry, no!" I threw myself on him, gripping his shoulders and pressing my breasts against his back. I laid my cheek against the soft cotton of his shirt.

"I'm going, Gloriana. I've said all I need to say."

"I hate to see you leave like this, still so angry." His muscles tightened under my arms as I held on to him. "Please stay." My breath hitched. If I slid down to his feet and begged, dragged him to my bed, I might win the night, but not the battle. And we'd both hate me for it later.

"No, Gloriana. There is no point. You need to be around Valdez without that demon inside you and see where things stand between you." He turned and took my hands, holding them between us. "*I* need to know where things stand."

"I told you." I gasped when Jerry shoved me away and opened the door.

"Oh, yes, you *told* me." His face was set, his lips firm. He let me see his pain and I bit my lip.

"Next time block your thoughts, Gloriana, if you don't want me to hear them. I'll be back in two weeks. By then, I hope you know who you want. Because if it's the shifter, I'll be relocating. I can't stay around here and watch." With one last look that made my eyes fill, Jerry turned on his heel and left, shutting the door quietly behind him.

I leaned against it, my cheek against the wood. Sweet God in Heaven. What had I done?

Three

"You okay, Glory?" Penny had obviously taken out her earbuds.

"As well as can be expected. Jerry's gone. Business trip." I headed back to the couch. I might never get dressed again. Maybe I'd sell my business. Become one of those weird vampires who lived in a cave and flew with bats. I was so depressed I was thinking about giving up cute shoes.

"Did you two break up?" Penny hurried into the kitchen and came out with a bottle of synthetic. She shoved it into my hand. "You look terrible."

"Thanks." I took a swig. "Not a total breakup, hopefully. Just a time-out. Don't worry about me. I always bounce back. I've had lots and lots of practice." I pushed down the urge to throw myself on the couch and cry bitter tears. Nope, I had a job to do here. Might as well get on with it. But two weeks with Jerry gone. I ached already.

"So you guys have split before?" Penny peered at me like she was trying to break through my mental blocks. No way was I letting her into my thoughts again, though constantly keeping her out was a pain and a half. Literally. It always gave me a nagging headache and vamps can't exactly take Excedrin.

"We're taking a break. We do that sometimes. He'll be back." I stared down into my bottle, then determinedly shook off the urge to smack myself with it. "Now tell me about your transformation, Penny. How did that weird vampire get hold of you?"

Penny sighed and sat across from me. "This story won't cheer you up. It was pretty pathetic."

"I understand pathetic. I just barely stopped short of grabbing Jerry's ankle and having him kick me off. And looking like this." I waved my hand at my rat's nest of a hairdo. "Spill."

"I had a blind date. The only kind I ever have lately." Penny made a face. "Surprise, surprise."

"Nonsense. You're full of potential. Jerry has a sister with hair that color. The Scots love it." I smiled encouragingly. "Keep talking."

Penny sighed. "Thanks. Anyway, I have had boyfriends, other lab rats who don't notice things like how I fill out a pair of jeans."

"News flash, Penny. I never met a man yet who didn't appreciate a woman's assets." I looked her over. "I just don't know why you're hiding yours in baggy sweatpants and a sweater that's two sizes too big." I kept my feelings about her horizontal stripes to myself.

Penny blinked. "You want to hear this or not?"

"Sorry. About that night." I waved my hand.

"Anyway, as I was starting to say, my usual dates had never taken me to a fraternity party." She sighed. "Just once I wanted to have a normal college experience, you know?"

"Not a clue. Never got a whiff of college myself, but I can imagine your sister is living it up. Am I right?" I bet Jenny, so cute in that cheerleading outfit, never missed a Saturday night out.

"Of course she is." Penny frowned and picked at a pull in her sweater. Where had she found it? The last-chance bargain rack in a thrift shop? I wanted to rip it off and use it as a dustrag. "So when I had an opportunity for a blind date at a frat party, I jumped at it."

"I get that. I hear about stuff like that from students all the time. Sounds like they have fun." But if Penny had gone looking like this . . .

She gave me a look. "Your block is slipping, Glory. I didn't wear this. Jenny picked out a cute outfit for me. White jeans and a red-and-white-striped top."

"So what happened?" I heaved my block back into place. White on that butt? Sister Jenny wasn't doing this kid any favors. And the stripes too? Well, well. Made me wonder.

"But Jen didn't want me to go. She said she'd heard rumors this wasn't a regular frat party. I ignored her. I'd spent way too many nights chained to my computer working on my latest project." Penny leaned forward. "I've got a grant to study the molecular structure of . . ." She obviously saw my eyes glazing over. "Never mind. I get really wrapped up in it."

"Fascinating. If Ian MacDonald were here, he'd be thrilled to talk to you about it." I shook my head. "But let's get back to the vamp connection. So what about this blind date?"

"Turns out it was one of those parties where the guys at the frat house are supposed to bring a loser, try to get them drunk and then do ugly things like drive them out to the middle of nowhere and dump them. You know, cruel jokes." Penny shuddered. "I'm pretty unaware of social things, but I thought this guy might be into me. He was cute, bringing me punch. Dancing with me."

"And he was setting you up for some kind of mean prank?" I felt my fangs go down. "We are so dealing with this loser."

"I was clueless. The punch was spiked, I should have noticed when I couldn't grip the cup anymore. And when he dragged me out to the parking lot to make out, I mean"—Penny flushed—"did I really think he was going to kiss me?" She covered her face with her hands. "I'm a total idiot," she mumbled into her palms.

"Stop it! No, you're not." I was up and put my arm around

her. "He's a jackass. The guy needs to know he can't get away with this."

Penny looked up, her face splotchy with embarrassment. "No, I deserved what I got. I threw up next to his car. He was disgusted. I didn't blame him." She took a shaky breath. "So I got in the car and shut my eyes. Never asked where we were going, just assumed he was taking me home."

"But he didn't." I patted her shoulder.

"No, he drove to a hilltop and stopped the car. It was quiet, creepy, but he went around, opened my car door and helped me out. I was dumb enough to just go along, thinking maybe there was a romantic view or something. Then he just jumped back in the car and drove off. He never even looked back." Penny shuddered. "I *would* like to teach him a lesson."

"Now you're talking. We won't kill him. Just scare the little prick and let him know he can't get away with treating women like that." I was imagining all kinds of scenarios that would make this frat boy have nightmares for years.

"Sounds like fun." Penny finally smiled but it didn't last. "Anyway." She shook her head. "I sat there, on the grass, too sick to move until I heard something. A man walked out of the woods and stared at me. I wanted to run, but I was paralyzed. When he got closer, he smiled and I saw these gigantic fangs." She took a shaky breath. "That did it. I screamed, then blacked out. When I finally woke up, I heard him talking to me but nothing made sense and there were those fangs. I just conked out again."

"Yes, I can see that it would freak you out." An older vampire's fangs are huge. On top of that, Penny had been drunk, traumatized . . . My heart went out to her.

"When I woke up enough to look around, I realized I was in a shack, no idea where. But I had the most agonizing thirst." She glanced at me. "And it wasn't for water."

I squeezed her shoulders. "Two assholes in one night. How lucky can you get?"

"I did get lucky. I staggered outside and another vampire smelled me." Penny made a face. "I know that sounds gross. I do bathe, you know. But that's what she said. She was flying over and got a whiff of a new vampire and headed down to check it out. She's the one who took me to Damian."

"You'll soon learn to be able to identify other paranormals by their smells." Jerry might be gone and I ached from my head to my heart, but I had Penny here and a real mission. It was a distraction I needed. "I'm getting dressed and we're going to deal with that dickhead who started this. Are you with me?"

"Sure. But I have a question first." Penny was on her feet, following me to my bedroom.

"Ask me anything. If I think it's too personal, I'll tell you to mind your own business."

"Fair enough." Penny glanced at the door. "Look at me. Look at you. Not that you're not cute and all, but you're no size zero and I'm just the same as when that guy sank his fangs into me." She sighed. "Yet every male vampire I meet is drop-dead gorgeous and has the body to match. Even the creep who turned me was easy on the eyes once you looked past those fangs. What's up with that?"

"Life isn't fair?" I laughed at her expression. "Oh, come on. I'm kidding, even if it is true. When we're turned, we're stuck however we are at that moment." It was my turn to sigh. "Oh, our hair still grows"—I grimaced—"everywhere. And our nails. But the rest of us? Doesn't change. Not a pound, not an ounce."

"You're kidding me." Penny collapsed on my bed. "No hope then for this?" She grabbed a handful of excess flab at her waist.

"Not really." I sat beside her. "Trust me. If I'd only known, I would have laid off the clotted cream and jam on my scones and dropped a few pounds before I let Jerry turn me." I made a face. "Of course back in those days, a well-rounded woman was a sign of prosperity. And, hello, when I met Jer, I hit the mother lode." I winked. "In more ways than one."

"Yeah, he's a hunk all right." Penny leaned against me. "No wonder you let him turn you. And if he was rich . . ."

"Oh, he was. And I was a poor widow. He was an answer to my prayers." I sighed, remembering. "But money wasn't the issue for me. It was love at first sight. The vampire thing scared me at first, but I just couldn't resist him."

"Lucky you." Penny stood and looked down. "But bottom line—and I do mean bottom—is that I'm now stuck with this spare tire and big butt?"

"Afraid so."

"Damn." Penny stared at my size-twelve—okay, more like a fourteen—hips.

"On the bright side, you never have to exercise again." I laughed and got up to rummage in my underwear drawer. "Because a sit-up can't tone you and running can't make you lose a single ounce."

A slow smile spread on Penny's face. She really did have a pretty smile and you could see how she resembled her cheer-leading sister when she used it.

"Well, now. You just made this whole thing way more tolerable."

"That's him." Penny gave me an elbow in the ribs when a stocky blond emerged from the frat house and walked to a black SUV in the parking lot. We'd been hiding in a tree near the house for about an hour and it was after midnight. The guys had been drinking and having a fine old time re-hashing the Ugly Chick party of the weekend before. It was all I could do not to burst through the door and clean house.

"What's his name?" I jumped down and waited for Penny, who was a little less secure in her skills. She climbed down cautiously.

"Josh Hansen."

"Watch and wait right here. I'll bring him to you." I strolled over to the car with a twitch of my hips. "Hey, good-looking."

Josh turned at the sound of my voice as he fumbled for his keys. The yahoo didn't have any business driving in his condition. Too many beers. I could smell the alcohol from here. Maybe the best revenge would be to let him get on the road, then get a policeman to stop him. No, he might hit an innocent person on his way to getting caught.

"What?" He finally focused on me. "Hi, there." He smiled.

No surprise, he was interested. I'd worn a low-cut top and a short skirt that shouted "slut looking for a good time." Josh was obviously up for that.

I was close in an instant and ran my hand down his chest. "I was hoping I'd find someone to talk to. It's late and I'm, um, lonely." I licked my lips and Josh got the message loud and clear.

"Uh, yeah, I could give you a ride somewhere." He held up his keys and grinned. "We could talk at my place. I have roommates, but they're cool."

"How about my place? It's just up the street." I grabbed his hand and tugged him toward the tree where Penny waited out of sight. "Closer." I rubbed against him suggestively. "No roommates."

"Yeah, yeah." He stumbled after me until we were on the other side of the enormous oak.

"Josh! Remember me?" Penny was suddenly in front of us, fangs down.

"What the—?" Josh peered at her. "Poppy? What happened to your lips? You go freaky?"

"It's Penny, you dipshit, and I went totally freaky, thanks to you." Penny slammed her fist into his stomach. He leaned over and retched, emptying the contents of his stomach next to his shoes.

"Hah! How'd you like that, you bastard?" She grabbed his hair, then hit his face, drawing blood. "You have no idea what you did to me."

I latched on to her arm before she could hit him again. "Penny, stop. Read his mind." I'd focused on him while Penny had gone on the attack, figuring she should be allowed to get a few licks in for what he'd done to her.

"What do you mean?" Penny kept staring at the blood at the corner of Josh's mouth. "Who cares what he's thinking? Do you smell that?" She lunged toward him.

"No, you don't, girlfriend. He's not the main course on the midnight buffet." I held her away with one hand while I lifted Josh's chin with the other so I could stare into his eyes. I did my thing, making sure he couldn't run away screaming.

"What did you just do? I love that he's not moving. Just waiting for me to take him down. I'm going to drain that creep dry." Penny tried to wrestle her way out of my grip. Not happening. I was that much stronger. I put both hands on her shoulders and shook her.

"Calm down. Listen to me." I stared at her. "I used the whammy on him. Mesmerized him, I guess you'd call it. He's in a kind of dream state so he won't run screaming back to the frat house for reinforcements. I really don't feel like taking on a dozen drunk frat boys. This guy reeks enough." I nodded toward where he leaned against the tree trunk, a vacant expression on his face. "You don't want to drink from him, he's loaded."

"So? Maybe I'll get a buzz too. I could use it. This has been the worst week of my life." Penny gave me a sour look.

"I know. But we were just going to pull a prank here, not kill him. Remember?" I stayed between Penny and Josh. She had a wild look in her eyes and I expected her to try to jump me at any moment. I'd hate to have to hurt her, but would do it if she forced the issue.

"Just move, Glory. Let me at him. Mesmerized? Cool. So he'll just stand there while I sink my fangs into his neck and . . ." Penny snarled. "Damn, he smells like beer but under that is the most delicious aroma . . ." She tried to pry at my hands on her arms with her fingernails. "Let me at him."

"Stop it." I shook her until her head snapped back on her

shoulders. "Get a grip. That's your bloodlust talking. I understand. But I want you to look at Josh and read his mind. He's not what you think."

"Not the asshole who drove me to the middle of nowhere and dumped me so a vampire could ruin my life?" Penny's voice rose and I looked around, afraid the guys in the nearby house would hear us. Luckily they were into loud music and a game that required a chant that drowned out Penny's whine.

"Just look at this guy and listen." I aimed her at Josh and we both tuned in to his mental ramblings.

"Beer pong. Cole's turn. Need to give up beer. Look what happened at Ugly Chick party. Hated it. Got drunk and took girl to Mount Bonnell. Drove down the hill. Supposed to leave her. Rules of the party. Couldn't do it. Not to any girl and she was nice. Liked her. Damn, I was sloshed. Got lost, couldn't find way back up. Lost her. Tried to call, tell her, but no cell signal. Finally got up there, but she was gone. Guess she got signal, ride home. Must have better cell provider. Need new phone. Droid."

Josh sighed and the chanting stopped for a moment. Then a new one started. *"Bucky. He'll win. Next year I'm prez. Stop Ugly Chick thing. Makes frat look bad. Never shoulda left that girl. Bet she freaked. Gotta quit beer pong. Makes me hurl and act stupid. May hurl again. Damn beer."*

Penny turned to me. "He went back to look for me."

"Seems like maybe Josh is basically a nice guy when not under the influence. Might even have boyfriend potential if he wasn't a mortal." I let her go but kept a close eye on her. There was still the bloodlust problem and we both had our fangs down.

"He *is* cute and smart. He's a junior engineering major and makes the dean's list." Penny dragged her eyes from his bleeding lip down his body. "Does that mean my days of having a human boyfriend are gone forever, Glory?" She looked at me, her eyes filled with tears.

"Afraid so, hon. The only use you've got for mortals now is for feeding. And, personally, I don't think that's fair to them. That's why I stick to the synthetics." I glanced at him.

He had a great blood type but was soaked in beer. Even if I was starving, which I wasn't, I wouldn't go for him.

"Guess you wouldn't want to let me use him as a guinea pig then." She approached him, ran a finger through the blood on this lip and tasted it. "Pretty delicious, even with the beer aftertaste."

I sighed. Maybe Josh here owed her a meal, but I wasn't going to let it happen. Just then a group of frat boys emerged from the house.

"Hey, Josh's car is here, but I don't see him. Wonder what happened?" There was a bit of discussion as to whether he'd been drunk enough to wander away and fall asleep somewhere and I could see a search party forming.

I grabbed him and looked him in the eyes. "Josh, go back to your car, tell your buds you got sick, hit the tree and scraped your face. Now you need a ride home from someone who isn't drunk. You won't remember seeing us." I was about to shove him toward the parking lot when Penny grabbed him and took a turn with the eye thing.

"Tomorrow night you'll call that girl Penny and apologize for the Ugly Chick fiasco. You think she's cute and smart and you'll ask her out. Now go!" She aimed him so he wouldn't hit the tree and gave him a push with her boot on his backside. Then she followed me as we ran down the street toward my car.

"A date? You're not going." I glared at her when we were safely away from the house. We could hear the guys exclaiming over Josh's reappearance from down the block.

"Why not? If this whammy thing works and he's really going to do what we told him. Which I doubt." Penny flipped her hair back over her shoulders in a gesture that I bet her sister had taught her.

"Oh, it'll work all right. Vamps have the power to plant suggestions with mortals. I assume he has your number." I stopped next to my convertible and unlocked it with a click of the remote.

"Yes, so why not let him be my practice mortal?" Penny

climbed into the passenger seat. "So I won't go nuts when I finally get to see Jenny."

"You can practice a thousand times and I still won't let you tell your sister about our world. Not till I know more about her and whether she can be trusted to keep our secret." I sighed and got in the car. "We stay off the grid, Penny. Besides, it's too soon for you to go testing yourself. When he calls, you can turn him down. Call him an unfeeling bastard for dumping you up there. It's what he'll expect."

"No way. He's the perfect candidate to test whether I can be with a mortal without draining him dry." She grabbed my arm as I started the car. "Of course you'll have to go along as chaperone."

"You're kidding, right?" I gave her a look and Penny let me go to fasten her seat belt. Chaperone. Nothing like making me feel every one of my advanced years.

"I'm going to see my sister eventually, Glory. So I guess I have to prove to you that I can be around mortals without endangering them. Better to practice on Josh than on Jenny, don't you think?" She lifted her chin as I headed toward Sixth Street.

Brainy brat. "I suppose. But sounds like you're trying to call the shots. *I* decide when things happen in this mentoring business, not the other way around." I stopped at a light and gave her a serious look. "You don't have a clue what you're getting into."

"I'm not a kid." Penny crossed her arms over her chest.

"To me you are. In vampire years you're an infant." I grinned as I drove down the street with the top down on my red convertible, happy that I'd gotten in the last word. It was a really snazzy car for a poor shop owner and I loved it. I'd gotten it after working on a video for a billionaire and the Energy Vampires, a group of local vampire gangsters who I had owed a favor. The EVs weren't to be trusted, but I'd *needed* the car and for once the creeps had kept their end of a deal.

It was a Monday night and my shop was closed but Rafe's club was open. N-V was doing well and Monday was a night with a DJ. Teens could get in but not drink alcohol, of course. I decided to stop and see if Jerry had been right. If Rafe and I did have more going than friendship. And I could introduce Penny to him. It wouldn't hurt to have help keeping an eye on her. We'd be around lots of mortals in the club and Penny could show me if she had a handle on her self-control. I found a parking place along the busy street, even though it was after one in the morning.

"You ever been in the new club N-V, Penny?" I smiled at her as I turned off the engine.

"No. You mean we're going in there? I don't exactly look right for the place." Penny frowned down at her clothes. "When I woke up a vampire, I decided maybe I should go Goth but haven't had time to shop. Damian had someone go to my apartment and grab this stuff. I may be fashion challenged, but I've been around Jenny enough to realize I'm not exactly rocking this look."

I grinned, loving this opportunity. "Well, then. Lucky for you, my shop is just down the street. And *real* vampires try to avoid looking like a stereotype. We let the fakes have the Goth look. If we hurry, we can get you fixed up and still get in before the club closes. I want you to meet one of my best friends. He's the owner of N-V."

"Your shop. Vintage Vamp's?" Penny climbed out of the car and looked around. "Let's go. I love old clothes."

Like I couldn't have figured that out. But Penny would soon learn that my taste was less Salvation Army and more upscale retro. I unlocked my front door, punched in my alarm code and turned on the lights. Penny hurried to the black clothes; I hurried to the warm autumn colors. If I had to whammy her to prevail, I would. This girl was not going to be the poster child for bad vampire stereotypes.

"Go wash your face and brush your hair first while I pick out something for you to try on." I pushed her to the back room. "Bathroom's in there. I'm taking you to my hairdresser as soon as I can get you an appointment. Who's been cutting your hair?"

"I cut my own." Penny frowned. "You want me to wash off my makeup?"

"You have beautiful skin. You don't need base or powder. And black lipstick is horrible on fangs. I have some mascara and a nice coral lipstick in my purse. That's all you need." I grabbed a green silk blouse and black pants in a size I figured would fit her and took them into the back. Shoes. The combat boots she had on were not made for dancing unless on someone's grave.

"Green? I like green. And I thought you wanted me out of black." Penny snatched the clothes and pulled off her old ones to reveal the saddest bra and panties I'd ever seen. We definitely needed a trip to Wally World for some better ones. But not tonight.

"Black pants are a staple. Those should fit. Try them." I darted back into the shop and grabbed some black flats. "The boots have to go. See if these work. Unless you can wear heels."

"No, I fall down. Flats are fine. How are you getting the sizes right?" Penny's skin and hair had come alive as soon as she put on the green. And the black pants fit as if tailored just for her.

"I'm in retail and have waited on a lot of women. I can guess pretty accurately." I grinned. "And you forgot to block your thoughts. You should hear them, very chaotic. Don't be so uptight about shopping. A size is just a number. So what if you buy a sixteen one day and a fourteen another? Some brands run large, others run small."

"Yeah, and I'm this size now, forever." Penny sighed. "Guess I'll just have to deal."

"Yes, you will. Ready?" I put my arm through hers. "You can't see yourself, but you look fabulous. Josh would so not take you to that awful party looking like this."

"Thanks, Glory." Penny hugged me. "Let's go. I've been dying to get into N-V but didn't think I'd get past the doorman."

"Well, now you will. Even if you're under twenty-one, you can whammy a mortal doorman. And if a paranormal is at the door, you just walk on up and they'll know you're a vamp by smell. Since Rafe and Nadia own the club, we're always welcome. Nadia is a vampire and Rafael Valdez is a shape-shifter." I added a gold jacket to my outfit to tone down the slut factor.

"Shape-shifter?" Penny waited as I punched in the security code and locked the shop door behind us. "You mean they're real too?"

"Oh, yes. Weres too. Rafe can change into any form he wishes. So can you when you get the hang of things." I started down the sidewalk. "I didn't like to shift at first." I laughed. "Well, for the first four hundred years actually. But it's such a great defensive tool I had to get over it. Now I can do it when I have to. It does take a lot of energy. We'll work on it."

"How totally cool. I can't see why anyone wouldn't want to be a vampire." Penny paused as we got to the block where the red neon proclaimed we'd arrived at N-V.

"Don't kid yourself, Penny." I gripped her hand. "Just a couple of hours ago you were crying about those morning coffees with your sister. And now you'll never give your parents grandchildren, will you?"

"Geez, Glory, rain on my parade, why don't you? I was trying to make the best of it." Penny jerked her hand from mine. "Let's go. It's late and I want to see the inside of this place."

"Fine. But also remember this is a test. You'll be surrounded by mortals. Let's see you rock that self-control you're so sure you have." I stalked up to the door, then smiled at the shifter standing there. "Hi, Trey, Rafe working tonight?"

"Sure is. Come on in." He sniffed. "Your friend here

should probably show some ID but I'll stamp her hand since she's obviously not going to be drinking alcohol anyway." He reached out. "Hi, pretty lady. I'm Trey."

Penny flushed and let him take her hand. "Penny. I'm new at this. Can you really tell what I am from my, um, smell?"

"You bet." Trey grinned. "You want some lessons in how to tell the difference? I'd be glad to tutor you. I'm off on Wednesday nights. Call me." He pulled a card from his jeans pocket and handed it to her.

"Thanks." She tucked it into the black clutch I'd found for her.

"Anytime." With a wink he glanced into the club. "Oops, here comes the boss man. Talk about sense of smell. When Glory is in the vicinity, he knows instantly. Right, Glory?"

I patted Trey on the shoulder, really happy with him for making a pass at Penny. She was positively glowing from the attention. And Trey was a hot guy. It had certainly taken her mind off the whole vamp issue and the mortals crowding around her. Her fangs were nowhere in sight.

Still, I'd keep a close eye on her while we were here. I wasn't sure I'd been wise bringing her to a place with so many temptations. But I had made her down an extra bottle of synthetic from my back room fridge before we'd left the shop. Hopefully that would help her stay under control.

"Yes, you're right. Penny, Rafe was my bodyguard for five years. He's pretty well programmed to sense me from blocks away. Guess it's a hard habit to break."

"Impossible to break." Rafe snagged me around the waist and gave me a squeeze. "Good to see you here. Who's this?" He smiled at Penny.

"Penny Patterson. I'm mentoring her for the council. To make up for the recent debacle with the red eyes." I gave Rafe a nudge. He was part demon himself and could make his own eyes red when things got dicey. "But I'm happy to help out a fledgling."

"Hi. You must be the former bodyguard." Penny was gaz-

ing around the club as we moved inside. It was pretty spectacular with deep purple walls, those red neon N-Vs and lots
of chrome and strobe lights, along with loud music and a
throbbing beat. The place was packed.

"That's me, Rafael Valdez, at your service." He shook her
hand. "I mean it. You need anything. Can't find Glory and
need help, come here. If I can't help you, someone else here
will. I'll pass the word. Paranormals stick together." He said
this quietly and there were no mortals near enough to hear
him over the music.

"Place seems to be doing well." I was very conscious of
Rafe's arm still around my waist. I should move away. Put
space between us. The fact that I hadn't rebuffed him from
the get-go bothered me. Maybe Jerry had been wise to give
me space. I needed to get my Rafe attraction settled once and
for all.

"Business is booming. Even DJ nights like this one. We've
got live acts lined up for every weekend for the next few
months too." Rafe found us a table near the dance floor.

"Good to hear." I realized my toe was tapping. I did love
to dance. I looked around and saw Trey had pulled Penny out
on the floor. She was shaking her head and he was showing
her some smooth moves.

"Trey's a nice guy. She could do a lot worse." Rafe slid his
hand up to my shoulder.

"She's really confused right now. I have to keep a close eye
on her because she has a sister . . ." I couldn't concentrate
with Rafe's finger trailing up to my ear. "Rafe, stop it."

"Let's dance then." He pulled me onto the floor, and as if
he'd willed it, the music changed to a slow song and the
lights dimmed.

I looked up at him accusingly but he just grinned and
shook his head, then pulled me close, his warm chest firmly
against mine. It felt too damned good. And he danced too
damned well. I gave in after I checked to make sure Penny
was still on the dance floor. She was, with a dreamy look on

her face. Hmm. Well, I'd make sure she went home with *me*. I leaned against Rafe, enjoying his heat and his own smooth moves.

"Jerry left town tonight," I murmured as I laid my head against his shoulder.

"Is that an invitation?" He ran his hand up my back, then down, but not so far that I felt compelled to stop him.

"No, just a heads-up. He's still upset with me, us, for what happened last time he left." I had my thumbs in Rafe's belt, my fingertips in his back pocket. His butt was a work of art I could visualize only too well.

"Yeah, I bet he is. It would take me a century to get over something like that. If ever." Rafe growled and nipped my ear. "So are you two taking a break?"

"I guess we are." I sighed. "Don't do that, Rafe, it drives me crazy."

"That's the plan." He licked the spot he'd bitten.

"I've got Penny in the spare bedroom now and she's only one reason I'm not going to be playing games in mine." I slid my hands up Rafe's back. The music was coming to an end and so was this conversation.

"And the other?" Rafe stopped dancing and pushed me back so he could look in my eyes.

"I have to be loyal to Jerry this time. I won't play him false again." I sighed.

"Sounds like you're doing penance instead of acting on your true feelings, Glo." Rafe ran his thumb over my cheek. "Keep me posted on how it goes. I'll be here."

"Uh, Glory, thought you might like to know." Trey was suddenly right next to us as the lights flashed and the music sped up.

"What, Trey?" I tore my gaze away from Rafe's and the urge to pull that thumb into my mouth.

"Penny said she was going to the ladies' room but she headed outside instead."

Four

"You're kidding me. She took a hike? How long ago was this?" I ran toward the door, Rafe right beside me. My fault. I'd let myself get distracted and hadn't kept an eye on her. Even going to the ladies' room had the potential to be dangerous. I should have warned Trey . . . Hindsight. Which wasn't worth my time.

"What's the problem, Glory?" Rafe stopped me with his hand on my shoulder.

"She has a twin sister. Hasn't told her yet and thinks the thing to do is to turn her." I glanced at a couple of mortals who were just leaving the club. "You know what I mean."

"She's just five minutes ahead of you. Maybe I can track her for you." Trey frowned. "I'm sorry. You should have told me you didn't want her to leave without you. I would have stopped her."

"No, it wasn't your job to ride herd on her, Trey." I sighed. "I need her sister's address. That's where I'll find her. At this time of night, Jenny will probably be asleep and Penny will have to wake her up to tell her. What a shock that will be." I turned to Rafe. "Can we use the computer in your office?"

"Sure, let's go." Rafe turned to Trey. "You're off the hook.

But if you want to help, stay for closing because I'm going with Glory. Nadia's off tonight so it's on you." He tossed Trey a large key ring.

"Wow. Thanks, boss. I'll do it right. I promise." Trey's eyes gleamed like this was a big deal. And it probably was with bar receipts and all the other responsibilities that go with closing a club of this size.

I glanced at Rafe. As usual it was Rafe to the rescue. His partner, Nadia, hated that he did these kinds of things for me. I started to say something but he was already in his office in front of his laptop.

"Her name?"

"Jennifer Patterson, student at the university."

"She's staying in her sorority house. Does that sound right?"

"Yes, that's her."

"Okay, got it. I know where this is. Let's go." He jumped up and I was on his heels as we headed outside and around back.

We shifted into birds and in minutes were behind a large white house that was dark except for a light in one downstairs room. Penny stood outside the back door, her shoulders slumped. I nodded at Rafe and shifted by myself, landing next to my fledgling.

"Going somewhere?" I dropped my hand onto her shoulder.

She turned to look at me, tears running down her face. "No. I can't do it." She leaned against me and I put my arm around her. "What the hell am I doing here at almost two in the morning on a Monday night?"

I led her away from the house before we woke up someone. Rafe had shifted and stood waiting for us on the sidewalk.

"You're a night creature now, Penny. This is prime time for you." I squeezed her shoulders. "I'm sorry, I know this is a rough thing to face." I looked at Rafe.

He pulled out a cell phone and made a call. "Come on, Penny, Glory and I'll show you how beautiful this time of night can be."

Penny looked at him, her face wet. "Beautiful? Nothing looks beautiful to me. Don't you get it? I've lost everything I ever cared about. My family, my career, you name it, I can't do it anymore." She pulled away from me. "You can't distract me with some freaky trick."

"Freaky trick?" Rafe glanced at me. "Let me clue you in, little girl. Those freaky tricks can save your immortal life. Am I right, Glory?"

"Yes. Took me long enough, but I learned that lesson." I shook my head. "I know you're angry and frustrated, Penny. But you haven't lost your career or your family. Not yet, anyway. We'll figure out a way for you to stay in touch with them."

"Sure you will. Until it's obvious that I'm not aging and they are. Then what am I supposed to do? Just disappear? How would *that* make them feel?" Penny looked around, wild-eyed, like she wanted to scream or maybe hit somebody.

"We need to move out. Here comes our ride." Rafe nodded as a black SUV pulled up. A shifter got out, left the motor running, then walked away with a nod. "Let's go."

"Where are you taking me?" Penny dug in her heels when I pulled her toward the car.

"What difference does it make?" I wasn't about to let her get away from me again. "Get in the freakin' car, Penny." A light had come on in an upstairs room in the house. "Now." I shoved her into the backseat, hopped in the front passenger side, and Rafe hit the gas pedal. We were out of there just as the back porch light came on.

Penny looked back. "Guess they heard the noise. Damn it, I can't do anything right."

"Spare us the pity party." Rafe drove and I didn't bother to ask where we were going. "Glory, I hope the council is paying you for this mentoring responsibility."

"They should. I'll check with Damian." I smiled back at Penny. "Come on, vamp girl, lighten up. You're going to have to learn to deal with your new reality and there are some cool perks. Trust me on that."

"Yeah, right. Trust you. Like vampires are so trustworthy. I'm the undead proof of that." Penny kept staring back toward the sorority house.

I decided to let that one go. She needed time. I got that.

Penny finally turned around to frown at me. "So far this 'new reality' sucks and I don't understand half of it. I was offered a teaching assistant's job for the fall. Forget that now. Not unless they gave me all night classes." She slumped in her seat.

"Sounds like a drag. Grading papers, trying to make bored college kids pay attention to someone younger than they are." I reached back to pat her hand. "You dodged a bullet."

"I wasn't seriously considering it." She shrugged. "I prefer research. And grant work can be done anytime, anywhere. I have a few irons in the fire." Her mouth trembled. "But that doesn't mean I didn't want to have the choice."

"Quit whining." Rafe was obviously all for tough love as he pulled into a deserted area on top of a hill.

I recognized the place. He'd gone ballistic here once when I'd let him know our relationship was going back to being friends without benefits. There was still a charred stump as evidence. Hmm. I gave him an inquiring look but all I got back was a bland smile.

"So what are we doing here?" Penny finally sat up straight and looked out the window.

"I'm going to teach you to shape-shift." Rafe opened his car door. "I had to work with Glory to get her comfortable with it, so I figured I'd help with this part of your education. What do you say, Glory?"

"Sure, go for it. You need to learn this, Penny." I got out of the car and waited while Penny climbed out.

"You're serious. You're really going to make me turn into something else. What? A bat?" She looked down at her green blouse. "Will we have to strip off? No way, no how. I'm not comfortable with that."

I laughed. "Luckily, we can do it wearing what we have

on, even down to our shoes. Believe me, if I had to go skinny shifting, I'd never have made it a habit."

Rafe winked at me. "Not saying it isn't more comfortable that way, though. And fun if you're doing it with the right person."

"Okay, Rafe, let's just get on with it." I turned to Penny. "Shifting is good for defense. It can help you escape when you're in a tight spot."

Penny frowned. "What am I going to be defending myself from? I can take down a frat boy now with my handy-dandy new fangs." She gave us a demo with a snarl. "And I seem stronger too. I'm not one to go to a gym, but my punch had some power behind it tonight."

"You hit someone?" Rafe looked from Penny to me. "What's been going on?"

"I'll tell you later." I smiled at him. "Now, Penny, let's pretend you're surrounded and outnumbered by people brandishing stakes. We can be killed with a wooden stake to the heart. That part of the vamp mythology is true."

"Gross." Penny looked around, searching the shadows. "You mean there are people out there who know vampires exist and hunt them?"

"A few. Luckily most of society doesn't believe them. Writes vamp hunters off as crazy." Rafe smiled. "Or considers the stories about you guys pure fiction."

"Obviously it's not." Penny sighed. "This is almost too much to take in."

"You can handle it." I patted her shoulder. "You have to. Now back to defense." I stepped back and looked around, pretending I was surrounded. "Vamp hunters everywhere, but they're mere mortals. Too many to fight, but you can escape. What do you do?"

"Shape-shift?" Penny looked interested. "But forget flying. Not my thing."

"Why not? You need to move in a hurry. Flying is a good way to escape and I prefer doing it as a bird. Though you can

become a bat if you don't mind being a cliché." I studied the
sky. It was a clear night with a sliver of a moon. "This is a
perfect night to practice. No wind."

"I told you. Forget flying. Can't I shift into other animals
and just scare the hell out of them? How about a panther?"
Penny also glanced at the sky, but not appreciatively.

"You can shift into whatever you want, but what's wrong
with flying?" I got close to her. "You afraid of heights?"

"I'm acrophobic, okay? Deal with it." Penny's chin lifted.
"I don't do airplanes or roofs and I'm sure not going to do, uh,
birds or bats. Trust me, if I hadn't been scared, I'd have jumped
out of my bedroom window earlier tonight and gone to see
Jenny then. I actually opened it and tried to take the leap, then
chickened out."

"Give me a break." It had never occurred to me that she
might have gone out her window.

"You give me one. No flying." Penny had a mulish look
and I figured arguing was futile.

"Now that's a problem." I glanced at Rafe. "Got to be
honest with you. Once I got past my own reluctance, flying
out of trouble saved my butt a time or two."

"She's right, Penny." Rafe and I exchanged looks full of
memories. "Something like a panther might scare away a pred-
ator, but it's also a pretty big target. You could try sneaking
away. Become something tiny. Like an ant or cockroach." He
frowned. "Of course you can get stomped or kicked. Right,
Glory?"

I shuddered; Penny too. "Ancient history, Rafe." I'd done
the roach thing and had an unhappy ending. Literally.

"I'd much rather work the fear factor." Penny had obviously
been thinking this over. "Panther, lion, cheetah. Obviously I'm
partial to cats."

"That could work. But a hunter will just pull out a conventional weapon and shoot you. You could be wounded, which
would slow you down." Rafe was solemn, all business. "Honestly, you need to try to get over this height thing. Now that

you're a vampire, your perspective might have changed. Go for the bird, Penny. At least once. Are you game?"

Penny sighed, her shoulders tense. "Okay, I'll try. But no guarantees."

"That's a given." I smiled encouragingly. "Now pick a kind of bird and get it in mind."

"Fine. I've always liked bluebirds. Like that bluebird of happiness that dumped on my head a few nights ago." Her smile was wry. "Now what?"

"Now you visualize that bluebird. I mean, really see it in your mind and imagine *becoming* the bird from the claws up to the beak. Then flap your wings and fly up to a branch in that tree over there. Rafe and I will meet you. We'll still be able to talk to each other in our minds." I watched Penny. She closed her eyes, her forehead wrinkling as she concentrated, her fists clenched. Nothing happened. Finally she opened her eyes.

"What's wrong? Why am I still a person?" She looked down and stomped her foot.

"I think you're trying too hard and worrying too much about the flying." I smiled, totally sympathizing with her. I'd freaked out when I'd first tried to shift, sure I'd be stuck forever as a bird or a bat. Not that I was sharing that concern with her. "Take a few breaths, relax and picture yourself that beautiful blue. Feel your feathers, the air under your wings. Now close your eyes and let yourself transform."

Rafe gave me an elbow. "Can't believe you're actually pretty good at this. I thought I was going to be the one giving the lessons."

"I'm just telling her what you told me to help get me over my own phobia." I grinned when I saw Penny suddenly change. She looked down at her feet, now claws, then up again.

"Am I . . . ?"

"Yes, you're a beautiful bluebird. Now flap your wings and see if you can fly." I did my thing, becoming a mockingbird and Rafe became a blackbird. We did a few laps around the hilltop before we settled on a branch near the top of a tree to watch.

"Come on up!" I was talking in my mind now. We all were.

"I—I can't." Penny sounded panicked. *"Get me the hell out of here!"* She looked up at me, then hopped a few steps. I flew down to land beside her.

"Calm down. Take it easy. Hey, you did shift. Great first step. But if you could just flap your wings and come up a foot or two, I know you'd like it. It's really amazing to fly." I took off and soared above her.

"Says you." She sat in the dirt. *"I'm not flapping anything. How do I get back to me?"* Her voice was shaking and I could see panic about to set in.

I landed beside her again. *"Okay, Penny. Just relax. Maybe we tried this too soon."*

She stabbed me with her beak. *"Get me back to myself. Now!"* Her bird eyes were wild.

"Calm down and we will." Rafe flew down to her other side and his quiet voice finally seemed to penetrate her panic.

"I'm a failure." Bird tears dripped off Penny's beak. *"Intellectually I should be able to overcome this ridiculous phobia. Talk myself out of it."* She trembled, her feathers quivering. *"But, but I can't."* Big birdie boo hoos.

I wanted to reassure her because I'd been where she was now, but I still smarted from that stab with her beak. Hey, she'd drawn blood. I let Rafe handle her.

"No, you're not a failure." Rafe moved closer. *"Glory's right. We did rush you. Now let's get you back to your human form. Imagine yourself Penny as usual. Don't overthink it, just picture feet, body, head. I'm right here, watching you."* Rafe spoke gently, with an assurance that didn't allow for doubt. Then he took off. I bet he was remembering how I used to have meltdowns, positive I'd never look human again. He'd talked me through the whole thing.

I sat beside Penny, proud of her when she suddenly transformed without a hitch. I did the same, totally at ease with it now.

"Fantastic. You're a natural." I patted her shoulder, deciding not to mention the puncture wound on my arm that was already healing.

"Oh, my God! That was a total freak-out! I'm not turning into any more flying things, but now that I know I can get back, I can see shifting is definitely doable." Penny wiped tears off her cheeks. "What else can I be? What else have *you* been, Glory?"

"You can be just about any animal you're familiar with. Rafe was a Labradoodle for years. I tried my hand at being a golden retriever." I smiled. "You could be a cat too, a house cat. I'm sure your own pet would find that interesting."

"No kidding." Penny shook her head. "Don't think I'll go there."

"Isn't this just the coziest scene ever," a male voice said from the other side of the clearing.

"I'm getting teary just witnessing all the bonding going on." Another male voice.

Rafe and I stood in protective mode between the voices and Penny, when two men shimmered into view. One was tall and lean with long dark hair and an expensive black suit. His white shirt and gold tie were immaculate. The other man was a bit shorter but not by much. He was more casually dressed but you could tell he had an expensive tailor too. His trousers had an Italian look and his sport shirt was silk. He was dressed all in black, down to his leather loafers. But his hair was a golden blond. Both men were handsome enough to make Penny shove at me so she could get a better look.

"Well, well, I knew this was a demon's playground and here's the demon spawn himself with some of his playthings." Blond guy flicked his hand at the burned bush Rafe had taken out when I'd tried to dump him. Oops. Rafe had warned me that act might have stirred interest in him down below. So these guys must be ambassadors from hell. A slight breeze brought a whiff of sugar to me. I recognized it instantly. Demons put on the sweet smell along with a beautiful façade when they came up to be around mortals.

"Glory?" Penny tapped me on the back.

"Hush. Rafe and I will handle this." I hoped and prayed we would anyway.

"Gloriana!" The dark one strode across the clearing, his hand outstretched. "I'd never have recognized you from Alesa's description. Though she was a bit rattled by her visit here, there is no excuse for missing the mark like she did. You are obviously a natural blond." His gray eyes swept over me, like he'd peeled the clothes right off to see down to my skin underneath. Rafe growled and stepped between us.

"You've gone far enough, Caryon." Rafe held up his hand. "What the hell are you doing here?"

"Steady, demon child." Blond guy was at his cohort's side. "We're here on legitimate business. Some with you, some with the delicious Gloriana here." He smiled at me, suddenly around Rafe as if he didn't exist. "Alesa says hi."

"I'll bet she does." I didn't smile back. "I have no business with the likes of you. Go back where you came from." The sugary smell was so strong it was nauseating.

"Get away from her, Spyte." Rafe thrust an arm between us.

"Spite? Carrion? Are you kidding me? What is this? A bad comic strip?" Penny made the mistake of giggling.

"Oh, does the new vampire need a demo?" Caryon smiled, suddenly showing a mouthful of deadly looking fangs. His hunky façade vanished and he was the stuff of nightmares, all scaly skin and snout. Beside him, Spyte chuckled when Penny clutched my skirt, then sank to the ground, whimpering.

"Quit it!" I don't know where my nerve came from, maybe from carrying around one of their evil sisters for weeks. "State your business and then go."

Caryon was back to his pretty-boy self. "Rafael, aren't you proud of your woman?"

Rafe glanced at me, sending me a mental message to be

careful. "Of course I am. She's not afraid of your butt-ugly self or interested in your pretty one. Now what do you want? Come to collect a debt for Lucifer?" He glanced at the bush he'd burned with a look from his eyes when they'd gone red with fury that night. "For flaming that thing?"

"That will be collected at a date to be named later." Spyte laughed and brushed an insinuating hand down Rafe's black N-V T-shirt.

I grabbed Rafe before he could start something he'd regret, my stomach heaving at the idea of hell's payback. Then I looked around. "Penny! Where—"

"The little rat scurried away into the brush. She's cowering over there. Thinks we can't find her." Caryon smiled. "Don't worry, little girl, we're not interested in you tonight. Just your mentor."

"What do you want with me? And you will leave Penny the hell alone." I stayed shoulder to shoulder with Rafe, though I knew he wanted me behind him. Not happening.

"Oh, Alesa was so right." Spyte put his hand on Caryon's arm. "She *does* have a weakness. Glory, we are so glad to know that."

Rafe growled and surged toward them until he was suddenly turned to stone. It was a demon trick and I was surprised the two hadn't whipped it out sooner. Rafe was frozen in place, only his eyes moving. I knew they could have relaxed their hold enough to let him talk, but obviously I was the one they wanted to chat with this time. I felt chilled right down to my black boots.

"Weak? I don't think so. I handled Alesa and I can handle you two." I glared at them though I knew I hadn't exactly been a tower of strength when the female demon had taken up residence inside me. Still, she hadn't managed to turn me into one of her disciples of evil either. So I considered it a victory for the good guys. "You're wasting your time here. Go back to hell where you belong."

"No, not yet. Your weakness is so obvious." Spyte moved in a blur and returned the same way, a wiggling white rat in his hand. "For example, check out this cute little rodent. Look in her eyes. Recognize anyone?"

I hate rats, even the obviously pet kind, but I recognized the frantic golden brown eyes. Penny. She sent me hysterical mental messages as Spyte held her, first by the tail, then in his hand, alternately squeezing then petting her.

"Put her down!" I lunged toward him but he danced back. Caryon slipped his arm around my waist, anchoring me in a death grip that I couldn't escape.

"Ah, yes. Glory loves her little and not-so-little friends." Caryon glanced back at Rafe, whose eyes glowed red. "Some more than others, eh, Rafael?" His laugh was full of innuendo and I felt like he'd watched me in dirty videos. What had Alesa told these bastards? Oh, God. And what was Spyte going to do to Penny?

He dropped her in his pants pocket and grinned at me, letting me see his real teeth, sharp and horrifying.

"Morning snack, right, Car?"

"Chopped up in an omelet?" Caryon smacked his lips. "Garlic or cilantro?"

"Both. I saw the most wonderful recipe on this cooking show—"

"Stop it! What do you want?" I jerked against Caryon's hold, the reek of him this close making me gasp, like I'd been dropped in a vat of boiling sugar. I swallowed bile.

"We come with a proposition. From the big boss down below." Caryon frowned at me. "Don't you dare throw up on my new shoes. Italian leather, custom-made." He thrust me away from him. "Stay."

My feet stuck to the ground but at least I could inhale fresh air again. I saw Spyte's pants wiggling and he grimaced. Guess Penny had bitten him through the cloth. Good for her. But I sent her a mental message to be still. He could kill her with a hard smack against his thigh.

"What's the proposition?" I didn't want to hear it. Would never do anything for the Devil or Lucifer or whoever was calling the shots down there. But I'd play along for Penny's sake.

"Lucifer. Lucifer sent us." Spyte smiled. "You know we can read your thoughts, don't you? Your puny vampire mind blocks don't work on us so don't even try it."

"Whatever. Just spill it." I feigned a yawn. "Is there anything more boring than carrying on over a lost cause? Just release Rafe from that stupid freeze thing and let Penny go so she can shift back. She's new and now I'm afraid you've traumatized her for the rest of her immortal life." At least they'd left my arms and head loose from the freeze. I glanced back at Rafe and gave him an encouraging smile. Then I put my hands on my hips to show I still had attitude. "Well?"

"You're all about others, aren't you?" Caryon shook his head. "This may not work, Spyte. If she's really"—he shuddered—"good, how can she do the job?"

"There's only one way to find out. Tell her." Spyte dragged Penny out of his pocket. "This damned rat is showing potential. She actually gnawed a hole in my pocket and broke skin." His black eyes twinkled. "She was going for my family jewels."

"That's my girl. She probably thought that ripping them off and tossing them to me would be a nice parting gift." I nodded at her proudly. "Since you seem to be determined to keep her."

Caryon laughed. "Glory, Glory, you are such a hoot. Do you think we'd ever be afraid of you or your little fledgling?"

"You know, I'm thinking. If Glory won't do this job, maybe Miss Penny here will. I *would* like to keep her. You should hear her vocabulary. And she bit me, Car. Me! I'm really impressed." Spyte's gruesome mouth was a perfect O of surprise.

"It's an idea. A backup plan." Caryon studied Penny with an interest that made me desperate to snatch her away. If I could only move.

"Back up to this shoe, Caryon, and I'll shove it up your backside when you have the guts to unfreeze me." I gave him my best snarl. "Leave. Penny. Alone."

Caryon just smiled as he focused on me again. "I will if

you take our deal. Lucifer wants you to gather souls for him. You know so many interesting people. Alesa gave him quite a list of potential donors. And he thinks you're in a good position to be a harvester for us."

"You're out of your freaking mind." I watched Penny lying in Spyte's hand as he stroked her between her ears. She was shivering. "Never."

"We can't *make* you do it." Caryon looked up at the night sky. "There are these aggravating rules in place. But we can bribe you, and Alesa suggested a really good one."

"I can't imagine what you could offer me that would tempt me to lure my friends and acquaintances over to the dark side." I wasn't really listening. I was trying to keep my mind blank since I knew they could read it, though I desperately wanted to get us out of there.

"Gloriana St. Clair," Caryon intoned with the voice of an announcer on a quiz show. "How would *you* like to be a size six?"

Five

"You have got to be kidding me. *That's* your bribe?" I stared at Spyte.

"Yes." He frowned down at Penny, who was gnawing on his thumb. "Alesa assured me that was one of your heart's desires. That's how we get people on the give-up-your-soul train. Dangle something they really, really want in front of them and—bam!—they're ours. Ouch?" Black blood began to ooze from the wound Penny had made.

"Penny! Don't drink a demon's blood. I'm here to tell you it can have bad consequences." I was relieved when I saw her back away from the droplets. Spyte tossed her to his other hand with a grimace.

"That wasn't nice, Glory. Demon blood is delicious." He sniffed, then stuck his thumb in his mouth to lick off the blood.

"Nice? You expect me to be nice to you? I've been a size six before, for about five minutes. *It* was nice. I even loved it. But I won't sacrifice my friends for it. No thanks." I put out my hand and realized I could almost reach Rafe's arm. "Please let us go now." I looked up at the sky. We had a few hours before dawn, but not so much that it didn't occur to me that these demons could leave me like this to fry when the sun came up. And Penny. What would happen to her? Fear slammed into me like a stake in the heart.

Caryon smiled. "Aw, Glory, don't worry. We aren't here to terminate you." He exchanged glances with Spyte. "Yet."

"You said you can't force the issue." I hated that my voice quavered.

"A technicality. Unfortunately." Spyte frowned when Penny began to dig her claws into his palm. "But we can offer incentives. You'll see. The first one is a surprise. Next time you're in your shop, or even at home, look around. You might see something unexpected." Spyte handed Penny to me. "I do like the rat. She's a tough little thing. I'm keeping an eye on her."

"And, Glory, don't dismiss our proposition out of hand. You don't have to harvest souls from your friends, you know. Just from the people you meet who you think deserve hell. You'd be doing a public service." Caryon smiled, giving me another glimpse of jagged fangs that made me shudder. "Simon Destiny ring a bell?"

"Simon? I figured he was already marked for hell." He served a goddess who came from down there, so it was a no-brainer.

"Oh, he is. But he's playing for the wrong team. Lucifer wants him on ours. We have kind of a competition going on down there. Each god and goddess in the Underworld has its own turf. And collects its own, um, victims." Big smile from Spyte. "Nobody trusts each other on the accounting thing so we have a scorekeeper. He posts quarterly stats. Right now, well, let's just say Luc doesn't like to fall behind and leave it at that." He and Cary shuddered and didn't that make me wonder how Lucifer expressed displeasure.

"It spices up what could be a rather dull existence." Caryon sighed. "You know roasting, filleting, slicing and dicing. And the screams are endless." He arched a brow at Spyte. "Some of us have started to tune it out."

"Can I help it if I got caught with my iPod during playtime? Drawing and quartering is so archaic. And when they get out the cattle prods . . . I mean who wouldn't yawn? Get over it, Cary." Spyte huffed.

"I'll get over it when the job's done. We're working off seventy demerits here. Demerits you got us, Spyte." Caryon turned his back on his cohort. "New recruits give us some bragging rights, points."

"And entertainment," Spyte added.

"Exactly." Caryon rested his hand on Spyte's shoulder. "Simon's so deliciously bad. Worth a bundle to Luc. All the Energy Vampires are. And we have a feeling you could recruit Simon for us, Glory. You know you'd love to bring him down." He winked. "And I do mean down."

"Not denying that. But why do you want immortals anyway? Seems like you'd have a long wait. Like forever." I dropped my arm so Penny could scurry down my leg and into the brush again. She could hide there until these yahoos left. If they ever did. I glanced at the sky again.

"You know as well as I do that immortals bite the big one all the time. Like Miss Penny's sire did the other night. He's down there serving time right now." Caryon raised his voice. "Bet that makes your undead heart sing, doesn't it, furry one?"

Penny walked out from behind a bush, back in human form again but obviously shaken. She sucked it up though and actually walked right up to stand next to me and squeezed my hand.

"Sure does. Tell me he's roasting over a pit or something."

"Or something." Spyte smiled and looked her over with that nasty X-ray vision of his. Oh, how I wanted to rip out his throat. I'd even risk sucking in some demon blood to do it.

"We don't share all the details of the joys of hell with potential, um, members, Penny, dear." Caryon whipped a black card with gold letters out of his breast pocket. "Here's my number. Call if you wish to talk. About anything."

"Don't touch that!" I strained against the freeze that kept me glued to the ground. But Penny just grabbed the card and stuck it in her pocket.

"I have a question for you." Penny glanced at me. "Why

bother Glory here? Why don't you just recruit this Simon character yourself?"

"Hmm. Good question. She's a smart one." Caryon glanced at Spyte. "It's like this. We can't steal players from another team directly, you see. Stupid rule, but it's one we can't go around."

"That's right. So we have to get insignificants like Glory here to do the dirty work, so to speak. Leaves our hands clean." Spyte's laugh sent chills down my spine. "As if that concept matters down there. But somehow fair play is the one thing Luc insists on. Can you believe it?"

"No." I didn't believe any of this. "You're wasting your time here. I am not working for the Devil. Period."

Spyte laughed again. "We'll see. Oh, yes, we'll see." He looked down and set my favorite boots on fire. I felt the heat lick at my toes and bit my lips to hold back a scream.

Penny did screech and pulled off my jacket to smother the flames. "You creeps! What was that for?"

"Just a little reminder of who you're talking to and where we're from. This isn't a game, people. Take it seriously." Caryon waved a hand. "We'll be going now. You have a lot to think over, don't you, Glory?" Caryon ran a finger tipped in a black claw over my cheek, then simply vanished. Spyte gave us a little wave then disappeared as well.

"Son of a bitch!" Rafe jerked free and ran to me. "Are you all right?"

"I'm okay. Boots? Not so much." I fell to the ground, my toes stinging but not really hurt. Not like my boots were. They were a melted mess. Ralph Lauren black patent, found on sale, now history. I handed Penny the ruined jacket and risked singed fingers to pull down the zippers and get the boots off. Damned demons.

Rafe examined my toes, reassured himself that they were just a little pink, then stomped around the hillside. Of course it was futile. The demons were gone, the only other sign they'd ever been there the cloying scent of sugar that clung to the air, like we were downwind from a donut shop. Mortals would think that was yummy. Me? Since I couldn't eat a donut, it was nothing but more torture.

"That was strange and scary as hell." Penny sagged against me. "Uh, literally, I guess." I could feel her shaking as I hugged her and met Rafe's eyes over her head. He looked like he wanted to flame another bush. "When he threw me from one hand to the other, I almost died. Again."

"You certainly got to practice your shape-shifting. But a rat?" I pulled back and looked at her.

"We have them in the lab. It was all I could think of." Penny's hand went to her pants pocket. "Those demons blew my mind."

"Penny, give me that card." I gave her a stern look.

"No way. It's cool. A demon's card. It's going in my 'Oops, I'm a Vampire' scrapbook." She held her hand over her pocket. "I'm not going to call him. Are you kidding me? My grandpa is a Baptist preacher. He'd have a cow and calves." Penny sighed. "Of course what would he do if he saw my fangs?"

"You won't let him. And just because you're a vampire now doesn't mean you're bound for hell. I go to church. As many Sundays as I can. Night services." I felt Rafe's arm go around me. I turned to him. "You okay?"

"Sure. I'm worried about you. Getting attention like this from Lucifer is no joke. No, they can't coerce you, but evil is their specialty. They can apply lots of pressure indirectly to get what they want. Like the hot foot just now." He leaned down to kiss my cheek. "That bitch Alesa sicced them on you as payback for playing hard to get when she was inside you. Now they'll see you as a personal challenge." Rafe's frown was so fierce Penny stepped back from him. "They'll be back. I guarantee it."

"Way to make me feel better, Rafe." We climbed into his car. Penny peppered me with questions about Alesa that I didn't want to answer as the dawn dragged at me. Rafe drove fast, anxious to check with Trey on how the closing had gone. Reality. Unfortunately, we hadn't faced the last of it.

"Jenny called me six times while I slept." Penny shoved her cell phone in my face as soon as I rolled out of bed. "I don't think I'll ever get used to just dying at dawn."

"Can I brush my teeth before I deal with you and your sister drama?" I pushed her out of the way and staggered into the bathroom.

"It's not drama. It's my life, Glory." Penny stood in the bathroom doorway.

I ignored her and grabbed my toothbrush. I squeezed toothpaste, leaned against the sink, looked up and screamed.

"Glory! What happened?" Penny grabbed my arm and turned me to face her. "The demon's back?"

Okay, Penny was real. I touched her face, clear of makeup, and patted her tangled hair. Hairdresser. Calling her first thing. Then I slowly turned toward the mirror above the sink. No, not possible.

"L-l-look. What do you see?" I pointed at the mirror.

"You trying to torment me? I already brushed my teeth and washed my face. Talk about a freak-out. Checking the mirror and nobody . . ." Penny stared at the mirror and then at me. "Oh. My. God."

"What do you see, Penny?" I held on to the sink to keep from falling to the floor.

"You—you have a reflection. How did that happen?" Penny waved her hand in front of my face but it didn't show up in the mirror, only as a brief distortion in my reflection.

Me. My reflection. Of my face. I was seeing my face for the first time, except in that computer monitor, in more than four hundred years. I leaned closer. Scary. Not that I looked old. No, I was still a dewy twenty-two, though I guess I looked older by today's standards. I'd had no access to face creams or even decent soap back in the day. My hair was wild and I brushed it back. I needed my own appointment with the shifter who cut my hair. I wouldn't mind some highlights too and, geez, my brows could stand a serious plucking.

"Glory, snap out of it." Penny shook my arm. "Has this happened before?"

"No." I dragged my eyes from the mirror. "The demons said they had an incentive for me to become a size six. I guess this is what they were talking about."

Penny stepped out of the bathroom and did a quick tour of the small apartment. "Well, there's sure no full-length mirror in here. Guess to get the whole effect you'll have to go down to your shop."

"Full effect." I glanced back at my rear. "Those bastards. They want to torture me. Want me to look at myself and see how big I am." I picked up my toothbrush again. "Size six. Who wouldn't want to be a size six?"

"Yeah, I know what you mean. I haven't seen that number since I was thirteen except in the shoe department." Penny glanced down at her faded sleep shirt. "Jenny's a six."

"Of course she is. So's one of my best friends. Size six is gorgeous. Worshipped by the masses as perfection for some reason." This was a hot-button issue for me. Totally unfair, this obsession with size. Big bones, heredity. There were so many factors that went into a woman's size. My own was the result of Jeremiah Campbell not warning me that I'd be stuck when he turned me. And he'd chosen a day when I was bloating, for crying out loud. Stuffed me like a Thanksgiving turkey for weeks before my V-day too. Men. They just don't get it.

"It's so unfair!" Penny peered over my shoulder, as fascinated by the fact that she couldn't see herself as I was that I could.

"Exactly." I waved my toothbrush in front of the mirror, still thrilled that I could see the hand holding it, my face behind it, the whole enchilada. "But I'm not giving in to those evil demons. I'm not working for the Devil. I'm at peace with my chubby thighs." Couldn't believe I said that with a straight face.

"Guess we might as well be, we're stuck with them." Penny waved that black card in front of me. "You want to call Caryon and tell him so?"

"No, thanks. I'm ignoring him and his torments. Tonight we deal with your sister. Did Josh call too?" I brushed my teeth, listening as Penny described the message from the frat boy. Seems he'd left a long apology, then a stammering request for a real date. If she could forgive him.

I rinsed out my mouth and turned to face her. "Call him back and say no."

"I already called him back and said yes." Penny glared at me. "He's cute. He's nice. I want to give it a shot." She toyed with that damned black card. "And his blood smelled delicious."

"That last sentence just sealed your fate, Penny. Not gonna happen. When is he supposed to pick you up?" I managed to snatch the card. I wasn't ripping it up. The number might come in handy.

"It *is* gonna happen, Glory." Penny turned and stomped into the living room. "We're meeting in your shop at nine tonight. Hitting a late movie. Deal with it."

"Deal with this." I was on her heels. "You will not taste his delicious blood. You will not drink from mortals. You will only drink synthetics while you live under my roof."

"You're kidding me. I can't believe all those vampires I saw at Damian's stick to synthetics. In fact, it was obvious that they didn't." Penny's hands were fists. "There were mortals around that I'm sure were providing meals for some of them."

Okay, I had to admit even Jerry did the mortal thing from time to time and Damian's crowd had been known to keep mortal pets. Nice that he'd let Penny see that. "You're right. A vampire with experience can drink from a mortal." I grabbed one of Penny's fists. "But you, my dear, are about five minutes old and haven't learned to control your bloodlust. Put you close to a mortal and you're liable to go too far. You want to kill Josh?"

She sighed and unclenched her hand, drawing it away from me. "I did. When he left me on that hilltop. But now I just want a date with a cute guy. Is that so horrible?" Her eyes filled with tears. "I want to be normal."

"The normal train left the station the night you were turned." I pulled her down to the couch. I hoped this didn't turn into a sobfest. "Tell you what. Meet Josh. I'll follow you every step of the way. I'll do you a favor and stay out of sight unless I see you start something that will become dangerous to him. I'm afraid that's as close to a normal date as you're going to get right now." I hit the fridge and grabbed a cold bottle of synthetic. "Did you drink one of these yet? You need to fill up before you get close to him."

"Thanks, Glory. I'm sure you have better things to do tonight than trail after me." Penny twisted off the top of her bottle.

"I do, but I'll deal." I opened my own bottle and noticed I was running low on regular synthetic. "Hey, stay away from the Blud-Lite, it has alcohol in it."

"Glad you warned me, though I kind of figured that out from the name and the label." Penny smiled. "Blood with alcohol. They make vampire drugs too?"

"Yes. That Simon Destiny the demons want is a vampire drug dealer. Vampire Viagra is his big moneymaker."

Penny grinned. "You're kidding. Vampires need Viagra? My illusions are shattered."

"No need." I smiled back. "I don't know if you're, um, experienced or not . . ." I remembered that nineteen in this day and age wasn't the same as it had been way back when. I'd married at sixteen, been widowed at twenty, and had found Jerry and bliss at twenty-two.

"I'm not a virgin." Penny winked. "I even lived with one of my lab-rat boyfriends for a while last year. My parents stroked out, but they got over it. Sending me away to college when I was so young, they had to get used to the fact that I was going to try everything I could as fast as I could, you know?"

"Not really, but let's try to slow down on the vampire thing, okay? Just know that vamp men have got it going on and on." I actually flushed. "Never mind." I sat on the couch. I could see myself in a mirror. Wow. I grabbed my purse and pulled out the compact I carried strictly for the powder. I opened it and gazed into the mirror I'd never bothered to look in before. My skin was so pale. When summer got here, maybe I'd try one of those spray tans.

"Earth to Glory." Penny sat beside me. "You've really not been able to use a mirror in hundreds of years?"

"Nope." I snapped the compact closed. "Wonder how long this'll last. The demons have got to know I'm not harvesting souls for them, no matter how bad the person is who crosses my path."

"But maybe you'd be doing a service. For the Lord." Penny looked serious.

"Penny, don't even think about it. The Lord wouldn't want you to even speak to a demon, much less trust one. You can't do anything connected to hell without payback. I had a demon inside me and I got to know their kind way too personally. It's an impossible situation. There's no way I could just merrily send bad guys to hell and not get sucked down there myself. Besides, who am I to decide who is good and who is hell-worthy? I sure don't want that kind of responsibility."

Penny's phone rang. She picked it up off the coffee table. "It's Jenny. I've got to answer this."

"Fine. But you can put her off if she wants to meet. Until after your date with Josh." I sat back and waited for her to answer the phone.

"Hey, sis." Penny listened to her sister exclaim over how hard it had been to reach her. "Yes, I was in the lab. Had to turn off my phone."

"Someone saw you outside the house late last night. Bein'

pushed into an SUV. Are you okay?" Jenny's voice sounded a lot like Penny's only with a bit more Texas twang.

"What? Outside the sorority house? Someone's been taking those weird sleeping pills again." Penny laughed and rolled her eyes at me. "What would I be doing lurking outside your house? And in the middle of the night?"

"I know. Sounds nuts, doesn't it, Pen?" Jenny laughed. "So where are you? Can you meet for coffee? I got the cutest new blouse to show you. And there's this math test comin' up. I just can't get the hang of this one type of equation. I know you could explain it and it would click. We are always on the same wavelength. Am I right?"

Penny's eyes filled and she shook her head. "Can't meet tonight, Jen. Sorry about the math test. Judith in your sorority can help you. Go to her. I've got a date. Really cute guy. I'll tell you all about it later. Oops, got to go. He'll be here soon and I'm gonna jump in the shower." She ended the call, then sobbed.

"Aw, Penny, I'm sorry." I rubbed her arm.

"M-m-math! I always help her with math. But now I can't because I might bite her on the neck and d-d-drain her dry." Penny fell over and cried on my shoulder.

"No, you can't because you have a date. All in all, you handled that very well." I patted her back as my robe got damp.

"I lied to her." Penny sat up and wiped her eyes.

"Get used to it. It will become your way of life with mortals." I glanced at the clock, then got up and walked toward the bathroom. "If you're serious about going on this date, we'd better get moving. My hot water heater is ancient. It has only one long hot shower in it or two short ones. I'm taking a quickie, then you're next. Wash your hair and let me see what I can do to fix it."

Penny jumped up. "You really hate the way I look, don't you?"

"I didn't say that."

"Didn't have to. First you take me to your shop and pick

out new clothes. Next, you tell me to wash off my makeup and then give me your lipstick, muttering about your hairdresser the whole time. Now you tell me you're going to fix my hair like I'm a freakin' Barbie doll!" Penny stomped toward her bedroom. "Give me some space, Glory. You're my mentor, not my mom." The door slammed.

"Thank God!" I yelled down the hall. Well, how was that for gratitude? I gathered up some clothes and went into the bathroom, stopping for several minutes to study my face in the mirror. Size-six Glory had had cheekbones, none here. No, not tempted. The price was too high. But having a reflection was so unbelievably cool. How long would I have this unexpected treat? No telling. But I was going to make the most of every second. I stripped and tried to see more of me in the small glass. Forget it. There was way too much Glory and not nearly enough mirror.

I hurried through my shower and jumped into my clothes, then knocked on Penny's door.

"I'm sorry, Penny. I'm bossy. What can I say? I took my mentoring job off the rails to where it didn't belong." I turned the knob and poked my head inside. If she'd run again . . . But, no, she was lying on the bed, staring at the ceiling.

"I'm not an idiot."

"That's obvious." I sat on the foot of the bed.

"I know I look better in green than in horizontal stripes."

"It's not polite to read my mind." I sighed and jiggled her bare foot. "But I have a clothing store. I'm really into fashion and have been trying to disguise my own figure flaws for centuries, Penny. So maybe I wanted to pass on some hard-won information."

"I get that." She sat up and looked at me. "I want to look good for this date. Really good. I know nothing can come of it. He's a mortal, I'm a freak. But for once I'd like a hot guy to be into me. A guy who doesn't buy his clothes at Goodwill or pay more attention to his hard drive than to the woman sitting next to him at the computer."

I grinned. "I am so there with you." I held out my hand

and helped her get up. "Now go shower, wash your hair and blow it dry. I'm going to nip down to the shop and pick out a few things for you to try on. Okay?"

"I'd love that. Last night that cute guy Trey really looked at me, danced with me too. And I know it was the green blouse and your lipstick." She poked me on the arm. "I admit it. You seem to know what you're doing."

"Wow. Ya think?" I grinned at her while she dug into the clutch I'd given her the night before.

"Here's my credit card. Put whatever you think I'd look good in on there. I have a nice limit. My grants are big." She grinned back at me. "I did mention I was a genius, didn't I?"

"Yes, you did." I gave her a quick hug. "Feel free to raid my makeup bag while you're at it. It's on my dresser in my bedroom. Please stay away from the Goth look." I picked up the worn bra on the foot of the bed. "And, Penny, we're going to have to buy you some new underwear soon. Been a while since you've lived with that boyfriend?"

"Yes." She sighed. "And it didn't last long. He was more of a slob than I am. Imagine two geeks who never remembered to buy the coffee or wash the sheets living together. It was a nightmare." She brushed past me on her way to the door. "I was much happier with a cleaning service and my battery-operated friend."

"Too much information, Penny." I shoved her toward the bathroom, stopped to throw on my own makeup, then headed downstairs. I loved a makeover and Penny was ripe for one. It took me a little longer than it should have because the full-length mirrors in the shop kept stopping me. Oh, woe is me. That could not be my hips and butt. In the fifties and sixties, I'd worn a panty girdle. I'd hated it, but maybe it was time to pull it out again. Of course it would push everything up to a muffin top . . .

I was thoroughly depressed—which I figured was what the demons had wanted when they'd given me my reflection—by the time I took Penny my clothing choices for her date. She actually accepted my advice without argument. At nine o'clock she was blown dry, dressed right, and ready to meet Josh. He didn't recognize her in the pale blue cardigan and dark-wash jeans.

She tapped him on the shoulder. "Hey, remember me? I'm Penny, the girl you—"

"Sorry, guess I had way too much to drink that night." Josh turned red to the roots of his blond hair, then he smiled. "Looking good, Penny." He glanced around the shop. "First time I've been in here. I'm not sure I get the vintage thing. I mean, they're like strangers' hand-me-downs."

"Vintage is cool, Josh." Penny led him toward the door. "Retro chic is very in right now. But obviously not for everyone." She smiled as he opened the door. "What movie did you want to see?" She totally ignored me as I lurked near the dresses.

I signaled my night clerk and headed out after them. Josh helped Penny into his SUV, acting like a gentleman. I was glad to see him treating her with respect. But I wasn't so happy as I probed Penny's mind. She'd forgotten to block her thoughts and they were all about trying to control her fangs as he shut her inside the dark car and strolled around to get in. Penny had a bad case of the "I want to taste a mortal" cravings.

I jumped into my convertible I'd parked at the curb and followed them at a discreet distance. Yes, this felt weird, but I wasn't about to let Penny dine on this guy. He pulled into a space at a mall that had a multiscreen cinema and parked. Soon they were headed for the theater. I paid for my ticket and tried not to roll my eyes when I saw we were actually going to see the latest vampire flick. I wondered whose idea that had been.

Josh bought popcorn and drinks. Penny forgot and sipped hers, coughing until Josh pounded her on the back. Too bad. She'd been pretty cool up to that point. After that she just pretended to drink, shaking her head when he offered her popcorn, though I saw her nose twitch and her eyes water. I could sympathize. It smelled delicious. I had to give her props for playing mortal like a pro as I trailed them into the theater, one of dozens of women and a few men. Josh was really taking one for the team with this show. Obviously it was a chick flick.

I settled two rows behind them, ready to critique the vamp action on the screen and in front of me. No fangs on the vamps? Like I'd gnaw a vein open. But the fight scenes were great. Loved the werewolves. I was so engrossed, I almost missed Josh making a move on Penny. Hmm. His arm was around her and she leaned into him. Sweet.

Then I got caught up in the movie again. A love story. I'm a sucker for romance. Especially since my own love life is a twisted tale of— Wait a minute, where had they gone? Penny and Josh had managed to slip out before the movie was over. And I wasn't going to get to see which guy this girl picked? Damn it!

I jumped up and stepped unapologetically on numerous feet to get out of there. I ran across the lobby to the parking lot and saw that Josh's car was missing. How long had I been watching the screen and not my fledgling? I looked around and realized no one was nearby so I shifted into my bird form, flying up so I could look for that black SUV. Oh, great. There are only thousands of black SUVs in Austin. I tried to figure out the logical places Penny might go with Josh.

His place? He'd said he had roommates. Definitely not my place, though I'd given her a key and the alarm code for the building. So her old place? Totally a possibility. I landed next to my car and quickly shifted back, then hit speed dial for Damian.

"Hello, Gloriana, how goes the mentoring?"

"Oh, fine, fine." No way was I admitting failure to the head of the council. "You *are* paying me a stipend for this, aren't you? This girl's really racking up expenses. Synthetics, utilities, not to mention part of the rent. I was about to bring in another roommate when you dumped her on me. A paying roomie." I heard Damian say something about submitting receipts. "Sure, whatever. You know, I was following her over to her old place to pick up the rest of her stuff and lost her in traffic. Could you give me that address?"

"Certainly. And as to a stipend . . . Well, I suppose that could be arranged. Half your rent, anyway." Damian rattled some papers. "Here's her address." He read it to me. "The council is impressed that you were willing to do this. But there are still concerns. There have been reports of more demons scented in the area. Do you know anything about that, Gloriana?"

"Demons? You know how I hate those things. If I do run into them, I'll tell them to fly straight back down to hell where they belong. You know that, don't you, Damian?" I got into the car and started the engine, thinking about the address and trying to figure out where it was. I knew it was near the university, but that was a big area. Fortunately, Austin is laid out logically with numbered streets.

"Yes, Gloriana. Just be careful. Your last run-in with a demon should have convinced you how serious a problem they can be. By the way, Florence and Richard should be back soon from their honeymoon." Damian seemed inclined to chat and I didn't have time.

"I know. Can't wait to hear all the details. Listen, got to go. Penny's waiting. Talk to you later." I hung up and headed out. If Penny hadn't taken Josh back to her place, I had no idea where to look. And if she had, what was I going to do? Burst in on them? She already thought I was overprotective and interfering. But she had no idea what a dangerous situation she was in. Talk was cheap. Until she experienced it, she probably didn't believe me about bloodlust. It wasn't easy to control even in an ancient vampire. For a new one? Impossible.

I got onto a freeway and gunned my turbocharged motor. And what else was up here? My fledgling couldn't even sit through a whole movie on a first date? I'd be damned if I'd mentor a slut. Okay, I realized that was a little bit of the pot calling the kettle. But, hey, rational thinking had been left back at the mall parking lot.

Maybe Penny was discovering the famous vampire libido along with the bloodlust. I hated to rain on that parade, but she just wasn't ready for it. Not sex with a mortal anyway. If I could hook her up with a paranormal, she could have at it. I heaved a sigh of relief when I saw the exit for Penny's street and crossed two lanes of traffic to take it. In minutes I'd found her address and followed my sense of smell to the right apartment in the vintage building. I should have known Penny would be on the ground floor. That height aversion.

She'd put on music and I heard her laughter behind the door. I knocked and she stopped laughing. I waited, tapping my foot in time to the tune, a top-forty hit. I knocked again, hard enough to rattle the doorframe. The music clicked off.

"Open up, Penny, or I'll knock it down." The door jerked open and Penny stood there, her fangs gleaming in the light from a dozen candles.

"What the hell are you doing here?" Penny growled.

"Thought you'd given me the slip? As if." I shoved past her to see Josh sitting on the couch, the telltale look on his face that meant she'd whammied him. Yep, my little fledgling had put the guy into a trance. I didn't see fang marks yet. I turned and reached behind her to slam the door shut.

"First, *you* tell *me*. Why the whammy, Penny? What's Josh going to do while you have him under your little spell?" I stared hard at her.

"What do you think? That I'm so desperate I've got to put a guy in a trance before he'll have sex with me?" She flounced over to the couch and sat close to him, even put her hand on his thigh. "I'll have you know he was all over me before I did this to him."

"Yeah, I'm sure he got the message that you were good to go when you agreed to leave the movie before it was over." I sat across from her in a sagging leather chair. A fat orange cat stared at me from under a table across the room. I ignored it.

"I'd seen it before. Jenny dragged me to it the first week it was out. I wasn't into vampires then and this time I could see how fake it was." She rubbed Josh's leg. "Isn't he cute?

He offered to take me to the vamp movie because he'd heard girls like it. You did such a great job of making me look good, he couldn't keep his hands off me."

"You do look good." I shook my head. "But then you had to screw things up, didn't you?"

Penny frowned. "What do you mean? You're the one who burst in here, checking up on me."

"Come on. Admit it. Josh is sitting there looking zoned out for only one reason." I leaned forward and gave Penny a hard look. "Despite my warning, you were about to test drive your fangs on this mortal, weren't you? You think I can't see them?"

Penny swallowed and looked everywhere but at me. Finally she turned, chin up. "Yeah, so what? I can control myself. I'm not your ordinary fledgling, Glory. I can do this. Watch me." She put her hand on his jugular.

"Stop right there." I gripped her wrist. "This isn't some intellectual exercise, damn it. This is bloodlust. Your eyes are dilated. Your fangs are down and I can see you're about to lose it."

"So?" Penny snarled. "Feel him. He's so incredibly warm and that's his heart pounding under my hand. Then there's the smell." She inhaled and a look of near ecstasy came over her face. "God, but he's, he's driving me crazy. He's alive!"

I kept my grip on her, though she was trying to pull away. "Forget it, Penny. You can't do it. Let him go. Plant the idea in his mind that he liked you, but he can't call you again because you dumped him. You just can't forgive him for leaving you on that hilltop. It's the right thing to do."

"No. I want to see him again. He—he makes *me* feel alive." She leaned against him, gasping when he fell over to land on the couch. "Geez, this is ridiculous." She grabbed him and straightened him back to a sitting position.

"That's because he's basically unconscious with his eyes open." I sat on his other side to keep him propped up. "Give it up, Penny. Don't you think it's a little creepy to accept a date with a guy and then take advantage of him by drinking his blood?"

"Maybe." Penny showed me her fangs. "But he left me on that hilltop, you know. No excuse is good enough for that. Especially considering what happened there. So maybe he owes me this. I can *hear* the blood going through his veins, his heart pumping. It's calling to me. I . . . I want it. Need it. Bloodlust? What the hell? It's fantastic." She kept brushing her thumb over his jugular, then leaned in and inhaled again before she shuddered, forcing herself to sit back.

I knew what she meant. Wasn't immune myself. But I'd had a long, long time to gain control over my urges. In a way, I almost envied her the newness of this experience. But it was a dangerous thing, easy to get out of hand.

"Slow down, Penny. I get it, I really do. But you're letting your baser instincts take over. That's not like you, is it?" Not according to what she'd told me, this genius teen.

"Maybe becoming vampire has changed more about me than just my sleeping and drinking habits." Penny sighed, still staring at Josh like he was the last cookie in the jar. "Come on, Glory, you saw that movie. So much blood. Is it weird that it made me thirsty?"

"No. Even though I knew it was all faked, it made me thirsty too. But I can ignore my thirst when I have to." I wondered if I should give in on this. At least I was here to stop her before anything too drastic happened. "You had two bottles of synthetic before your date. You aren't really hungry, Penny, just drawn to the real deal. Am I right?"

Penny frowned like she was doing a gut check. "Guess so." She kept stroking his jugular. "I can feel his pulse. So strong, so warm."

"I may be sorry, but I'm going to teach you how to drink from a mortal safely. Even I realize I can't dog you every waking moment." I glanced at Josh. He was a healthy mortal, a fairly big guy who could spare a pint or two.

"No, you can't. Better to train me than to just ignore the

fact that I'm going to have this bloodlust issue." Penny actually smiled, sure she'd won something here. "Do I just lay his
head back?" She gazed at him hungrily. "Oh, God, thanks,
Glory. I thought I was going to have to fight you for him."

"And that wouldn't have ended well, Penny." I didn't say
that I knew I could take her. Let her keep her illusions. "Forget
the neck for now. Too dangerous. Pick up his wrist." I grabbed
his other arm for a demo. "Find his vein. You can see it and feel
it, of course. Easy, isn't it?"

"Sure, it's practically calling my name." She pulled his
arm up close to her mouth and her eyes closed. "Mmm."

"Now open your mouth and your fangs will know what
to do." I sighed, not allowing myself to join in on the fun.
"I'll tell you when to stop and you'll obey me if I have to
physically pull you off to get you to do it."

"Got it. I don't want to kill him, Glory. He's told me over
and over again how sorry he was about that night on the hill.
He'd just had too much to drink. He never should have been
driving at all." Penny's hand was shaking as she held his
wrist. When her fangs sank in, she was obviously surprised.
Then her eyes closed and she moaned. I didn't need to read
her mind. A new vampire's appreciation of real blood bor-
dered on orgasmic. Penny gulped and sighed and clung to
Josh's arm like she'd never let it go. But I knew she'd have
to and well before she'd want to.

"That's enough."

Her eyes popped open and she glared at me. She kept
drinking.

I stood, one hand on Penny's shoulder, one on Josh's arm.

"I said let him go."

Penny's mental message was colorful and boiled down to
"Ain't no way."

"You asked for it." I gripped her hair, giving it a sharp tug,
then ripped Josh's wrist away, leaving her mouth smeared with
blood.

"Bitch!" Penny snarled and hit at me, trying to make
contact with Josh's bleeding wounds again.

"I'll slap the shit out of you, Penny. Calm down. Take a breath. I need to show you how to close these punctures." I gave her hair another hard jerk and her eyes watered.

"*You* calm down. He's mine. Give him back." Her eyes narrowed and we were playing tug-of-war with poor Josh's arm. She didn't have my strength though and even one-handed, I was winning.

"What's going on here?"

Both of us froze, Penny's face smeared with blood, Josh's arm between us. I knew at once who stood in the doorway staring at us in horror.

I paused to toss Josh off the couch and out of Penny's reach, then grabbed the newcomer before she could run away screaming. I clamped a hand over her mouth and wrestled her inside, kicking the door closed behind us.

"You wanted to see your sister, Penny? Well, here she is." I stared into big blue eyes, well aware that all the excitement and blood in the room had my fangs on full display. Yep, that did it. Jenny, Penny's twin, slumped to the floor.

Six

That snapped Penny out of her bloodlust.

"Glory, what have you done?" She jumped up and ran over to Jenny, rolling her over to stare down at her pale face.

"Not a thing. She fainted." I dragged Josh up off the floor where he'd landed after our little tussle and sat him in a chair. He was still staring blankly into space. To my amusement, the cat jumped into his lap and made himself comfortable. If Josh had been awake, I'm sure he'd have let out a few yelps as paws trod over his crotch.

"Jenny." Penny patted her sister on the cheek. "Wake up."

"Don't think I'd be in such a hurry to do that. You've got blood smeared all over your face." I checked Josh's wrist, which was still bleeding sluggishly. I forced back my fangs when all I wanted to do was take up where Penny had left off.

"I'll go wash it off." Penny turned toward her tiny kitchen.

"Not yet. Get over here and do what I tell you." I was not a happy camper. Can you tell? "You've got to close these wounds so that when Josh wakes up, he won't be wearing evidence of your snack time."

"But Jenny." Penny squatted down again. "I can't just leave her on the floor."

"Pick her up and put her on the couch. You've got vamp strength now, should be easy to tote around that lightweight. If she starts to wake up, you'll have to use the whammy on her until we figure out what we're going to do with her." I tapped my foot and looked around. A luxury condo, this wasn't. And a housekeeper, Penny wasn't. I was surprised she'd brought a man back here.

A big computer setup held pride of place on the small dining room table and it was surrounded by a sea of papers, boxes of books, notebooks and stacks of more papers on the floor. Penny might have big grants, but she sure didn't waste them on interior decorating. The sagging couch looked like it had come from a charity store, as did the rest of the furniture. I could see an unmade bed in a tiny bedroom next to the kitchen with a sink piled with dirty dishes. Clothes were draped on a chair next to that double bed.

Penny heaved Jenny over to the couch and arranged her head carefully on a throw pillow that was the only bright spot in the avocado green and brown room. Too bad the burnt orange UT pillow wasn't Jenny's color.

"She's still out. Guess the sight of your fangs, which are way bigger than mine, blew her fuse." Penny stumbled over to my side. No coffee table, which was a good thing. Otherwise poor Josh would have a bruise to add to his bite marks. "Now what?"

"You have a healing agent in your saliva that makes bite marks disappear. You should always lick wounds closed after you feed from a mortal. Not that you should make that a habit." I grabbed her shoulder as she leaned forward to take his wrist again. "Do *not* be tempted to take another drink. I swear I'll knock you against that wall if you try it."

"Geez, Glory, go all Terminator on me, why don't you?" Penny carefully reached for his wrist with two fingers then really looked at Josh's pale face. "Oh, God, what did I do? I was the Terminator, wasn't I?"

Great, here came the waterworks. But, no, she sucked it up.

"How long? How long can I safely drink from a mortal and not kill him?" She ran to her dining room table and snatched up a notebook and pencil.

"What? You're taking notes?" I sighed. I guess I should have expected this from a brainy scientist. And it sure beat tears. But if I hadn't followed her and been on the scene, she could have killed Josh, no doubt about it. Fledglings made those kinds of mistakes.

"Josh here might have been okay after three minutes, but two to be on the safe side. Trust me, you weren't in control enough to watch a clock, Penny." I gave her a fierce look and waited until she stopped writing and glanced at me. "I don't care how smart you are in your old world. In this new world, you're dumb as dirt. When bloodlust takes over, you can't just stop on a dime. At least not until you've learned to get a handle on it. Tonight, if I hadn't been here to get you off of Josh, you would have drained him dry. Then you'd have had to figure out how to dispose of his body."

Penny swayed, dropped her notebook and pencil, then sank down on the floor. "Oh, God. Oh, God."

"I'm sorry, but that's the truth." I sat beside her and put my arm around her. "You see why I'm trying to stay close to you when you're around mortals? You can't think your way through this. It's an instinct. Primitive and not easily controlled. Until you can convince me you're managing your thirst like an adult vampire, you're going to be stuck with me."

Penny leaned against me. "Thanks, Glory. I had no idea." She took a watery breath. "Just, uh, thanks."

"No problem, kiddo. I had Jerry do it for me." I smiled, remembering. "Now let's handle this situation, okay?"

"How? Here's Josh, looking pale and probably weak and now I've got Jenny. Obviously I don't want to tell her about my new status until I can look at her and not want to bite her." Penny stood and picked cat hair off her jeans. "Guess I've finally come down to earth."

"Josh's okay. He's a big dude. He can handle losing the

little bit you took. But if you attacked someone small like your sister, a minute or two too much could do her some serious harm." I stood too. "It's all about percentages."

"I get that." Penny grabbed her notebook again and scribbled, then ran to the kitchen. She came out with something clutched in her hand and dropped it into her purse.

"What's that?" I was suspicious of everything Penny did now and, looking at Josh's pale face, rightly so.

"A kitchen timer." She grimaced. "Okay, so I'm thinking ahead. But maybe I'll get another chance to—"

"Bite Josh?" I really wanted to scream. But what good would it do? Penny was used to being the smartest kid on the playground and in her new world she still thought she could beat the system. Who was I to doubt her? I just shook my head.

She'd pulled the timer out and stared down at it. "Mom gave me this timer. I used it to b-b-bake brownies." Tears. Now these I could understand. My mad evaporated and I patted her shoulder.

"Brownies. Little squares of chocolate heaven. I've never even tasted one. Just smelled them." I took the timer and dropped it back in her purse. "Now let's finish with Josh and get this"—I looked over at Jenny, still out, but showing signs of coming back to life—"mess cleaned up."

"What do you want me to do?" Penny stared at her sister too. "I can't believe Jenny just showed up here. This late. Guess I didn't do a very good job of putting her off."

"Well, we'll handle it. Now lean in and lick away the evidence that you were ever at Josh's wrist. Got it?"

"Got it." She took a steadying breath and did what I told her. "God, his blood still smells so . . . delicious. What blood type is he? I like it a lot."

"Josh's is one of the rare ones and my personal favorite if you must know. AB negative. The synthetic of this type is expensive. It's like a fine wine. To be sipped and savored, not gulped." I kept my hand on Penny's shoulder. Good intentions or not, I was relieved when she dropped his wrist and ran her fingers through her cat's fur.

"Look at this, Booger likes Josh. I take that as a good sign." She smiled at me. "My old boyfriend has the claw marks to prove the B-man doesn't take to just anyone."

"Doesn't matter in this case. We're going to escort Josh out to the hall and you're going to give him the suggestion that you dumped him. Remember?" I pulled Josh to his feet, dislodging the cat in the process. "Sorry, fur face, but the mortal has got to go."

"I don't remember agreeing to that. I told you, I want to keep Josh. As a boyfriend. Or a pet. This guy was into me, Glory. Surely I can figure things out so that I can keep him." Penny kept glancing back at Jenny, who hadn't opened her eyes yet. "I'm worried about Jenny. She's not the fainting type."

"It's only been a few minutes. But we need to hurry. We can discuss Josh's fate later." I steered him toward the door. "Mortals as pets would be damned complicated and I, for one, have never had the patience to even try it. Stick to synthetics. It's a better option."

"But some vampires do keep pets? Like those women at Damian's." Penny waited for my reluctant nod. "I knew it! There are too many Goths desperate to join the vamp fan club." Penny looked Josh over speculatively, obviously picturing him in leather and a choke collar, with AB negative on tap.

"Stop thinking, Penny, and start getting this mess untangled." I'd been watching her sister and saw her eyelids flicker. "For now, go out there, look him in the eyes and tell him you two did a little necking but you called a halt because you don't fall into bed on what was your first decent date. If he's got even a tenth of your gray matter, he'll realize that fiasco where you ended up abandoned on a hilltop didn't count. Am I right?"

Penny shrugged, obviously not happy.

"You know I am. Then tell him to wake up, kiss him good night and send him on his way. Got it?"

"Okay, I can do that." Penny got a sly look on her face like maybe she'd add a suggestion or two of her own.

"I've got vamp hearing, Penny. I'll be listening to everything you say. You screw this up and I'll take care of Josh my way later. I'm sure I can find him." I grabbed her arm. "And I'll be in here with your sister. Don't forget that."

"You wouldn't hurt Jenny, would you?" Penny's eyes narrowed.

"Not without provocation." I kept my thoughts blocked, determined to get the upper hand in this mentor relationship early. No need for Penny to realize I was far from the badass I was pretending to be. "I didn't survive four hundred years by letting some upstart newbie endanger me with her bloodlust *or* her libido. Keep that in mind."

"Fine." She ran into the kitchen and washed her face and hands. "Am I clean?"

"Yes. Lipstick's gone, but after your make-out session that's to be expected." I nodded toward Josh.

"I just look into his eyes and tell him what I want him to remember, right?" After I nodded, Penny dragged Josh to the door and out into the hall. I heard her tell him he'd had a wonderful time with her and all the rest we'd agreed upon. Then there was silence, which I figured was her getting the kind of kiss she wanted.

"Whoa, I have to come up for air. For some reason, I'm dizzy." Josh laughed. "Don't tell my frat brothers, they'll think I'm a wuss."

"Your secret's safe with me." Penny laughed. "You okay to drive? Maybe it's low blood sugar. I could get you some juice." She sounded anxious. "If I had some. Darn it, I've got to get to the store."

"That's okay. I'm fine, seriously." More silence. "See? Not dizzy this time. Thanks, Penny. I'll call you." Josh sounded like he meant it. Then I heard him walk away.

Penny stepped inside, closing the door behind her. "Happy now?"

"You did fine. Now let's see about your sister." I gestured toward Jenny, who was struggling to sit up.

"Jenny, are you all right?" Penny sat beside her and brushed back her hair.

"What happened? And who is this woman?" Jenny's eyes widened and latched on to me. "I saw something. The strangest thing. The two of you . . ." She went silent when Penny stared at her and obviously put her into a trance.

"We have to erase her memory, don't we?" Penny looked up at me, her eyes swimming with tears. "I don't want her to remember me with my face covered with blood, fangs down like that, before I have a chance to explain things."

"I'm sure it was a pretty horrifying sight to a mortal who has no clue we really exist." I sighed. "And there's no need to explain any of this tonight. Give yourself a break. One thing at a time. You can tell her you're moving in with me. That I have a great location, a cheap room to rent and you decided you were tired of living alone." I looked around her place. "Surely you won't be sad to leave this behind."

"Hey, it's not that bad. Though I admit I don't keep it as clean as I could. Jenny and I never could share a room at home. She's a neatnik." Penny sighed and sat her sister up, arranging her like she would a pretty, life-size doll.

"I'm not a neatnik, but you will have to keep your mess confined to your bedroom at my place." I frowned at her computer station. "Guess I'll concede my dining table to you, though. We don't need it for a meal, that's for sure."

"Thanks, Glory. And my parents will be tickled at the news. They've been living in fear that I'll get another guy in here. As it was, they never told Gramps that I had Albert as a roommate for a while."

"Gramps the preacher. I can see where that would cause a stir at prayer meetings." I sat in Josh's abandoned chair and got a visit from Booger. The cat was growing on me. He licked my hand with a sandpapery tongue and I stroked between his ears.

"A stir? Me living in sin would have called for a candle-light vigil." Penny sighed. "Jenny would never disappoint Gramps by shacking up with a guy before marriage." She looked at me. "She's the one who always gets the smiling pictures and features in the local paper. Of course she was homecoming queen, head cheerleader."

"But you're the one who has grants and degrees." I looked from one twin to the other. Hard to believe they'd popped out during the same birth. They were so different. Yet there was a slight similarity to the tilt of the chin and the curve of the brow. Of course Penny's eyebrows were dark and hadn't been properly shaped.

"Whatever. We don't compete. We accept our differences and love each other for them." Penny put her arm around Jenny. "No way am I letting her grow old and die when I won't."

"You may not have a choice in that." I felt the cat purring in my lap. "It will be Jenny's decision when the time comes. And it's way too soon for you to ask her to make it."

"Why? I'm stuck in this nineteen-year-old body." Penny looked down. "Not the one I might have wished for, but look at hers. It's perfect. Who wouldn't want to be stuck like that?"

I had to admit she was right. Jenny could have posed for a magazine ad. She *was* the size six the demons had tried to tempt me with but taller than I was by a few inches.

"You have to give yourself time to get used to your new life. I'm not allowing you to tell Jenny anything about vampires until I get to know her better and see what kind of risk we'd be running telling her about us. That is nonnegotiable." I gave Penny my sternest look. "If you want to keep seeing Jenny on a regular basis, it's going to have to be playing Penny as usual, no vampire vibe visible at all. Got it?"

"That's never going to work." Penny gave me a venomous look. "I get that my bloodlust is a problem, but otherwise . . .

Come on, Glory, she's my twin. We don't keep huge secrets like this."

"You do now. You're the brain around here. Quit arguing and start doing. Erase her memory of the scene she walked into and wake her up. Introduce us. Tell her about the new living arrangement. Your new life starts now." I sat back, cat in my lap and waited.

"I hate you." Penny stood, her hands fisted by her sides.

"I can live with that. Just do it." I ran my hand across Booger's back while Penny told her sister she had just walked up to the door, had felt dizzy because she'd skipped dinner and Penny had caught her when she'd passed out. Then she told her to wake up.

"Jenny, I hope you're feeling better." Penny handed her sister a bottle of cold water from her refrigerator and a protein bar.

"Yeah, I know better than to skip a meal." Jenny twisted off the cap and took a deep drink. "Thanks. You sure you can spare this bar?"

"You left it here. I'd rather eat the wrapper. Of course I can always zap you a frozen pizza. Sausage." Penny smiled like this was an old joke between them.

Sure enough Jenny shuddered. "*I'd* rather eat the box."

"This is Glory St. Clair." Penny waved in my direction. "Glory, my sister, Jenny, who made that dramatic entrance. She's on a vegetarian kick. That's why the shudder."

I smiled. "I get it. I have dietary restrictions myself." I ignored Penny's gasp. She'd just have to get used to vampire humor. "Nice to meet you. Penny and I have known each other awhile. I've persuaded her to move in with me. Share the rent. She's moving in tonight."

"No kidding?" Jenny's eyes went wide. "That's odd. I thought you liked it here, Pen." She gazed around the cluttered room and winced. "Though I never could understand it. Where's your place, Glory?"

"On Sixth Street in an apartment over my shop, Vintage Vamp's Emporium." I put Booger on the floor when he scratched my hand to be let down. He ran to Jenny and hopped up into her lap.

"I love that store. Perfect for finding a Halloween costume. You own it?" She gave the cat a quick pat. "Down, big guy, you're shedding all over my new skirt." She sat him on the floor.

"Yes, vintage clothes are my thing." I could see at a glance that everything on Jenny was brand-new, right down to her silver thongs. Her toenails were painted a hot pink to match her clingy T-shirt. The skirt she didn't want decorated with cat fur was a dark-wash denim and now had orange hair on it. She got busy plucking it off and dropping it on the rug.

"Well, now you can mention Penny's name and get a discount." I kept smiling but Penny's sister was a little too perfect and perky for my taste. I didn't read her mind. I wasn't in the habit of prying unless I felt it was absolutely necessary.

"That is so cool." Jenny frowned when Booger tried to jump up into her lap again. "You are letting her take the cat with her, aren't you? I just can't have him with me in the sorority house."

"Of course. I had less of a problem with the cat than with what she calls her big-ass computer."

Jenny laughed. "I know what you mean. What a mess." She patted Penny on the arm. "She says she knows where everything is in that pile of junk, but beats me how she finds anything."

"Speaking of, I need more boxes and to get packing. Did you still need help with that math, Jenny?" Penny glanced at her watch. "It's getting late."

"No, I've got it. Just wanted to touch base. You said you had a date. How'd it go?" She looked around, like maybe she doubted the date story.

"It was fine. It's the frat guy I saw last weekend. Josh. We hit it off." Penny edged away from her sister.

Surely she wasn't being hit by the bloodlust again. After taking Josh down a pint or more? I jumped up.

"I met him. He's cute and into Penny. Which is great. Right, Jenny?" I watched her reaction.

She gaped at the open bedroom door. "You brought him here? You didn't—"

"No! Geez, Jen." Penny flushed. "Give me a little credit. Yeah, I'm a slob, but guys don't notice stuff like that. He said he'd call me."

Jenny pasted on a bright smile and jumped up to hug her sister. "Then I'm sure he will. Guess I was wrong about that party after all. I wish I had time to hear all the details. Call me tomorrow and we'll dish." She brushed at her skirt. "I've got to go. Need my beauty sleep, you know. It *is* late. Surely you're not going to move stuff tonight."

"We'll just take a load or two." Penny ignored the party comment. "Glad you stopped by. You can always text me when you want to get together but I'll be super busy for the next two weeks. This grant project is coming to a head. If we meet, it'll have to be at night."

"Sure. And I've got finals looming." Jenny looked me over, taking in my vintage designer jeans and red sweater. As usual I'd gone for a V-neck and a color that was good for me. I might not be a six, but I knew how to work what I had. "How did you and Penny meet, Glory? I'm sure it wasn't over a dress rack. Though I bet you're the one who got her into flats. Am I right?" She winked at me.

"Yes, Jenny hates my boots as much as you do, Glory." Penny hunched her shoulders and I felt sorry for her.

"*Hate*'s a pretty strong word. But Penny looks good tonight, doesn't she, Jenny? Josh couldn't take his eyes off of her. And she had another guy hitting on her last night at N-V." I couldn't resist. Jenny was just too cute, and Penny, when she'd shown up on my doorstep, had been far from it. Why the great divide? "Trey couldn't wait to get her on the dance floor."

"You went to that new club last night?" Jenny's eyes were saucers. "You're kidding me."

"Oh, we were there. Glory's best bud owns it. Rafe's cool.

And Trey's a hunk, isn't he, Glory?" Penny's shoulders were back again and she was smiling.

"I've never been." Jenny looked me over speculatively. "You already out of school, Glory?"

"Oh, yeah. I'm way out of school." I gave Penny a look that kept her from jumping into the conversation. "Actually, Penny and I have a mutual friend. He put us together. You know how these things work. I had an extra bedroom and needed the rent money." I swept my gaze around the cluttered living room. "And Penny needed to live with someone who could keep her environment reasonably organized." I grinned. "Someone your grandfather would approve of."

Jenny laughed. "Oh, I get that. Good luck to you on the organization thing. I gave up years ago."

"Hello. I'm in the room." Penny glowered at both of us. "Laugh all you want. But when I'm rich and famous and cure the incurable, we'll see who's laughing."

Jenny planted a kiss on her sister's cheek. "My bets are on you all the way, sis. Now I've got to go." She turned to me. "I'll be praying for you, Glory." She hit the door and left without a backward glance.

"That went well. She never really questioned my decision." Penny collapsed on the couch.

"Good thing. Because she wouldn't have gotten any answers."

"Am I a total pervert for having a moment or two where all I could think about was tasting her blood? I know Jen's blood type. It's not exotic like Josh's. It's just plain old B positive. But I had to fight my fangs when I got too close to her and the sound of her heartbeat . . ." Penny stared at me. "Damn, Glory, it sounded loud as a drum to me."

"Only natural. Now you need to grab what you want to take right away. We'll get Damian to arrange for the rest of your stuff to be moved." I glanced at her computer. "You can come tomorrow night and supervise." Booger rubbed against my leg. "You have a cat carrier? We might as well take this guy with us."

"Sure. I have to use it when he goes to the vet. Pick him up first. If he sees me get the carrier out of the closet, he'll hide and we'll never find him." Penny walked into her bedroom.

I grabbed Booger and hugged him. "Such a sweet boy and such an ugly name. I think I'll call you Boogie. Like the way I danced during the war."

"Which war was that?" Penny was back and I felt Boogie stiffen, his claws digging into my arm.

"WW Two, of course. I was over in England and helped keep the troops happy in the USO canteens. I love to dance." I dropped the cat into the carrier and slammed the lid shut while Penny gathered food, litter and the litter box.

"Amazing. I can't imagine what a long life you've had." Penny had her arms full. "Let's go. I have enough underwear in my backpack for tomorrow and you bought me those new clothes. Please call Damian when we get back to your place. I really want my big computer with me. I've got my laptop, but my major work is on Chuck here. I guess it's never too late to call a vampire."

"As long as it's between dusk and dawn, we're good." I lugged the carrier to the door. "You have a car?"

"Yep. It's a relic, but it runs. Should I park on the street in front of your shop?"

"No, there's parking in the alley behind it." I shivered. There'd been a lot of bad things that had happened in that alley. It was almost a death trap. "Follow me and, when you get out of your car, stay alert. I've had some trouble back there so pay attention. I'm sure the demons aren't through with me, for one thing."

"Now you're creeping me out." Penny locked the door with her key as she followed me out to the curb and watched me stow the cat in the passenger seat of my car.

"I'm glad. A vampire can't just walk around without watching for danger. Just like a woman by herself on a dark night in an alley can't." I slammed the car door. "Understand?"

"Only too well. I know Sixth Street gets its share of crime too." Penny pointed at the apartment lot. "That's my car, the blue Ford."

"Must get good mileage." It was an economy car and not old, but it had more than its fair share of scrapes and dings.

"It does. The battered look is courtesy of my inattention to detail when I park." Penny made a face. "That's what Dad says anyway. He gave up fixing the cosmetic stuff. Says I have to live with it, warts and all."

"Guess you think too much." I grinned. "About things other than the world around you."

"Exactly." Penny laughed, for once in sync with me. "I'll meet you there." She walked over to the car and I saw her add a scratch when the edge of the litter box bumped the rear door. I was watching her carefully near *my* new car.

I drove home with Boogie griping the whole way. He was obviously very worried that I might be taking him to the vet. I tried to reassure him, but talk was cheap in his world. By the time I parked, he was yowling. Penny pulled in a few moments later. I had deliberately parked between two cars so Penny couldn't park next to me. I heard a *thunk* as she opened her car door into the side of the Dumpster.

"Aw, Booger, is Glory being mean to you?" Penny stuck a finger into the carrier. "Ow! Don't bite me. This is not the vet's office, you ungrateful feline."

We both were distracted by Boogie's yowls so, when the man stepped out of the shadows, it was only natural that we jumped and yelled.

"Hyyyy-yah!" Penny swung into action with a karate move that impressed the hell out of me. The man fell flat on his back and grabbed his stomach where her kick had landed.

"Stop, vamp girl. I know this man and he's no danger to either of us." I grabbed her arm and pulled her back to keep her from landing a kick to his head while he was down.

"What?" Penny looked down at her victim, keeping a good distance from his arms as he struggled to sit up.

"Glory? Who the hell is this?" Nathan Burke took the hand I offered him and got to his feet.

"A fledgling I'm mentoring." I smiled at her. "Good work, Penny. I didn't know you had it in you."

"Self-defense classes. My folks wouldn't let me come to the big city without them." She smiled tentatively at Nathan. "Sorry if I overreacted. Obviously you and Glory know each other." She offered her hand. "Penny Patterson." Her nose twitched and I knew she was taking a whiff of her second delicious and rare mortal of the night. Another AB negative. She gave me a wink like maybe she thought I'd kept this guy a secret, as my own pet.

"Penny, this is Nathan Burke, a friend, not my blood buddy." I watched them shake hands, then stepped between them. "Nathan, be careful around Penny. You may not remember this, but new vamps have a problem with self-control around mortals."

"Some not-so-new vamps do too." Nathan ran his hand over his close-cropped hair. "That's why I'm here. Ray's way out of control and I need your help."

"Can we go upstairs to discuss this?" I gestured at the cat carrier where Boogie still wailed his distress. "I think the neighborhood may be getting ready to call animal control."

"Sure. Let me carry that." Nathan reached for the crate.

"Careful, he may try to scratch you." Penny relinquished the handle.

Nathan just shook his head. "I'll deal, but if he draws blood, don't think it's an invitation to dine." He grinned at me. "Glory has first dibs. Am I right?"

"Don't start putting ideas in Penny's head, Nate. Come on up and tell me about Ray's crisis." I helped Penny unload the rest of the cat paraphernalia and we trouped up the stairs.

Once Boogie was in the apartment, we let him loose and he ran to hide under my bed. We settled in the living room and Penny was all big eyes and curiosity.

"Who's Ray?" she asked first.

"Israel Caine. Nathan's his best friend and manager. I was

Ray's mentor too. And, for a while, we pretended to be engaged, for the media." I grabbed a bottle of synthetic and one of the beers Rafe had left in my fridge. I handed the beer to Nate, who opened it gratefully.

"Are you telling me that Israel Caine, the rock star, the legend, is a vampire?" Penny was on the edge of her chair.

"Unfortunately." Nate took a deep swallow of his beer and sighed. "He's really into the synthetic with alcohol now that he's discovered it."

"I was afraid that would happen." I glanced at Penny. Might as well tell her the rest. "Ray was close to having to go to rehab for alcoholism when he was turned. Being a vampire was no more his choice than it was yours. He earned his fangs in an act of revenge by a woman who thought he deserved to lose daylight."

"As revenge, she got it right. He's still brooding about it. Getting suicidal again. Really into the daylight drug and I'm afraid he's going to fall down drunk outside some morning and just fry." Nate took another gulp of beer. "I've hired people to watch him, just in case."

"Oh, Nate." I was beside him on the couch and I put my hand on his knee. "This has got to be killing you."

"I was hoping you'd help me snap him out of it." Nate gave me a sad smile. "You know he loves you. Still."

"Doubt it. We really didn't part well the last time he made a move on me." I'd laid it out pretty clearly that I was either all for Jerry or even Rafe before I'd take a chance on a rocker with Ray's history of love 'em and leave 'em.

"I know you're not going to go back to him as his woman or anything like that." Nate grimaced. "Ray shared some of what went down with you. One night when he was bombed it came pouring out. I don't think he remembers telling me or he'd be embarrassed. Anyway, you always had a way of making him remember what he has to live for." Nate looked at Penny. "You guys have forever. But if you've lost what you value most, I guess that's not such a good deal, is it?"

Penny sniffed. "No, it isn't. I'm still trying to figure this

out. How am I going to handle it when my parents die? My
friends? Hell, I have a twin sister. Glory won't even let me
clue her in yet about this freakin' change I've gone through."

"Listen to Glory." Nate put his hand on mine and squeezed.
"She's been through a lot. She knows. I saw her handle Ray
when I couldn't and he's been my best friend since grade
school."

"I want to help him, Nate. Seriously. But how? Last I
knew he was with Nadia and having a fine old time learning
the ropes and chains and you name it of her freaky sex-
perience." I eased my hand from his. "He's been living here
in town and hasn't even called me, even though we're supposed to be friends."

"Nadia got tired of Ray's drinking and dumped him. I
told you, he's out of control. Won't rehearse. Isn't writing
the songs we need for the new album. Told the band to take
a break so they're about to head out. He's pushing everyone
away. You're not the only one." Nate shook his head. "Here's
the worst. He even talked to Ian MacDonald about coming
here to Austin. Ray offered to be the guinea pig if Ian would
move his lab so they could work to make the daylight drug
last all day. I think Ian's going to come check out the city."

"No way." I jumped up. This was bad. Definitely suicidal.

"What's this daylight drug?" Penny just had to ask.

I'd been so into the Ray thing I'd almost forgotten she was
in the room. "It's a drug that will let vampires stay awake
long enough to watch the sun rise. Out of direct sunlight, of
course. You let the sun's rays hit you and you're toast."

"Wow. This Ian must be a genius with chemistry." Penny
looked really interested.

"He is. You'd probably love him. I think I already mentioned that." I really didn't want her meeting the man. We
needed to head Ian off at the pass.

"Have you tried it? Are you sure it works and isn't just an
urban legend?" Penny was up now too, on my heels as I paced.

"Yes, I've tried it." I grabbed her. "Stop following me.
The drug worked for a little while. It costs the earth. I can't

afford it on what the shop makes so I put it out of my mind. Rich vamps can blow their money on a few minutes of daylight but I won't."

"So your boyfriend paid for it." Penny's eyes were shining, and I again got the feeling that her wheels were turning. That giant brain was trying to figure out what Ian had done to let vamps see daylight.

"Yes, one of them did. Think about it, Penny. After four hundred years, seeing the sun again can be a big deal, worth whatever the price if you've got it." I sighed. Might as well spill all the beans. "Ian's got a weight-loss drug too. I tried it. It worked. Actually got me down to a size six."

"No way." Penny was riveted, eyes wide, her hands on my arms.

"Oh, yes." I looked at her hands and she let me go. "But it was temporary. Also expensive and Ray picked up the tab for that one." I made a face. "Ian's a businessman, in it for the money. Which I get. But he's also a genius and dangerous as hell. He surrounds himself with bodyguards and he's a vampire with lots of weapons at his disposal. Not someone I'd like to see you mess with."

"Sounds fascinating." Penny grinned at Nathan.

I grabbed Penny by the shoulders and looked her dead in the eyes. "Stay the hell away from him."

"Make me." Penny jerked free, snatched up her cat, who'd finally come out from under the bed, and ran for her bedroom.

I flopped on the couch next to Nate. "You see what I'm up against?"

"Wait till you see what Ray's doing. Penny's just a kid acting out." Nate looked tired and worried. "Come tomorrow night. Last performance before the band breaks for vacation. A venue out at Zilker Park. General admission. I really didn't want them to do it but Ray insisted. He likes Austin. Plans to stay here to cut the album so he wanted to give back." Nate shook his head. "Ticket prices were ridiculously cheap. It'll be a mob scene."

"I'll be there, though I'm not sure what I can do to help." I leaned back and glanced toward where I could hear scratching at Penny's bedroom door. Obviously Boogie wasn't happy being shut in. "Sometimes people need to make their own mistakes."

"Thanks, Glory. If there's anything I can do for you, just let me know." Nate yawned, obviously exhausted.

I leaned against him and inhaled, telling myself I was never going to drink from this mortal no matter how delicious he smelled. I got up, grabbed my bottle of synthetic and chugged it.

"Just leave before you become my late-night snack." I pulled him up and walked him to the door.

Nate grinned and kissed my cheek. "You wouldn't. Though you're more than welcome. Have to tell you though." He lost his grin and shuddered. "The truth is, I knew Ray was losing it when he threw me down and drank from me last night." He winced when I gripped his hand and let my horror show. "Yep, his best bud. Luckily one of the shifters I'd hired to watch him ran in and wrestled him off me or I'd be dead, drained dry." Tears sheened his dark eyes. "I had to be driven to the hospital for a transfusion, Glory. I was that far gone. We had a hell of a time arranging that too. Fortunately, I know a doctor . . ." He shrugged, trying to go for casual, and failing. "I'm scared, Glory. For Ray, for our friendship. This time he went too far."

"Oh, Nate. I'm so sorry." I pulled him into my arms and just held him. Ray had crossed a line and I was wondering if he could be pulled back. If the council got wind of this, they'd take a hard look at Ray. Because he was an inch away from going rogue. I shuddered. And there was only one outcome for a rogue vampire in Austin. That was at the end of a stake.

Seven

I had to put some time in at the shop. At least I didn't have to worry about Penny. She was busy supervising her move, nervous about her computer and her research. I'd arranged to meet Nathan at ten o'clock near Zilker Park. When the sweet scent hit me, I was going over receipts near the register while my night clerk, Erin, helped a customer.

"Not avoiding that full-length mirror, are you, Glory?" Spyte came through the door first. He was a vision in blue tonight. His baby blue satin shirt clung to broad shoulders and did great things for his eyes, which were blue tonight, and his honey blond hair. His navy trousers had a sheen that shouted Italian silk.

"Nonsense. I bet she's already bought one for upstairs. Am I right, Glory dear?" Caryon wore a silver gray suit and black shirt. His tie had a stripe that pulled it all together. The pair drew admiring looks from my female customers. If they only knew . . .

"That's what you wanted, wasn't it? For me to obsess about my fat butt?" I came out from behind the counter and, yeah, tried not to catch a glimpse of my reflection just visible down one aisle. Big butt, thighs, and why had I ever thought

I could wear this shade of gold, which made my hair look dull and my skin washed out? I was definitely changing tops before I met Nate.

Spyte's smirk propelled me toward the back of the shop. "Follow me. We can't talk out here." I gestured toward the door that led to my storeroom.

"I think we're making progress, Spyte. Yes, I do." Caryon was on my heels after I murmured to Erin where I was going.

"In your dreams." I smiled and opened the door. "Come inside. I don't want to run off my customers. If they keep inhaling your stench, they're likely to discover a craving and head next door for a muffin."

"Yes, we do have that yummy thing going on, don't we?" Spyte wrinkled his nose. "Holy hellfire. *Here's* a stench. Do I smell mothballs, Glory? Where *do* you get your stock? Dumpsters?" He picked up a vintage shirtwaist dress that had indeed come from a street person who'd found a box of great things on a curb destined for the garbage.

"Never mind that. I want to make it clear, hellboys, that I am not and never will work for Lucifer. Now you can clear out and take your mirror tricks with you." I threw the dead bolts and opened the back door. To my shock, Rafe was standing in the alley like he'd been about to use his key.

"Sorry, Glo, but I'm here with orders from down below." He smiled ruefully. "Remember that payback I told you about? Yeah, it's a bitch." Rafe took my arm and stepped inside, throwing the bolts home again. "Hey, Frick and Frack. See you're still on the case too."

"Some respect would be nice." Caryon sniffed. "I don't think you can afford to be flip, Valdez."

"And I don't think you can afford to piss me off, shitface." Rafe's eyes glowed red.

"Uh, guys, calm down. I really don't want my shop going up in flames. Again." Or my shoes. I had on some nice platform heels. I stepped between them. Maybe not my smartest move, though I knew Rafe would never hurt me. But Caryon's eyes sparked red now too and the place was heating up.

Unfortunately, my shop *had* gone up in smoke before. Fire-bomb. My budget couldn't handle another rebuilding.

"We're going to cooperate now, aren't we, fellas?" Spyte stepped into the fray, flicking me aside like an irritating gnat.

"Rafe, what is this about? Surely you're not here to persuade me to be Lucifer's trash collector." Tears popped into my eyes. Not Rafe, my best friend, a man I'd depended on and who I knew in my heart was a good guy.

Rafe finally gave up his stare-down with Caryon and turned to me. "I'm sorry, Glory. You think I want to do this? I'm stuck with a debt that I have no other way to pay. You know I have demon blood and used my powers when I shouldn't have."

"That demon stuff is his best part." Spyte dared lay a hand on Rafe's shoulder and I thought the flame-throwing was going to start then and there. But Rafe just shrugged it off.

"Not going to waste time arguing that." He took my hand. "You know how I feel. Better that I jump in here than let these two loose on you. I think I've figured out a way we can satisfy my deal and get Lucifer's bootlickers—"

"Hey!" Now Spyte shoved a shoulder between us, his eyes shooting off sparks.

"Chill, honey, I want to hear what *our* little bootlicker has to say." Caryon's smile was the stuff of nightmares. I shuddered and clutched Rafe's hand like a lifeline, even though Spyte stood with his back to me and face-to-face with Rafe.

"The day you get what I decide is too close to me or Glory here is the day you find out what hell is really like, you piece of shit." Rafe hit both demons with a glare that could have peeled the paint off the walls. Now I was really worried. For him. To my shock, Caryon merely nodded with what might have been respect and Spyte snorted but moved out of our space. Hmm.

"Go on," Caryon ordered.

I kept my mouth shut, trying desperately to stay out of this pissing contest. If I'd had the power of invisibility, I'd have been wallpaper. I was so clearly outmatched when it came to powers here. Even if I shifted into something tiny enough to hide or dangerous enough to attack them, they'd be able to stomp me, freeze me, fry me. The options were endless.

"As I was saying . . ." Rafe put his hands on my shoulders and gave me an encouraging smile. Like that was going to make me relax. Hah! "Glory, what would be the harm if we could at least bring them the one they're jonesing for?"

"Simon. He won't deal with us. What's his motive for changing sides?" I focused on Rafe, desperate to ignore the demons, who seemed to be crowding too close to me.

"I've been thinking about that." Rafe seemed to realize what I was doing. "Back off, creeps. Give Glory some breathing room."

"She doesn't have to breathe." Caryon scratched his earlobe. "I want to hear this."

"One soul? Not nearly good enough to satisfy Luc. And you know, Valdez, that if you don't bring this assignment in successfully, there *will* be hell to pay." Spyte managed a toothy grin, though he was obviously pouting. He sat on my table, the shirtwaist a mangled mess under him. I had a feeling the bootlicking comment had struck a nerve. Maybe he didn't like the taste of leather.

"What does he mean, Rafe?" I really didn't like the sound of Spyte's threat.

"Ignore him. Now Simon's got a son, Freddy. Do you think he wants a relationship with him?" Rafe had clearly decided to take his own advice and ignore the demons for now.

"Most men would." I was getting an idea and saw where Rafe was headed. "And Freddy is a good guy. Never would want to have anything to do with the Energy Vampires. Money and power aren't his thing."

"Sounds like a sorry excuse for a son to me." Spyte started juggling a fireball and I gasped when it danced close to my hair.

"Hush, Spyte. I think they're going to work for us." Caryon smiled. "Start with Simon. We already told you we want him. Pull him over to us and all will be cool. For a while, anyway." He flashed me with a little crackle heat from his red eyes. I jerked and blinked, my eyelashes stinging. Surely he hadn't . . . "But don't think you'll be totally off the hook. Especially you, Valdez. You can't just use your demonic powers and not pay and pay, now can you?" He winked.

"Simon should be enough for you. Let Glory help with this and then forget her." Rafe kept me close by his side. "What do you say, Glory? Are you up for getting Simon as Lucifer's plaything?"

"I hate Simon. Don't care where he ends up, as long as it's somewhere down below. But you and I both know, Rafe, that a deal with a demon isn't worth shit." I knew Rafe could feel me shaking from the truth of that statement. Example: Why were my eyelashes now crumbling crisps? That was a damned mean trick and totally undeserved. I shot Caryon a hard look and a pithy mental message. Of course both of these creeps were reading my mind.

"If you're looking for guarantees, Glory dear, you can forget it. And you can buy excellent fake lashes at your nearest drugstore. Doesn't hurt to have a reminder that we're powerful enough to make you miserable if you think to wriggle out of any deal we make." Caryon laughed when Rafe frowned, studied my face, then bit out a colorful curse.

"Relax, Valdez, they'll grow back. Now you two get busy. And, Glory, there's a bright side. You have your reflection." Cue maniacal laugh. "Think. You're going to give us the king of the EVs, who you yourself acknowledge is an evil man. He'll only get what he so richly deserves—a hellacious afterlife." Spyte hopped around in what could only be described as a demon version of a happy dance.

Caryon frowned at him. "He's right. You know Simon's goddess, who is a major slut, by the way, had probably planned to give him a cushy spot enjoying sizzling sex with her when he finally gets that stake he's been cruising for all these years."

"Yes, I bet she does. He worships her and has fed her energy for centuries from the poor saps he captures. He almost got *my* energy once." I held on to Rafe. He'd actually come up with a solution I thought I could live with. But how did we pull this off? What did you do to get someone to sell his soul? Barter? Coercion? Would it help to do a web search for deals with the Devil?

"Relax, dear girl. We have a contract. When the time comes, we'll make sure you know what to do." Caryon clapped his hand on Spyte's shoulder when he started to levitate. "Calm down, my man. You're embarrassing yourself."

"Can't help it. Lucifer is going to be *so* happy." Spyte grinned, all fangs and candy breath. "Maybe he'll even shut down the karaoke for a while."

"Silence? That would be too much to hope for. One more screaming version of 'Endless Love' and I'm going to . . ." Caryon rubbed his forehead. "Never mind." He gave Rafe and me a stern look. "This isn't a done deal yet. And the penalty for failure is steep. Valdez is Exhibit A, Gloriana." He glanced at Spyte and sighed. "Don't you dare reveal your true nature!"

"I can't resist, Glory doesn't like them. Look at her, she's freaking." Spyte now wore face paint, red pants, a green polkadot shirt and a blue bow tie. He squirted us with water from his bright yellow flower, then tooted a horn, which made me flinch.

I clung to Rafe. Spyte was right, I didn't like clowns. Yes, maybe it was a stupid phobia, but I'd never been comfortable around them. Leave it to a demon to zero in on it and take advantage.

Spyte danced closer to me and laughed when I cringed. "Going to cooperate now, Glory?"

"Leave her alone. She's going to. Aren't you?" Rafe looked down and I managed a weak nod. "Now back off, asshole." He put his hand on Spyte's loud shirt and shoved.

"Takes one to know one." Spyte giggled and did a flip,

landing on my table and squirting Caryon and Rafe with his flower.

"Now you know what we endure down there." Caryon sighed and wiped the moisture off his face. "Clowns. Hell is full of them, the kind who like to torment kids. They actually have contests to see how many of them can fit into those little cars, then race, running over toys and Christmas ornaments." He shuddered. "Exhausting."

"Not as exhausting as watching you channel that loan officer who came down last week. Too bad you aren't buying your apartment, Glory. Cary just loves a foreclosure." Spyte gave me a creepy smile. "So he's really pissy this trip. Even for you, Cary, that eyelash thing was low."

"I left her eyebrows!" Caryon poked Spyte in his bulbous red nose.

"You sure you weren't aiming for them?" Spyte squirted Caryon in the eye before they both vanished.

I surprised myself with a giggle, then buried my face in Rafe's shirt. Before I knew it, I was crying bitter tears. Rafe's arms were strong as he rocked me against him. I finally pushed back and took the tissue he'd grabbed from a box on the table. I blew my nose and wiped my wet cheeks.

"Sorry for the meltdown."

"You earned it. That was pretty intense." He leaned down and picked up the dress Spyte had knocked to the floor. "At least they're finally gone."

"But they can pop back in at any time." I sat on the one chair in the room. "A deal with the Devil? You have any idea how that freaks me out?"

"Of course I do." He knelt down in front of me and took my hands. "And I know this is my fault. Alesa came here for me and landed in you."

"Well, now. I guess you owe me, don't you?" I kept my face solemn and saw his stricken look. "Oh, relax, Rafe. You know I don't blame you. Stuff happens. We all have baggage and you never could have predicted what she'd do. And I was the one who made you so mad you used your demonic powers.

So I guess I can take some of the blame here." I kissed his lips, briefly, not letting it get into too much.

"I appreciate your attitude. But I can't let you accept any of this responsibility. Corralling Destiny for Lucifer is going to be tough. I have no illusions about that. I just want this to go away so I can keep you safe, damn it. I don't want to lose you." This time Rafe leaned forward, one hand threading through my hair when he took my lips, his mouth lingering as he plundered mine. I felt that kiss all the way down to where he'd worked my knees apart and slid in between them.

I wrapped my arms around his waist and sank in, meeting his greedy kiss with my own. Yes, I wanted him. Jerry had been right about that. And I loved Rafe. Enough to . . . ?

A knock on the door pulled us apart.

"Glory, you told me to remind you when it was nine thirty." Erin called through the door.

"Thanks, Erin. I'll be leaving from the back in a few." I sighed and touched Rafe's cheek. "Got to go."

"What's up?" He brushed back my hair.

"I'm meeting Nate. He asked for my help with Ray. Our rocker is back on the sauce, vampire-style." I stood, with Rafe's help, and walked over to the mirror above the bathroom sink.

"Oh, God! Look at me! Damn, Caryon. I can't believe he took my eyelashes." And of course my hair was a fright too. Add to that the fact that Rafe had kissed away my lipstick and I was a total freak show. I rummaged in the makeup bag I kept back there but didn't hold out much hope.

"Wait here, I've got an idea." Rafe patted me on the back and headed into the shop. I repaired my lipstick and got rid of the remains of my eyelashes with my powder puff.

"Here, put these on. You're going to a rock concert. You'll fit right in with the crowd there." He handed me a pair of vintage Ray-Ban sunglasses.

"Shades?" I grinned at myself in the mirror. "Brilliant. And you're right. Ray's friends totally wear these at night. Especially if they're hungover."

"There you go. Now tell me something." Rafe grinned at me in the mirror.

"Anything." I attacked my hair with a brush.

"Two things." Rafe turned my face toward his. "Holy crap. You really can see your reflection. I heard Spyte say something, but I guess I wasn't really thinking about the ramifications. Doesn't it just blow you away? After all these years?" He laughed.

Tears sprang to my eyes. Of course Rafe understood. He knew me so well. "Yes. But it's a double-edged sword." I turned back to check my face in the mirror. "I want to be able to do my makeup without that computer thingy Ian made for me but then I see that I never should have bought this sweater. Gold is not my color."

Rafe frowned. "I see what you mean. I like you better in blue or red. Want me to run out to the shop and get you a different one? I know you like to look good when you see the rock star."

I threw my arms around Rafe's neck and smeared my lipstick kissing him again. "You are absolutely the best friend I've ever had."

"And an idiot." He laughed again and pulled back. "I know your size, which I realize you don't like for me to say out loud. Just promise this is a mission of mercy and you won't fall for that asshole again."

"I promise." I grinned, dropped the sunglasses, then turned to repair my lipstick again. In moments Rafe was back with a blue sweater that I'd been thinking about keeping for myself anyway. I swear the man was way too observant when it came to me. I blocked my thoughts. Jerry wouldn't have a clue what size I wore or what color to choose for me. But were those necessarily qualities I needed in a mate for life?

Rafe grinned and ripped my gold sweater off and over my head in a smooth move that made me shiver. His admiring look and clever touches when he saw my cream silk bra made me do more than shiver. Okay, so maybe Rafe was more than a friend with good taste and an excellent memory. We definitely had chemistry and he had a libido to match mine.

As I playfully snatched that blue sweater and tugged it on, he pulled me to him again and told me about his club and what had been going on there. I was interested. We were both business owners and struggling to get things going in a new town. We had a lot in common and I was as comfortable with Rafe as I was with Jerry. More comfortable, actually. Because I didn't ever have to worry that Rafe would try to order me around or control me. Hmm.

Well, maybe that wasn't entirely accurate. Rafe could be pretty bossy when he was in protective mode. As usual, I was letting chemistry cloud my judgment. I put some space between us and pulled on those shades again.

"Got to go, Rafe."

"Me too. If I didn't have to be back at the club, I'd go with you. Have to admit, I'm curious about Caine and this breakdown. I thought he'd gotten a handle on the vampire experience." Rafe walked with me to the back door.

"So did I. But then I spilled the beans about the synthetic blood with alcohol and his old dependencies came into play. I felt guilty about telling him at first, but that stuff was served to him at Flo's wedding anyway, so it was only a matter of time before he found out about it."

"Right. You aren't that guy's keeper, Glo. This mentor thing has to have an expiration date." Rafe had always made it clear he didn't like my relationship with Ray.

"He's my friend too, Rafe. I care what happens to him." I sighed. "Anyway, alcohol can bring on depression. It definitely made Ray think about what he's lost." I stopped next to my car. I wasn't about to shape-shift out to the park. It was a beautiful spring night and I wanted to drive out there with the top down.

"The sun. I remember. Your friend Caine was all about the sun. Even owned an island in the Caribbean, didn't he?" Rafe opened my car door for me and watched me fasten my seat belt.

"Guess he still does." I smiled and touched Rafe's hand. "You and I will have to get together tomorrow night and talk over this deal with Simon. You know he wanted to recruit me into the Energy Vampires. I guess we could use that to make contact. Some would consider the invitation to join a real honor."

"But I bet you already told him where to stick that invite, didn't you?" Rafe frowned. "Think he'd believe in your sudden interest?"

"Maybe. But the father-son angle is our best bet. I want to talk to Freddy and see how he feels about his father. If there's a chance for them to have a relationship away from the Energy Vampires, then that would be a powerful motivator for Simon to switch sides." I sighed. "If Simon has a natural father's instincts. Who knows?"

"Can't say I'm crazy about the idea of you and Simon within a hundred miles of each other." Rafe leaned in and kissed me lightly on the lips. "But I was desperate to get your tail out of a sling tonight."

"Great image, Rafael." I started the car. "Just promise me that none of this slips around Penny. My fledgling is mixed up enough as it is. I'll just tell her the demons went back to hell after I refused to work with them."

"She's pretty smart. Won't be easy fooling her." Rafe watched me lower my convertible top with the flip of a switch.

"She's got lots of school work coming up. I hope she'll be too busy to notice what we're up to." I grabbed Rafe's hand. "Ray's trying to get Ian MacDonald to come to town. When Penny saw my computer mirror, she was intrigued by the guy who invented it. Can you imagine if she and Ian got together?"

"I'm afraid to. Didn't you tell me she's into chemistry too?"

"Yes, they'd be quite a pair." I heard the click that meant the top was secured and I was good to go. "We can worry about that if it happens. Got to run. Call me tomorrow?"

"Sure. Be careful around Caine." Rafe slapped the car hood as I backed out. "A drunk vampire is unpredictable as hell."

Unpredictable as hell. I'd just had a demo of how unpredictable hell could be and it didn't exactly encourage me. When I got to Zilker Park and realized I'd be one of a cast of thousands, I wondered if driving had been such a great idea. I parked in the darkest area I could find, near some trees, and shifted so I could fly up close to the stage and spot Nathan. A local band was opening for Ray and had the crowd dancing and pushing toward the stage.

Just as I saw Nate talking to the members of Ray's band, the local musicians came to a loud and successful conclusion if the roars of the crowd were any indication. Lights came up, along with an announcement that there would be a brief intermission before Ray and his band performed. I found a spot to shift back and strolled up to Nate, my shades firmly in place.

"Hey, look, it's Glory. Long time no see, babe." I was wrapped in strong arms, then passed around among the guys in the band. I sure didn't mind it. They were all good-looking and nice when they weren't high. Which none of them were tonight I was happy to notice. No sign of Ray. Finally I was left with Nate.

"Great to see all of you. Break a leg or whatever." I waved them off as they went to gather their instruments before the performance started.

"Glory, am I glad to see you." Nate grabbed my arm. "Come with me." He hustled me toward an RV parked at the curb near the back of the stage. The area had been cordoned off and few vehicles other than the large trucks that had hauled in the sound equipment had been allowed to park there. Beefy security guards kept the curious away.

"Where's Ray?" I looked around but didn't see him. I did, though, seem to sense another vampire in the area.

"He's in there. And he's not alone." Nate frowned and knocked on the door.

"Go 'way." Ray's voice. Though it was slurred, I'd know it anywhere.

"Ray, let me in." I banged on the door with my fist. "It's almost time for you to go on."

The door was flung open. "Glory, babe! Come in and join the party." Ray swayed in the doorway. He wore his favorite black silk boxers and nothing else. He frowned when he saw Nate beside me. "Hey, buddy. Best stay outside." He shook his head. "Fangers only, you dig?"

Nate gave me a look. "You okay with that?"

"Sure. Go take care of band business." I squeezed his hand. "How long before he needs to take the stage?"

"Thirty minutes, max." Nate backed away from the doorway. "Be careful, Glory." He finally looked at Ray, his best friend. "Damn it, Ray, pull yourself together." Then he turned and walked away.

"What's he pissed about?" Ray pulled me inside the cramped trailer. "Come meet Tiffany. Tiff, this is Glory, my mentor."

"Hey." The woman lounging on the small bunk at the end of the bed wore less than Ray and didn't bother to cover herself.

I nodded, trying not to stare at her perfect breasts on display or her slim hips, which were clad in nothing but a scrap of black lace.

"Ray, we need to talk. Tiffany, would you excuse us? Maybe Nate can find you a good spot to watch the concert." I managed a smile.

"Fine." Tiffany began to gather her clothes, which included a very brief skirt, tiny top and a pair of five-inch heels. In less time than it took Ray to refill his glass, she was dressed and at the door. "Later, Ray."

"You bet." He met her at the door, squeezed her perfect ass, then watched her step outside. He turned and frowned at me. "So what's this about? I don't usually let someone else run my women off like that." He took a deep swallow of what I could tell by the smell was the synthetic that had alcohol in it.

"Your drinking." I moved closer and grabbed his glass, throwing it into the small stainless steel sink. "Damn it, Ray, what the hell are you thinking? You've got a concert in less than half an hour and you can barely stand."

I swear Ray growled at me, but seemed to catch himself. He looked down at the floor, then at me. We were almost toe to toe. He reached out and grabbed me around the waist then yanked me to him.

"I'm standing. And I'm sober enough to take you that way too. What do you say, Glory? You did it with the shifter. How about trying it on with me?" He leaned in, sliding his fangs along my throat when I jerked my face away.

"Stop it! You really think I want you in this condition? You're staggering drunk." I shoved at him and he proved me right, grabbing hold of the counter next to him before crashing into the small table that was bolted to the floor. Discarded glasses flew everywhere and shattered. He finally landed on the padded banquette next to the table, a scowl on his face.

"No need to get mean about it. Just say no. I can take it. I took it before." He tried to pull himself up to a sitting position and it took three efforts before he made it. "What the fuck?"

"You're trashed, Ray. Obviously you've been drinking since the sun went down." I stood next to him and finally gave in to the urge to smooth his hair back from his forehead. He looked lost and confused.

"Help me up. I can shower. That'll get me sober. I've got to go on in a few." He licked his lips and I saw him eyeing the bottles stashed next to the sink.

"Nothing else to drink." I helped him to his feet, ignoring the totally hot body he exposed when he shucked his shorts and stepped into the tiny shower stall next to the kitchen. He turned on the cold water and stood under the spray, his face directly under the showerhead. He swayed there for a good five minutes. It obviously wasn't doing much for him and I finally reached in and turned off the water, helping him wrap a towel around his waist. I rubbed another towel through his long dark hair, then handed him a comb. He barely bothered to run it through and he usually tied it back anyway.

"What are you going to wear?" I glanced in the tiny closet. The choices were similar and when he didn't answer, I grabbed dark jeans and a blue silk shirt the color of his eyes. I looked back and he'd fallen onto the bed, those beautiful eyes closed, the towel a heap on the floor.

Of course I looked my fill, savoring the way his broad shoulders tapered into a lean waist and his muscular legs ended in narrow elegant feet. And then there was that package with a piercing you know where. He'd added a diamond to the loop since I'd seen it last, and it sparkled . . . Never mind. Time was marching on and this man was still in no shape to sing. I knew of only one way to get Ray sober and ready in time.

"Ray, wake up." I climbed on the bed and jiggled his shoulder.

"Glory, babe." He wrapped his arm around me and pulled me on top of him. "Finally, I've got you where I want you. What's with the shades?" He grinned and pulled them off, tossing them on the floor. "What the hell?"

"A little accident." I sighed as he slid one hand under my sweater. "Stop it, Ray."

"No way." He found my breast, then grabbed my butt with his other hand. "Feel sooo good."

"Forget that." I propped myself up to get some space, desperately trying to ignore his clever hands, one of which had unclasped my bra, then gone to work on my breasts again. "You've got to drink from me."

"Ah, love that." His fangs were sliding out and rasping along my jugular in an instant. "You are so sweet." Then he was taking my blood, sucking it in with a hum as he slid his fingers inside my jeans and stroked my bum. I moaned, not immune to the pull of his mouth or his hands on my body.

I knew I wasn't going to let him do more than this bit of foreplay, but if I made an issue out of stopping him now, he might quit drinking, and he needed my blood.

The weakness that comes from maybe a little too much giving and not enough taking began to creep over me, making me lethargic. I gently pushed him away, finally having to use force because he was really into drinking from me. He collapsed back on the sheet, his eyes slitting open as he looked up at me.

"That was so fine." He grinned and then leaned up to kiss me, one of his hands grasping the back of my head to make sure I wasn't going anywhere. He put some serious effort into the kiss, like maybe he thought he was going to finally have me where he wanted me. I sighed into his mouth, wiggled against his questing hand, which had worked its way inside my panties, and almost didn't have the strength or will to roll away from him.

"How do you feel, Ray?" I dragged myself off the bed and stood next to it. The room spun and I had to hold on to the built-in bedside table to keep from falling over.

"Better, but not as good as I'll feel when we finish what we started." He grinned and held out his hand. "Come on, babe, don't be a tease."

"I'm not. You needed my blood so you could go out there and sing. I don't want you to disappoint your fans. That's all there was to that. Anything sexual was all on your part, not on mine. I just felt sorry for Nate, stuck with you and the fallout if you were a no-show." I stomped over to the kitchen, hoping to find at least one bottle of synthetic blood that didn't have alcohol in it. No luck. But I couldn't wait, so weak that I twisted off the top of the other and took a swallow.

"Good old Glory. Always the mentor. Shit." Ray got to his feet and stepped into his jeans, not bothering with underwear. Next he grabbed his shirt. "How kind of you." He took the bottle I'd opened and drained it. "Quit doing me favors.

You putting out for Nate now? I know he's your favorite blood type."

I stared at him, my mouth open. "You know better than that. Don't be a jerk. And where's my thank-you? Don't you care that there are thousands of people out there who paid good money to see the famous Israel Caine perform?"

"Big fuckin' deal." He grabbed another bottle and opened it.

"Stop it!" I lunged for the drink. "I'm about to fall down, you drank so much, and you're going to ruin it by drinking that poison again? No way!"

"You are not my keeper, Glory St. Clair. Get the hell out. Tell Nathan to quit running to you to save my ass. If I want to kill myself, I will." He took another deep swallow of the synthetic. "Got it?"

"No. I can't let you do that. Why, Ray? Why are you so bent on self-destructing?" I didn't try to hide the tears that filled my eyes. "You have people who love you. You'll live forever. It's a gift."

"It's a fucking gift I didn't ask for and don't want." He finished the bottle and threw the empty against the wall, where it shattered. "Now get out. I've got a set to do. Go watch. You always were a fan." He grinned but it looked more like a grimace. "I'm good to go. Hell, I can do these things in my sleep."

I wiped away my tears, obviously wasted on him. But my heart broke. For Ray. I wasn't getting through to him and I guess it was true that an alcoholic had to ask for help and truly hit bottom before he would. I picked up my sunglasses and trudged to the door.

"Fine. I will watch." I opened it and almost bumped into Nate, who'd been about to knock. "I did the best I could. Good luck." I turned and looked at Ray, who was on yet another bottle. "I love you, Ray. Please remember that before you walk into the sun or whatever you think you're going to do to end this. Nate here does too. And your parents, fans. I guess none of us count, though." I sighed. He didn't even turn around or acknowledge what I'd said.

I joined the crowd, finding a spot next to Tiffany in the VIP section. The band was tuning up and the crowd was getting restless. When Ray finally staggered onto the stage, I knew this was going to be a rough night. I just didn't know how rough.

Eight

The set started off well. The band sounded great, Ray was energetic and the crowd went wild. Guess Ray had been right; he could do these things in his sleep or drunk. But he had a look in his eyes that I recognized. A dangerous look. He was on the sixth song, a fast one, when he started working the edge of the stage, leaning down to touch the women in the crowd who reached up to clasp his hand or tossed him a pair of panties or a bra.

It was actually pretty common at his concerts and he usually played it for laughs, tucking the thongs in his pocket with a wink or pitching the bras to his bass player, who sometimes wore the big ones like a cap.

Not this time. This time Ray leaned down to kiss three different women, lingering long enough that the crowd went completely insane. The big screen monitors over the stage gave everyone a good view of deep kisses with plenty of tongue. I wasn't jealous but worried. Ray looked wobbly and I had no idea if he could control his fangs when he touched these mortal women. The best I could hope for was that he didn't make them bleed and looked in their eyes at the end of the kiss to erase their memories of those sharp pointy teeth.

Luckily, song seven was a ballad and he staggered back to sit on a stool to sing with his lead guitarist. The occasional screams made him pause but he got through it, forgetting the words only once. Didn't bother this crowd. They knew his songs by heart and prompted him. He grinned and waved a thank-you, which just got the women in the audience even more excited.

Finally the end of the set was in sight. I knew it because Nate whispered in my ear that they could wrap it up with this song. It was Ray's greatest hit from last year, a fast, loud rock number that got everyone dancing, Ray included. His hip thrusts made the women squeal and reach for him, begging him to dance right into their arms.

His shirt was unbuttoned and he jerked it off, tossing it into the audience. The blue satin was shredded in seconds, leaving several women clutching pieces of it, tears streaming down their cheeks as they screamed his name. He never missed a beat, just kept singing and dancing along the edge of that stage like a tightrope walker. So dangerous.

I jumped up, afraid to lose sight of him when he bent down to kiss yet another woman. Damn it, he really was staggering now. More women grabbed at his black boots and snug jeans but he skipped out of reach, teasing them until he stumbled. He didn't fall though, just grinned and saluted, then aimed for the other side of the stage.

The music soared toward a dramatic conclusion and I tried to relax. Okay, he was going to make it. I guess I hadn't given him enough credit. Ray was a professional. He'd done this for years. And he'd done it drunk more than once when he was mortal too. Nate had told me that. As a vampire, Ray was stronger than he'd been before. I guess I should quit trying to mentor him and just let Ray go, let him live his own life.

Then he reached down to kiss one more woman and he disappeared, falling headfirst into the crowd. I held my breath and heard Nate curse beside me. Surely Ray would pop up any second now and wave to us, assuring everyone that he was all right. But it didn't happen. The crowd where Ray had landed was thick, too thick to give anyone space to work a way in. Unless they had a vampire's special gifts.

I whammied a path to Ray, staring into wide eyes and commanding obedience, until I got to where he lay on the concrete, stricken women hovering around him. The band had gone silent, clearly stunned that their lead singer had literally taken a dive midchorus.

"Move. Give him air," I said as I shoved the women back and looked down at Ray's pale face. He had a pool of blood under his head and had obviously been knocked unconscious when he'd fallen.

"Back up, let us through!" Nate's voice. He'd found the paramedics who were always on hand at these concerts and he managed to beat a path to where I knelt next to Ray. A woman shrieked Ray's name and that did it. Screams and shouts sounded from every part of the area. The women who could actually see the blood under Ray's head sobbed uncontrollably.

"Calm down. He'll be okay. Ray's tough." I tried to smile, but couldn't manage it. "Let the paramedics get to him." The women did shuffle back, clinging to each other.

Two men carrying a first-aid kit and a litter stopped next to Ray and started to assess the damage, pulling out equipment I knew would be useless. This was impossible and I knew what I had to do. No matter what was wrong with Ray, a day's sleep would take care of it. For now, we had to get away from these mortal witnesses. I gazed into their eyes, then told the paramedics to put Ray onto the stretcher without checking his pulse or whatever else they usually did. Nate and I stayed close as they carried him to his trailer. I would handle things from there.

The crowd got really quiet as a path opened in front of us. I heard the clicks that meant that pictures of this were going to show up in the tabloids. No help for that. Ray deserved whatever bad press this brought him. Nate and a pack of bodyguards kept the paparazzi at bay as we crossed the parking lot. Curious bystanders probably wondered why we didn't load Ray into the waiting ambulance but a brief comment at the trailer door took care of that. Nate just put out a statement that Ray was already awake and refused to be transported.

Inside, I threw a towel under Ray's bleeding head and had the confused paramedics lay him on his bed. The fact that the wound was still bleeding freaked me out. Vampires usually quit bleeding in moments, even from head wounds.

"We should—" The paramedic never got to finish whatever he wanted to say. I got in his face and took care of business again. Nate hovered behind them and escorted them out the door with the empty stretcher. After I'd finished with them, all they'd remember was that Ray was fine, awake, with no sign of a concussion. He'd just gotten a little bump on his head.

Actually, he was still unconscious and I was going to have to find him some decent blood to drink. Not from me; I'd already given my quota for the night and still felt shaky. What I drank to keep me on my feet was from Ray's stash, full of alcohol, and I was feeling the effects. I grabbed another bottle and drained it. Nate was close beside me again and smelling way too delicious.

"What can I do, Glory?" Nate stared down at his friend. "He's not, uh, dead, is he? You wouldn't let the paramedics do anything. Not even take his vital signs."

"Nate, his signs aren't vital. He's a vampire, remember? And immortal. Unless he fell on a stake or the sun came out, he'll live. But I don't like how he's looking." I put my hand on Nate's arm. "Blood pressure, temperature, they're not going to be in the normal range. Those results would have freaked out the paramedics." I sighed. "But there is something you can do. Have you been drinking tonight? Drugging?"

"What? I don't do drugs. And, while I could use a stiff drink, especially tonight, I always wait till after the show is over." Nate looked from me to Ray. "Shit, I get it. You need my blood. For him to drink. What about yours?"

"I already fed him before the show. To get him sober enough to perform. I can't give again tonight." I touched the oozing cut on the back of Ray's head. It was healing now, but slowly, and I didn't even have enough juice in me to speed up the process. "I know you're not enthusiastic, especially after he attacked you before, but it will save him. I don't know how serious this head injury is, but he's not coming around yet. I don't like that. He'll live, but I've seen impaired vampires who never healed properly for one reason or another. I don't want Ray to end up less than he should be."

"God, no." Nate shucked his suit jacket and sat on the side of the bed. He always dressed like the business manager he was and didn't go for a casual look. He unbuttoned his cuff and rolled up his sleeve, then offered his wrist.

"Thanks. I'm sorry if this hurts." I bit into his wrist, ignoring how yummy his blood tasted, then pressed the open wound to Ray's lips. "Come on, Ray baby, drink for me."

No response. This was not normal, not by a long shot. Usually one whiff of an exotic type like Nate's really did it for a vampire. I lay on the bed next to Ray and pried his mouth open, no fangs in sight.

"Run your wrist under his nose. Let him get a good sniff." I looked down at Ray's chest. Was he even breathing? He didn't actually need to but I pushed on his sternum to move things along. Nate shoved his wrist under Ray's nostrils.

"Come on, buddy. This is good stuff. Glory's favorite. I hear it's rare and expensive." Nate glanced at me. "I think his nose twitched."

"Yeah, and his fangs are coming down. Brace yourself, this won't be pretty." I winced when Ray latched on to Nate's wrist with a growl, sinking his fangs in deep. Nate shuddered, then reached out and took my hand.

"I can handle it." Nate did hang on to me though.

I watched to make sure Ray didn't take too much and color gradually came back into his cheeks as he drank. When his eyes fluttered open, I wrenched Nate's wrist away from him and licked the wounds closed. Ray made a grab to get the wrist back but I pushed him onto the bed again, my hands on his shoulders.

"Forget it. You've had enough."

"No." He tried to get past me, almost knocking me off the bed.

"Yes." I sat on his chest. "Get out of here, Nate. I've got this."

"You sure?" Nate grabbed his suit jacket, obviously glad to leave Ray in my hands.

"Yes, I'm sure. Does Ray have any more obligations tonight?" I didn't turn around, just stared down at Ray, daring him to buck me off like I could see he was thinking of doing.

"No, he's done. The band is taking a break, like I told you. The roadies will pack up the equipment and it's going into storage until we need it again. I'll handle it all from here. Ray's free and clear until the end of the month." Nate stood at the foot of the bed. "You okay, buddy?"

"No, I feel like shit. Get back here and let me have some more of your juice. I'm hurt, can't you see that?" Ray's voice was rough. Obviously the set had strained his voice.

"No can do. Glory says that's all you need. I have to take her word on that." Nate kept his distance. "As for being hurt? It's your own damned fault. Deal with it."

I dug in my pocket, peeled off my apartment key, then tossed him my car keys. "Could you get someone to drive my car to my place? It's a red convertible. I parked it in the far corner of the lot, almost in the trees."

"No problem." Nate moved to the side of the bed but still out of Ray's reach. "Thanks, Glory. I'll say it, even if Ray won't."

I smiled at him, then turned and frowned down at Ray, who'd made a grab for Nate again.

"Yeah, yeah, it's unanimous, I'm a bad boy. Now get off me, Glory, so Nate and I can have a little business meeting." Ray put his hands on my butt and tried to shove me off. He obviously didn't have any strength and cursed when he couldn't budge me.

Nate strode to the door. "Here's what I'm going to do. I'll take care of the press, spread the story that you're okay, but already on the way to the hospital to be checked out anyway. Should keep the vultures away long enough for you to make a move." Nate sighed. "It's what you'd do if you were *human*, Ray."

"Well, I'm not human so get back here," Ray growled.

"No, thanks. You about took my arm off. Not exactly eager for a replay." Nate didn't try to keep the anger out of his voice as he jerked open the door.

"Pussy," Ray snarled.

"Asshole." Nate slammed the door and was gone.

"Get off me. Unless you're ready to spread your legs and let me inside." Ray's smile wasn't a bit loverlike.

"Like you could even get it up, hotshot. And no thanks anyway. Right now you're about as appealing as roadkill." I stayed where I was. "You couldn't thank Nate? And we *are* human, Ray. I'll set Nate straight on that later." I glared down at him. He was obviously in pain so I let my anger go. I reached back to gently explore the back of his head. "Hmm. Hit the concrete pretty hard, didn't you? Admit it. You had it coming, strutting along the edge of the stage like an idiot."

"My fans expect it. The ladies loved it." He licked his lips and grinned, finally showing some of his famous charm. "Want a sample? Or should I say a reminder? You seem to like kissing me. And sure I can get it up. Give me a minute and something to work with." He grabbed my hair and wound his fingers in it. "Still wearing those shades? Lose 'em." He used a thumb to send them flying.

"Careful. Those are vintage. And I'm not interested in kissing you. You made a fool of yourself. I hope no one took video of that performance tonight, but I'm betting it'll be all over YouTube by morning. Israel Caine staggering around until he falls off the stage."

"Hey, no such thing as bad publicity. I bet I have a thousand get-well cards and e-mails by the end of the week. Enough to freeze up Facebook." He slid one hand down to my jugular, clearly thinking to take another drink from me.

I heaved myself off him. "You're probably right. Most women are stupid over you. Not me." I rescued my shades. "Can you stand?"

"Don't know. My head hurts like hell. Bring me a drink." Ray tried to sit up but didn't quite manage it.

"Not happening. You're coming home with me and putting some nonalcoholic synthetic in your system." I grabbed his hand and pulled him up.

"You goin' to let me sleep in your bed?" Ray grinned when I swung his legs to the side and tugged him to his feet. "'Cause that's the only way I'm leavin' here with you, babe."

"Of course, Ray." I didn't hesitate to lie to him. Whatever worked at this point. I slung his arm over my shoulders, relieved that he had enough steam to actually walk beside me to the door. Even enough to make a lunge toward the booze on the kitchen counter. He was still too weak, though, to resist when I kept it out of his reach.

"Can't shift. To, um, dizzy." He leaned on me as we stumbled down the steps. I was glad that Nate really had managed to keep the paparazzi away and the parking lot was deserted.

"This your car?" I nodded toward a black SUV. Good grief, the things were everywhere, obviously a macho must-have.

"Yeah, keys are on the visor." Ray was heavy and he was barely able to shuffle his feet. I was glad to dump him into the passenger seat and buckle him in. He leaned back and closed his eyes. "Head hurts like a son of a bitch."

"I'm sure it does. Remember that the next time you decide to lock lips with one of your fangirls." I said this as I snatched the keys and latched my own seat belt.

"No need to be jealous, babe. Just part of the act." He opened one eye and looked at me. "Usually."

"You *are* an asshole." I started the car with a roar and reversed out of the parking lot. Ray just chuckled, then groaned, closing both eyes again.

What was I doing taking him home with me? Penny would be there and I shouldn't let him within miles of her. I drove there anyway, alternately worrying about Ray's condition—he seemed to have lapsed into unconsciousness again—and having him around Penny. He was the worst example possible for a new vampire. He was profane, liked to flaunt his hot body and would no doubt do his best to drink his way through my supply of alcoholic synthetic. The first thing on my agenda would be to hide that.

By the time I dragged him upstairs to my apartment, I was almost frantic. I couldn't get more than a groan from him. I blamed his recent diet of alcoholic blood on his poor healing and myself for not letting him take more from Nate when he had the chance. I was relieved when I saw my door ajar, sure I was going to have to drop Ray on the floor to dig out my key.

I kicked the door open so I could shoulder him inside, not even stopping to wonder about the lack of security that easy access implied. I'd just managed to dump Ray on the couch when I realized I was being watched from the kitchen doorway.

"This is interesting."

"Jerry!" I straightened, brushing back my hair, and suddenly realized I'd lost my sunglasses somewhere between the car and the apartment. "I thought—"

"That I'd still be in Florida, taking a break?" He strode over to me, a bottle of synthetic in his hand, and looked down at Ray sprawled on the couch. I hadn't bothered to put a shirt on him and one of his legs had fallen to the floor. He still hadn't moved.

"Well, yes, that's what you said you wanted." I inhaled, savoring his nearness. I'd missed him so much I felt tears pop into my lashless eyes. I hated for him to see me like this. No doubt he'd decide to make the break permanent. And here I was toting around Ray, a man he hated.

"What's the matter with Caine?" Jerry nudged Ray's foot with his boot. "Not dead, is he?" I knew I didn't imagine the hopeful note in his voice.

"No, but he was hurt tonight, during his concert. And drunk. He fell off the stage and hit his head. He needs more blood but I've given him all I can." I put my hand on Jerry's arm, unable to resist touching him. He wore a short-sleeve knit shirt in a deep red that looked wonderful with his dark hair and eyes. My heart leaped at the way he studied me for a brief moment. He frowned when he noticed my lack of lashes, but he was wise enough not to mention it. I wanted to bury my face against his wide chest and just breathe him in. But then he looked away, down to the bottle in his hand.

"Blood. This stuff sure won't do it for him. It's too damned weak." He set the empty bottle on the coffee table with a grimace.

"He took some mortal blood from Nathan but I was afraid he'd get carried away and stopped him, maybe too soon." I couldn't help it. I moved in and slipped my arms around Jerry's waist. I just had to hold on to him. To let him know in a small way that I was only here as Ray's mentor, nothing else.

"Yes, he'd take too much if he could, especially if he'd overindulged in the alcoholic brew. It lowers your inhibitions." Jerry smiled down at me. "And from what I know of Caine, he has damned few of those sober."

"True." I snuggled against Jerry. "I'm so glad to see you. It's been a rough night." I was desperate to ask him why he was here but scared of his answer. It was enough that he smiled at me and kept his arm around my shoulders instead of pushing me away.

"Obviously. Caine needs vampire blood to heal properly."

"I'm sure you're right." I sighed. "I know you don't like Ray, Jerry, and that the feeling is mutual. I don't expect you to . . ."

"Just my dumb luck to show up here when you've got this lackwit on your hands." Jerry put some space between us and rubbed my cheek with his thumb. "I'm sorry you've had a bad night."

I blurted it out, just couldn't stand it. "Why are you here, Jerry?"

"Because I got to Florida and then wondered what the hell I was doing. I don't run away when I want something." He ran his thumbs up and down my neck, making me shiver. "I stand and fight for what I want."

"And what is it you want, Jeremiah Campbell?" I knew the answer, saw it in his eyes and read it in his mind as he opened to me. My own eyes filled and I trembled.

He pulled me closer until our chests met and I had to look up at him, the gleam in his eyes taking me back centuries to the first moment I saw him, so handsome, so determined to have me.

"You, woman. I want you, Gloriana St. Clair. Any way I can get you. So I'll woo you and win you, by God. Against all comers." He leaned down, kissing my cheeks, my chin, then my lips. He seduced my mouth open to take it completely.

I moaned and climbed his body, trying to show him how desperately I wanted and needed him too. How his words had thrilled me and calmed a terror I'd been feeling ever since he'd left. I hadn't even dared acknowledge it, the awful dread of what life without Jerry, truly without Jerry, would be like. Now I wouldn't have to face it. I clung to him and poured my heart into that kiss.

"Uh, hate to interrupt, but I'm coming through." Penny's voice penetrated the fog that had made me forget everything but Jerry. "Oh, my God! Is that Israel Caine on the couch?"

I eased away from Jerry's arms and turned to see Penny, followed by two burly shifters carrying boxes.

"Yes, that's Ray. Just finish up. Is that your last load? You only have a few hours until dawn, you know." I sounded like a snippy house mother, which I was at the moment.

"Yes, last load. Fellas, the boxes go back here. Follow me." Penny smiled at Jerry, gawked at Ray, then headed toward her bedroom.

Jerry and I just stood there silently, patiently waiting until the two men left and Penny had closed the door.

"Uh, hi, Mr. Blade." Penny flushed. "Sorry if I'm in the way here. I'll be working on my laptop." She held up earphones. "These are noise-cancelling. Top of the line. Going to my bedroom now. Music on. Loud." She headed toward the hall. "'Night."

"Thanks, Penny. I'll explain about Ray tomorrow. I promise." I smiled at her gratefully. She really was incredibly bright. When she'd disappeared, her door closing with a click, Jerry moved away from me to sit on the coffee table near Ray's head.

"Now I'm going to prove just how much I love you, Gloriana." He bit his own wrist, then shoved it into Ray's mouth. "Drink, you sorry bastard. Drink and heal so you can get the hell out of here."

I stared at Jerry, my mouth open. As proof of love, this was a doozy. Jerry giving his life force to Ray. And of course Ray latched on. Jerry's ancient blood was irresistible. Ray gulped and swallowed, taking it in and healing, almost before our eyes. The cut on top of his head vanished and the circles under his eyes disappeared. He had his healthy tan back too, the tan he'd had when he'd been turned vampire. I dragged my gaze from that miracle to move behind Jerry, running my hands through his soft hair.

"Thank you. This means—"

"What I said. That I love you. That I'll do whatever it takes to prove that." He jerked his arm away from Ray, swearing as his skin ripped. He kept a hand on Ray's chest when Ray tried to go for another drink. "Cease your whining, Caine. You've had enough." He leaned down and stared into Ray's eyes, now bright and alert. "Sleep. When you wake up tomorrow night, you should be good as new. Whatever the hell that means to you."

To my astonishment, Ray meekly closed his eyes, apparently down for the count.

"You whammied him." I stepped back when Jerry rose and pushed the coffee table out of his way.

"Aye."

"I didn't think that was possible with another vampire. Especially one like Ray, who wouldn't want to do anything you ordered him to do." I glanced at Ray again, who was clearly sleeping peacefully.

"He's still weak, has enough of my blood in him to be susceptible to me, and no will to resist." Jerry scooped me into his arms and carried me toward my bedroom. "I'm hoping that last one applies to you as well."

"Wait a damned minute." Even I realized there was no heat behind my protest. I grabbed the doorframe as he stepped over the threshold, stopping us before he was actually inside the bedroom. I had to at least make a token attempt to slow this down.

Jerry grinned down at me. "You want me to leave? After I went against every instinct that said let the bleeding sod rot? I fed him for you, Gloriana. I'd hoped that would prove something to you."

"It proved, Jerry, that you like to make grand gestures. No news there." We both knew Ray would have healed on his own. Eventually. There was no need to bring that up.

"Can't say I wasn't impressed." I stroked his cheek. The roughness of his late-night beard was just another sign of his virility. He was so strong, so all male. I loved that about him. "But do you want me to fall into bed with you in gratitude? For saving Ray?"

"I'd take it." He laughed when I hit his chest. "For a start." He leaned down to kiss me in that hot and effortless way he had that curled my toes and made me grasp his hair. "But I imagine I could get you to invite me there for other reasons with a little time and persuasion."

"I'm too easy for you. You left me here crying your name." I punched him a little harder this time. He'd hurt me but not nearly as much as I'd hurt him when I'd turned to Rafe. I couldn't deny that.

"I'm sorry for that, Gloriana, but I needed to get some things straight in my mind. A man has his pride, you know."

His arms tightened around me and I knew his pain was still raw and would be for a long while yet. If inviting him to lie with me now would make it less, I was more than willing. Who was I kidding? I wanted him with everything in me. I ached for him.

"A woman has her pride too." I pressed a soft kiss to his lips. "But where you are concerned I have none, it seems. Take me to bed, Jeremiah. Make me scream. If Penny hears too much through her earphones, let her be jealous that I have the most delicious, the most expert lover in the world."

"Most expert, eh? Now there's a high mark." Jerry was beside the bed in three strides. He laid me gently on the coverlet and gazed down at me. "I have to ask. What the hell happened to your eyes? They look strange."

"I lost my eyelashes. You don't want to know how." Demons. Jerry would go insane when he realized hell had come calling and that Rafe and I would be working together again.

"Don't I?" He crawled on the bed, his hands on either side of my head, his knees bracketing my hips. "Why do I think the shifter is responsible for this?"

I put my finger on his frowning lips. "Stop. The shifter cannot be here now. Not when I'm thinking I wear too many clothes and so do you."

"You're right. I'm going to make love to you, Gloriana." Jerry smiled and glanced back at the candles I'd placed on my dresser, left over from an exorcism.

Oh, definitely not thinking about demons now, not with the candles suddenly lit and the overhead off. I liked the romantic lighting, much more forgiving as he eased off my sweater and dropped it beside the bed. Another glance from Jerry got soft music from my bedside radio.

"How did you do that?" I sighed as he released the clasp of my bra. Sometimes it felt more like a cage on my too-full breasts.

"I have more tricks than you can imagine." His grin was wolfish as he tossed the bra aside and leaned down to trace the marks left by the underwire with his tongue. "I don't know why you bother wearing such torturous devices. Your breasts are perfect."

"They bounce. Not cool." I shoved my fingers in his hair. "Tricks? I figured you'd shared pretty much all of them over the years." I gasped when he ran his fangs back and forth across first one nipple then the other.

"Why don't you just relax and enjoy, lass." Jerry's eyes gleamed as he slipped open the button on my jeans, then eased down the zipper. "Let me do all the work tonight."

"Work?" I tugged on his hair. "Since when is lovemaking work to you?"

"Clearly I am talking too much." Jerry swooped down, silencing me with a hungry kiss.

He was right, of course. No more talk. I pushed my hands under his knit shirt to explore the taut muscles of his back, the ridge of an old scar, the bumps of his spine.

He was taking care of my jeans and panties, getting me naked with an efficiency that was no trick at all. When he released my mouth to explore my breasts again, I managed to tug his shirt up and off him, then took care of the fastening of his jeans. He sucked my nipple into the warmth of his mouth and I moaned, the flick of his tongue and the pressure making me clench between my legs.

Jerry obviously knew that because he stroked me there, his clever fingers finding just the place that needed attention and, oh, yes, pressure until I gasped and writhed in his arms.

"Jerry!" I wanted to touch him, to make him lose his mind like I was losing mine. To hell with this "make Glory wild" mission. Suddenly I resented it, resented the way every man in my life—well, make that Jerry and Rafe—always had to be in the driver's seat. Even in bed. Sure it was all about my pleasure. Yeah, right. But you can bet the farm Jerry would get his rocks off long before dawn and more than once.

I guess I stiffened or something because Jerry pulled back and stared down at me.

"What's wrong, Gloriana?"

I almost didn't say anything. He wouldn't get it. In Jerry's worldview he was making a big sacrifice here. Giving Glory the big O with all the bells and whistles. I reached up and touched his cheek.

"I love you, Jerry. You don't have to prove anything to me." The truth was I had everything to prove to him. But I wasn't getting into our issues now. Talk about ruining a mood.

"I wasn't—"

I shut his mouth with a deep and, okay, desperate kiss, then eased off again.

"You know what I want?"

"I hoped I was getting there." His hand rested on the damp curls at the juncture of my thighs. He leaned on one elbow and tweaked one of my nipples and, yes, I shivered.

"Okay, yes, that." I nudged his erection with my knee. I'd gotten his jeans off somehow. We were both naked, good to go. Why was I talking? Oh, yeah. "But can you forget tricks and special effects and fantasies and whatever cute things you might have up your sleeve and just *be* with me?"

Jerry frowned. "First, look, no sleeves. Second, I set a scene, wasn't much of a trick there. And, third?" He lay beside me and pulled me into his arms. "There's nothing I like better than just *being* with you. I love you. Do with me what you will. But don't expect me to just lie here and take it." He rolled me on top of him. "You've been known to inspire me."

"Back at you." I smiled and slid down his body to take him into my mouth. His gasp and groan were my reward. He only allowed it a few moments before he turned me so he could taste me as well. We drove each other wild with our fangs and our tongues until I finally pulled away to sit astride him, impaling myself on his rigid cock.

"Jerry!" I sighed as he filled me, sure no one else quite made me feel this complete. He held my breasts, his fingers clasping my sensitive nipples as he looked at me with love in his eyes.

I couldn't imagine why I still held his devotion. I had tested it and would continue to strain this relationship. I leaned down to kiss his mouth as we moved, my body convulsing just as his did. We were so attuned, so in sync. If only we could forget everything but the here and now. Finally I trembled and lay in Jerry's arms, too languid to do more than kiss his damp shoulder.

"I will never be able to look Penny in the eyes again."

Jerry grinned, took my hand and placed it on his chest. "Move in with me and leave her here. Then you won't have to."

"Can't. I'm her mentor, remember?" I sat up and stared down at him. "And don't rush me. A half hour ago I thought we were no longer a couple."

Jerry glanced at the clock on the bedside table. "That was more like an hour ago. And we will always be a couple. Make no mistake about that." He stretched, his naked body a thing of beauty and, wow, pure sex on a stick. "I'm spending the day. You couldn't blast me out of here. Not with Caine on your couch."

"Did I ask you to leave?" I glanced at that same clock. Another half hour or so till dawn. I got up and opened the bedroom door, glancing down the hall. Penny's music was so loud, I could hear it out here. I guess if she were mortal, I'd worry about hearing damage. I grinned and went to check on Ray, not really worried that I was naked. If he woke up and peeked, Jerry would have a good excuse to knock him in the head again. I would probably enjoy watching that.

But Ray was still out. I put a hand on his chest and could tell it was a natural sleep, not yet the death sleep that would hit him when dawn came. I took a quick detour to the kitchen, dragging every bottle of synthetic with alcohol into a bag, then grabbed an ordinary one for myself. I picked up the bag and carried it into the bedroom.

"What's that?" Jerry had propped himself up in bed.

"Blud-Lite. It has alcohol. I'm hiding it in my closet. So Ray can't get into it. I'm going to help him dry out if he'll let me." I dumped it in the bottom of my clothes hamper, then threw a dirty towel on top of it.

"You're kidding." Jerry jumped out of bed, slid a bold hand over my backside just to show he'd noticed I was naked, then took the bottle of synthetic out of my hand and twisted off the top. "You really think he'll let you do that?"

"Doubt it, but I'm going to offer. I still feel like his mentor, Jer." I took the bottle he held out to me and took a swallow. "Ray knows I'm not into him." I grinned. "Not like I'm into you." I rubbed my bare breasts against his chest.

"He'd better." Jerry jerked me against him. "Come back to bed."

"Oh, I am. Just needed to get my strength back." I quickly drained the bottle, then set it on the dresser. "You've fed Ray, I've fed Ray. I think we both need to take a rest from feeding tonight." I ran my finger down the center of his chest to his navel and twirled a curl there. "But not from any other sort of fun."

"Fun. Yes, I've got some ideas about that and I think it's my turn." He backed me toward the bed and rolled us until I landed on top of him. "Remember some of the fantasies we've tried?"

"Oh, yeah. What can we manage in twenty minutes?" I laughed when Jerry listed four that made me shiver. Oh, yeah. My guy was serious about keeping us together. Now if I could just make sure not to mess this up. Of course there was always help with that.

Nine

I had a new definition of hell: four vampires, one bathroom and an ancient hot water heater.

"Look, it's my apartment so I go first." I gave Jerry, then Ray, an uncompromising look. "And, no, I don't need company in the shower."

Penny giggled. I swear she hadn't taken her eyes off Ray since we'd all popped awake at sunset. Well, Ray hadn't exactly popped. He still showed some effects of a rough night before, lounging on the couch and trying to weasel information from a dazzled Penny about my stash of alcoholic synthetic. Someone should run downstairs and get the man a shirt. Penny glanced at me and winked. Hmm. Maybe not.

"Go ahead, Gloriana. I'll make sure Caine behaves himself around your fledgling." Jerry plopped himself in the chair nearest the couch. I swear if he'd brought his broadsword, it would be resting across his knees.

"Right, babe. Go for it. I'm not sure I can stand alone in a shower anyway." Ray leaned back to smile at me. "When it's my turn, you'll have to go in and hold me up, scrub my back."

"Like hell." Jerry pulled a knife from the sheath he kept at his ankle and began to clean his nails. "I'll dump you in the tub, Caine, and hose you down with the showerhead myself. Water should be good and cold by then." He grinned and waved his knife at me. Even from the doorway I could see that it was wickedly sharp.

"Put the knife away, Jerry." I sighed and took advantage of the lull to grab my clothes and hurry into the bathroom. What a circus. Oh, no. Bad choice of words. Because who should jump out from behind the bathroom door and cause me to drop my underwear and dress but Spyte?

"Israel Caine." The demon wasn't in clown costume today but black jeans and T-shirt. He shouldered the door closed and we were shut inside together. How creepy was this?

"What about him?" I picked up my dress and hung it on the hook on the back of the door. "Get out of my bathroom." I could barely move without touching the demon and I sure wasn't taking off my robe with Spyte the spy in here.

"He's a hell-raiser. A prime candidate. We could make every song he puts out an instant hit. Or we can give him his mortality back. Tell him that. Reel him in for the big guy and you'll be shrinking before you know it." Spyte gave me a hip bump in case I missed the point.

"Ray is basically a good person. He's just a little depressed. I won't be the one to send him to hell." I set my underwear on the back of the toilet, then sat on the closed seat. "Get out of here. I need a shower and you're not invited."

"Too bad. Curvy women were once my thing." Spyte stared at my robe and I figured he could see right through it. "True hell is when you still appreciate the view but can't do anything about it. Trust me on that."

"And that's what you want for Ray?" I jerked my robe closed, even though I hadn't even been showing cleavage. "Get out. Leave my friends alone. You approach Ray and no way I'm helping with Simon. That's our deal. Don't drop in here again. You screw this up and I bet Lucifer will be mighty unhappy with you. Am I right?"

"Yes, of course. But then he's always unhappy and bored. Takes a lot to amuse him. It's a hell thing. Sure, he gets a charge now and then when we bring him somebody unexpected. Like a do-gooder who does bad or a really public figure who falls prey to one of our seductresses." Spyte gave me another once-over. "You seem to keep your guy happy in the sack. We've got a job opening in that department. Pay's lousy but there are benefits you wouldn't believe." Spyte's leer made me shudder. "Lucifer likes to interview applicants himself. I've heard those one-on-ones can be quite an experience."

"Get. Out." I hopped up and opened the lid of the toilet. I pointed to the water. "I'm sure you know the way."

"Funny girl. Hurry with that shower. Your bud Valdez is on his way and I don't think your lover is going to be happy to see him." With an evil grin, Spyte vanished, just not into the bowl.

I looked all around, even behind the shower curtain, then stripped and turned on the water. So what if the water was still cold? I had to hurry. Rafe and Jerry in the same room. They needed a referee and Penny wasn't up to that task.

To my surprise my fledgling had come through with a pair of false eyelashes her sister Jenny had given her. Getting those on straight slowed me down, but I'd just made it into the living room when there was a knock on the door. I knew who it was so I sent Penny into the bathroom for her shower before I let Rafe in.

"It's Rafe. Stay calm, Jerry." I gave my lover a warning look.

"What the hell's he doing here?" Jerry jumped up to stand by my side. Ray just smiled. He'd taken off his boots and had his bare feet propped on the back of the couch.

"This is gonna be good. Oh, how I wish for the days of popcorn and beer." Of course Ray knew all about my fling with Rafe. It had infuriated him and hurt him at the time. Now he just wanted to see how Jerry handled it.

"Shut up, Ray." I unlocked the door and opened it. "Come in, Rafe."

"What is this?" He looked from a glowering Jerry to a grinning Ray. "An ambush?"

"No." I put my hand on Jerry's chest and felt the rumble of a barely suppressed growl. "Not at all." I stared up at his frowning face. "Jerry, maybe you should head home and take your shower there."

"Not likely." He smiled suddenly when he saw Rafe sniffing the air and obviously picking up on something that caused a furrow between his own dark brows. I'd showered off my hint of sex, but Jerry reeked of me and how we'd made love the night before. Ray had probably noticed, but no longer cared enough to even give me grief about it.

"Glory and I have business to discuss. It's none of yours." Rafe shut the door behind him. "I believe she asked you to leave."

"I'm going to have to tell him what's going on, Rafe. No more secrets." I felt Jerry's hand slide into mine. Possessive. I understood and accepted it.

"He's going to blow a fuse." Rafe glanced at Ray. "And what the hell is *he* doing here?"

"I'm here for the show. I can't wait to see how Glory keeps the two of you from killing each other." Ray sat up, looking more alert by the minute. I saw that he had finished one bottle of synthetic.

"Think you can walk, Ray? Go lie on my bed. We don't need an audience." I nodded toward my bedroom. Maybe that wasn't a good idea with the alcohol stashed in there, but Ray wasn't budging.

"No, too weak. I'm still sick. Either bring me a real drink or call me a cab." Ray patted his pockets. "Hell, I don't even have my phone or wallet."

"Yes, I know. You're here to dry out. If you think you can handle it." I really didn't want to get into this now, especially not with this audience. Rafe and Jerry both looked ready to reach for cab fare and to haul Ray to the street.

"I can handle it. But I don't want to." He rubbed his forehead. "Whatever. Go ahead, do your thing. I'm going to bed." He heaved himself to his feet and staggered toward my bedroom. He hit the wall on his way and I ran to help him, tossing back the covers to the clean sheets I'd put on the bed after Jerry and I had gotten up at sunset.

"I'm sorry, Glory. Call Nate. He'll come take me off your hands." Ray pulled my fingers to his lips.

"Not right now, Ray. I've got my hands full." I sighed. "Rest. I'll check back with you in a few minutes. Okay?"

"I feel like shit. What's the matter with me? I'm supposed to heal." His eyes fluttered closed and I pulled my hand out of his.

"You've abused your body. Even vampires have limits." I turned and left the room. No time for this. At least the living room was quiet. Which meant Rafe and Jerry weren't fighting. Yet.

"Now, Gloriana. Want to tell me what you and Valdez are working on together?" Jerry gestured for me to sit on the couch. Of course he was beside me, too close beside me, in an instant.

Rafe sat in the chair Jerry had used earlier. He studied me with his warm brown eyes and I knew he was hurt and not a little disillusioned. I could easily read his thoughts. There Glory goes again, back to Blade and her old dependent ways. I sat up straight and slid into a corner of the couch, using my knees to put some space between Jerry and me.

"Okay, here's the deal. Alesa, the demon who possessed me before—"

"Valdez's ex-wife." Jerry glared at Rafe.

"Yes, she was that. Anyway, she went down to hell after we drove her out and apparently bragged about how strong I was." I looked at Rafe for help.

"Knowing her kind, that was to save face. She was trapped in Glory for a good long while. Any demon worth her salt should have been able to jump right back out again after what happened. Instead, she was stuck in Glory. Couldn't get back to hell until we used extreme measures."

"Right. The exorcism and the power of love." Jerry looked

beyond grim. "This all goes back to you and your demon origins, Valdez."

Rafe leaned forward, his elbows on his knees. "Which you knew about and appreciated when you hired me to look after Glory. Thought my powers might be useful."

"Okay, so that's a standoff. Am I right?" I didn't like the heat rising from Rafe or the way Jerry's fangs were glinting in the lamplight.

"Not exactly. What has that to do with now? You sent this demon bitch back where she belongs. So you're done, Gloriana. Valdez no longer works for me. He's no longer your bodyguard or your lover. Am *I* right?" Jerry stared at me, almost daring me to close my mind to him.

I didn't. I opened it wide. "No, he's not my lover. That's history." I turned to Rafe. "I'm sorry, Rafe, but Jerry and I are together now. What you and I did . . ." I stopped. No need to dredge that up. "Anyway, I'm committed to making our relationship work now."

"Committed. Working. Fine. Have at it. But you and I are in a hell of a mess." Rafe glared at Jerry. "Sorry, but we're committed too. And if I don't help you, Glory, we're both up shit creek."

"Explain." Jerry bit off the word.

"Alesa did such a sales job on me that two demons showed up, determined to make me an offer I couldn't refuse." I sighed. "They want me to work for Lucifer, to collect souls for him."

"That's ridiculous." Jerry smiled. "Anyone who knows you would never expect for a moment that you'd go over to the dark side."

"Exactly!" I wanted to reach over and hug him. But I didn't. Rafe was here and I wanted to keep the tone of this meeting as neutral as possible. "They even tried bribing me. Said if I did this, they'd make me a size six, permanently." I laughed. "Like that would do it."

"I remember when you went down to that size, in California." Jerry reached over and rubbed my bare knee, exposed by my skirt. "You were too thin, lost your full curves. You weren't the Glory I knew and loved."

"Well, maybe not physically, Jer, but, no matter the size of my outside, I'm always the same inside you know." I frowned, hearing myself. Hello? When I was right, I was right.

"I could have told you that, Blade." Rafe just had to put his two cents in. He nodded at Jerry like get a clue.

"Don't start, Rafe." I sighed. "In that world, Hollywood, surrounded by so many glamorous stick-thin women? It was important to me. And, I admit it, ultracool. A dream come true." I sighed again. Too bad it hadn't lasted. I'd always consider Ian MacDonald a genius for creating a vampire diet drug that worked. But so temporary and so outrageously expensive. Ray had paid for it. Which reminded me. I could see that he'd shut my bedroom door. What was he up to in there? If he was hunting for my Blud-Lite . . .

"Regardless, she turned them down flat. Even though they gave her another incentive." Rafe smiled at me. "She can see herself in a mirror. Actually gets a reflection."

"I don't believe it." Jerry gripped my knee.

"Oh, believe it. I'll show you later." I sat up straight, effectively getting away from Jerry's hold. I was afraid this next bit of news was going to make him crazy. "Then they called in the big guns."

"How so?" Jerry looked from me to Rafe.

"Me. I owe hell a favor." Rafe shot me a look that said it wasn't too late for me to abandon him. I sent him a mental message that he could forget it. "For using my powers. So I'm charged with helping Glory work for Lucifer."

"No, by God!" Jerry jumped up, gripping Rafe by his shirt front.

"You think I want her working for demons?" Rafe shoved at Jerry and the sofa moved.

I jerked the coffee table out of the way. I'd already lost one to a fight in here and I really liked this one.

"Calm down, both of you. There's nothing we can do except work to fix this."

"All of this comes down to this damned demon." Jerry snarled at Rafe.

"You brought me here. Let me get to know Glory, love her. This is your damned fault, Scotsman." Rafe was livid and he threw a punch that landed with a sickening crunch on Jerry's nose. Blood spurted and I screamed.

"If you love Glory, then get these hellspawn away from her. Do something!" Jerry roared and charged, hitting Rafe solidly in the midsection and reducing my chair to kindling as they hit the floor.

"Stop it!" I kicked at both of them but they didn't even notice, too busy pummeling each other as blood sprayed the wooden floor and pieces of chair crunched under their bodies.

"Nice." Ray stood in the doorway, a bottle of Blud-Lite in his hand.

"Damn it!" If that didn't just make this whole thing worse.

"Glory, your cell is ringing." Penny came out of the bathroom, my cell phone in her hand. I guess I'd left it next to my makeup bag. The mirror in there was now my favorite place in the apartment.

Jerry and Rafe cursed and rolled toward me. I threw up my hands and stalked around the back of the couch. To hell with them. To hell with Ray too, who now leaned against the bathroom door, flirting with Penny. I grabbed my phone, shoved Penny toward her bedroom and Ray into the bathroom, then slammed the door. I finally answered the phone, though I could barely hear over the grunts, curses and crashes from the living room.

"Hello?"

"Glory? It's Erin. We've got an emergency in the shop. You'd better get down here."

"What kind of emergency? I've got a situation up here that's pretty bad at the moment." Damn it, there went my lamp. Jerry was paying for a new one. I was pretty sure he'd started this brawl with his attitude. Then Rafe's red eyes started heating up and I was afraid he was going to owe hell even more favors. I had to stop this, right now.

"Paparazzi. Seems you and Israel Caine are back together again if the fact that his SUV is parked behind this building is any indication. Which is way cool. But you know what happens. We're swamped. You went to that concert and someone got a picture of the two of you right after he did a header off the stage. Is he okay?" Erin sounded breathless. "Yes, ma'am, this is her shop. Oh, yes, I'll ring you up." I heard the rustle of fabric. A sale.

"Erin, I'll be down in a few. Ray's fine. But we're not—" I almost fell in when the bathroom door opened behind me. Ray came out wearing nothing but a towel around his waist after what had to be his quickest shower ever.

"Damn, that water's cold." He snagged me around the waist. "Let me call Nate and get some clothes up here."

I heard more glass breaking in the living room. "Erin, hang in there. Give me five minutes to kill a few men and I'll be down." I shut the phone and handed it to Ray. "Knock yourself out."

"Thanks, sweet thing." He gave me a smile and a squeeze. "Better do something about your guy in there before he kills your dog."

"You are such a jerk." I took his hand off my waist and charged into the wreckage of my living room. "Stop!"

Jerry rolled off Rafe and lay panting on the floor. His shirt was ripped and bloody and both eyes were swollen to slits. Obviously he'd been ready to call a halt or he'd never have obeyed me. Rafe lay on the floor where Jerry had left him. He had long gashes in his skin where obviously Jerry had used his fangs to good effect, and he was bleeding all over the floor and what was left of his ripped shirt. His lips were cut and swollen to double their normal size.

"Aren't you a pretty pair?" I put my hands on my hips. "And look at the mess you made." I figured the only piece of furniture still worth keeping was the couch. Both chairs had been destroyed, along with my lamp and various decorations I had used to make the living room homey. My coffee table hadn't survived either. Damn it. "Did this solve anything?"

"Sorry, Glory." Rafe winced as he sat up. "Guess we should have taken this outside."

"Ya think?" I kicked the broken lampshade aside to make a path. "You will pay for every bit of damage. Both of you." I glared at Jerry, who was getting to his feet. I saw him bite his lip against the pain but didn't have much sympathy for him. His temper had started this.

"Of course. Send me half the bill." Jerry held on to the wall as he staggered. "The shifter can pay the other half."

"It should all be on you." Rafe was on his feet now and grabbed a kitchen towel to wipe the blood off his arms. "You put your hands on me first. I don't take that shit from anybody."

Jerry smiled. "You just took it from me. How'd you like the beat-down?"

Rafe growled, obviously about to launch himself at Jerry again.

"No!" I jumped between them. "I've got to get to the shop. Apparently Ray and I are an item again, according to the tabloids, and all hell has broken loose down there."

"Seems hell has broken loose up here too." Penny stared around the room in dismay. "You didn't bump into my computer, did you?" She picked her way to the kitchen table and anxiously checked the new setup there.

"See? See what you've done? Is this an example to set for a fledgling, Jerry?" I thumped him on his bruised chest and had the pleasure of seeing him wince. "And, Rafe, get that smile off your face. You threw the first punch and owe me for half. Make no mistake about that." I grabbed my purse, which, luckily, had been in a chair safely near Penny's computer. I stomped back to the bathroom door and held out my hand. Ray, having just ended a call, slapped the phone into it.

"Nate coming?"

"No. He's pissed at me. Says for me to stay here and dry out." Ray shook his head. "What the hell is the matter with him? Where's the loyalty?"

"I think you drank it, Ray. Right out of his veins." I clomped into my bedroom, picked up the bag of Blud-Lite that Ray had obviously unearthed from my hamper, and hefted it. "This is coming with me. Take Nate's advice and dry out. I'll check in on you later. You and I are a couple again." I brushed my hand on his cheek. "Sorry, sweetie. I know this is going to be rough. Please try to stick with it."

His answer was a lunge for the bag that made him stagger.

"Glory, I need to leave and work on my research at the lab at school. My computer is okay now, but . . ." Penny glanced at Jerry and Rafe.

"Oh, they are both leaving. Immediately. Don't touch this mess. One or both of them will come back later and help me clean it up." I grabbed the doorknob and opened the door. "Am I right?"

Jerry nodded. "Of course I'll be back. Don't expect the shifter though."

"We still need to talk. I don't want her involved with these demons any more than you do, Blade. I told her that." Rafe glanced at Jerry, then me.

"Yes, well, I can't let them torture you when I . . ." I shook my head. Jerry didn't need to know the details of why Rafe had lost his cool and used his powers. "You're my friend. I don't abandon friends who need me. Get it, Jerry? Ray, you hear that?"

"Glory the good witch," Ray muttered as he staggered over to fall on the couch. "I hear you. Thanks, I guess."

"Gloriana, you need to think about this." Jerry glared at Rafe. "Valdez is letting you off the hook."

"I know. Not accepting that. Now I've got to get down to the shop." I shoved them both out to the hall. "I suggest you each go upstairs, shift and disappear that way. I have a feeling the paparazzi will be camped on my doorstep waiting for a Glory sighting. I really don't want to be seen with either one of you looking like you've been mugged. They'll assume Ray took you on and won."

"Hey, I like that." Ray grinned, but the effect was ruined when he lurched to his feet and ran into the bathroom. We could all hear him heaving into the toilet. Uh-oh.

I hurried to look in on him. "You okay?"

"Yeah, yeah. Get out of here. Clear everyone out. Guess it's what I deserve." He looked up at me, a towel in his hand, his face pale. "The fewer who see me like this, the better. You dig?"

I ran cool water on a washcloth and wiped his face. "I really will come up and check on you in a while. There's plenty of regular synthetic if you feel like it."

He grabbed my hand. "Thanks, babe. I know you and Nate mean well."

"Yeah, we both love you." I brushed his hair back from his face. "Need help getting back to bed?"

"No, think I'd better camp out here next to the john for a while. Go. I mean it." He leaned back against the bathtub, managing to flash me. Ray as usual noticed me looking and winked. "Or stay if you can get rid of the brawlers out there."

"Gloriana?" Jerry was suddenly behind me in the hallway.

"I'm coming. And you're leaving." I shook my head at Ray and pushed Jerry toward the door. When Jer leaned toward me as if he thought to kiss me good-bye, I held up my hand.

"No, not going to happen." I whipped out my compact, checked my lipstick and dabbed some translucent powder on my nose. "You're bloody and I'm mad at you. Penny, will there be mortals at the lab?"

"Uh, no. Too late for that. I'll be alone. I've got a key card and the security code. This won't be the first time I've gone in late to work." She picked up her laptop and stuffed it and some papers into a canvas bag. "And I drank two bottles of synthetic in case I run into anybody."

I stared at her, pretty sure she was up to something, but just didn't have the time to deal with her right now. "Okay, take off and make it soon. Ray would like some privacy. Just don't mess with any mortals. Remember the council's termination policy."

That got her attention. "Yeah, sure. Just need to do something in the lab. Not thirsty at all." Penny glanced at the bathroom. "Will he be all right?"

"Hopefully. Try to ignore him and just go." I wasn't sure I trusted Ray not to try to talk her out of her cell phone to get some alcoholic brew delivered. I didn't say it, just got both men out the door, slammed it, then waved my hand at a frowning Rafe and Jerry. "See you both later. Don't call me, I'll call you."

I strutted down the stairs, the effect ruined when I had to drag my bag of Blud-Lite behind me. Did you think I was going to toss it down the garbage chute? Are you kidding? That stuff costs the earth. I'd just stash it in the fridge in the back room of my shop. I braced myself, then opened the door to the outside. Sure enough, there was a gaggle of cameramen lying in wait for me.

"Glory! Is it true you and Israel Caine are back together again?"

"Glory! Where's Caine? How is he? What hospital did you take him to?"

"Glory! Look this way! Tell us about Caine!"

I held up my hand. "When Ray was hurt, I couldn't just stand by, not knowing how he was, whether he was seriously hurt. Naturally, I rushed to his side." I put on a stricken face and it was funny how silent these creeps got, the only sound the clicks of their cameras.

"Imagine how horrified I was to see the blood under his head as he lay on that hard concrete, so still, looking almost"— I took a shuddering breath—"dead." I dabbed at my eyes, careful of those temporary lashes and trying not to drop my sack or my purse. "But head wounds do bleed profusely, even when they're not serious." I sighed. "Thank God Ray's injury wasn't." I smiled. "He's fine now. Just resting after a concert and, admittedly, a rough fall." I waved and stepped toward the door of the shop.

"Glory! Are you two back together? Did this tragedy spark a new romance?"

I stopped in my tracks. "I will always love Israel Caine. Who doesn't? His music speaks to me. And"—I looked down at my feet and that damned heavy bag of booze I'd finally had to set down—"he's so very charming." I looked up again. "But we'll just have to see how things work out. Ray and I agreed to go our separate ways a while back. It was for the best then and it's probably still for the best. I'm just a simple shopkeeper. The life of a rock star is pretty intense. I'm afraid his lifestyle isn't for me."

"But, Glory, he did move to Austin. Don't you think that meant something? That he wanted to put things back together with you?" This from a local reporter who'd been pretty good about promoting Ray's music and was definitely a fan. I didn't mind answering him.

I smiled. "Ray's a complicated man. And Austin has a great music scene and good studios. He likes Austin. And we'll always be good friends. Now I've got to go to work. You want to help me? Spell the name of the shop right. Vintage Vamp's Emporium on Austin's Sixth Street. Bring me more business." With that I shoved my way through the crowd and made it into the store.

Wow. And the place was full. Nothing like being a rock star's main squeeze to pull in business. I stashed my booze and my purse in the back room and went to work. It was great therapy. I could almost forget for a while all the stuff going on in my life. Yeah, right. That is until CiCi, the Countess Cecilia von Repsdorf, dropped by to pay me a visit. Talk about perfect timing. CiCi was Simon Destiny's ex-lover and the mother of his son. She could give me the lowdown on how things were between the EV leader and Freddy, his son.

"*Cheri*, you are radiant. I guess the rumors are true then? You are with this sexy rock star?" CiCi looked me over.

I had to admit I'd picked a dress in Jerry's favorite blue, a color that brought out my eyes, and in a style that hugged my waist. Of course the deep V-neck got attention where it needed to be and not on my hips. I was still dodging those full-length mirrors but had known I wouldn't be able to dodge those cameras.

I looked around and realized we were in a lull. "Come in the back with me and I'll tell you all about it." Since my best bud Florence was still out of town, CiCi was a good shoulder to cry on. I led the way to the back room.

"Gossip, I live and breathe for it. Tell me all." CiCi sat on the only chair, happily accepting one of my bottles of booze while I stuck to the straight stuff.

"Jerry's back and he's responsible for my glow."

CiCi leaned forward and clinked bottles with me. "Excellent. You know I've always wanted you two together. Keep talking. What about the Israel Caine rumors stirring up again?"

"Ray's an alcoholic and he's on the sauce again, vampire-style. I was his mentor and now I hope to help him dry out. He's upstairs right now thinking about it." I took a swallow. "Or at least I hope he is. I didn't leave him with many resources, but he *is* a vampire. He might take off anyway."

"Sounds like you have your hands full. With Jeremiah back and this handsome singer there too? What does your Scot think about your helping another man this way?" CiCi peeled at the paper label on her bottle with a scarlet painted fingernail.

"He's actually pretty okay with Ray. It's Rafe, Valdez, he's freaked about. He and Rafe got into it tonight. I thought they were going to kill each other." I drained my bottle and set it aside to recycle.

"Ah, because you were unfaithful with that shifter." CiCi had never approved of my affection for a man who was not vampire.

"Of course. And now Rafe and I are involved again because, uh, CiCi, the demons are back." I hated to get into this. What would CiCi think? I knew she was deeply religious.

Don't laugh. A lot of vampires, who were people first, you know, hang on to their mortal values and faiths after they get their fangs.

"Why? We routed that horrid creature, Alesa her name was. And you said demons. More than one?" CiCi set her bottle on the floor. "What have you gotten into now, Gloriana?"

"I didn't get into anything. That bitch Alesa went back to hell bragging about how I held her against her will inside me." I huffed. "As if I wanted her in here." I thumped my stomach. "It was the most miserable time of my life."

"I know, *cheri*, I still think she is why you had the affair with that shifter." CiCi delicately wiped her lips with a hanky from her designer clutch.

"Well, whatever, I thought I was totally through with all things from hell, but it seems her big mouth got me some unwelcome attention from Lucifer."

CiCi shuddered and crossed herself. "I cannot imagine being discussed by such creatures. What has happened now?"

"Two of his minions came calling and made me an offer. They will give me a reward if I gather souls for the Devil." I sighed. "I refused, of course."

"Certainly you did." CiCi reached forward and patted my knee. "And was that enough for them?"

"Of course not. So they put on the pressure. Gave me an incentive. I can actually see my reflection." I grabbed CiCi's hand and tugged her into the bathroom. "Look!" I stood in front of her and gazed into the mirror above the sink. Oh, I had a smudge of pink lipstick on my tooth. I wiped it away and turned to look at my friend. She had tears in her eyes.

"C'est impossible!" She peered around me, did the hand-waving thing in front of my face, then sighed. "You really do have a reflection."

"I know. Isn't it great? It makes you realize how people are seduced into deals with the Devil." As usual I had to literally tear myself away from the mirror, finally shoving CiCi out of the bathroom and shutting the door.

"Yes, it *is* the work of the Devil." More frantic making of the sign of the cross and CiCi pulled out a gold crucifix from the bodice of her cream silk blouse and clutched it. "These demons, you must get them away from you. I'm afraid"—she shuddered—"I'm afraid for your soul, Gloriana."

I hugged her, then settled her back in her chair. "Relax. I'm not tempted even one little bit by their caper. But I'm going to have to do something to placate them and send them on their way before they do real damage around here. They threatened Rafe. And I know you don't think much of shape-shifters, CiCi, but he's saved my life more times than I can count. He's a dear friend and I'm going to help him gather at least one bad guy for Lucifer. Someone I figure is already bound for hell anyway. Someone you know, actually." I bit my lip.

Could she still harbor some residual feelings for creepy Simon? I figured the only way she'd ever had an affair with him in the first place had been if he'd been in one of his disguises. In his normal persona, he was about as appealing as a zombie after a hard Halloween.

"Who? Who are you going to try to send to Lucifer?" CiCi rummaged in her purse and came out with a rosary. "I'm sorry, Glory, but you are making me nervous. Ever since your exorcism, I have been carrying around these religious objects. Just to be on the safe side, you understand." Her hands were shaking and she looked around the room. "Are you sure we aren't surrounded by evil now?"

"No, I'm not sure. Hell, they pop in whenever they feel like it." I looked around too. Spyte and Caryon could be anywhere, and I did have a tingling feeling, like I was being watched.

"Relax, Glory, honey. You *are* being watched, but it's by the good guys this time." The Texas twang had a comforting familiarity that brought tears to my eyes. I looked up and saw a pair of boots dangling from the top shelf behind CiCi's chair.

"Emmie Lou!" I jumped up. Another pair of boots appeared next to hers. "And Harvey! I thought you went to Heaven permanently."

"Gloriana? Are you mad?" CiCi grabbed my arm. "Are they here? The demons?"

"No, look up there." I pointed at the shelf where my ghosts, the two who had haunted the shop for years, had suddenly reappeared. They were dressed in brand-new cowboy duds, matching red-checkered shirts with blue bandannas and white cowboy hats. Their boots were shiny black and they each sported a pair of filmy white angel wings.

"Angels? You have angels to look after you!" CiCi grinned and gave me a hug. "Now that makes me feel better."

"Me too. How did this happen?" I pulled CiCi down to sit beside me on the table.

"Someone up there doesn't like the way you're being bullied by someone down below." Harvey Nutt wore his usual suspenders on his jeans. He popped them, then winced. Guess they were too new to be adjusted quite right. "Anyway, we're here to keep you safe in the shop. We can't leave here, but as long as you're inside, we can keep them demons from doing any of their ugly tricks to you or your friends."

"That's right, Glory gal. They won't be lightin' any fires or hurtin' any of your pals while they're in here, I tell you that. Consider this your safe place. It's the power of goodness and light. Evil don't stand no chance agin that." Emmie Lou hopped down and flew around the ceiling before landing on the chair. "How do you like them wings? Ain't they a doozy?"

I laughed. "Beautiful." She was so tiny, all I could do was grin at her, a hug would crush her. "Thanks, guys. I feel better already. Now let me tell CiCi who I'm trying to get for Lucifer. Maybe you could kind of go invisible and keep an eye on things out in the shop. Okay?"

"Fine. We got your back, Glory, and that's a fact." Harvey snapped his suspenders, muttered a "darn it" and disappeared, Emmie Lou with him.

"All right, Glory, now who is it you want to garner a soul

for Lucifer?" CiCi sat back in her chair again. I was glad to see the rosary had been put away.

"Simon Destiny. Do you care if I try to snatch his soul away from his goddess?" I braced myself. I was committed to this, but if I had to lose her friendship over it, I was going to hate it, really hate it.

"Simon?" CiCi pulled out that rosary again. "You have any idea what you're dealing with? Don't be a fool. Touch Simon and the only one going straight to hell is liable to be you."

Ten

"CiCi, I have no choice. Who else do we know that is totally evil?" I realized that sounded harsh, but the truth was the truth.

"He's the father of my child." Her voice was low and she wouldn't look at me.

"I know that. How does Freddy feel about his father?" I knew Freddy, and he was a fine man, nothing like Simon.

"Frederick's been reaching out to him lately. Which scares me, of course." CiCi looked up, her eyes filled with tears. "I told him not to, but it's only natural for a man to want to know his father."

"Surely he's heard the stories." I threw out my hands. "Hey, one trip out to the Energy Vampire headquarters should convince Freddy that he wants no part of that dynasty."

"Power can be very seductive, Glory." CiCi had the hanky out again. "When I told you that Frederick and Derek were on a road trip? The night we did your exorcism. That wasn't to Houston. They were out there, with Simon, enjoying all the favors the EVs can bestow." CiCi's hands shook. "His father is offering Frederick the world, *his* world. But it's evil. I'm praying my son sees that and turns away in time."

I grabbed her hand. "What if we can convince Simon to leave his goddess and come over to Lucifer? At least Freddy wouldn't be exposed to the Energy Vampire thing anymore."

CiCi looked up with a frown. "You think that creature will just let Simon walk away? Pah. Why should she? And Simon. He's got everything he's always wanted out there." She took a shaky breath. "When we were together in Paris, Simon would tell me about his dreams of power, to be the leader of the Energy Vampires. You won't believe me, but he can be very charming, very charismatic. I, I loved him. And of course I had no idea what his group really did. It was only later that I heard they took energy from innocent people to feed that monster from the Underworld."

"I'm sure he kept his true face and nature very well hidden so he could seduce you. Am I right?" I smiled sympathetically.

"Of course he did! I was mortal, naïve. When I became pregnant, he finally showed me what he was really like. He turned his back on me. No explanation. It was as if the love he had professed simply vanished." She began to tear apart her fine linen handkerchief. "I was glad when he left me and my child alone. Oh, he sent money and wanted reports about his son in return, but he didn't try to see him, not while he was young."

"Odd. You'd think he'd be thrilled to have a son." I wasn't really clear on the born vampire thing, though I knew the males could father children.

"It depends, Gloriana." CiCi sighed. "Frederick is a Halfling, you see, since he was the result of a born vampire and a mortal mating. Some Halflings become vampire when they reach puberty. Some do not. Simon was waiting to see how Frederick would turn out. To see if he was worthy of claiming, I suppose." She frowned. "Born vampires are very arrogant."

"So Freddy . . . ?" I figured any information I could get about Simon's family could be useful. Though I'd never involve my friend Freddy if I could help it.

"Is a born vampire. Of course then Simon wanted him.

Tried to take him from me." CiCi lifted her chin. "But I'd had time to prepare for him and was not so naïve. I'd married my count and had his entire family and their allies behind me. I wasn't about to let Simon have my son."

I leaned forward, riveted. "How could you fight him?"

CiCi smiled. "I was vampire too by then. And chose my husband wisely. He had enough connections and power to make it very uncomfortable for the Energy Vampires to remain in Europe. That's how Simon and his followers ended up in America." CiCi's dark eyes flashed, then filled with tears. "My dear husband is gone now, killed by an ancient enemy, and Frederick is a man with a mind of his own. When my son decided to come here, I was afraid he was planning to finally get to know his father. What could I do except come with him?" She smiled sadly.

"Let's get Freddy over here and see what he thinks about his father. Since he's been out to the EV compound lately, maybe he'll know if Simon might be interested in switching sides." I clasped CiCi's hand. "Will you call him?"

"Why not? It would be a way for Frederick to have a father, if we could lure Simon away from his goddess. I'd think he'd be tired of always pleasing a demanding mistress, wouldn't you?"

I patted her hand. "My thoughts, exactly. You said Simon moved his crew here from Europe. Does this goddess just pop up in any convenient sinkhole or how does that work?"

"I've no idea, but maybe the boys will know." CiCi put her hanky away and pulled out her cell phone.

I knew the "boys" were her son and his longtime partner, Derek.

"Derek loves Frederick, but hates his new fascination with Simon. Derek is a good man and he knows evil when he smells it. He's certainly not blinded by riches either." She hit speed dial. "I'll see if I can get them over here."

I stepped out to the shop and left CiCi to make her call. I should call Rafe and let him know I'd made progress. Then I'd run upstairs and check on Ray. I'd left the apartment in absolute chaos. What if a council member stopped by to check on Penny? I'd flunk mentoring, big-time. I was thinking about grabbing my purse when Erin waved frantically from the register.

"Glory, you have company." Erin rolled her eyes.

"Glory! Ooooh. I didn't realize till I saw the clip on You-Tube that you're the same Glory who used to go with Israel Caine!" Jenny grabbed me and jumped up and down like I'd just scored a touchdown. Three clones of her, only with varying hair colors, squealed and jumped too. Trust me, their boobs didn't bounce.

"Hi, Jenny. These your sorority sisters?" I smiled and reminded myself I had to get along here.

"Yes. Girls, this is Penny's roomie. Can you believe it?" Jenny had her arm slung around me like we were best buds and made quick introductions. The girls squealed again. I swear dogs could hear them in the next county. "Where's Israel?" Jenny looked around like maybe I'd hidden Ray under a dress rack.

"Oh, he's upstairs." Never should have said it. The decibel level rose to shattering-glass range and they surged toward the door.

"And is Penny up there too?" Jenny dragged me with them.

"No! She went to the lab." I put on the brakes and hid my smile at the moans of disappointment.

"I brought her a treat from home. Mom mailed it to me. Maybe I can take it up and leave it for her." Jenny pulled a tin out of her Coach tote. The way it rattled, I figured there were six cookies left in it, max, and the Christmas tin was a dead giveaway that this wasn't a recent care package.

"Give it to me. I'll make sure she gets it." I snatched it out of her hand and passed it to Erin. The werewolf stashed it under the counter and I knew she'd take care of it personally once the girls were gone.

"Has Penny met Israel?" Jenny raised her eyes toward the ceiling, like she wished she had X-ray vision.

"Of course. So embarrassing. She caught him coming out of the shower earlier." Sorry, but couldn't resist. My fledgling needed some points over the so-perfect Jenny and this was just too choice. Jenny collapsed on one of her friend's shoulders and all of them moaned in Penny envy.

"How long will he be staying with you?" Jenny was obviously trying to figure out how to meet Ray. "Penny and I really need to get together."

"Why don't you just call her and meet for coffee somewhere?" I smiled. "Ray's a private person. I'm sure you understand. Rock stars. It's a nightmare the way the tabloids hound us. I never give out his schedule." I gestured toward the three cameramen still lounging around the front of the shop, waiting for me to come out or, better yet, for Ray to emerge.

"Oh, my lips would be sealed." Jenny actually did the old finger-locking-the-lips thing. "It would be so cool if I could meet him, get an autograph. Maybe he could sing for our end-of-year social."

I laughed and walked the girls to the door. "Sorry, not happening. If you were on YouTube, you saw his horrific fall. Ray's still recuperating. That's why he's with me. In fact, I'm going upstairs in a few minutes to check on him. Shouldn't have left him alone this long." I patted Jenny on the back.

"But—" Jenny could see opportunity slipping away.

"So sorry to disappoint you. Maybe I'll get him to sign a few photos or CDs for you. Okay?" I eased them out the door, finally prying Jenny's fingers off my arm. "Bye. I've got to go get my purse. You should call Penny."

I shut the door and headed to the back room. CiCi was just coming out.

"They'll be here any minute." She looked stoked. "I told them to come to the alley door."

"Great." I hoped Ray was okay upstairs, but followed CiCi into the back room in time to hear a knock on the door.

Frederick and his partner were both handsome men. It made me remember Penny's comment about vampire males.

Yes, they usually were perfect specimens. What was up with that?

"Thanks for coming, guys. I've got a situation that I need help with. Did your mother explain, Freddy?" I settled on the table while CiCi took my one chair again.

"Something to do with my father? I hope you know I'm cutting all ties with him. I told him that the last time we were out there. I can't take all that Energy Vampire crap." Freddy glanced at Derek. "Derek made me realize I was letting Simon's power go to my head. The bastard was doing a mind-control thing on me, trying to get me to come on board as his successor."

Derek put his hand on Freddy's arm. "It was because he was proud of you. He thought the offer was an honor. But your mother raised you to be decent, Fred. Obviously you couldn't go that way."

CiCi dabbed at her eyes. "Thank you, Derek. You don't know what it means to hear you say that. I was so afraid . . ."

"Mother, I would never serve a goddess from hell." Freddy lifted her hand to his lips. "I wanted a father, but not one who could sacrifice people to feed a monster. I told Simon that."

"So you gave him an ultimatum?" I couldn't believe it. If I'd planned this, it couldn't have worked out better. Now if only Simon wanted a relationship with his son badly enough, maybe we could work a deal.

"Basically. But Simon can't leave the EVs. No one can. The goddess doesn't tolerate defectors. You sign on for life. If Simon tried to quit, he'd be terminated." Freddy's shoulders sagged. "I'm sorry. I really wanted to get to know him. He's a fascinating man. Brilliant, really. And he could do so much good if he hadn't tied himself to Honoria and her demands."

"He did that long before he knew he would have a family, Frederick. I'm sure he has regrets now. But it's too late." CiCi looked at me. "Unless . . ."

"I don't know. I guess the big question is, can she be taken out? That would free Simon from the EV thing." I remembered the setup out there. The gold dome where Honoria resided, the moans and groans coming from a dark hole in the earth. Supposedly she sucked the energy from her victims to survive.

"I tried to find out more about the EVs while we were out there, Glory." Derek sat on the table beside me. "That's one creepy place. It's not just a hole in the ground, it's a tunnel. Simon actually walks down inside it when he confers with her. Which shows he's either brave or nuts. I wouldn't get within a hundred feet of the place. I swear you can hear the screams of the damned coming from there."

"Wow. I had no idea. I had pictured a hose of some kind connecting to her. The Oreck from Hell, you know?" I shivered. "Guess the only one who could tell us how to take her out would be Simon. And that's if he's interested." I turned to Freddy. "What do you think? Would your father give up the EVs for you?"

Freddy looked thoughtful, then took his mother's hand again. "There's only one way to find out. Glory, you're going to have to ask him."

"Me?" I swallowed, trying to picture that conversation. Simon had such power that he could be one of Lucifer's demons. He could turn me to stone, read my mind past blocks, you name it. Probably all powers courtesy of Honoria. Yes, he scared me.

"Hey, this is your idea. I gave him my 'ultimatum,' as you call it. He didn't exactly fall to his knees and beg me to take it back. Just sat there, like he had to think it over. Right then I realized that I'd probably expected too much. Unless there's a way to kill the goddess, walking away from the EVs wouldn't give us time together. Simon wouldn't survive to be a father to me. Honoria doesn't allow for defectors."

"We don't know that, Fred." Derek frowned. "I say someone has to have a talk with Simon. Get some answers. You started this, Glory. Why not finish it?"

"Simon and I aren't exactly best buds." I could feel three sets of eyes staring a hole in me. Yeah, I'd started it. No, technically Rafe had started it. Me and my loyalty. It had really taken me down a dark and creepy path this time.

"But I think you're the one to do it." Freddy nodded. "Even if Simon survives leaving the EVs, you want him on Lucifer's team. Mother told me the demons explained that's what is necessary to get Rafe's debt clear."

"Yes, that's right." This was too messy, with way too much margin for error. Freddy put a reassuring hand on my shoulder.

"Relax, Glory. I'm assuming Lucifer can offer Simon some incentives to come over to his side after my father makes the break. Seems like that's for you to explain too. If Simon shows an interest in leaving the EVs." Freddy looked very serious and Derek jumped off the table to put his arm around him.

"He loves you, Fred. It was obvious to me that, if there is a way for him to make a relationship happen with you, he'll do it. Don't let pride keep this from working."

"It's not pride, Derek. But I don't want to beg him to make the choice. Let Glory handle it." Freddy leaned against Derek. "I've been without a father this long, I can make it without one forever if I have to."

"Ah, darling, I'm so sorry." CiCi stood and wrapped her arms around her tall son.

"Okay, I'll meet with Simon. See what he says." I took a shuddering breath. "You know how I hate this."

"Sure we do." Freddy smiled. "But don't worry. Simon likes you. Even talked about making you an EV. I think Honoria shot down the idea though. Pissed him off. That's another reason my father is ready to leave the EVs. He's tired of taking orders from a woman." Freddy glanced at his mother and then at me. "No offense, ladies."

"Oh, I get it. Typical Simon." I sighed. "Okay, I'll make a call. Soon. Now I've got to go. This is a busy night for me. Paparazzi out back?"

"You bet. They were all excited that Israel Caine's SUV is out there." Derek grinned, obviously determined to lighten the mood. "You are so lucky. Don't get jealous, Fred, but, Glory, any chance that bad boy swings both ways?"

"Not that I know of. But I'll check." I winked at Derek when Freddy popped him on the arm. "I'll let you guys know what I find out."

"Thanks. And be safe." Freddy kissed my cheek. "And I've been known to swing both ways. You get tired of Blade, let me know."

This time it was Derek who growled and hooked an arm around Freddy's neck. I left them wrestling while CiCi fussed and hit them both with her purse.

I grabbed my own purse, called Rafe to give him an update, then braced myself for the paparazzi gauntlet. It was fairly painless since I wasn't making statements and they had enough pictures of me without Ray. When I got upstairs, I unlocked the door and figured I'd have a mess to clean up.

To my amazement, the place was spotless, a little empty, but all cleaned up. No sign of blood on the hardwood floor and the couch was straight. Someone had moved the chairs that went with the dinette set in the kitchen to face the couch and there was a semblance of order in the living room.

"Okay, what good fairies have been at work in here?"

"Just one." Jerry came out of the kitchen, a wet towel in his hand. "I came to my senses and realized we couldn't leave you with this disaster." He turned to toss the wet towel in the kitchen sink.

"You look better too." I could see that he'd obviously been home to change clothes and his face had healed. That was probably due to a pit stop where he'd whammied some hapless mortal and taken a good long drink. I didn't comment, just walked up to him and wrapped my arms around his waist.

"I won't object if you examine me for injuries." His grin made me shiver.

"Maybe later. First, thank you." I kissed his smile. "I dreaded what I'd find when I opened the door."

"Not my finest moment, trashing your place. So I put in a call. You'll have two new lounge chairs, a coffee table and lamp by tomorrow night." He ran his hand up my back. "I'm sending half that bill to Valdez. We were idiots, but I admit it felt good. I needed to give that shifter a pounding. I had a lot of issues with him. Still do."

"Let's table that for now, Jerry. I've got a hell of a situation on my hands and that's a fact. I can't have boyfriend drama too. It's just too much. Remember that your territorial jealousy thing tends to end up with us taking breaks. You want that?" I looked up at him, really interested in his answer.

"I'd have an easier time reining in my jealousy if I didn't have your other men in my face all the time." Jerry rested his palms on my bum and pulled me against him. "And, yes, I plead guilty to being territorial. It's a Highlander thing. You've known that about me for centuries."

"Known it and not especially liked it." I kissed his firm chin. "Can you try to work your way through it without using your fists and fangs?" I angled my head when he leaned down to deepen the kiss. Why not? I enjoyed kissing him and needed a reminder while standing in my almost empty living room that Jerry was my guy. He pulled back first and smiled.

"Yes, I will definitely try to stay civilized. Though when other men put their hands on you, I want to break out a claymore and use it on the nearest man who even looks at you." He patted my bottom. "Patience, lass. I'm obviously a work in progress."

I pushed away from him. "I get that, but how many years should I give you? Two or three hundred?" I knew my smile was rueful as I kicked off my high heels and walked toward the bedroom. "Any word from Ray?"

"He's asleep now, finally resting." Jerry followed me. "Not sure I'd bother him. I took him another bottle of synthetic about an hour ago. He had the shakes and obviously was in the throes of some night terrors. Mortals call them delirium tremens. I looked up alcohol withdrawal on the Internet."

I turned and caught Jerry's grimace. "Seriously? You've been taking care of him?"

Jerry shrugged, obviously almost embarrassed. "Never thought I'd feel sorry for the bastard, but this might do it. He's got a rough road ahead. But clearly he needs to find another bed. This apartment is getting too crowded." He gestured at the couch. "Sit. You want a bottle of synthetic?"

"Sure, why not? Thanks. Not sure I can kick Ray out yet though. Not until he's over this stage. I still feel like his mentor, you know. And the paparazzi are lurking out there, waiting for a photo op." I sat on the couch, resisting the urge to check on Ray myself. Jerry had actually taken care of everything. I smiled at him as he brought me the cold drink, poured into a goblet. Nice.

"Then I'll move him back to the couch before it's time for us to go to bed." Jerry sat close beside me and slipped his arm around me.

"I got something started tonight to satisfy the demons. Freddy's been reaching out to his father. You can imagine how that's freaked out CiCi. We're going to see if Simon is actually interested in defecting. If so, we need to find out how to take out his goddess. That would end the EVs permanently. Then they can all sign over to Lucifer's team. I'm sure the demons have some incentives to offer them. I called Rafe and told him about it."

"All right. You brought it up. Let's talk about this demon thing." Jerry lost his smile. "How are they forcing you to work for them?"

I realized Jerry had gotten the shorthand version of what Rafe and I were doing. The full story wasn't going to go over well. And that was an understatement. "They can't force a good person to do the Devil's handiwork."

"Then you're out of it. Simply refuse and walk away. Let the shifter take care of Destiny and his goddess. Hell, Glory, you remember what it was like out there. No way are you getting anywhere near that cesspool again." Jerry snugged me closer.

"I can't abandon Rafe, Jerry." I knew he was going to hate this. "He can't refuse them. He used his demonic powers when I told him I wouldn't sleep with him again. Flew off the handle."

"Not against you." Jerry's arms tightened around me. "I've seen what the man can do. You wouldn't be here right now if he did."

"He burned a bush. That's all. It was freaky at the time, but I know in my heart that Rafe would never hurt me." I touched Jerry's tight jaw. "Take my word for that."

"So he's got to get them Destiny. Let him. It's none of your business." Jerry grabbed my hand. "You're risking your immortal soul trucking with those creatures."

"No, I'm not. I'm only making sure an evil person gets what he so richly deserves." I knew I'd never persuade Jerry to cut Rafe some slack. "And helping someone I care about at the same time. Let it go, Jerry. I'm doing this."

"It's insane. You know you can't trust these demons. They'll do anything to seduce you to their side." Jerry looked really worried. "We don't have any guarantees we'll live forever, Gloriana. Call me old-fashioned, but I always fancied seeing you in Heaven after this life was over."

"Oh, Jerry, of course we'll see each other there." I kissed his lips. "They've tried to get to me already and I laughed in their faces. I won't be tempted, no matter what they dangle in front of me." I shivered and looked around. Had I just waved a red cape in front of a bull? I braced myself in case Spyte and Caryon made a sudden appearance. When nothing happened, I relaxed.

"Then I'll do whatever I can to help you, Gloriana. The sooner this is done, the better. You want Simon Destiny? Just tell me what I can do. I've wanted to bring the man down for a long time." Jerry grinned. "And if we can speed up the process? Even better."

"God, Jerry. You realize the risk? I mean . . ." I grabbed

him and kissed him until we were both breathing hard. "Thank you, Jerry. I love you." I gave him a leisurely kiss this time that made me wish Ray wasn't in my bed. When we finally parted, we were both smiling.

"What's this?" Jerry looked down as Boogie strolled into the room.

"Penny's cat. Isn't he sweet?" I reached down and lifted him into my lap. "Poor baby. Did you hide under Penny's bed when all that horrible fighting was going on?" I glanced at Jerry. "It will never happen again." I stroked the cat's fur.

"I like cats." Jerry reached for the cat and rubbed him between the ears. The cat rewarded him with a loud purr.

"Good to know." I put the cat back on the floor. "I guess Penny fed him. Her sister came into the shop today. Penny wants to tell her she's a vampire but it's going to be a problem. I can see—"

The door crashed open and a wild-eyed Penny ran into the room. She dropped her laptop case on the floor, turned and threw the dead bolts.

"What is it? What's the matter?" I jumped up and grabbed her shoulders. She was shaking.

"I just did the most amazing thing!" She looked down. "Oh, no! I dropped my laptop." She picked it up, slid it out of the canvas bag and quickly turned it on. "Okay, no harm done."

"Penny! You ran in here like the hounds of hell were after you." I glanced at Jerry. "And, trust me, I know that's possible. What happened?"

"Well, you remember on the hilltop? When those demons had us?"

"Sure, who could forget?" I could feel Jerry's eyes boring into my back. I turned to look at him. "One of their tricks. You know how Aggie turns people to stone? Demons do it too. Rafe and I were statues."

"Yeah, and I was learning to shape-shift. Rafe and Glory were teaching me when the demons came along." Penny paced into the kitchen, clearly agitated, and I heard the fridge open and close. She came out with a bottle of synthetic and twisted off the cap. She took a gulp, then a breath.

"Anyway, at one point I shifted into a white mouse, just like the lab rats we use for our experiments." Her eyes filled with tears and she blinked rapidly, then took another chug from her bottle.

"Penny's a chemistry major, doctor of something." I couldn't take my eyes off her. She was clearly jazzed and positively beautiful with her eyes alight and her energy seeming to fill the room.

"I specialize in genetic engineering among other things. I'm working on a post-doc." She waved her hand. "The thing is I had an epiphany."

"About?" I sat on the arm of the couch. Her energy was wearing me out as she paced the perimeter of the room.

"Those rats, Glory! What had I been doing to those rats? Experimenting, causing mutations, giving them diseases!" Tears overflowed and ran down her cheeks. "God, I couldn't stand it."

I grabbed her hand to get her to stop. "Of course not. But you were trying to find cures. For mortals. It's what scientists do."

"But I can't do it anymore. Not after I knew what it was like from the rat's point of view. I was tiny, defenseless." Sob. "That demon just tossed me from one hand to the other like I was a thing to him, of no consequence." Another sob. "Then I went into the lab tonight and saw all those cages with all those sweet faces peering up at me." She dropped her head to my shoulder, unable to speak.

I patted her back and looked at Jerry. "Of course it would be impossible to do that anymore. I understand. Maybe you can change to a different kind of research. Use plants or—" I shut up. What the hell did I know about science?

She raised her head and grabbed a tissue from a box by the computer. Guess this wasn't the first crying jag to come up over the rat question. She blew her nose and the beauty thing vanished.

"Forget the research. I had to do something to save them. To keep them from any more pain." She tossed that soggy tissue and grabbed a fresh one.

"Save them?" I stepped back from her. "What did you do, Penny?"

"Well, first I disabled the security cameras." She smiled at Jerry. "I'm really good at that kind of thing and I don't want to be booted out of the program for theft, you know?"

"Certainly not." Jerry nodded. "Good to know you're skilled at security."

"Thanks. Anyway"—she wiped her cheeks—"I got a traveling cage and started filling it. It took three cages to get them all. A couple were too sick and I, I had to put them down." She took a shaky breath. "That was so hard, but the merciful thing to do. I wasn't going to allow them to suffer another minute for science."

I shook my head. I was no scientist and never wanted to be one. "So where are these rats now, Penny?"

"Well, I knew I had to be careful. These are domesticated white rats. Where could I take them that they'd be safe and cared for? And the university would find them if I just dropped them off at the local animal shelter. They'd demand them back."

"Yes, they would." Jerry spoke up. "I imagine they have identifying marks on them, don't they?"

"Yes, of course. They're tagged. That's important when you're running controlled experiments."

"So where are they, Penny?" I was very afraid I knew the answer.

Suddenly slumping and trying to put on a shy and supplicating façade, she looked at me.

"Oh, no, you didn't." I leaped over the couch and grabbed Boogie. "Your cat and I cannot live with a dozen white rats."

"Actually it's more like fifty-three." Penny's face was flushed.

"Fifty-three?" From the doorway, Ray's voice was strong,

his laughter the first sign that he might live through with-drawal. "Oh, Glory, and you thought *I* was a handful as a fledgling."

Jerry actually helped Penny drag three cages of white rats upstairs. Boogie and I retreated to my bedroom and closed the door. Sorry, but I just couldn't see cute and rat in the same sentence. I made Penny promise to keep them in her room. Which was going to be a squeeze. Too bad.

"She's going to have to buy more cages," Jerry announced once he coaxed me out of my bedroom.

"I can smell them from here. Boogie's pacing in front of her door, just looking for an opportunity to get in. Some fun, eh, Glory?" Ray patted my knee. He and Jerry were sitting on either side of me on the couch.

"The council is definitely compensating me for this. I'm calling Damian." I pulled my cell out of my purse.

"No! You can't. He won't understand and the fewer people who know about this, the better." Penny walked into the living room with Boogie in her arms. "I'll find a home for them. With one of the animal rights groups. Just give me time." She smiled and put the cat in my lap. "A few days."

"What's going to happen to your research?" I petted the cat while Jerry stared at Ray's arm on my knee. "Stop it, Ray." Jerry looked afraid to move, but his fangs were showing when he gave Ray a "grope her and die" look. Ray just grinned.

"It's ruined." Penny slumped into one of the chairs. "But that's okay. I'm vampire now. A whole new life. Don't know what I'm going to tell my folks though. They were picturing a Nobel Prize in my future. A cure for some obscure disease."

"Tell them you decided to join the animal rights thing. Saw the light." Ray grinned at her and threw his arm across the back of the couch to play with my hair. "Or maybe I can hook you up with my pal Ian. He'll be here this week. I convinced him to check out Austin. You'd dig his research. He's going to make it possible for us to walk in daylight someday."

"Glory mentioned that." Penny leaned forward. "It's true then that he's a chemist? She said this daylight thing was temporary though."

"Right now it is." Ray winced when Jerry gripped his wrist. "Okay, she's yours. I get it." He removed his arm. "But Ian is a genius. I bet he could use a good assistant. I'll arrange a meeting for you."

"Not a good idea." Jerry glared at Ray. "Never trust a MacDonald, Penny. They're double-dealing cattle thieves."

"Oh, well, then. Penny, listen to the man. Guard your cattle when you meet Ian." Ray chuckled. "Did you just *hear* yourself, Blade?"

"Stop baiting him, Ray." I patted Jerry's knee. "Jerry has his reasons for mistrusting Ian. There's an age-old feud going between the families. But also, Ian is tricky. I don't exactly trust him either and his diet drug gave me weird side effects."

"But he's brilliant. You said it yourself." Penny stood and walked to the breakfast room and her computer. "First, I'm finding a home for the rats. I can't take the smell and it's not healthy for them either, it's so overcrowded. I'm not sure where I'd find enough cages for them at this time of night though."

"I know where to go." Jerry got up and headed for the door. "Come with me, Penny. We'll take my SUV and get what you need." He turned and pinned Ray with a hard look. "Can I trust you to behave?"

"Really, Jerry, what kind of question is that?" I stood and marched to the door. "You can trust *me*. That's all you need to know. Now thanks for helping Penny." I kissed his cheek and watched them both head down the stairs. I knew he'd been trying, but as a "work in progress" he had a long way to go.

I shut the door and turned to Ray. "How are you feeling?"

"Not so hot." He stretched out on the couch. In low-slung jeans and nothing else, he was still a sight to make a girl drool. "I was putting on a good show, wasn't I? Didn't want Blade to know how bad I felt, it's a guy thing. Though he was actually pretty decent to me before you got home."

"Yes, you're obviously a good actor. Jerry doesn't bother to mask his feelings, the jealous ones anyway. But, like you, if he's in pain, he'd rather die than let on he's less than a hundred percent." I leaned down and touched his forehead under the silky hair that had fallen into his bright blue eyes. "You're very cold to the touch. Have you fed today? The Bulgarian brew has real blood in it. I'll bring you some."

Ray pulled me down on top of him, showing surprising strength. "I'd rather have some of what you've got. You know vampire blood heals us faster than anything."

"Ray, this isn't a good idea." I lay on top of him, inhaling him. This brought back some memories in a rush, some good, some not so great. He had the same charisma that always pulled me in, but then he could be a world-class jerk, especially to the man I loved.

"Please?" He ran his hand up under my hair and just smiled, such a sad smile, like he knew he'd never have me now. Okay, of course I was being manipulated but I went along with it anyway.

"All right. Take what you need. But this isn't foreplay." I started to offer my wrist but didn't bother. Why not let him take what he wanted from where he wanted it? It might keep him from turning back to the alcoholic stuff. I still couldn't get the visit from Spyte out of my mind. No way did I want Ray to sell his soul to Lucifer and there were things he'd do it for. Spyte had nailed it with that chance to live in the light as Ray used to as a mortal. Or maybe he'd choose to get his mortality back.

"There you go, Glory. Now you're thinking like one of us." Caryon stood beside the couch, watching as Ray sank his fangs into the vein at my neck.

I expected Ray to jerk and react but he started drinking with a sigh of pleasure, his hand on my back anchoring us together.

"Oh, he can't see or hear me. Just you can. But now's your

*opportunity. Yes, we can give him his mortality back. Or, if he
wants to stay vampire? He can get that gift of sunlight. Just like
we gave you your reflection. If Israel Caine will sell his soul to
Lucifer, he can become a vampire who can walk and play in the
sun."* Caryon laughed and I got chills. He was talking in my
mind and I answered him the same way.

"You couldn't really—"

"Need proof?" Caryon gave me one of his full-on creepy
fang smiles. *"Just look in your bathroom mirror."*

"Then Ray . . ." I felt his other hand slide down to pull me
closer, our chests and hips pressed against each other as his
mouth worked on my throat. I couldn't let him drink much
longer. He was enjoying this, his mind open as he wondered
if making a move on me now was worth risking being shot
down again. But it was a brief thought, most of him caught
up in the pleasure of taking in ancient vampire blood.

I knew how Ray would react to an offer of daylight. He
wouldn't hesitate. Hell? To Ray that would be an abstract
when he was all about the concrete, the here and now. And
he'd easily blow off immortality if he could have his old pleasures back. Ray was all about pleasures.

*"Oh, I see you know how seductive that would be to the rock star.
Do you dare make the offer? Think about it. You say you love
the man. If you truly do, why not give him his heart's desire?"*
Caryon began to fade away. He'd been in his usual dark suit
and tie, not a hair out of place. *"Make the offer, Glory. Then
Caine won't need to lose his mind and dull his pain with alcohol.
How do you like this proof that I can stay away from your friends?
This one, anyway."* That had sounded like a taunt just before
he disappeared.

I probed Ray's mind again and got a glimpse of yearning
that made me sigh. I knew what that felt like, to crave something just out of reach. But I also knew that this evil bargain
wasn't the way for Ray to get it. I shoved at him, suddenly
sure that I'd been so distracted that I was in danger of letting him take too much of my blood. I sat up and the room
swirled around me.

"You okay?" Ray held on to me when I bent over and rested my head on my knees.

"Bring me one of the synthetics out of the fridge." I took a breath, feeling queasy. I wasn't sure if it was from blood loss or Caryon's offer. Both were a possibility. Ray put a cold bottle in my hand, then went to answer the door when I hadn't even heard a knock.

"What the hell has been going on here?" Rafe was by my side. "Did you drain her dry, asshole?"

"Didn't think so." Ray sat on my other side. Seemed it was my night for being surrounded by hot guys. "Drink, Glory. Hell, I'm sorry. Guess I got carried away. You should have stopped me."

"You should have stopped yourself." Rafe looked like he wanted to start a fight with Ray when I glanced at him.

"No more fighting in here. I appreciate the concern, but I'm already living in a war zone with almost no furniture. I swear, if I inhale any more testosterone, I'm going to start scratching my crotch and craving Monday-night football. Now, chill." I drank my synthetic and felt better immediately, though Rafe's neck looked awfully tempting.

"You need to feed from me?" Rafe shot Ray a challenging glare. "Help yourself, sweetheart."

"That's all you need. Bite him, Glory, and let Blade walk in on that. There'd be a dog area rug here before you know it." Ray sat back and smiled.

"Son of a bitch!" Rafe jumped to his feet. He'd stayed shifted into dog form as my bodyguard for five long, frustrating years, and Ray wasn't inclined to let him forget it.

"I said chill. I mean it, Rafe. Jealousy is not sexy to me. And hurling insults is childish, Ray. A total turnoff." I drained my bottle and handed it to Ray. "Thanks. That did the trick." I sighed and leaned back. "Now, Ray, Rafe and I have some business to discuss." I glanced at Rafe. "Maybe you could give us some privacy."

"What? You have secrets from me? What's the big deal?" Ray looked like he didn't want to budge.

"We're dealing with some demon issues. Nothing to do with you. If you must know, they'd like your soul. Interested?" There, I'd said it. He did what I thought he'd do, he laughed.

"You're kidding, right? Demons from hell?" Ray got up and took the empty into the kitchen. "What else, angels? Are we living in a graphic novel?"

"No such luck." Rafe looked like he was grinding his teeth. "Remember, you used to think vampires were fiction. How's that working out for you?"

"Point taken." Ray sat in one of the chairs. "So demons are real. Angels too?"

"A couple are guarding my shop right now." I looked at Rafe. "Emmie Lou and Harvey Nutt are back and protecting it and us as long as we're in there. Seems a higher power doesn't like the pressure we're under."

"No kidding." Rafe grinned. "That's cool." He glared at Ray. "You going to mock that?"

"Naw. I'm open to whatever you guys are selling. This is a whole new world to me. How can I help?" He actually sat back and crossed his arms over his chest.

"Stay sober. Let us handle this and don't add to my load." Oops that had popped out.

"Well, shit, Glory. Didn't know I was a load." Ray was on his feet in an instant. He never had managed to get any more clothes and he still just had the black jeans and his boots, which were by the door. No shirt. "If you call Nate and tell him I'm sober, he'll pick me up." He looked around. "No, to hell with it. I feel good enough. I'm shifting out of here. From the roof."

"Ray, wait. I didn't mean—" I jumped up. "Don't shift. You haven't had enough time to fully recover."

"You got another idea?" He'd started pulling on those boots.

"Stop. You can't leave." I put my hand on his chest, knocking him back onto the couch. It was too easy; obviously he wasn't ready to go anywhere yet.

"I'm sober. What else do you need?" Ray glared at me as he pulled on his other boot.

"Proof you can stay that way. Damn, I wish we had vampire rehab." I stood in front of him, ready to knock him down again if he tried to get past me. Yes, I could call Nate to keep an eye on him, but a mortal didn't stand a chance in that situation.

"Maybe we do. Have rehab. Call Ian. He can set something up. He's a doctor and he's coming here anyway. Would that satisfy your urge to watch over me?" Ray stomped into his boots, then leaned back. "Hand me your phone and I'll put in his number, let you talk to him."

Ian was a medical doctor. And could be relentless. Maybe this would work. I dug in my purse and handed Ray my phone. "Do it. Dial his number."

"Shit. You really don't trust me." Ray obviously hadn't expected me to call his bluff.

"History tells me I'd be an idiot if I did." I smiled as he frowned and punched in numbers.

"Ian? Glory St. Clair here. I've got Ray Caine with me and he's in need of your help." I listened to the Scottish accent and ignored Ray's muttered curses as I described Ray's recent behavior and meltdown. "When will you be here?"

"That soon? Excellent. Oh, I'll tell him. Thanks so much." I ended the call, then smiled at Ray.

"He's flying out tomorrow at sunset. Seems he wants to help you. And needs you clean and sober if you're to be his lab rat for the daylight drug." I punched in another number. "Nate, can you have two shifters in the alley in five minutes? Ray's going home. He's sober now, and if you can keep him like that for twenty-four hours, Ian MacDonald will take over after that." I listened for a minute, smiled, then dropped my phone in my bag and pulled out a set of keys. "All set, Ray. Guess it's safe to give you these."

"What the hell?" Ray shook his head, then glanced at Rafe. "You hear a train whistle? I think I've just been railroaded."

"When Glory gets a notion, don't stand in her way. It's a

done deal." Rafe grinned, obviously glad to see Ray headed out the door.

"Your car is in back. Your wallet is locked in the console." I tossed him the keys. "I'm also calling Damian. No more booze deliveries."

"Gee, Mom. What about my diaper change?" Ray got up and strolled over to face me.

"You're welcome." I knew Ray was mad, didn't blame him. And treating him like a child right now didn't sit well with me either. I reached out to touch his cheek. "I'm sorry if this seems unnecessarily rough, Ray. If I didn't care about you, I wouldn't bother."

He tried for a smile and failed. "Yeah, I get that. Don't think I don't appreciate what you've done. I hit a low. Falling off the stage may have knocked some sense into me." He glanced at Rafe, then pulled me into his arms. "Thanks, Glory girl, for everything." He gave me one of his "you can have all I've got" kisses and my knees buckled. He grinned, settled me into Penny's computer chair, and saluted Rafe as he walked to the door.

I watched him go, not sure it wasn't to his doom. God, if Caryon or Spyte decided to approach him themselves and offered a trade—soul for sunlight—what would happen? I didn't want to think about it. And then there was his drinking. He closed the door and I tore my gaze from it to Rafe. How many times had he watched a scene like that and felt left out of the mix?

I shoved myself to my feet and stumbled over to him. I collapsed on the couch and leaned against him.

"Rafe, hold me a minute? I swear I didn't feel a thing just then."

"You know, you could go to hell for lies like that."

Eleven

I didn't bother arguing with Rafe. When he was right, he was right. I just headed down the hall and scooped up a frantic Boogie who'd started clawing at Penny's bedroom door.

"I have fifty-three white rats in my apartment. I think I'm already in hell." I sat on the couch again and kept a firm grip on the cat, trying to soothe him.

"You're kidding." Rafe laughed. "I thought it reeked in here."

I punched his arm. "Penny related to the little things after the hilltop encounter with our demons. Now she's rescued the batch in her lab. Jerry's gone with her to get more cages." I sighed when Boogie finally relaxed and began to purr.

"I've been thinking about getting Simon away from his EV goddess. I sure hope he knows of a way to take her out, because gods and goddesses are notoriously hard to kill." Rafe tried to pet Boogie and was rewarded with a paw swipe that drew blood.

"But if anyone knows how it can be done, it would be the king himself. That's Simon. If he decides he wants to be free, maybe he can take Honoria out himself." I fought back my fangs as I inhaled the rich scent of Rafe's blood.

Rafe grinned and waved his bleeding hand close to my lips. "Go ahead, taste. I can see you're dying to."

"No, we're having a serious discussion."

"Which you can't concentrate on because you're staring at my blood." Rafe shook his head. "Go for it."

"What can I say? It's my thing. Thanks." I pulled his warm hand to my mouth and licked off the too few drops. "Now where were we?"

"I think this all hinges on whether Simon is willing to leave the EVs to have a relationship with his son." Rafe leaned back into his corner of the couch like feeling my tongue on his hand was no big deal. Oh, yeah? Fine. I stayed in my corner and kept Boogie happy rubbing his ears.

"Who wouldn't want to be close to a man like Freddy? He's smart, successful and handsome. Any father would be proud to call him son. Simon even offered him the post as his second in command." I realized that was a huge deal. There were others in the EV ranks who would have squawked about that if Freddy had accepted.

"All right then. But clearly the demons aren't going to be satisfied with just one soul. Shutting down that goddess should give Lucifer a shot at all the Energy Vampires."

"I get the heebie-jeebies just thinking about that hole in the ground with the strange noises."

"Yeah, well, I was hooked up to the legendary energy vacuum pump once. Not that I actually remember it. Just woke up with an empty stomach, what looked like a burn there, and Simon gloating over the fact that he'd just about drained me." Rafe glanced down at his hand. "Sorry it already quit bleeding. But if you want more, you can always bite me. Anytime, anywhere." He leaned closer and the cat hissed.

"I think the cat senses your former dog persona." I smiled, tired of worrying about Simon, demons, all of it. "Usually when someone says 'Bite me,' it's not a come-on." I shook my head. "Let's stick to business, Rafe. I'm with Jerry now. End of story."

"Your story has many chapters, Glory. No end in sight."

He ignored the cat and ran his thumb along the side of my neck. "I'm patient and here for you. If the Scotsman lets you down, keep that in mind."

"Rafe, you're going to get hurt and very tired of waiting." His warm touch disturbed me just like it always did. Then there were his dark eyes on mine, reading me, trying to see if I was tempted and seeking ways to take advantage if I was. *If* I was? It took everything I had to shift my body away from his.

"I'm going to call Simon and ask him to come to the shop. Freddy says Simon was turned down by the goddess when he asked to invite a female Energy Vampire, but Simon doesn't know I know that. I'll use that as my opener. But what if he just tells me over the phone to forget it?" I threw out the question in a desperate attempt to get this conversation back where it belonged.

"Before all this came up, CiCi called me about a surprise birthday party for Freddy. She wants to hold it at the club. I'm sure she didn't plan to invite Simon but you can mention it and tell him you have the perfect gift for Freddy. Claim you can pressure CiCi to include him on the guest list. That should bring him around." Rafe relaxed at his end of the couch. Apparently he'd seen enough of my confusion to be content.

"Yes, that should do it. Not looking forward to this." I shuddered and finally let Boogie jump down and run back to Penny's door.

"I can be there with you." Rafe moved close again and picked up my hand. "I'm allowed to use my own demonic stuff in this case without worrying about payback."

"I want to do this on my own." I slipped my fingers from his; this constant touching was not a good idea. "But we've got to have something to offer Simon in return besides this relationship with his son. He seems to have everything he wants as head of the EVs. What else would Lucifer have to offer him?"

"I thought you'd never ask." A man shimmered into view

in front of us and I wished for my sunglasses. He glowed with a white light, almost blinding me. Finally he settled into a mortal form. But beautiful, so beautiful I wanted to reach out and touch.

"I wouldn't do that if I were you." Rafe held my hand again. "This is Lucifer, Glory. Just stay put. No sudden moves."

"Good advice, Rafael. You do the same." Lucifer smiled and his perfect teeth were a dazzling white. He had shiny blond hair, pale skin and brilliant turquoise eyes.

I licked my lips. I've known a lot of good-looking men, though my taste runs to muscular types who know how to fight. This guy was glorious, long and lean with hands that looked like they had never touched a sword or a plow. He was as pale as a vampire but without the fangs. While I watched, he added more muscles and stronger hands. Hmm. Perfect. I realized I'd leaned forward, straining against Rafe's hold on me.

"Don't underestimate my strength, Gloriana. I can break a man or woman with a fingertip, mentally *or* physically. Can't I, Rafael?"

Rafe swallowed. "Yes, he can. I've seen it. Lucifer has more power in his pinky than Simon's goddess could ever dream of."

"Good man, that's the party line." Lucifer smiled. "I would like to be rid of that vacuum-sucking sex addict but, alas, there are rules. You, however, could annihilate her and no one could object, now could they?" His grin dazzled me. "Do that and just imagine the rewards. I have the power to give anyone their heart's desire. Simon; even you." He waved his hand and I looked down.

I gasped. There I sat, a size six again. Small breasts, narrow hips and—I felt my face, yes!—cheekbones. I had on a different dress too. It was a chic Parisian number, red silk with the kind of tiny straps that didn't allow for a bra. My normal size would never have fit in it. I looked down at my feet and had the gorgeous designer shoes to match in a shiny red crocodile platform heel.

"How do you like that demo, Glory?" Lucifer's voice flowed into me, deep and resonant, stirring me like one of Ray's sexy love songs.

I dragged my gaze up to the gorgeous man again. "I'm tiny."

"Glory, take a breath. Easy now." Rafe squeezed my hand. "This is how he works. Hold on to your soul, honey."

"Now, Rafael, am I going to have to make you mute?" Lucifer clucked. "Guess so." He waved a hand and Rafe was a statue, his hand cold in mine.

I jerked my fingers out of his and skimmed them down this incredible new body. I did so love the way I looked now. I stood and walked into my bedroom where I'd put a mirror. Not full-length, no way, but a big one that I could use when I was doing my hair. I had a hand mirror too, for checking out the back, and I used it now to do a three-sixty. Oh, wow, how about that view? I *was* tiny. Flo and I could be a matched pair, even borrow each other's clothes. I teared up.

Lucifer appeared behind me. "Look at you. Why, you could be a model. Is there anything else you would like? Natural curl? A paler blond? How about long lashes again? That naughty Caryon, he can get carried away, can't he?" Lucifer waved his hand again and I had all of those. I blinked, fluttered those long lashes, and smiled with perfect gleaming white teeth. I almost didn't recognize myself.

I finally turned and looked up at him. He was irresistible. And he'd given me everything I ever dreamed of. I wanted him, wanted to throw my arms around him and kiss him with everything I had in me. I could drag him to my bed and make love to him. I bet he could make me feel wonderful and I could do things to him, wicked things I'd never even done to Jerry, and we'd both be more satisfied than ever before. I reached out.

Lucifer smiled. "Look but don't touch, Gloriana. Not yet. Of course I could make you feel wonderful. Beyond anything a mere man of *this* world could." His glittering eyes lingered on my breasts long enough to make them ache, then moved down until my thighs clenched and I had to lean back against my dresser. I had a naughty vision of us together and closed my eyes.

Yes, there we were, tangled on silk sheets. His mouth slid over my skin as he stripped away my dress. He tasted my breasts, between my thighs, everywhere, until I couldn't stand it and begged him to take me. He showed me ways to use my body that I'd never dared imagine. To reach a fulfillment that had me riding wave after wave of pleasure. I sighed and finally opened my eyes again. It was almost as if we'd actually been together, touched each other, done those incredibly erotic acts with more yet to come. I was damp, aching and trembling.

"Oh, yes, Gloriana, the rewards are unimaginable. But first you'd have to sign a contract. You've heard my boys mention it. Are you ready?" Lucifer's smile teased me to hurry so he could make my dreams come true.

Ready? Weak, shaking and still not sure where fantasy ended and reality began, I shuddered. I was tempted, so tempted. But I finally managed to shake my head.

He sighed and waved his hand. "So be it."

I looked down and I was back to my same old size, the one I'd been stuck in for more than four hundred freaking years. Unbearable. My bra strangled my heavy breasts, the straps dug into my shoulders to carry the weight. My panties cut into my upper thighs and into my waist. I wanted to tear them off and throw them across the room.

"Lucifer! Please! Wait! Can we talk about this? Where is the contract? How do I—" I searched the bedroom for him.

He was gone. No sign of him. The hall door opened and Jerry and Penny came in, dragging two metal cages apiece. I heard Penny chatter about how they'd fit them into Penny's bedroom. Rafe jumped up from the couch and ran to my side. He wrapped his arms around me and held me tight.

"Are you all right? I could hear what was going on but couldn't do a damned thing."

I shook my head. "Don't say anything to Jerry." I leaned against Rafe. What had just happened? In the moment, I'd almost been willing to sell my soul for a dress size. That and pleasure. Clearly Lucifer knew how to probe a person's mind, heart and dreams and then dangle paradise. Simon, who was a cold and greedy son of a bitch, didn't stand a chance.

I guess that had been the point of Lucifer's visit, though if we hadn't been interrupted . . . I shivered. What else would that Devil have offered that might have pushed me over the edge? He seemed to know me better than I knew myself. And that was his power, of course.

I looked down, then stared into the mirror. I saw myself as I'd been for four hundred plus years. I was fine. Men who I loved, had loved me just the way I was. I loved myself this way. This obsession with size was ridiculous. I wasn't about to trade what I hoped was an afterlife of ease and joy for the creepy tortures of the damned and a body, no matter how incredibly . . . No, not even going to think about it again. No freaking way. I ignored what was suddenly damned tight underwear and put some space between Rafe and me.

"Gloriana? What's going on?" Jerry stood in the bedroom doorway.

"Just showing Rafe my reflection again. I never get tired of it." I laughed and squeezed Rafe's waist like I always hugged him when I was excited. Which was true, come to think of it. Hugged him when I was scared too. He made me feel safe. Just like Jerry did. Both men were blessings in my life and I wasn't taking either of them for granted.

"Where did you and Penny get the cages?" I eased away from Rafe, then walked up to Jerry and kissed his lips.

"We went back to her lab. I figured since she'd disabled the security that was our best bet and I was right." Jerry studied Rafe, who'd put on an innocent face. "So now we're going in there and sorting out the animals. We picked up some supplies too."

"Good. I hope she can get them all new homes by tomorrow night, though." I walked back to the living room. "Boogie and I aren't comfortable with the crowd. Have you seen Penny's bedroom door? There goes my security deposit."

"I'd say you lost that a long time ago." Rafe grinned. "Didn't some of the broken furniture come with the place?"

"Why are you smiling?" I shook my head. "Jerry's ordered new and you're paying half. I hope it was expensive, Jer." I smiled at him.

"Of course it was. Only the best for my girl." Jerry kept his arm around my waist.

"Mr. Blade, will you bring those other cages? Boogie, no!" Penny sounded frantic.

"Duty calls." Jerry frowned. "I'll want an update on the demon thing after this."

"Of course." I glanced at Rafe. "We're going to go straight to the source. Ask Simon if he's interested in leaving his goddess. That will let us know how to proceed." I shooed Jerry down the hall when I heard a crash from Penny's room, then turned to Rafe. "Do you think Lucifer will come himself and make the offer to Simon once the goddess is dead?"

"He's not allowed to. Remember? We've got to get him to agree before the contract comes out. Part of their 'rules.'" Rafe collapsed on the couch. "I'm worried, Glory. Now you know how seductive Luc can be. Are you sure you can keep resisting him if he tries to reel you in again?"

"I have to." I sat and noticed how much space I took up on the couch. "I just have to."

The next night, I heard squeals over the roar of my blow-dryer and finally turned it off to investigate. I opened my bedroom door just as Penny came down the hall lugging two crates of rats.

"What's going on? The animal rescue people come through for you?" I was due down in the shop in a few minutes and running late because I'd taken time to supervise a visit to the beauty shop for Penny. The result was a cute haircut for her but I'd been left no time for my own cut to be blown dry. Now, if mortals were coming, I might need to call my clerk and let her know I'd be even later. I didn't trust Penny yet unsupervised. I'd been lucky the night before. She'd been so intent on the rat rescue, she'd left any mortals who'd crossed her path alone.

"No. I ran into your neighbor and she's found homes for all of them." Penny set the cages by the door. "That's the last. Don't know why they're so upset. Guess it's all the motion." She knelt down and tried to soothe the frantic rodents. "Can you believe the luck? Lacy says her family loves white rats."

"Lacy?" I stomped over to the hall door and jerked it open. "Where is she?"

"She's taking the crates down to her car. She'll be back up to get these in a minute." Penny sighed. "I wish I could keep at least one rat, for a pet, but Boogie has been crazed by this."

"Yes, and he was here first, weren't you, big guy?" I picked up the cat when he stuck a paw into the wire cage. "Have you e-mailed the rescue people yet to cancel?"

"No. I'll do it later." Penny stood. "This week has been insane. Jenny's been texting me every few minutes wanting to meet Israel Caine. More e-mails from the university. My advisor and everyone at the lab's freaking over the rats being stolen." She ran her hands through her hair. "I just got my hair cut by a shape-shifter. And . . ." She grinned. "Josh called and asked me out for Saturday night!"

"Wow!" I hated that I was about to add one more insanity to her list. "Congrats on the date. We'll talk about it later." I was sure she wasn't ready to be alone with him yet but she was so excited . . . I mentally went through my schedule. I wondered if Jerry would enjoy following Penny on her date. That image almost made me smile. Until the rats squealed again. "You'd better take these rats back to your bedroom."

"Why? I hear Lacy coming up the stairs." Penny looked puzzled.

I grabbed Lacy's arm and jerked her inside, then slammed

the door. "Okay, Lacy. Why don't you tell my roomie why you're so crazy about white rats? Why your whole family loves them?"

Lacy grimaced and glanced down at my hand on her arm. I let her go, but stayed in her face. She and I both knew that in a fair fight she could probably take me. She was a werecat who had some serious skills and I'm too softhearted to rip out the throat of someone I consider a friend. Lacy? I wasn't so sure she wouldn't get caught up in the moment and claw me to pieces. Her real disadvantage was that she worked for me as my day manager and beating up your boss didn't translate to job security. On the other hand, finding good reliable day help wasn't easy either. It was a standoff.

"Lacy? Is something up here?" Penny had quickly figured out that her rats weren't exactly going to a happy home.

"Oh, well, sorry I didn't tell you the truth." Lacy backed toward the door. "I'm, um, a werecat." She smiled and let her canines show. "White rats. To be honest? They're absolutely delicious."

"Oh, my God!" Penny clutched a cage to her chest. "You didn't— You haven't—"

"Relax. The tasty treats are still in the station wagon, waiting for Mom's secret sauce." Lacy winced when I kicked her in the shin. "I'll go get 'em."

"No. Stay here. Where Glory can watch you." Penny held out her hand. "Give me your keys."

"Car's not locked. Who's going to steal rats? Any other werecats in the area are, er, *were* invited to the barbeque." She sighed. "It's the red station wagon out back. Just wish I hadn't called Mom first. She's already fired up the grill and called the cousins."

"Ewww." Penny lurched out of the apartment holding her stomach.

"Really? Was that last necessary?" I frowned and grabbed Boogie before he could make a dash for freedom through the open door. "If you value your job, I suggest you disappear before Penny gets back up here, Lacy." I showed fang. "I'm not happy with you right now."

"It's my nature, Glory." Lacy shrugged and reached out to give Boogie a scratch under his chin. His purr was epic. "The newbie's gonna have to learn to deal."

"Lacy . . ." I really did need her at the shop or she'd have been fired on the spot. But what she said was true.

"Now if she ever wants to get rid of this sweet fella, he'd be treated like a king at Mom's place." She scratched him again and he closed his eyes in ecstasy.

"Get your freaky claws off my cat!" Penny had a cage in each hand as she shoved Lacy out of her way. The rats scrambled into a trembling pile, as far away from the werecat as they could get. "I'm doing a head count. If even one rat is missing . . ."

"Chill, vamp child. Like I said, Mom makes a secret sauce. It's killer." Lacy put up her hands when Penny dropped the cages and lunged at her. I jumped in between them.

"Stop! Penny, take care of your rats. Lacy, don't taunt her. Please?" I sent my manager a mental message to work with me here.

"Yeah, well, good luck, Glory. You'd better teach your gal here not to make idle threats."

Penny was right behind me, her fangs bared. "You want to try me?"

"No one's trying anyone. Good night, Lacy. Say hi to your mom for me." I looked back and gave Penny a mental message to chill.

"Sure. I'm outta here." Lacy held up her hands. "But now I've got to stop and pick up something else." She eyed the crates wistfully. "Salmon. Guess Mom can grill that." Lacy glanced at me. "Course these would have been free."

In the interest of harmony, I grabbed my purse and handed her a couple of twenties.

"Thanks, boss!" Lacy smirked at Penny and sauntered out the door.

I closed it, then leaned against it, hugging Boogie who was struggling to get to the rats.

Penny glared at me. "I can't believe that woman! And you gave her money?"

"She works for me and lives across the hall. It's important that we all get along." I stroked the cat. "And she would have mopped the floor with you, fledgling. Believe that."

"Humph." Penny took a minute to calm down and think that through. "But I'll get stronger as I get older."

"Sure you will. But each species of paranormal has its own skill set. There's lots to learn in this new world of yours. Werecats, werewolves, you name it, shape-shifters of all kinds exist and live in this building, Penny, along with other vampires. You should call Trey. Get him to help you identify the different kinds of paranormals by smell like he offered at N-V. And let him teach you some other things too, whatever he's willing to share." I glanced at the door. "That scent thing would have sure helped you tonight."

"You're right about that." Penny picked up two crates and started toward her bedroom. "You think that he meant it? That I could call him?"

"Sure. There aren't a lot of young, cute paranormals available. Trey was happy to see a new girl in town."

Penny stopped. "Oh. I get it. Supply and demand."

"I didn't mean to insult you. I'm stating a fact. Didn't you hear the cute part?" I let Boogie down, shutting him inside my bedroom. "Take advantage of the situation. And I have no problem with you dating a shifter. He can handle you if your bloodlust becomes an issue."

"Oh, yeah? What? Will he let me drink his blood?" She moved closer. "Have you had some of Rafe's? Would I like shifter blood?"

"Okay. First, let's not get personal. Second?" I thought about Rafe and his blood, so hot, so, um, delicious. I shook my head. "Yes, you'd like it. Shifters have a very fast metabolism; They have to in order to shift. So their blood is hot and, in my experience, pretty fine." I smiled. "But they have different types just like mortals do. With any kind of luck you'll live a long, long while. Plenty of time to try them all."

"So vampire blood . . . ?" Penny forgot about the rats for a minute.

"Is fairly cool, temperature-wise. And you already sampled the mortal kind. It's warm. So the shifter's feels hot in comparison." I sighed, remembering. I'd really miss that. But I just couldn't go there again.

"Interesting." Penny picked up her crates again. "Yes, I'll call him. I can't do research with the lab closed and an investigation going on. I texted Jenny that Ray wasn't here now so she's calmed down."

"You're not a suspect, are you? In the great lab rat heist?" I picked up the other crates and followed her to her bedroom. Phew. These guys had to go soon because it definitely reeked in here.

"No, my research was trashed by the theft. I'd be the last person they'd look at. So far it's a dead end." Penny clipped food and water trays to the crates and arranged paper and litter as it should be. "Poor babies. What a close call. I definitely need to know a werecat when I smell one."

"Yes, you do. And, seriously, don't blame Lacy. She needs prey, as you would if you didn't have the synthetic blood available. Neither of you can help what you need to live."

"I wonder. I'd like to run a chemical analysis on our DNA, among other things. The genetic changes since I've been turned vampire. The whole thing is fascinating. Our metabolism. You name it. Since my old research isn't satisfying me anymore, I figure I need to move on to something new." Penny opened her window, turned on a fan, and shut the bedroom door. She led the way to the living room. "Ray texted me. Ian MacDonald is here and will meet with me later tonight. I'm definitely going. I think I'd like to work with him."

I sank down on the couch. Of course I knew Ian was here. I'd talked to him at length about Ray's rehab. For once, I felt in sync with the Scottish doctor, though I hadn't shared that information with Jerry. My Campbell still had the MacDonald prejudice and couldn't see past an old feud.

"Oh, Penny, you have no idea what you'd be getting into with Ian. As much as I respect his brilliant mind, he has a pretty unique perspective on science. Instead of lab rats, Ian experiments with mortals and other vampires."

"That's radical." But instead of being horrified, Penny looked intrigued. "Not good that he uses mortals, though I can see he'd need blood samples for comparison. But the vampires are immortal, so how could he hurt them?"

I threw up my hands. "We're talking about people, Penny. Vampires are still human, my dear. And you're not going near Ian MacDonald without me."

Penny smiled. "Great. I admit I was a little scared about it. You and Mr. Blade keep throwing out dire warnings, though Ray thinks Ian's cool."

It didn't escape me that Penny was still calling Jerry "Mr. Blade" but had gone to "Ray" immediately.

"What time is this meeting? And how are you supposed to get there? Are you driving? The paparazzi are still camped outside, you know. Though they won't bother you, I don't think." They'd gotten shots of Ray leaving in his SUV out back. Some still followed me every time I left the apartment. They'd got a swell shot of me with a wet head after our visit to the beauty shop tonight. I kept hoping they'd give up. Business was still booming, though, which was why I really needed to get down to the shop.

"I'm meeting them at three." Penny sighed. "I guess I'm getting used to these crazy new hours. I didn't think twice when Ray told me that. The meeting's at his house on the lake and he said it was hard to find so he's sending a car for me before then."

"True. You're adapting very quickly." I gave her an encouraging smile. We were settled on the couch in my newly refurnished living room. The chairs were a beautiful caramel leather and the coffee table was a sturdy black enamel that could hold a man if he landed on it. My favorite new addition was the lamp. It was an Oriental ginger jar decorated with a red, caramel and black dragon design. I was grabbing it at the first sign of trouble next time. I figured Jerry had called a high-end furniture store and had a decorator pick these things. The only problem was that it made my thrift store couch look pretty sad. I was going to have to at least splurge on a new throw and some pillows.

I was about to comment on it when Penny's phone rang.

"It's my mom. She's been leaving messages. She wants to come check on me, especially after I told her about the rats being stolen and my research trashed." Penny kept staring at the phone.

"Answer it. We'll figure something out." I leaned back. Obviously I was going to be really late to the shop.

"Hey, Mom. Sorry I missed your other calls."

"Penny, why didn't you tell me you were moving?" Penny's mother had none of the Texas drawl I expected as I leaned close to listen in. I guess she was a Yankee transplant as they called them around here.

"It was kind of spur-of-the-moment. Glory and I clicked and she needed a roommate. It was a good deal for me." Penny rolled her eyes.

"Well, Daddy and I want to come up and meet her, see the new place." Mom obviously wasn't taking no for an answer. "How about Saturday? I'll bring a pot roast and we'll have lunch. I know how you miss my home cooking, honey. Jenny can come too."

"Sounds just wonderful, but that's not good for me." Penny heaved a big sigh that I was sure her mother could hear. "Still trying to deal with the mess at the lab and I have a big date Saturday night. I'll have to get ready."

"A date!" Mom was excited now. "Of course. Take all the time you need. Jenny could help you with that."

"Yeah, right." Penny looked at me. "Actually Glory has a clothing shop. She's been super helping me with my wardrobe. You won't recognize me when you see me. I'm totally transformed. Even got a haircut."

"That settles it. We're coming. Name the day. I mean it."
Mom sounded firm.

I grabbed the phone. "Hi, Mrs. Patterson? This is Glory
St. Clair, Penny's new roommate."

"Glory? Well, I'm glad to meet you. I hope Penny isn't
making a mess in your place." Mom laughed. "She does have
her mind on other things."

"I'm enjoying having Penny here. And she keeps her stuff
in her room except for that big computer. But I'm sure you
know how important her research was to her." I listened
while Mom lamented about the lost research.

"Well, why don't you and Mr. Patterson come on up this
Monday night? My shop's closed and Penny and I can have
you here then. In the apartment." I laughed at the look on
Penny's face. Obviously I'd just given her a deadline for having the rats gone and the place aired out.

"Oh, I love pot roast. With potatoes and carrots? Bring it
on. I can't tell you the last time I had a home-cooked meal."
I sighed. I couldn't have meant a statement more. "Yes, I'll
make sure Penny calls her sister and gets her to come too.
Penny says she's a vegetarian. Guess you know that, though.
More pot roast for me." I laughed. "See you Monday." I hung
up and faced Penny's glare.

"My parents are coming here? Monday night?" She looked
significantly toward her bedroom. "What am I supposed to
do about them?"

"Find them a home. Pronto." I got up and went to grab
my purse.

"And how are we supposed to eat pot roast?" Penny was
on my heels as I headed to my bedroom.

"We don't. We whammy the entire family to make them
think we did." I picked up my brush and finished fixing my
hair.

"Damn it, Glory." Her eyes filled with tears. "That seems
so creepy and like cheating."

"What do you want to do? Show them your fangs?" I put
down the brush. "You want creepy? Mom and Dad would

absolutely die. Maybe literally. I don't know what kind of shape they're in or how old they are, but . . ."

"Dad's had a few heart issues." Penny frowned. "Mom's in great shape. They're both teachers. Dad teaches math but Mom's sponsor of the cheerleading squad and coaches soccer. You can imagine what a disappointment to her I was. I'm not into sports."

"But I bet you're Daddy's little girl." I patted her shoulder. "Get over this. We'll handle it. Since your computer is on our table, we'll set up TV trays and pretend to eat. Figure something out." I was getting really tired of all these complications.

"Gee, Glory, sorry to be a complication." Penny stomped back into the living room and picked up the TV remote.

"Did you just read my mind?" I grabbed my purse and followed her.

"Of course I did. I do it all the time." She frowned when I snatched the remote and muted the Syfy channel.

"It's rude. You do that to some paranormals and they'll hand you your head." I tossed the remote on the couch.

"Well, now you tell me." She slouched on the couch.

"Yes, now I tell you. Pay attention. The only time it's okay to read someone's mind is defense. You can try it during this meeting with Ian if thing's get dicey, but he'll have his thoughts blocked anyway. Guys like that do as a matter of course." I stared at her. "Just like you seem to do."

"Well, sure. I don't want just anybody strolling through my brain." She finally managed a smile. "It's a jungle in there."

"Of course. And swear to me on your mother's life, and I do mean that literally, that you'll stay out of Ray's mind. Totally X-rated." I kept my eyes on hers.

"First, cool it with the dire threats. I've done enough unauthorized strolls through your thoughts to know your bark's way worse than your bite, Glory." She ignored my snarl. "And second . . . " Now she blushed and giggled. "Who could resist a chance to get inside Israel Caine's head?" She grabbed my hand. "X-rated? Is there such a thing as Z?"

Now she had *me* flushing.

Penny sighed. "Wow, Glory. If you didn't fall into that guy's bed, you're crazy."

"Guess I am. Crazy enough to see Ray for what he is, a man who will never settle down with one woman for the long haul." I leaned back, sighing myself. Oh, the memories. We'd had some really close calls, but I just never could let myself go with Ray. And my reasons had always been valid. "I was scared to love him too much because I knew he'd just break my heart."

"I can see your point." Penny sighed. "But what a fine time you could have short-term."

I smiled and patted her knee. "There are guys out there who are much better bets, for both of us." Penny was wearing black jeans I'd picked out for her. Tonight she had on a black cardigan and turquoise V-neck shell. She looked good, especially with her new haircut and simple makeup. She'd pulled out some dangly topaz earrings that matched her eyes, a gift from her parents that she never wore. I'd complimented her enough that I had a feeling she'd be wearing them a lot now. Funny how becoming a vampire had brought life to her look.

"Speaking of bets . . ." She leaned forward. "I've been thinking about this meeting with Ian. If he's a genius like you say he is, he could be on his way to figuring out how to resurrect a normal life for vampires. Maybe get me some quality time with my folks before"—her voice cracked—"before it's too late."

"It's a dream we've all had, Penny. Nothing more than that. I hate to see you get your hopes up just to be disappointed." I sighed when she shook her head.

"With science, anything is possible. Don't be so pessimistic, Glory." Penny crossed her legs and bumped her knee on the new coffee table. "Damn, that thing weighs a ton."

"Not pessimistic, realistic. But I've seen too many miracles in my long life to count anything out. So you can meet with Ian and see what he says." I got up and walked carefully around the table. What had Jerry told that designer about his requirements in a coffee table? It was too big and way too heavy for this room. But it was beautiful. I arranged my latest issue of *InStyle* in the middle of it, then set the remote on top. Penny was quiet and I finally turned to her.

"I'm going down to the shop. I'll meet you there at two thirty. Are you going to just stay here and watch the tube till then?" I could see she had a good six hours to kill. For Penny, that was plenty of time to get up to mischief.

"I'll call the rat rescue people again, tell them it's urgent, then I may call Trey, see if he has a break and if I could meet him at N-V for it." Penny grabbed the remote but didn't touch a button. "What do you think?"

"Sure, why not? But let me know if you go out. Please?" I knew that was asking a lot. "The council wants me to keep tabs on you for now. It's important."

"Fine. You *are* helping me." She glanced back toward her bedroom and wrinkled her nose. "And I am kind of taking advantage here."

"Great. That's all I ask, that I know your schedule. Just stay out of trouble and we'll be cool." I picked up my purse and headed out.

Penny and Trey. Surely they could hang out without fallout.

Oh, Glory, when will you learn not to tempt fate?

Twelve

The shop was busy as usual for a Friday night, so it was almost midnight before I got a chance to call Jerry and let him know about the meeting with Ian. I hated to do it. He'd want to tag along and I wasn't going to allow it. So we'd fight. I was right, of course.

"Seriously, we'll be fine. No need for you to go with us, Jer." I had taken this call to the back room since we were in a brief lull. Erin was handling the front.

"I don't like you doing anything with a MacDonald when I'm not around. I'm coming over." Jerry was in command mode.

"No, you're not. This is important to Penny. She wants to meet Ian, scientist to scientist, and, if you're there, it will be all about old feuds and macho posturing." I frowned at the phone. I could practically hear Jerry seething. "Ian has no reason to hurt me. So you have no need to start up another war. Let me handle this."

"It's not 'macho posturing' if the man is a danger to you, Gloriana. The MacDonalds and the Campbells never miss a chance to hurt each other. I've told you that time and again. Remember the pain his diet drug caused you?"

"That was a fluke. And your feud is old news. You and Ian are ushering in a new age. A rational one." I sank down in a chair. "Come on, Jer, relax. I'll give you a full report when I get back. Better yet, come by the apartment and see the new furniture. I love it. We'll be back before dawn. Use your key, let yourself in and wait for me. We can have some alone time before the sun comes up." I picked up a black silk camisole that had come in from a shifter wanting to sell some old things. I loved it and it fit. I was going to put it on under my zebra print blouse, without a bra, and let Jerry discover it. Something to look forward to.

"You'll call me if you need me? Where does Caine live now?"

I could tell I'd dangled the right bait and he was calming down. "No idea. I'll call you from the car with the address. That way if I do need you, you can fly right out. How's that?"

"It makes me feel better. Should make *you* feel better too. Don't suppose Valdez is going along?" Jerry's voice had hardened. He'd hated to ask that question, but actually probably hoped Rafe was doing guard duty.

"No, and I won't ask him. It's Friday night. A busy night at his club. He needs to stay there." I opened the door into the shop and could see a new group of customers had just come in. "And we're busy too. Got to go. I love you, Jerry. See you later?"

"Count on it. Take care of yourself, Gloriana. And the fledgling too." He hung up.

I did feel that responsibility for Penny weighing heavily on me. She'd called at eleven and said she was heading over to N-V. Trey had been happy to hear from her and invited her to come listen to the band, then spend his lunch break with him at one o'clock. Penny had sounded thrilled and I sure wasn't going to forbid her.

I had called Rafe and warned him that my fledgling was still shaky on the bloodlust thing and to let his waitstaff know to keep an eye on her around mortals. He'd have them serve her plenty of the synthetic they kept on hand for vampires, only without the alcohol. Fortunately, he'd been too busy to talk for long or he might have pried out of me my plans for later in the evening.

I didn't need another of my overprotective males putting doubts in my mind about this meeting with Ian. I had enough of those already. Sure Ian was being great about re-habbing Ray, but he had his own reasons for wanting the rocker clean and sober. If he was going to use Ray as a guinea pig, he'd want him to be drug- and alcohol-free. Or at least that's what Ian had told me on the phone. Worked for me as long as Ray benefited in the long run.

At least the shop was busy and I made some good sales to the Friday-night crowd. Time flew by so I was surprised when the phone rang and I noticed it was two o'clock already.

"Rafe? What's up?" I knew this was closing time at N-V. He had to be really busy.

"Trey's not back from his break. He left with Penny an hour ago and now he's late. This isn't like him, Glory. He knows I need him here for closing." Rafe shouted at someone in the club. "Hang on."

I could hear noise in the background as Rafe issued orders. Trey and Penny late. Surely they hadn't . . .

"Okay, I'm back. I can't leave but there's a place not far from you where the shifters here like to hang out. The green belt along Town Lake. Can you go check it out? Trey's not answering his phone. Maybe you could try Penny's first."

I looked around and seemed to be alone. "You don't think the demons bothered them, do you?"

"I wouldn't put anything past them. But they can't do harm, just make their propositions."

"Are you sure? Alesa didn't abide by that rule. She attacked me when she was here. I also have a pair of ruined boots that proves they play fast and loose with the 'do no harm' clause. Damn it, Rafe, if they try to lure Penny to the dark side . . ." I hurried into the back room and grabbed my purse. "Where's this place?"

"A few blocks over, the park that runs between First Street

and the lake. You can't miss it. Shift and you'll see it from the air." Rafe cursed. "If I could get away, I'd do it myself, but Nadia's out of town and I have to be here."

"I get that. I can handle this." I stuffed my keys and a credit card in my pants pocket, then left my purse in the back room. When you shift, you really don't want to deal with baggage.

"Thanks for calling, Rafe. I'll let you know what I find out." I shut off the phone, tried Penny's number and got her voice mail. Not a good sign. I stuffed my phone into another pocket in my black jeans and hoped my blouse covered the bulges.

Damn it. The last thing I wanted to do right now was to confront a pair of demons. With luck, this was just Penny and Trey getting too friendly, too fast. I could understand that. The vampire libido and I were well acquainted. I'd already put on that cami and my bra was in the back room. Yeah, I was living on the edge, Glory-style. I'd let the girls loose for Jerry, but Ray would undoubtedly appreciate the view too.

I told Erin I was taking off and asked her to have Ray's driver wait if I ran late. Then I headed out the back door. I was thrilled that no paparazzi were waiting to ambush me as I stepped behind the stinky Dumpster and shifted. I flew toward First Street just a few blocks away, staying close to the treetops once I saw the water. The lake here near downtown looks more like a river and they'd made a park out of the green belt on both sides of it. A small group of people clustered near the Congress Avenue Bridge, known for its bat colony. Maybe Trey had decided to show that to Penny.

I flew down for a closer look. No, I knew immediately from the smell that these were mortals and they weren't into bathing. I flew along the water's edge until I saw another group under some trees. Okay, now this looked promising. As I got nearer, the sugary smell hit me and I screeched.

"Guess we have company." Spyte frowned at me as I landed and shifted.

"You bet you do. What the hell is going on here? You are supposed to leave my friends alone." I saw Trey, frozen in place, but he blinked at me in a silent plea to get him out of there. Penny was rooted to the ground, but obviously had the use of her hands and head.

"Glory, these creeps think I'd be interested in their work. Can you believe it?" Penny growled at Caryon, who managed to look bored.

"It was worth a shot. You had such spunk the other night I figured you'd make a good harvester for us. I admired how you bit me." He smiled at me. "And we've got Glory working for us now, so anything's possible."

"No! Glory, you're working for them?" Penny's eyes widened. "He's got to be lying."

"I'm only getting one really rotten soul for him. To save Rafe from boiling in oil or whatever nasty things they might do to him." I stalked up to Caryon and poked him in the chest. "I told you to leave my fledgling alone."

"And I do what you tell me to, why?" He flicked me with a look that made my skin crawl. "What are you going to do to me?"

"This isn't my first rodeo, you know. When Alesa was stuck in me, I learned what gave her heartburn. How'd you like a Bible verse marathon? Those give these losers migraines, Penny. And they really hate the 'G' word." I glanced at Penny. "You got one for him?"

"Sure. Twenty-third Psalm. The Lord is my—"

"Not that again." Spyte covered his ears. "Didn't take this girl five minutes to figure out how to hurt us. She's been saying that one over and over again ever since we showed up here. The girl's a Bible-spouting torturer."

"Oh, I've got thousands of them." Penny grinned. "But 'Fear no evil' seemed to fit the situation."

"Seems like you're wasting your time, fellas." I glanced at Trey. "And what about the shifter here? Did you proposition him too?"

"Of course." Caryon grimaced. "Seems he's just as good as

the rest of your friends. No fun at all. Didn't even cry when we set his tail on fire."

"His tail?" I glanced from Trey to Penny.

"We were shifting. He was a fox." She flushed. "I was a hound chasing him when the saccharine Satans dropped by."

"But he turned them down." I smiled at Trey. "Now that makes me happy. Let him go, Caryon. He needs to get back to work."

"Whatever." Caryon flicked his wrist and Trey was free.

"You son of a—" Trey lunged for the demon, but I got between them.

"No, just take off. Go back to the club and help Rafe close. I've got this. Penny and I have an appointment in a little while anyway. Date's over." I felt Trey's anger vibrating through him. "Please. If you get into it with these two, you'll only make it worse on all of us."

"Penny? You want me to stay?" Trey turned to her and took her hand. Her feet were still firmly planted.

"Thanks, Trey. I'm so sorry you were caught up in this mess." Penny glared at the demons, then at me. "Not anything else you can do here. Go, save your job. You've been absolutely great about this."

"Call me later, please. Let me know how you are." Trey leaned forward and kissed her on the lips.

Penny flushed. "Sure. Take care." She watched as he shifted and flew off into the night. "Wow. He really is a nice guy."

"Gag me." Spyte staggered like he was going to fall down as he held his stomach. "Where do you find these creatures, Glory, Penny? Wimps R Us?"

"He's no wimp. When you surprised us, he would have torn you apart if you hadn't paralyzed him." Penny glared at him. "That's such a cowardly way to deal with people. Makes me realize who the real wimps are here."

"Penny, why don't you just be quiet so we can get out of here?" I put my hand on her shoulder. She was right, but that didn't mean we were going to stand around and trade insults with these demons all night. So far they'd just talked.

But I still had a pair of ruined boots to remind me they could
do worse. And Alesa had almost ripped me to pieces in my
shop when she'd arrived in town. Murder was definitely in
their playbook.

"Fine." Penny lifted her chin. "Let me loose so we can
leave or I'm singing 'God Bless America' again."

"There's an incentive to hurry. The girl's got the pipes of
an orangutan in heat." Spyte waved his hand. "I'm muting
her." And Penny was frozen head to foot.

"What now?" I put my hands on my hips. "I thought you
wanted my cooperation?"

"We do." Caryon smiled at me. "Progress report, Glory."

I glanced at Penny, who, even frozen, fairly radiated fury
and disappointment. With me. I was going to have to fix this
with her. Later. I turned to Caryon as he looked significantly
at my eyebrows.

"Fine. Progress. I'm calling Simon. He wants a relationship with his son and there are signs it's badly enough to give
up his goddess. If he gets free, it's on Lucifer to get him on
his team. So either of you got any ideas how we can destroy
the queen of the energy vacuum pump?"

"You're thinking of taking out the goddess herself?" Spyte
rubbed his hands together. "Bold. We can't help you with
that. Rules."

"Lucifer loved the idea. But he agreed. It's all on me and
my friends. Didn't seem worried about luring Simon over
later. The man's nothing if not confident of his persuasive
abilities."

Ah. That got a reaction. Cary and Spyte exchanged glances.
"Oh? Didn't you know Luc and I had a little chat?" I smiled.
"He's obviously lost faith in your ability to handle this on your
own. Wasn't entirely happy with what you did to my lashes
either, Cary." At least I'd gotten proficient with the fake ones.
No sign yet that my own were growing in.

"You're lying. Luc would never demean himself by coming to see you." Spyte nibbled at one of his black claws.

"Oh, he did. Showed me what I'd look like as a size six.

Tried to tempt me with all kinds of, ahem, lures. Guess he really wants Team EV out of the way. Or it was just a slow night down at the old torture chamber." I couldn't look at Penny now. The memory of what had happened with Lucifer was too raw and even now the temptation was too shameful.

"Read her mind, Spyte. She's telling the truth. We're doomed." Caryon sank down to the grass. "It's the fiery furnace for us."

"No, no, no, that's so last century. Now he does this thing with electrodes and acid." Spyte shuddered. "Fire would be like a cool bath on a hot summer day."

"So now you know. Stop harassing me and my people." I glanced at Penny. "I've got places to go, people to see. Keep distracting me and I'll never get this done."

"Whatever." Caryon waved his hand and started muttering about power surges and microchips.

Penny was immediately free, jerking away from me when I tried to touch her shoulder.

"Let's go." I didn't look back as I followed Penny to the street, which was deserted this time of night. She ran toward my shop, cutting through alleys and side streets. I decided that my high heels weren't going to cut it and shifted, flying over her head, but keeping an eye on her. When she finally got to the shop, she was a little winded, but seemed okay. That is except for her attitude toward me. I ducked into an alley and shifted back, then approached the shop on foot.

"Penny, can we clear the air?" I waved at Erin through the window before we climbed into the back of the limo Ray had sent for us. Paparazzi shouted out questions about where we were going and asked for Penny's name as they snapped pictures. I ignored them while Penny just got flustered. When the car took off I could see we were being followed. No big deal. I'm sure they'd staked out Ray's house already.

"How?" Penny glanced at the partition between us and the driver. It was up and we could speak freely. "You spoke to Lucifer. You're doing the Devil's work. I really don't like where this is going."

"Neither do I, but I didn't have a choice." I sighed and leaned back. I needed to call Rafe and let him know we were okay, free and clear of the demons. In a minute. And were we free and clear? Good question.

"According to my grandpa, we always have a choice." Penny picked at her black jeans. "But I guess I'm undead proof that sometimes we don't." She looked up. "This Destiny character is a really bad man?"

"The worst. And he and his followers are the only ones I'm helping the demons with, I swear." I grabbed Penny's hand. "Now you swear something."

"What?" She looked alarmed and I realized I was gripping her too hard. I eased off.

"That you'll keep an open mind about Ian. Just because he's a scientist, don't jump on whatever he's offering. If he even offers you something." I let Penny go. This was so complicated. I couldn't dictate her life. She was basically an adult. And she needed to make her own decisions. But she was so new to this world. And Ian was so . . . not. He was a master manipulator.

"Can you just relax and let me meet the guy and talk to him without freaking out?" Penny finally relaxed. "Tell me more about him. You took his diet stuff. And it worked. Any idea how?"

"Not a clue. But it gave me nightmares. Can you imagine? During my death sleep." I checked the supplies in the mini-fridge in the space in front of us. Oh, yeah. High-quality synthetics in every blood type. I picked out two bottles of AB negative and handed one to Penny.

"Nightmares? When dawn hits, I'm dead. No dreams. Nothing." Penny twisted off the cap from her bottle, took a sip and sighed with pleasure. "Mmm. This is the good stuff."

"Only the best for Ian MacDonald. And, yes, that's exactly what happens. Dawn hits, we die. You heard me, we call it the death sleep. So when I suddenly got nightmares after four hundred years, I couldn't believe it." I savored the taste of that superfine synthetic for a moment. "They were horrible. Terrifying."

"Interesting side effect. What did Ian say about it?" Penny was obviously fascinated.

"Oh, he wanted to study me. Turn me into one of his personal lab rats. Claimed none of his other diet patients had ever experienced the same reaction." I was having trouble slowing down on this delicious drink but I knew these were the only two bottles of this type in the fridge.

"Yes, you were an anomaly then. He'd want to know why. Did you at least let him have a blood sample?" Penny had already gulped down her bottle and set the empty in a drink holder. Typical newbie lack of control.

"No, I didn't. He and Jerry have issues. An old clan feud. I couldn't cooperate with Ian on anything, not with a war about to break out. Speaking of, I've got to call Jer and let him know where we're going." I pushed the call button for the driver and got Ray's address, then pulled my cell out of my pocket.

"You were smart. I left my purse back at N-V. In the employee break room." Penny sighed. "Trey and I went over to the park, to practice my shifting. We were having fun and then those two bozos showed up."

I laughed. "Well, one bozo and a freak." I explained to her about Spyte's clown persona.

"This job for Lucifer isn't endangering your immortal soul, is it, Glory?" Penny put her hand on my arm.

"I hope not." I shook my head. "No, of course not. I won't let it. I'm just helping Rafe pay off a debt. Nothing more." I looked out the tinted window and watched the houses get farther apart as we headed toward Ray's rented home in the hills. I hit speed dial for Jerry and told him where we were going, listened to yet another lecture about Ian, and managed to leave out any mention of Penny's run-in with the demons. I ended the call, then made a quick one to Rafe, ending it just as the limo stopped in the curved driveway in front of a large home built of native limestone. Bodyguards kept the paparazzi outside an iron gate.

The driver opened the car door and helped us out. Ray must have heard the car arrive because he was smiling as he stood in the doorway. I noticed two more bodyguards, these Ian's, patrolling the grounds and pointed them out to Penny. They were blond surfer types, vampires of course, and Ian's trademark.

"There you are. I was beginning to worry." Ray kissed me on my cheek and did a fist bump with Penny. "Thought maybe you'd talked the kid here into chickening out."

"No, she's not a kid, as she frequently reminds me. And she deserves to meet Ian if she wants." I walked inside and gasped. The wall of windows exposed a panoramic view of a lake. No telling which one, Austin has several. Didn't matter. The moonlight on the water and the sprinkling of stars above and the few lights from houses rimming the lake below made for a beautiful setting.

"You like?" Ray kept his arm around me.

"Love it. This is even nicer than the last house you rented." I moved toward the terrace, a stone one easily accessed from doors off the living area. "Great for parties. The steps go down to a boat dock?"

"Of course. I've got a new boat on order. You know me. I like loud and fast." He squeezed my waist. "In my women too. Though once I've got 'em, I like to slow it way down."

"Ray!" I glanced at Penny.

"Hey, don't mind me. I can read his mind, remember?" She laughed. "Oops, I promised I'd quit doing that."

"It's not advisable to intrude uninvited." The deep voice sounded amused and we all turned to see Ian MacDonald stroll into the room. Ian was yet another handsome vampire. He looked more Viking than Scot, as if a Norse raider might have made a pit stop at the MacDonald castle back in the day. His light blond hair, piercing blue eyes and sharp nose, along with his deep tan were enough to make any woman sigh. Penny actually did, then she laughed in embarrassment.

"Sorry, I'm still learning. Only been a vampire for two weeks." She held out her hand.

"Uh, Penny, don't do that." I stepped between Penny and Ian with a smile. "I keep forgetting to tell you things. Some powerful vampires, like Ian here, can use touching your hand to take command of your will."

"Now, Gloriana, is that any way to introduce me to your fledgling?" Ian smiled and bowed in Penny's direction. "I never have to take command of a lovely woman. Women are usually quite happy to give me what I wish."

Penny laughed again, this time with genuine amusement. "Are you kidding? You've got to be kidding. Does that line work? Seriously?" She glanced at me. "Uh, maybe I'll shut up now."

"No, you've just made me proud." I grinned at Ian. "Modern women and even us ancient ones who've figured out how to get with the program are way over that command thing, Ian. You really do need a new line."

Ian exchanged looks with Ray. "Say what you will, Gloriana. I think most women do like a man who takes charge. At least when there's trouble. Your Campbell seems to hold your interest and he certainly is that type."

"Yes, well, that tendency of his has caused us some problems over the years." I really wanted to change the subject. "But Penny's here to talk to you about your research. And I know Ray's interested in it too. What do you think of Austin?"

"I like it. Property's certainly cheaper than it is on the West Coast." Ian looked out at the lake. "And I like settings like this one. Isolated. Yet close enough to an airport and technology to support my needs."

"Exactly. That's what I've been telling you." Ray stepped closer. "And, Glory, you'll like this. Ian says I've got to be off the sauce if I want to be part of his daylight experiments. That's why he was on board to do the rehab thing with me."

"That's great, Ray. At least the rehab part of it. I can tell you're off the sauce. You look good." I turned to Ian. "Daylight experiments. How experimental?" I hooked my arm through Ray's. "I really don't want to lose this man to a sunburn."

"Nothing dangerous. But, as I explained to Caine, I can't have extraneous chemicals in his system when I'm using my own formulas on him." Ian studied Penny. "You're blocking your thoughts, but I know you wanted to ask me about my work. Why don't you and I sit down and I'll show you some of my notes? Explain some of my projects." Ian glanced at me. "We'll be in Caine's study. Is that all right with you, Gloriana?"

"I don't need her permission, Mr. MacDonald." Penny shot me a look.

"Of course not," I said quickly.

"It's Dr. MacDonald, Penny. I have several PhDs and got my medical degree some decades ago as well. When you're immortal, you can indulge all your curiosities." Ian smiled. "But call me Ian, of course.

"Thanks, Ian. And it's Dr. Patterson since I got my own PhD," Penny said proudly. "But of course you can call me Penny. I'd been thinking about going to medical school myself before I got the big bite. I'd love to know how you managed it at night." They wandered off toward where I guess Ray had a study.

"Looks like a match made in heaven," Ray said quietly.

"Maybe. If I trusted Ian." I sighed. "This is a beautiful place. Much as I hate the water, I could even go for a boat ride on a night like this."

"How about skinny dipping?" Ray had that look in his eyes, that twinkle that always made me wish for a little more with him.

"That water's got to be frigid." I leaned against the wide stone wall. "Remember our run-in with Aggie during a midnight boat ride?" The Siren had had a crush on Ray, but that hadn't stopped her from forcing us to do her bidding or else suffer dire consequences. In hindsight, I understood. She'd been cursed, put into a hideous body by a jealous goddess.

Kind of like how I'd been stuck with the demon Alesa. Things like that made you desperate, and you did stuff you normally wouldn't do. Though Aggie wasn't all sweetness and light even after her curse was lifted.

"Who could forget? She was one creepy sea monster. I'm glad she doesn't live in this lake." Ray chuckled. "I admit I keep expecting her to climb onto this terrace some night and try to seduce me."

"If she's in her hot human body, you'll probably let her." I gave him a hip bump.

"Maybe." He slid his arm around my waist again. "Thanks for helping me dry out this time. I'm still struggling with it, but Ian's given me the incentive I needed to stick with it. He's got some meds too that helped me with withdrawal. I'm doing better than I thought I would."

"That's wonderful, Ray." I leaned my head on his shoulder. "I was so worried about you."

"Good to know." He pulled me close and looked into my eyes. "I'm not going to tell you your business, Glory, but here's my take on your situation."

"Oh, great. Here it comes." I frowned. "Go ahead."

"Blade. He's a stick. Old-fashioned and not the best guy for a woman like you." Ray rubbed his thumb along my jaw to my chin. "You've moved along with the times, just like you told Ian. I don't see that happening with Blade. I'm just sayin'." He leaned forward and kissed me with a soft rub of his lips against mine, then trailed a path down my neck.

"Ray, you can't begin to understand how hard it is to have lived so long, to have seen as much of life as we have." I didn't move away, which is what I should have done as Ray nuzzled my neck, then kissed a sweet path along my cheek to my ear and down my throat to the pulse beating there.

"No, I don't understand. Don't need to. I just see the woman here in front of me. I see the woman who really gets me, who cares about me like no other woman has in a hell of a long time. Damn it, I don't have a lot of real friends. I'm closer to you and Nate than anyone else. And Nate doesn't really understand what I've been going through since I was turned. You know?" Ray was back at my mouth again and lingering a little longer, going a little deeper this time. Then he pulled back, his hand on my neck now, massaging, coaxing, while his lips danced along the other side of my face.

"Yes, I know. Of course I care. I care about my friends. It's, it's what I do." Oh, God, but he was sliding his fangs along that sensitive vein in my neck. And his other hand was easing along the silk of my blouse, almost touching but not quite the center of my breast. I couldn't breathe. Didn't need to. But if I did, would that push my nipple into his palm? I gasped.

"I'll always be your . . . friend, Glory. You need me? I'm there. Remember that."

"Ray, we can be friends without the sexual thing, you know." I kept my eyes on his, knowing it was important that I say this.

"With a woman?" He smiled. "Can't imagine it, babe. You're too soft, too delicious for me to just ignore what's right . . . here." He pressed his hand against my breast for only a moment, then let it trail away, down to my waist. "You didn't wear a bra tonight. Was that for me?"

He didn't give me time to answer, his mouth back on mine, gently insistent as he deepened the kiss. He pulled me into his mind, reminding me of how we could laugh together, play together. Sober, he was as dangerous a man as I'd ever met. He had too many moves, too many ways he could entangle my senses until I couldn't imagine why I was still leaning against a stone ledge and not lying on the silk sheets in his bed upstairs.

"Glory?"

I opened my eyes and staggered in an effort to end this without damaging either my feelings or Ray's or the stone ledge I'd been about to fall back on.

"Penny." I eased away from Ray and focused on her. "What?" Okay that didn't sound happy, but she had eyes. She had to know she'd interrupted something interesting.

"Ian's invited me to work with him, maybe come see his lab in California eventually. Isn't that great?" Penny and Ian stood in the doorway. Ian had a smirk that meant if he'd had Blade's phone number, he would have taken a picture of that clench he'd just witnessed and sent it straight to his ancient enemy.

I cleared my throat, which seemed to have closed. "Sounds like you two hit it off."

"We did, actually." Ian glanced down at Penny. "Your fledgling has a fine mind and some excellent ideas that may be an asset in my research. She could very well be the assistant I need if I set up a facility here. And her research at the university is obviously at an end."

"Good. The setting up the facility here part." Ray frowned when I put some space between us. "So you're staying for a while to scout locations?"

"Yes. And to complete your rehabilitation. Surely you realize you're a long way from ready to go it on your own. Don't you, Caine?" Ian strolled over to look at the lake. "Gloriana, what do you think?"

"I think Penny will need something to do as a vampire and working with you might be a good place to start." I glanced at her. "How this will work with her grants or whatever I have no idea. We have a thing with her folks on Monday night, but after that . . ." I saw her nibble a fingernail. "Ian, are you sure about staying in Austin? This seems sudden. What about California?"

"I'm a practical man. And perhaps it makes me happy to rub Campbell's nose in my presence." Ian grinned at me. "Jeremiah give you grief about coming here tonight?"

"Of course. But I haven't forgotten the nasty problems I had with your diet drug." I sighed. "Though I did get thin for a nanosecond."

Penny smiled. "Ian's been working on some amazing things for vampires. He even gave me some free samples."

"Are you kidding me? Give them back." I stalked up to Ian. "What did you give her? Daylight? Diet? What?"

"Better than either one, Gloriana. Penny told me her parents are coming to dinner. How would you like to be able to eat like a mortal for just one meal?" Ian grinned, looking almost boyish for a moment.

I guess I must have been slack-jawed. Ray laughed out loud.

"Holy shit, Glory. You should see your face! If Ian had just handed you a million bucks you couldn't look more stunned." Ray gave me a bone-crushing hug. "Honey, you're too cute."

"Cute, hell. If you're toying with me, Ian MacDonald, I'm coming back here with one of Jerry's knives and carving my initials in your backside." I held out my hand. "Give me that sample."

"Gloriana. So bloodthirsty. Obviously you've been hanging around a Campbell for too many centuries." Ian took a vial of clear liquid from Penny and put it into my hand. "It works for one hour. You may eat whatever you like for that hour."

"Can I gain weight from it?" I stared at the bottle suspiciously. I did have that history of side effects from Ian's brews.

"No one else has, but, with you, I guess anything's possible." Ian glanced at Penny. "Perhaps you should use this as a chance to study the drug. Monitor both yourself and Gloriana for side effects, during and after."

"Yes, will do." Penny was clearly elated. "Just think, Glory, another way to get vampires back to mortal life. What a breakthrough."

I looked at Ray, who let me see the lingering lust in his eyes. He was still thinking bedroom not dining room. Once again I'd started something I wasn't going to finish. Why did so many people . . . Hmm. No, it was always other men. Okay, so why did so many men think I'd wasted my time with Jerry? Just a line? Then why was it that the more I heard it, the more it made sense to me? I shook my head, to Ray and to myself. I loved Jerry, I did. And he was waiting for me right now. I walked over and gave Ray a quick kiss good-bye.

"I'm so glad you're sober, Ray. Stick with it."

"You don't have to go now." He pulled me close and made sure I could feel how I'd affected him. "Stay."

I just smiled and shook my head. "Sorry. Not tonight. Let's go, Penny. Good night, Ian." I held up my sample. "Thanks. If this works, I may volunteer to be your lab rat."

Ian laughed. "Can I have that in writing?"

I felt my nerves twitch. That had sounded way too much like a certain demon I knew. "I'll get back to you on that," I said as Penny and I climbed into the limo.

Penny talked excitedly about her meeting with Ian the entire ride back to the apartment. She had every reason to be happy. This was a real opportunity for her. To continue research. To see a life for herself after getting turned vampire. Her depression about her undead life was lifting. We were almost to Sixth Street when she just had to ruin everything.

"So now all we have to do is tell Jenny about this and turn her. Then everything will be perfect." Penny bounced in her seat.

I just stared at her. Perfect? Perfect in hell, maybe.

Thirteen

I took off my high heels as I followed Penny up the stairs to my apartment. I figured we had an hour until dawn. I stopped her when we got to our floor.

"Okay, here's a test for you. What do you smell?"

Penny inhaled and wiggled her nose. "Geez. First, front and center, are the rats. I'm getting them out of here Sunday night. The animal rescue people told me of a place and I'll see if Mr. Blade will let me use his SUV to drive them over there."

I kept my snark to myself. Like Jerry would trust his very expensive vehicle to my fledgling who could put a ding on a car just by looking at it.

"Okay, that one was obvious. Now see if you can figure out who's inside. And there's more than one entity there." I had picked up on that before we'd reached the landing.

Penny grabbed my arm. "Oh, God, the demons aren't back, are they? I know I put on a brave front, but they freaked me out, Glory."

"No, not demons. The Cookie Monster reek would be too easy and there's not a whiff of it." I smiled. "Come on, use your nose. Didn't Trey get around to those lessons?"

"He tried, but there were too many mortals in the club and I was fighting my fangs. What can I say? I'm still all about the bloodlust. That's why we went to the park." Penny shrugged, then wiggled her nose again. "I think Trey's here! I recognize his scent." She grinned. "How cool is that!" She grabbed the doorknob and turned it. "Not locked. I wonder how he got in."

"Jerry's here too. And Rafe. They both have keys." I put my hand over hers. "Listen before you go inside."

"No crashes. Guess the coffee table's safe. And I hear the TV. Buzzing. Motorcycle races maybe?" Penny shook her head. "At four thirty in the morning?"

"That's cable for you." I stepped back and let Penny open the door. No crashes. That didn't mean Rafe and Jerry hadn't already demolished my new living room. But the scene we walked into was surprisingly civilized. Of course the three men had heard us approach, heard us talking in the hall too. They were on their feet and facing us as we walked in.

Jerry and Trey stood in front of the couch. Jerry had commandeered the remote and now turned off the TV. Rafe lounged in the doorway to the kitchen where he'd obviously unearthed yet another package of Twinkies left from when he'd lived here. They all stared at us like we'd made them wait. I just dropped my shoes by the door and stared back, not about to make excuses or rush into explanations. Penny and I had obviously survived and I needed a drink. I eased past Rafe and headed for the refrigerator.

"Trey! What are you doing here?" Penny rushed forward, not shy about getting right into it.

"I found your purse in the break room." Trey picked up the black clutch from the coffee table. "I knew you'd want your stuff, at least your cell phone."

"Sure. Thanks." Penny glanced at Rafe. "I guess Rafe showed you where I live."

"Sure did. When we got here, I ran into Blade and he told me what you two were up to. I decided we'd just stick around and see how things shook out." Rafe stuffed a Twinkie into his mouth, chewed and swallowed. "Looks like you survived MacDonald." He stopped me in the doorway with a hand on my shoulder as I twisted the top off a bottle of synthetic. "You could have told me where you were going, Glo. Maybe I could have shaken loose. Done backup for you."

"Not necessary, Rafe, but thanks. I knew you were needed at the club and this was just a quick meeting." I smiled at him. "Ian was a perfect gentleman. He and Penny talked and I visited with Ray. It was no big deal."

"See? No big deal. Which means you can get the hell out of here, Valdez." Jerry inserted himself between us, practically shoving Rafe out of the way. He tugged me into the living room while he examined me with narrowed eyes, like for wounds or signs of abuse.

"Hold on. Don't take off yet, Rafe." I gave Jerry a look that said to quit manhandling me and he let me go. "I think it would be nice if we could all just sit down for a minute or two. Make nice." I smiled, deciding I really didn't like Jerry making my arrangements for me. Yes, Ian's last remark still stung. That I liked a man taking command of me. "Sit. Relax. Don't even think about testing the new coffee table."

Trey looked from Rafe to Jerry, clearly picking up on the vibe between them and not sure what the coffee table had to do with anything. Penny grabbed his hand and pulled him toward the hall.

"Ignore them." She grinned at Rafe, then Jerry. "Love the new furniture, guys. Now, Trey, wouldn't you like to come see the rats I told you about? If you can stand the stench." Penny nodded down the hall.

"Yeah, sure. Wish I could help you out with that. Knew somebody who could take them off your hands." Trey never looked back, just followed Penny.

"Now, why don't we sit down and talk for a minute, all three of us?" I gestured toward the couch. Then I walked over and carefully put my vial, cell phone and keys on a shelf next to a book. This one I needed to reread immediately: *Finding Your Inner Peace*. Right now my insides were churning and burning. I blamed it on that testosterone in the air again and the way Rafe grinned and Jerry frowned. I was so not in the mood to referee.

"Hold it. What's that?" Jerry just had to notice that vial. "Is that something from MacDonald? One of his drugs?"

"Glory, you're not going to experiment with some of his shit again, are you?" Rafe was right beside me.

"Cool it, both of you. It's nothing you need to worry about. Penny and I are going to try it. It's a one-shot deal. No biggie." I glared at both of them. "And none of your damned business."

"What does it do? Not more of that weight-loss junk, is it?" Rafe said as he and Jerry exchanged glances, for once allies.

"No, I gave that up. You both claim to like my curves." I ran my hand down my side. Oops, not smart. They'd both just noticed I hadn't worn a bra. That got Jerry's eyebrows up and Rafe's grin wider while I settled into a chair.

Jerry stomped over and picked up the vial. "Doesn't look like the daylight drug. And I still have some of that if you want to try it again. With me, of course."

I sighed. "Forget it. Please? And since you're not against all of Ian's drugs, you just made my case for trying something else of his."

Rafe frowned at Jerry. "Tell us what it's for, Glory, and maybe we'll back off. It's not like you to take a risk. And to let your fledgling—"

"Give it up, Rafe. We're doing it." I yawned. "It's been a rough night. Did Trey tell you guys that the demons caught him with Penny in the park and propositioned them?"

"They approached your fledgling?" Jerry finally sat down again on the couch, forgetting about the vial for the time being, which had been my aim in bringing up the demons. "What did Penny do?"

"Turned them down, of course. She's had a strong religious upbringing. Now she's none too happy that I'm helping them snatch Simon's soul." I shook my head. "But I think we've smoothed things over. I let her know I'm doing this just once, for a friend. Simon was bound for hell anyway."

"I'm sorry, Glory. This is getting way out of control. Let me approach Simon, no need for you to involve yourself." Rafe sat on the other end of the couch and leaned forward. "I don't want you messing with demons any more than Blade does."

"Listen to him, Glory." Jerry pinned me with a look, willing me to take the offer.

"No, I'm in this to the end. You know Simon wouldn't meet with you, Rafe. Both of you need to accept that this subject is closed. Right now I'm starting to feel the dawn." I stood and frowned at Penny's bedroom. "It reeks in here, doesn't it?"

"Yes. Come home with me. If we shift, we can be there in minutes." Jerry stood and held out his hand.

Rafe's face hardened, then he shrugged. "Wouldn't blame you. Want me to grab Trey and make him leave with me?"

"Would you?" I smiled at him gratefully. "That would be great. I know Penny's an adult, but I don't feel right just taking off and leaving her here. Like I'm giving permission for them to, you know."

"I get it. Go. I'm on top of this. Don't know how she's sleeping in that bedroom. Bet she jumps at the chance to use your bed. But I'll let her know the offer's good only if she's in it alone." Rafe glanced at Jerry. "I know you don't get this, Blade, but Glory and I are friends. I do things for her, even when I'm not getting sex. Go figure."

Jerry growled, not liking the reference to sex despite the fact that Rafe had just admitted he wasn't getting any.

"Jerry, let's go." I walked around that enormous coffee table and gave Rafe a hug. "Thanks, buddy. I appreciate this. And, both of you, love the new furniture." Rafe's hand lingered at my waist until I pulled away to grab my keys and cell phone. Jerry just stood at the door, watching silently.

"Yeah, Blade did all right. But you should see the bill. I expected to see diamonds inlaid on that damned coffee table."

Rafe shoved his hands in his jeans pockets, his face giving away nothing as he watched me join Jerry at the door.

"I told the designer to select a sturdy table." Jerry slipped his arm around my waist. "We would do well to take our next fight outside. It did cost a pretty penny."

"You both have to promise me there won't *be* a next fight." I looked up at Jerry. "I mean it. This tension between you is getting to me and I don't need it. Not on top of everything else."

"I can make the promise that I won't throw the first punch." Rafe smiled at me. "But can you, Blade?" He shifted his gaze to Jerry and his smile disappeared.

Jerry stared at Rafe, and I didn't doubt there were some pretty pithy mental messages being exchanged. What did I expect? Jerry's pride still smarted from my brief affair with Rafe. And there was something in the way my former body-guard treated me now, a familiarity that almost shouted, "I've had her." It was subtle, but, to a man like Jerry, it was like a jab with a well-placed sword every time he saw Rafe and me together.

"Can you at least act civilized around each other? Please? I don't expect you to be friends but both of you are in my life to stay. I hope you can accept that." I put my hand on Jerry's chest.

"For you, Gloriana. Only for you." Jerry nodded at Rafe. "I won't fight with him again. Unless he starts it."

"There you go, Glory. You can even bring him to the club if you want. See how civilized I can be?" Rafe sat back on the couch and picked up the remote. "I'll let Trey and Penny have a little more time before I pry him out of here. Take off. I think we've said all we need to."

"Thanks, Rafe. I mean it." I wanted to hug him again, but knew Jerry had just about reached his limit. "Good night."

"Good night." He turned on the TV, obviously determined to act like he didn't care what I did. But I saw through it.

Damn, I hated hurting him, but he was a man who had known the score when he'd tried his luck with me. It had been Jerry who'd hired Rafe to protect me in the first place and I was sure my sire had made it clear he expected the bodyguard to know his place. Now Jerry's arm tightened around me, strong, possessive. I shrugged it off, not happy with this last overt sign of one-upmanship from him, and eased the door closed. Then I led the way up the stairs to the roof.

It was still a beautiful night but awfully close to dawn; no wonder I felt out of sorts, off-kilter. We shifted and flew as fast as we could, arriving in record time on Jerry's back porch. Lights were on and we could hear loud rock music. So much for a peaceful ending to a tense night.

"Seems my daughter is entertaining. She won't appreciate it if I check up on her or interrupt." Jerry frowned down at me. "Is there nowhere we can be alone?"

I smiled, the brief flight having done a lot to blow away my bad mood. What could I say? Two handsome men wanted to be with me. It wasn't exactly the worst problem in the world.

"Is your window locked?"

"I don't know, but I can afford to have it fixed." He glanced up at his second-story bedroom and saw what I'd seen. It was a fairly easy climb to get to his window if we used the ladder he kept in the garage. In minutes he had the ladder out and we were on our way up. Jerry went first and did have to put his fist through the pane to unlock the window. He shoved it open then climbed inside, reaching out to pull me in.

His room was dark but we didn't need light. I reached for his hand and licked away the blood from the cut where the glass had sliced him.

"Mmm. Delicious." I smiled as he tried to unbutton my blouse clumsily with one hand.

"What's this? You know you were driving me mad with the way your breasts moved under your blouse."

"You told me I didn't need a bra. So I left it off. That's a camisole. Do you like it?" I sighed as he palmed my breasts through the silk and lace. I shoved my hands up under his shirt to touch his smooth skin. We always had this need for each other, this instant chemistry.

"I'll like it better once it's on the floor." Jerry leaned down to kiss my nipples through the sheer fabric and pulled first one and then the other into the warmth of his mouth. His fangs were a delicious torture as he ran them around the sensitive tips. I explored his chest, then pushed my hands into the back of his jeans, loving the flex of his hard muscles.

"Told you I heard something up here." Lily's voice made us jump apart. "Just the old man and his lady getting it on."

Jerry turned and hid me behind him. His daughter and two vampires I didn't recognize stood in the doorway.

"Lily. We didn't want to crash your party downstairs." Jerry reached down and grabbed my blouse, handing it back to me. I shrugged into it.

"Hey, Glory. Don't worry, Dad. We won't cramp your style. Just thought someone was breaking in." Lily turned around and said something to the men. They all laughed. "The guys and I were about to call it a night. Just go back to doing what you were doing."

"Maybe you should introduce us to your new friends." Jerry glanced back to make sure I was buttoned back into my blouse, then strode over to the door. He'd had issues with Lily's former friends. That's why he'd invited her to move in with him.

"This is Matthew and his pal Red." Lily waved a casual hand toward me. "My dad, Jeremy Blade, and his main squeeze, Glory St. Clair."

"Hey." The guys offered Jerry a fist bump, which he ignored. He was busy assessing them. Since they weren't drunk or stoned or cursing a blue streak I guess they passed muster.

Jerry just nodded. "It's fairly close to dawn. What are your plans?"

Lily grinned. "Well, Matt here is spending the night and Red is taking off. That was the plan, unless . . . Red?"

The men took one look at Jerry's stony face and straightened from their slouches. They made quick excuses and backed toward the stairs.

"Now what did you do? What mental message did you send them?" Lily cursed and threw up her hands. "I'm an adult, you know. I can do a threesome every night if I want." She turned and hurried down the stairs after the men. "I need my own place, Dad. This isn't working for either of us. Ask Glory."

"She's right, Jerry. The woman is several hundred years old. She can't be treated like a child." I walked over and wrapped my arms around his waist.

"I'm not treating her like a child, Gloriana. I'm asking her to value herself. You think I couldn't tell she only picked up those men tonight? She holds herself too cheaply." Jerry ran a hand through his hair. "Where's her pride?"

"You're right. And she's playing a dangerous game, bringing strangers into your home. But good luck playing the father card. She needs time to get used to you, Jer. Lily didn't even know you were her biological father until recently." I hugged him. "Maybe you can teach her to appreciate her own worth."

"Why in the hell does she act like this in front of me?" Jerry stared out at the hallway where Lily had disappeared. "Threesomes? I really didn't want to know that."

"She's hurt, Jerry. Confused. Since Mac died and she found out he wasn't really her father, Lily seems determined to punish her mother for lying to her and you for not figuring out she was yours. This wild behavior is the only way she knows how, I guess. Embarrassing you, an honorable man." I kept my arms around him and laid my head on his chest.

"I try to be. And I would have claimed my child, if I had known she was mine. But Mara lied to all of us—Mac, me and Lily. Guess it's no surprise my daughter is a bit of a handful with that cold bitch for a mother." Jerry ran his hands up and down my back but was obviously still thinking.

I didn't bother to hide my smile. At last Jerry was admitting what I'd known all along. Mara was a cold, manipulative woman and not for him. Yes!

"Just rent Lily her own place. Let her develop a decent relationship with you over time and things will smooth out." I looked up and traced his frown with a fingertip. "Maybe some of your honorable ways will rub off. And she'll get tired of the game playing."

"I can only hope. But those men. I didn't recognize them. Where did they come from? I should have asked questions, not let them take off like that." Jerry ran his hand up my back, then around to fondle my breast, but I could tell his mind wasn't on his work.

"And alienate Lily even more? I don't think so." I blocked my thoughts. Matt had had the blond surfer-dude looks that I'd recognized instantly. I'd have bet the castle that he was one of Ian MacDonald's bodyguards with a night off. Just Lily's luck that she'd hooked up with one of them. Or was it? I'd mocked the Campbell-MacDonald feud, but maybe Ian had his own thoughts on that rivalry.

Of course Matt was good-looking and buff, just Lily's type. Red was probably one of Ray's bodyguards. So he'd volunteered to show Matt around. Surely it was all a coincidence. They'd probably met Lily at N-V, the only club in town now that encouraged vampires to hang out. I'd question Lily on my own later, not about to share my worries with Jerry.

I did what I always did when I wanted to distract my guy. I slid down to my knees and headed south. Oh, yeah. Not all of his thoughts were on his wayward daughter. I soon had him moaning and picking me up to carry me to his king-size bed.

It didn't take long for us to shed our clothes until we were naked, skin to skin. I sighed when Jerry kissed a path down my body, using his tongue and fangs to drive me wild. The dawn was too close for us to do much more than take each other in conventional ways. But it was enough. When I lay sated on his wide chest, I kissed his lips, then sat up so I could look into his eyes.

"I didn't hear Lily come back. Did you?"

Jerry smiled. "Who can hear when you're working your magic, lass? I went deaf, dumb and blind for whole minutes there." He ran his hands down to my hips and pulled me tight where we were connected. How could he possibly still be hard? Yet he was.

"Guess she found a safe place to spend the day." I sat up and moaned as he pushed deep inside me. "I know I have."

"You can always feel safe with me, Gloriana." Jerry reached up to hold my breasts. "And you're right. I need to find Lily her own place. Trust her to live on her own and take care of herself. She has for hundreds of years."

"Fledglings like Penny and even Ray just don't understand what it's like to have lived so long. Have so much history together. Especially like you and I have." I stopped moving, feeling like maybe there was something important I needed to say here. A message for me and maybe Jerry if I could just get it out.

"Aye, we do have that. I've certainly lost count of how many times we've lain like this." Jerry pulled my head down and gave me a kiss that touched my soul as much as it touched my lips and my tongue. By the time he drew back I'd lost the words I wanted to say. "Being with you never fails to please me, to make me want more of you, Gloriana. Other women never hold me like this, keep me in thrall. You are my soul mate, as they say. Do you believe in such a thing?"

"Jerry. Jeremiah. Of course I do." Tears blurred his face below me as I pressed my hands on his broad shoulders. He moved again, seemingly determined to take me higher one more time before the sun rose and sent us both into the death sleep. I felt the tension coil inside me, the thrill, and the impossibly intense pleasure that was almost pain. He was right. Neither of us ever failed to feel this. It was more than sex, more than a physical connection. It was two becoming one. I screamed his name as the waves broke and I felt his release inside me surging strong and sure.

How I wished I could have given him a child. A beauty

like Lily. Or a strong son to stand by his side against dangerous enemies. But turning vampire ended all hope for me ever
having children. Had killed his swimmers too. Lucky for
him he'd sired Lily before he'd been turned.

Death pulled at me, trying to claim me. But I resisted,
needing to hold him against my heart. Needing to press my
lips to his for one more moment. I loved this man, seemed
to have always loved him. Yes, he commanded me. But in
some ways I commanded him. We would call it a draw if this
were a game, neither of us the loser. I smiled as I fell on top
of him and let the darkness claim me.

"I can't meet him here." Penny paced around the living
room. "No amount of air freshener can mask the smell of
those rats. And I change the litter in their cages several times
a night!"

"I know you do." I looked her over with a critical eye.
Hair shining and bouncing in the new layered cut that still
hit her shoulders but curved toward her jaw to flatter her
round face. Her black sweater was a wrap that did nice things
to her figure. The tie at the waist promised a man that if he
tugged he'd get an even better view of the cleavage, courtesy
of a new push-up bra she'd picked up at the mall. Her black
and yellow print skirt stopped above her knees at just the
right spot to show off surprisingly trim legs. And, yes, I'd
talked her into some heels, but they weren't so high that she'd
fall on her face when she walked. Her pacing was practice.

"So you're meeting him in the shop again. How'd you
explain that?" I put my hand on Jerry's shoulder. He'd driven
me home and I'd nagged him into making our Saturday-
night date into a "let's follow Penny" excursion. Not that we
were telling her that.

"I told him we were repainting. In honor of my moving
in. That things were a mess." Penny wobbled for a moment,
looked down at her shoes, then sighed. "Maybe I should
change into my flats."

"No, you're doing fine." I glanced at Jerry. "Men love women in heels. Am I right?"

"Absolutely. They make your legs look longer. Very sexy. You look good tonight, Penny. Where's this man taking you?" Jerry squeezed my waist. He hadn't quit touching me ever since I'd walked out in my red dress with the plunging neckline and my black lizard high heels that said "Do me."

"He didn't say, but Jenny says his frat is having a party. Seems like that's where we'll go." Penny glanced at a silver watch on her wrist. It was delicate, a far cry from her usual black and functional one that could do everything from tell the room temperature to determine the altitude. This one merely gave her the time.

"Guess you'd better head down. Have fun. Jer and I may go to N-V. They're having a good band tonight and Rafe actually invited us." I smiled at Penny, not even feeling guilty as I told the lie. Which maybe wasn't. If she wound up this date in time, we were definitely giving the club a visit.

"You mean it? You're going to trust me to be around this guy without dogging me?" Penny picked up her black clutch, then stopped in front of me. She narrowed her gaze. "Yeah, right. Give it up, Glory. You're blocking your thoughts, which you usually don't bother to do. I know that effort gives you a headache."

"Busted. Fine. So I don't trust you yet. Do you blame me?" I stood and walked to the door. Jerry knew enough to keep silent, but he was right behind me.

"When am I going to get some privacy?" Penny's jaw was set, her eyes flashing.

"When you prove yourself." Jerry put his hand on her shoulder when it looked like Penny was getting a little too close. "Calm down, fledgling. Think about it. The man is a mortal, your favorite flavor from what Gloriana tells me. Even *she* would be tempted. And you've barely broken in your fangs. It makes sense that we'd feel compelled to 'dog' you awhile longer."

"Come on, Mr. Blade. How would you like to have someone trailing you on your dates? It's humiliating. I won't be able to relax and enjoy myself." Penny stomped her foot, then staggered. "Damn these shoes!"

"Sure you will enjoy yourself." I put my hand on Penny's elbow to help her regain her balance. "Forget we're around. We'll make sure no one, especially Josh, sees us. We have supersonic hearing, remember? We won't interfere unless we sense you're losing control."

"You swear?" Penny looked from me to Jerry. Her makeup was perfect and I almost said something. No, she'd get self-conscious and maybe go add a layer. Right now I wasn't exactly the one she wanted to please.

"Yes, we both swear. Out of sight, totally laying back. Josh will never know we're there." I held up my hand, then put it over my heart. Jerry grinned and did likewise. If there had been a Bible handy, we would have broken it out. "Now head out. We'll be down in a few." I watched her practically bolt out the door. Did she think she could make good an escape? As if.

"What's the plan? I really want to take you somewhere like the club. Wouldn't hurt my feelings to rub Valdez's nose in the fact that you're mine." Jerry dragged me close. "I'd kiss you, but I can see you took special care with your lipstick."

"Can the attitude." I shoved against his chest. "You are not, repeat, not rubbing Rafe's nose in anything. If you can't swear to be charming to my friend, I'll trail Penny on my own and you can be alone this Saturday night." I put my hands on my hips.

Jerry held his own hands up in surrender. "It was reflex. Didn't mean a thing. But I'm going to hate the shifter for a long while yet, Gloriana. He had you and he wants to have you again. It's there in his eyes every time he looks at you. You deny that?"

I felt my cheeks grow warm. And Jerry had his answer. He shook his head.

"So, to please you, I'll keep my comments and my fists to myself. And even take you to his damned club because there's nowhere else for vampires to go and be served a decent beverage. But don't expect me to be friends with the shifter."

"No, obviously that's never going to happen." I touched his jaw and felt the tension there. "I know being around him keeps you pretty tightly wound. And I'm sorry for it, but he's in my life to stay."

"You've made that very clear." He grabbed my hand. "I know better than to ask you to make a choice. So I'm working on keeping my anger under control. For you." He looked down at the shadow between my breasts and then up to my lips. "Damn, but I want to kiss you."

"Go ahead. And thanks. For trying, Jerry. It means a lot to me." I smiled and pulled his head down to mine. "I can always redo my lipstick in the car." I gave him a deep and satisfying kiss. Maybe not a smart move. It got Jerry going and might make us too late to catch Penny and Josh. But we finally came up for air and ran down the stairs. We were just in time to see Josh help her into that black SUV.

"Don't you want to go to your frat's party?" Penny was asking as he held the door for her.

"Naw. It's always the same old, same old. And that's getting to be a drag. Nothing but kegs and a DJ with the music too loud and everybody getting drunk. How about we go somewhere we can talk?" Josh slammed the door and walked around the car, whistling.

Both of us saw Penny's disappointed look before she pasted on a smile as Josh got into the vehicle.

I turned to Jerry. "Damn it, what he just described was the perfect frat party. The kind Penny's been dying to finally attend. Go somewhere to talk is code for 'Let's go parking and make out.'"

"How do you know that?" Jerry stared down at me.

"Never mind. Just run and get the car and pick me up here. I'm going to watch and see which way he goes." I tapped my foot. Damned user frat boy. Not go to his own party? It didn't take a mind reader to see where this was headed. Penny was going to be so upset and I had a feeling she'd already figured the whole thing out.

She'd told me she hadn't read his mind before. Well, I bet she was paging through that dipstick's frontal lobe right now. And getting steamed. No way should she be alone with him once he stopped the car. I anxiously watched the car head down Sixth Street. It turned right several blocks down just as Jerry roared up in his own SUV, black of course.

I jumped in the passenger side and told him where to turn. It didn't take us long to catch up but we stayed a few cars back. Josh's car had tinted windows and it was impossible to see what was going on inside, but I soon had a pretty good idea where they were headed and I couldn't believe it.

"Jerry, they're going back to where that creep dumped Penny, the hilltop where he abandoned her the night she was turned."

"You're kidding me. The man has to have shit for brains. What woman would find that romantic?" Jerry reached over and took my hand. "Do you think Penny suggested it?"

"Had to. If she's read his mind, she's bound to have figured out that Josh is a loser with some insecurities." I realized I was grinding my teeth.

"Insecurities? What do you mean?" Jerry made a turn as we left the main highway and followed a narrow track up the hill. He turned off his headlights, not really needing them with his vamp vision and clearly getting off on playing private eye as he tailed Josh.

"The guy obviously likes Penny, but doesn't have the guts to be seen with her. Because she's not the same size six that most girls the frat boys date are." I sighed and looked out the window as we bounced along, noticing the brush and trees that lined the rutted road. The isolation was either creepy or romantic depending on your agenda.

"That's ridiculous. She's very attractive. I've always been partial to redheads." Jerry reached over and tugged at one of my curls. "After blondes, of course."

"Thanks. But you're old-school, Jer. Bless your blind eyes

and Neanderthal outlook. Josh is a twenty-first-century guy and he wants someone model-thin on his arm. At least in front of his posse." I ran my tongue over my fangs, down at the thought of that idiot's attitude and how he was hurting Penny. My vulnerable fledgling's new fangs were probably already aimed at Josh's jugular. And she'd drain him dry unless we got there in time to stop her.

"He's ashamed to be seen with our Penny?" Jerry's hands tightened on the steering wheel. "That bastard! I'll teach him to toy with a woman's affections."

We were nearing the clearing where Penny had lost her mortality. Sure enough, she and Josh were already out of the car and he was lying flat on the ground, staring up at her like he couldn't believe she'd managed to put him there. Jerry pulled the car to a stop and we both jumped out.

"Stop! Penny, what are you going to do?" I ran up to her. Jerry was on her other side but neither of us touched her. She had tears running down her cheeks and a shoe in each hand.

"Help! The chick's gone psycho on me. First, she says let's go park, then she throws me to the ground and threatens me."

"Death by Payless?" I snickered. "Were you scared, fella? How'd a little thing like Penny manage to throw you anywhere?"

"Caught me by surprise is all." Josh wouldn't look at us. He just got to his feet, keeping a good distance between himself and Penny, and brushed off his expensive khakis. "What are you doing here? Oh, never mind. Guess that's obvious. This is a prime make-out spot. But I'm not letting her get in my car again. Can you take her home?"

"You thinking of abandoning your date? Up here?" Jerry grabbed Josh by the front of his designer shirt.

"What else can I do? She's nuts. Look at her. She tried to put a high heel into my skull." Josh's eyes were saucers as he focused on Jerry. "Uh, what the hell's going on here?" He'd finally noticed Jerry's fangs. And, yes, they were huge.

"I'd say you are about to enjoy a little payback for disrespecting Miss Penny here." Jerry lifted Josh by his shirt and deposited him in front of Penny. "Do what you will, Penny. I certainly won't stop you."

"Jerry! I'm supposed to be mentoring Penny. 'What you will' sounds a little too much like carte blanche." I put my hand on Penny's shoulder. She was shaking.

"You think I'm going to kill him?" She managed a laugh. "As if."

"What? Kill me? No, hell no." Josh struggled but Jerry wasn't letting him go. When the fancy shirt ripped, Jer just shifted his grip to the man's arms, which made Josh screech.

"Settle down. It'll only hurt for a short while. Then . . . nothing. If you're lucky." Jerry smiled at me. "Gloriana, I believe you were given a description of hell recently. Will Josh here enjoy it?"

"Doubt it. Seems there are all kinds of upgrades. Fiery furnace is out. New tortures are in. The punishment fits the crime." I gave Josh a thorough head to toe. "Nice-looking. Demons will go for you. So I'd guess if you're an asshole in life . . . ? Well, I just don't want to think about what the lowlifes in hell would think you'd earned as your reward down there." I had no pity to spare for Josh as he began gulping back sobs.

"He was ashamed to be seen with me, Glory." Penny dropped her shoes and stepped into them, then turned to look at me, her eyes bleak. "That theater in a mall halfway across Austin? To a movie that none of his frat brothers would be caught dead seeing? It was all so no one would catch him with that fat girl he'd invited to the Ugly Chick party."

"No, I didn't mean it. I liked that movie. It was the only place it was still playing." Josh took a big, watery gulp of courage. "You want to go to the party? Let's go. You and me, right n-n-now."

"Too little, too late." Penny wheeled around and got in his face. "Listen to me, Joshua. I can read your thoughts. Get it? Yeah, I'm a genuine freak. Something you've never seen before. And something you won't remember after I get through with you." She glanced at me. "I haven't totally lost my mind, Glory."

"Good to know." I stayed out of this, pretty sure Penny was in control.

"F-f-freak?" Josh craned his neck, trying to get another look at Jerry's fangs. His eyes rolled back in his head and I thought he was going to faint, but he had more stones than I'd given him credit for. He gasped when he glanced back at Penny. Now she was letting her own fangs show and they were glistening in the moonlight.

"Yep, I'm a vampire. Newly made the night you dumped me out here." She poked him in his chest. "I drink blood and your type is extra delicious." She opened her purse, pulled out a timer, set it and handed it to me, then jerked his hand to her mouth and sank her fangs into the vein at his wrist.

"My God! My God!" Josh screamed and the sound echoed over the hilltop.

"Got to admit, he's taking this better than I would have thought," Jerry said conversationally.

"Yes, and Penny is keeping her head." I patted her on the back. "Good job, fledgling."

Josh stared at me wild-eyed. "This is not happening. Bad acid. Maybe one of the guys slipped something into my water bottle."

"Sure, Josh, that's it." I grinned and winked. "And that sucking sound Penny is making? That's a vampire version of a hickey on your wrist. You headed up here with the bright idea that you could make out with her, then take her home. Maybe take it all the way this time. Fat chicks have to be desperate. Am I right?"

"No. I offered to take her somewhere." He jerked when the timer buzzed.

Penny dropped his arm and raised her head, sighing with pleasure before she took the timer from me, opened her purse and dropped it in. Then she pulled out a wipe, tore it open and blotted the blood off her mouth.

"Delicious. What a shame this didn't work out. I was sure he'd make a good pet. But who needs this kind of douche bag for any purpose?" She glared at Josh. "Yes, he offered to take me somewhere. Let's see. Bowling at a lane on the other side of Austin. Or maybe we could hit a game room, same area." She closed her purse with a snap. "Meanwhile, all his buds are living it up at the frat house with a live band, no DJ, and open bar. Forget the keg."

"How did you—" Josh winced when Penny jabbed a finger into his midriff.

"Shut the hell up, you lying loser. My sister is going to that party. My *twin* sister. I thought we'd meet up there. Guess we won't now." She abruptly turned her back on him so that he wouldn't see the tears that suddenly filled her eyes. "I've had enough fun. Let's get out of here."

"Two things you need to do first, Penny." I was still in mentor mode. "Remember?"

"Oh, yeah." She blinked, then turned and grabbed his wrist. He tried to wrench free but it was useless. She sneered, then licked the puncture marks closed and they disappeared. Finally, she sighed. "I really wish he could remember this. The whole lesson."

"Let me take over." I gently moved her out of the way. I stared into Josh's eyes until he was under the whammy. "Josh, you brought Penny to this hilltop thinking to score but she told you off. Told you that she had figured out you were a loser and she could do way better. Then she got a ride home with friends who'd followed her up here so she wouldn't have to waste another minute with you." I turned him toward his car. "Now you're going to get in your SUV and you're driving straight to the frat house. There you're going to tell all your frat brothers and everyone else at the party that your heart is broken because the beautiful Penny Patterson dumped you on your sorry ass. Got that?"

"Penny dumped me? Heartbroken. Must tell all the brothers." Josh nodded and walked to his car. He started it and headed down the gravel road.

"Wow. He'll do it? He'll tell the whole frat that we dated and I dumped him?" Penny was actually smiling now.

"Yes, indeed. Our power of suggestion isn't. A suggestion, anyway. It's a command." I hooked my arm through hers and shared a smile with Jerry. "Now get in the car and fix your face. Jerry and I are taking you to N-V with us. You look too cute to waste it and I want to dance. I bet Trey gets a break sometime tonight and he'll want to dance too."

I gasped when Penny crushed me to her in a hug. "Glory, how can I ever thank you? I thought this was going to be the worst night of my life and you just turned it around."

"The night is young." I climbed into the car and checked my own lipstick in the makeup mirror. What a rush. First time to do that in a car. Jerry winked at me, easily reading my mind. Too bad it reminded me of the demons and that issue yet to resolve.

"Yes, Penny, Gloriana and I have learned that a night can turn to crap in a heartbeat." Jerry patted my knee, then started the car.

"Amen to that, Jer. Amen to that." I sighed and put my lipstick away. It would be too much to hope that we could just enjoy an uneventful night out.

Fourteen

"It's a good thing you know the owner." Rafe grinned at me as he had one of his shifters squeeze a table into a corner of the balcony. "I wouldn't do this for anyone else."

"And I appreciate it." I saw Jerry slip a tip to the man who put our spot together. "Thanks, Rafe. You sure it's okay if Penny just sits at the bar? It won't get Trey in trouble?"

"No, he's one of my most reliable guys. And he has a break coming up. He seems into Penny, was really glad to see her." Rafe quit smiling as Jerry put his arm around me. "I'll send you a waiter. Got to go."

"Appreciate the table, Valdez." Jerry held out my chair.

"Whatever makes Glory happy." Rafe nodded and headed downstairs.

"Gee, is it chilly in here?" I rubbed my arms.

"You expect me to be friends with the man?" Jerry sat and moved close enough to lean against me. "Never happening. I did thank him. And I can keep you warm if you're really cold. Though the heat from all these mortals is getting to me. We'd better order some synthetic before I give in to my urges that you don't approve of." He looked significantly at the next table where a rowdy group of men and women were obviously not on their first round of drinks. Definitely mortal and even tempting to me.

I put my hand on Jerry's arm. "Yes, order something. I don't want to worry if you head to the men's room and are gone too long." I glanced around the packed club and over the railing, where bodies positively seethed to the loud music. A band that had just hit the charts with their latest single was scheduled to perform in a few minutes and there was still a line at the door with people willing to pay for standing room.

Jerry signaled a waitress just as I heard the hum of my cell phone vibrating in my purse on the table. I pulled it out, checked the caller ID, and grinned. "Guess who." I answered the call. "Flo! Where are you?"

"Ricardo and I just got back in town. Where are you? I want to tell you all about our honeymoon." She laughed. "Well, not *all* about it. But we went to the most beautiful island. *Stupendo!*"

"Jerry and I just got to N-V." I looked around. I bet two more chairs could fit at our table. "Why don't you come over? The band should start in about thirty minutes. There's going to be dancing."

"On our way. I missed you, *amiga*." Flo laughed. "Ricardo is frowning. Doesn't want to get dressed. As if he wore much of anything on that island. I'll get him there if I have to drag him by . . . Never mind. He is throwing on clothes. Ciao!"

I was smiling as I turned to Jerry. "You heard?"

"So Flo and Richard are back. Then maybe she can talk you out of this nonsense of helping Valdez with the demons." Jerry had leaned in and spoke softly so that no one nearby could hear.

"Don't start, please. Can't we just enjoy the night?" I touched his cheek. "When you order drinks get the kind with alcohol. I wouldn't mind a little buzz." I looked up when one of Rafe's paranormal waitresses appeared at Jerry's elbow. He placed our order, then stood.

"Fine. Let's dance." The lights had dimmed and the song

was a slow one. Jerry gave me a hungry look that made me wiggle in my chair. "I want to hold you. That dress is driving me crazy. I can't wait to see what you have or don't have on under it later."

"Good to know." I smiled at him and held his hand as we walked downstairs. Earlier, I'd watched him get dressed in his dark trousers and white silk shirt. The open throat showed off his strong tanned chest. He looked pretty yummy himself and turned more than a few heads.

Downstairs, I was happy to see Penny dancing with Trey. They held each other close and were obviously feeling some chemistry. Good for her. She needed a guy showing her some appreciation after the humiliating experience with Josh.

Jerry and I danced to two songs before I felt a presence nearby. I turned and Flo grabbed me, dragging me off the dance floor. Richard and Jerry just shook their heads and followed us.

"Tell me everything." I laughed as Jerry went to find someone to bring us two more chairs.

"Aye, *Dio*. My husband outdid himself. We went to this little island in the Pacific. We had our own private cabana, our love nest. Eh, Ricardo?" She held out her hand to Richard.

Her tall husband looked more than pleased with himself. "It was that. I made sure Florence had some shopping close by too. I know my bride."

"Yes, the sweetest designer boutiques." Flo ran a hand down her size-six body. "You like my dress? My shoes? I got them there." She looked perfect in a copper silk sheath that hugged her curves and ended midthigh. Her heels were designer cages made of three kinds of metal. Only my friend could have walked in them and not fallen on her face.

"You look great." I wondered what Flo would do if offered the chance to see herself in a mirror. What a temptation that would be. But Richard was a former priest and still very into the church. And Flo herself would be horrified that I'd been approached by the demons. She'd been the leader in the exorcism that had finally managed to get Alesa out of me.

I was blocking my thoughts, of course, and glanced around. If Caryon or Spyte picked up on them, would they get the idea that Flo might be open to a deal with the Devil? No, no, no. I felt like making the sign of the cross or something but knew better than to let Flo see me upset.

Flo just kept talking as the table was rearranged, more drinks were ordered and we all settled down. "We were close to entertainment too. I know you can't, but we went gambling and I won! This honeymoon was lucky for me."

"No, I can't gamble, can't even handle a nickel slot machine without trying to pour my life savings into it." I sighed. I have this addiction. One of the reasons I'd left Las Vegas. It had taken twelve steps and years of paying off credit cards to break me of that dangerous habit.

"Well, there were shows in the casinos too. Great entertainment. We had many choices of whatever we wanted to do." Flo smiled and looked at Richard. "Not that we left the cabana all that often."

"Nice job." Jerry slapped Richard on the back.

"I have to say I highly recommend honeymoons. It seems to stimulate . . ." Richard looked up with relief when the waitress arrived with our drinks. "Anyway, if you and Glory want the name of the island. I'll e-mail it to you."

Jerry glanced at me. "It would be nice to get away for a while. Do that."

"You know I can't leave things here. Certainly not my business again. I already took one trip recently. That one to Los Angeles." I looked up when I saw Penny approaching us. "Here comes someone I want you to meet, Flo." I held out my hand. "Penny, this is my best bud, Florence da Vinci Mainwaring and her husband Richard. Flo, this is Penny Patterson, a fledgling I'm mentoring for the council."

Richard and Jerry had jumped to their feet, forever gentlemen. Penny grinned at them. "Sit, please. I'm happy to meet you, Mr. and Mrs. Mainwaring. I'm living in your old bedroom, Mrs. Mainwaring. Ruining it actually."

"What's this?" Flo looked at me. "And call us Florence

and Richard. We may be old, centuries, you understand." She glanced at the tables surrounding us and laughed. "Kidding. But we look young. No?"

"Yes." Penny was checking out Flo's jewelry, which had probably come from yet another boutique. The chunky necklace was obviously one of a kind and very expensive. "Young and very stylish."

"Thank you. I have made it my life's work." Flo put her hand to her dark hair, swept into an updo to show off the matching earrings.

"Trust me, she has. I have the bills to prove it. But I'm not complaining. I get to be seen with her." Richard laughed. "Won't you join us?"

"Well, thanks. But I really need to talk to my mentor. Glory, if you could come down to the employee break room with me for a minute? I hate to interrupt your party, but . . ." Penny squeezed her purse, crimping the leather.

"No, I'll come with you." I got up and grabbed my own purse. "Be right back. I'm so glad you came to me, Penny." I sent Jerry a mental message to come after me if I was gone more than ten minutes. "See you soon." I leaned down and hugged Flo, then Richard. "So glad you're back. Off to mentor." I gave them a wave, then followed Penny. She was obviously upset and this couldn't still be Josh, could it? She'd seemed to be having a good time with Trey.

We hit the door of the employee break room and, with the band scheduled to start in a few minutes, it was empty. Penny collapsed on a gray sofa.

"Jenny texted me a few minutes ago. Josh actually followed your orders. He went back to that party and told everyone I dumped him. She said the guys razzed him and he defended me. Declared I was beautiful and might even be the one for him. But he'd blown it, been a jerk." She had tears in her eyes. "I just can't believe it."

I sat beside her. "Believe it. That's how the vampire whammy works. We can wipe out memories and plant new ones. Mortals are pretty much putty in our hands. We have tremendous power, Penny." I squeezed her hand. "Are you thinking of taking Josh back?"

"No. I can see now that a mortal and a vampire can't work. We're from two different worlds and I'd be too tempted to drink from him, then manipulate his mind." She slumped against the cushions. "But imagine having a man you could make do whatever you wanted."

"That would be a first." Penny and I exchanged wry smiles, woman to woman. "But I'm honest enough with myself to know I'd never be happy with a man I could push around." I made a face. "So I get things like fistfights in my living room."

"And new furniture." Penny laughed. "I'd say you do more than all right in the man department. You're my role model." She nodded. "So I'm moving on. To Trey. He's got his own powers and we have fun. I can relax around him and don't have to worry about hiding my fangs." Penny put her hand on my arm. "He asked me to go out with him after the club closes tonight. Some of the people who work here are having a party. I may not come home afterwards. Do you think I'd be safe if I, uh, died at his place? For the day?"

"If he were a vampire, I'd say no problem. But a shifter wouldn't have the precautions you need. To keep out the daylight. I'm not about to tell you how to run your love life." I patted her hand. "If you're ready to go there, have at it, but you'd better ask him to get you home before dawn. Just to be on the safe side."

"Yes, I guess you're right." Penny frowned. "Why's this vampire thing have to be so complicated?"

"Just is. And maybe Trey's been around long enough to know how to take care of a vampire during daylight hours." I knew a rebound when I saw it but then again Penny had never really had a relationship with Josh, just a couple of dates. If getting close to Trey made her feel better, so be it. "But why take that chance?"

"You're right. And we may not . . . Well, I'll see what happens." Penny put her purse down beside her and looked me straight in the eyes. "Glory, the real reason I asked you down here is that Jenny's on her way. I texted her that I was at N-V and could probably get her and her date in. She was all over it and insisted she was coming to join me." Penny lost her nerve and looked away.

"Penny, what are you thinking?" I grabbed her shoulders and made her face me again.

"I'm thinking it's time I told her the truth. About what I am. See if she wants to join the club." Penny's eyes filled. Oh, great. Here came the waterworks.

"Not tonight. You've got the date with Trey to look forward to. Telling her now would totally screw that up. Put the Jenny thing off. Maybe tell her tomorrow night. Ask her over after the rats are gone. Better yet, after you get settled in with your job with Ian. And after the semester ends. Doesn't she have final exams coming up?" I was trotting out every delay tactic I could come up with.

"Oh, gosh, you're right. I totally spaced on that. With the lab closed, I'm out of the loop at school. And there's the dinner with Mom and Dad. Jenny would never be able to keep this kind of secret from them." Penny sagged against the sofa cushions. "Wow. Thanks for talking me down, Glory. It's just that Jen and I have been so close all our lives and I hate to see us grow apart like this with a monster secret between us."

I kept my opinion to myself. Which was that a "close" sister would have helped Penny look a heck of a lot better than the Penny who'd arrived on my doorstep. And it wasn't as if my fledgling didn't want to look good. She'd taken every bit of my wardrobe advice to heart and had been thrilled with the way she'd attracted male attention since then. Made me wonder why the perfect Jenny hadn't steered her sister along the same path.

"Fine. So you can introduce Jenny to Trey tonight. Won't that be a rush? He's cute. On top of Josh's big confession, it's become obvious that you're turning into a regular femme fatale." I grinned at her. "And you can always whammy her again if Jenny sees something she shouldn't here." I got up. "I need to get back to my friends. Are you okay now?"

"Guess so." Penny grabbed her purse. "I want to watch the band. It's starting soon and I need to get with Trey and arrange for Jen and her date to get in." She jumped up and hugged me. "Thanks for talking me off the ledge, Glory. I get so overwhelmed sometimes. You know?"

I patted her back. "Sure I do." I thought about the demons and how pressured I felt. "I really do. One word of advice. Don't go to the bathroom with Jenny. No reflection in those mirrors and wouldn't that raise questions? And of course there will be a bunch of other mortals in there too. Not only will you have the mirror thing to explain but—"

"Bloodlust." Penny made a face. "I'm doing better. Honest. The bartender is a vamp and he's been pumping me full of synthetic. He's cute too. If this thing with Trey doesn't work out . . ." She opened her purse and pulled out a cocktail napkin. "He gave me his number." She grinned. "What is it with these paranormals? Don't they notice the junk in my trunk?"

I laughed. "Lucky for us, a lot of them are ancient and have that old-time love of a well-rounded woman. And I don't mean a woman with a lot of interests." I hooked arms with her. "Now get out of here, have fun, but be careful. I'll want a full report tomorrow night."

"Thanks, Glory." She opened the door, then took off.

I was feeling really ancient myself as I walked out of the room and ran straight into Rafe.

"Oh, hey, I was hoping I'd get a chance to see you without your lord and master." Rafe looked me over with an appreciative smile. "You look amazing tonight. New dress?"

"Yes, Penny and I hit the mall. And thanks. But not for the lord and master slam. You know that wasn't nice." I backed up, pressed against the wall when Rafe moved close to let a group of giggling college students go past on their way to the ladies' room.

"You let Blade get away with that possessive crap, so I

figured you got off to it." Rafe didn't move back now that the hall was clear, just stayed in my space.

"No, but some battles just aren't worth fighting." I put my hand on his chest with the intention of pushing him away.

"I get that, I so get that." He dug in his jeans pocket. "Here, I have something that belongs to you. Taking it was stupid. I realized that after the fact. It was something Blade would do."

I looked down and saw the vial Ian had given me. "What? You stole this out of my apartment?"

"Yeah. Protecting you from yourself." Rafe made a face. "I said it was stupid. But you know how I feel about Ian's shit. You had bad side effects from his diet drug. Remember?"

"Sure I do. But good ones from his daylight thing. It worked and it was amazing, my glimpse of the sun was longer than Ian's clients usually get. Still, it was too short for the cost." I sighed. "I can't believe you took this, Rafe. What were you thinking?"

"Wasn't. It was me doing the bodyguard gig. Can't seem to drop the act, you know?" He gave me a rueful smile. "Now I'm giving it back, but I'd like to know what in the hell it's for. Come on, Glory. What is that drug going to do for you? And you said Penny has a vial too. You're actually condoning your fledgling taking Ian's drug? Wonder what the council would say about that." Rafe stared at me with a mixture of accusation, concern and, okay, a bit of a threat.

"You going to rat me out? Oh, cute, rat, yeah, I should sue the damned council for sticking me with a fledgling who brings home fifty-three freaking rats." I glared at Rafe. "I can't believe you'd do that, Rafe. Seriously."

"No, I'm not going to tell anyone what you're up to. But I wish you'd confide in me. Let me be around when you take whatever this is. In case there's fallout." Rafe was all concern now, his hand on my shoulder.

"I appreciate your protective instincts. I do." I felt the steam go right out of me. "But Penny's a scientist and Ian is

offering her a job. I don't think he'd be poisoning her. Right?"
I waited for Rafe's reluctant nod. "So just trust me now and
back off." The truth was I knew I was probably taking a chance
with this drug of Ian's. We did have a history and Rafe had
been a witness to the side effects Ian's concoctions could have
on me. But for the chance to enjoy real food and sit around
eating with mortals, like I was part of a family . . . Something
inside me just couldn't turn down that opportunity.

"Backing off." He held out his hands and took two steps
away from me. "Do what you want. You have my number. If
this goes down poorly, though, I hope you'll call me." He
shook his head. "Yeah, I'm a fucking glutton for punishment." He turned and I knew he'd be gone in a moment.

I blinked back tears and grabbed his arm. "Stop."

He looked down at my hand. "Why?"

"You're just being a good friend. Don't think I don't appreciate it. It's just—" I sniffed.

"That you're going to do whatever the hell you want to
do." Rafe shook his head. "I hope you don't regret it."

"Me too. I, uh, thanks for caring." I let him go when a
waiter called his name from the end of the hall.

He said something over his shoulder, then rubbed his
thumb over my cheek. "Yes, I care. But it would be better for
us both if I didn't." He gave me a crooked grin, then strode
off down the hall.

I took a shaky breath, stuffed the vial into my purse, then
pulled out my compact. I hated to think that he was right.
Where would I be if Rafe suddenly didn't give a damn what
I did? Could I be indifferent to him? Not a chance in the
world. I looked down the hall but he'd disappeared into the
crowd. I opened the compact, figuring the best I could do
right now was repair the damage the last few moments had
done to my makeup. I sure wasn't going to solve any of my
major issues standing here.

"Gloriana St. Clair. What are you doing?"

I glanced up from powdering my shiny nose. Flo gaped at
me from a few feet away.

"Uh, fixing my face." I snapped the compact shut.

"I saw you look into the mirror and wipe lipstick off the corner of your mouth. Like you could see it." Flo grabbed the compact, opened it and stared into the mirror. "Pah! No magic there." She held it up to me and gasped. "No, I don't believe it." She waved it in front of me, then in front of her, back and forth five or six times, testing it.

The same group of students surged out of the bathroom again and I pulled Flo into that empty break room.

"Come here. Let me explain." I really didn't want to, but what choice did I have?

"Jeremiah got up to come see about you, but I insisted it was a woman's matter so I came instead. And I find this!" Flo staggered over to the couch and collapsed. "You tell me. How did you get a reflection, Glory?"

"Uh, well, I—" I stammered, not sure where to start.

"Let me, dear girl." Caryon shimmered into view, Spyte by his side. The room filled with a cloud of sweetness that tonight had a hint of cinnamon.

"You like? We followed you to the mall, Glory. They make those giant cinnamon rolls. They smell sooo delicious. It does give us a little something extra, don't you think? To add a little flavoring?" Spyte settled next to Flo on the couch. "Picked up a few souls while we were there. Those crafty creatures who man the carts. Very eager to make a deal for extra profits, don't you know." He smiled at Flo, showing her his mouthful of fangs.

"Get away from me, you hell creature!" She jumped up and grabbed my arm. "Glory, what are they doing here?"

"They are the ones who gave me my reflection. They're trying to persuade me to do Lucifer's work. To get me to harvest souls for him."

"Hah! You are barking up the wrong tree stump here, you creatures from the black lagoon! You monsters from the depths of wherever!" Flo clutched me to her bosom, so overwrought she wrinkled her dress. "You cannot have my BFF. Go back where you came from. Roast your skinny asses somewhere else." Flo's eyes were shining and she actually stomped her foot, her metal shoe rattling.

"Now, Florence, is that any way to talk to someone who could make your own dreams come true?" Caryon's voice was smooth as butter melting over a stack of pancakes.

I eased away from Flo and looked into her eyes. "Careful now, Flo. Don't listen to him. He's going to give you his sales pitch." I gasped when I felt a sucker punch in the stomach. I looked down. Nothing there, but Spyte blew on his fist, like maybe he'd done it with the power of his thoughts. As if a little pain could stop me. But he sent me a mental message to watch my mouth or I could be a statue in a heartbeat. Okay, I got that.

"Sales pitch? I have resisted the best saleswomen in the world, you dung-heap dweller!" Flo stalked up to Caryon and had the nerve to poke him in his chest with a copper-lacquered nail. "I have listened to them claim I looked good in chiffon poofs. Hah! You think I didn't know better? Poofs on my butt? 'Try them,' they said. 'Exquisite.' Unloading last year's rejects. I see through that. And I see through you."

"But I see through you, dear lady." Caryon ignored Flo's finger stabbing and grinned at me. "Such spirit. Such fire. She will soon be Lucifer's favorite."

I started to say something but Spyte hit me again, a real stomach burner, and I gasped, breathless and speechless.

"Oh, yes, all your dreams will come true, dear lady." Caryon sighed. "Just think for a minute."

"What are you talking about? I have everything I ever dreamed of. A wonderful husband, a new house with the most magnificent closet—" Flo grabbed my arm. "Glory, I didn't tell you. While we were gone, Ricardo had the bedroom next to the master made into this closet. It *is* a dream. All organized and filled with my things. *Magnifico!*"

"Yes, Glory, you really should see it." Spyte danced around the room, finally landing right in front of Flo. "It even has a three-way mirror at one end. So the lady of the house can see herself from every angle." He pulled a face. "Except the designer didn't know that *this* lady can't see a damned thing, can she, Florence?"

"What a shame." Caryon studied the polish on his brown wingtip shoes. His suit was a cream silk, his tie a brown, peach and silver work of art. "And that meant you left the house tonight with a thread dangling loose on the back of your skirt."

"No!" Flo twisted, trying to see what Cary was talking about. "Glory, look, is there . . . ?"

"How do you know what's in her house?" Suddenly I was allowed to speak.

"Basic research, Glory dear." Cary inspected his perfectly manicured nails. "I can describe the homes of all of your nearest and dearest. Right down to whether their toilet paper rolls over or under."

"Glory, please. Is there a thread?" Flo grabbed my arm.

This time my stomach heaved without Spyte's help. Demons spying on all my friends? Flo's nails dug into my skin so I glanced and, sure enough, a thread stuck out from the center back seam.

"Yes." I sighed. "Sorry, Flo. I can't pull it or it might damage the fabric, make it pucker."

"I am not *perfetto*!" Her eyes filled.

"Of course you're not. How can you be when you can't ever see the total picture?" Caryon smiled, never letting his true ugly nature show. "Look at me. I'm wearing a custom-tailored Italian suit. My suit, my tie, every part of my outfit is perfectly fitted and coordinated. And, of course, my hair is just right. I hate to tell you, but the back of your updo is a giant don't." This time his smile showed just a hint of fang.

"What? Glory?" Flo put frantic fingers to the back of her hair.

"Okay, Cary, cut it out. When she got here, her hair was fine. You obviously messed with it." I could see that, yes, he'd done a number on her hair, turning it into a rat's nest. "Relax, Flo, you can fix it."

"Stop torturing me." Flo's lips quivered. "I will never

help a demon. I am good. My husband is a saint. There is no way I can work for the Devil. Go away."

"Of course. No problem." Spyte pointed at the full-length mirror on the back of the door and Flo shrieked.

Suddenly, she could see herself, from head to toe. "*Mio Dio.* Is it me, Glory?"

"Yes, Flo." I glared at Spyte. "What's up? Why are you doing this? I told you to leave my friends alone."

"And we obey you because?" Spyte laughed. "Come on, this one looks like an easy takedown."

Flo was busy with her purse, reapplying her lipstick, fussing with her eyebrows and straightening her hair. She leaned closer to inspect her skin.

"Flo, honey, step away from the mirror." I walked up behind her and grasped her shoulders.

"Look at us, Glory." She smiled at our reflections. "We are beautiful, no?"

"Yes, you are, anyway. But this is the Devil's handiwork. These guys are trying to lure you over to the dark side. What would Richard say?" I tried to pull her back but she wasn't budging and she ignored what I'd said completely.

"I think I look old. Do you have any idea how many hundreds of years it has been since I've seen myself? I had forgotten . . ." She leaned forward, peering intently at her teeth, her fangs. "This is not good. I must get some of those whitening strips, I think."

"Flo, listen to me. This is a slippery slope." I looked around but Cary and Spyte had disappeared, obviously sure that they'd laid the groundwork. I was afraid they were right.

"You must come to my house. See my new closet. After the band and the dancing." She finally dragged her eyes from the mirror. "See, the *diavolos* are gone. It is a little gift. I don't know why they are toying with me and I don't care. If they can see through me, they must know I am not going to do anything for *them*. Ever. But, in the meantime, they gave both of us a reflection. We can enjoy it and not feel guilty." She grinned and bounced on her weird metal shoes. "I am happy.

We will go to my house and see ourselves in the three-way mirror. Just wait."

I followed Flo upstairs, amazed that she could chatter with the men and fool even her husband into thinking that everything was normal. Demons never did anything without expecting payback. If Flo thought she could just enjoy her reflection and not suffer for it? Well, I could tell her there was no way in hell that was happening.

It took some doing, but we got the guys settled into Richard's man cave in front of his big-screen TV and a car race before Flo and I headed upstairs to see her closet. This was the first time I'd been to Flo and Richard's new house and I was impressed. It was obviously expensive, on a hilltop with a spectacular view of the lights of the city.

"Damian found it for us. You know my brother owns houses everywhere in Austin. He sold it to Ricardo for a good price." Flo was practically running as she headed upstairs. "This is the master bedroom." She threw open double doors. A king-size bed dominated the large space. There was a terrace and balcony off the bedroom to take advantage of that view, but I could see automatic blackout drapes that would close at sunrise.

"It's gorgeous." I wasn't lying. The cream and gold room was decorated with fine antiques, and an Oriental rug covered most of the hardwood floor. My fingers itched to touch some of the lacquered boxes that rested on the long dresser, not to mention the jade and ivory carvings displayed in a tall shelving unit.

"The pretty pieces from the Orient are Ricardo's. He's collected for centuries. One of his hobbies. I had no idea when I married him that he had so much in storage." Flo threw this information over her shoulder as she hurried to another set of double doors. "There's a decadent bathroom over there with a Jacuzzi tub, steam shower, you name it, and a closet I gave to Richard." She sighed and paused for dramatic effect. "But this is mine, all mine." She threw open the doors.

My jaw dropped. What had obviously been a good-size bedroom was now a walk-in closet painted in shades of cream and turquoise. It had shelves for purses and shoes with racks for dresses, pants and blouses. A dozen drawers were closed but labeled and I could see that she had many for lingerie, scarves and belts.

Flo had made a beeline for the three-way mirror at the end of the room. It was flanked by large windows with their own blackout drapes.

"Look at me. Ah, scissors." She pulled out a shallow drawer filled with every kind of manicure accessory and found a pair of sharp scissors. "Will you cut off the thread? Carefully, of course. I have to go back to the men wearing this same dress."

"Sure. Stand still." I said this because Flo was so hyped on adrenaline, she was practically vibrating. I clipped the offending thread, then handed her the scissors. "This closet is the most amazing thing I've ever seen."

"Isn't it? You see why I love Ricardo so much? He understands me and indulges my passions." She winked at me. "All of them."

"You are very lucky." I unzipped her when she gestured for me to. "What now?"

"I've got to see myself in . . ." She began going through her racks. "Oh, which one first? My wedding dress. The most special night of my life." She blinked as tears filled her eyes. "No, what if I think I could have done better? This? I wore it to a coronation. No, no, I'd better hurry. What if they take this away?" She began flipping through dresses, becoming almost manic until she tried holding a few up in front of the mirror.

"This color! What was I thinking?" She crammed the dress into a small trash can but I rescued it. Definitely could sell it in the shop.

"I did the same thing, Flo. Gold. Not my color." I settled

on a zebra-print velvet bench in the middle of the room. "Take a breath and try something on." I had to admit, seeing my tiny friend running around in a bra and bikini panties was depressing. She was so totally unaware of her body. And why not? From where I sat, it was perfect.

"You are right. Calm, must stay calm." She patted her cheeks and sat at the built-in vanity. "Makeup. I should never wear a coral blush again. Rose or pink, I think." She turned from the mirror to me. "This is a wonderful thing. This reflection."

My stomach sank. "No, Flo, it's an evil thing. From the Devil. Demons gave it to you and they can take it away." My throat started to close. "Uh, try on a dress." This came out as a croak.

"Yes. One I bought last week. Those clerks." Flo made a hand gesture as she jumped up and dug into her dress section one more time. "They will say anything to make a sale."

"Well, thanks a lot. I'm a clerk too, you know. I've been known to tell the truth and lose a sale." My voice was back. I guess as long as I didn't dis the demons, I was good to go. Flo stopped with the dress in her hand and gazed at herself in her underwear.

"*Aye de mi.* What is this?" She looked down and grabbed the skin at her waist. "I am fat!"

"Don't cry to me." I laughed. "Honey, if that little bit is fat, then I'm an elephant." I shook my head. "Just put on the dress. I'm sure Richard doesn't complain about your waist-line."

"No, of course not. He's not stupid. But what does he know?" She stepped into the dress and backed up to me so I could zip her up. She turned and faced the mirror. "I knew it. I hate it. The print makes my butt look huge."

I'd glanced at the price tag still hanging from it. I didn't know what currency they'd been using, but it obviously wasn't cheap.

"First, your butt isn't huge and couldn't look that way if

you tried. And, second, that blue is really your color. Third? No one is going to be focusing on your butt with the front dipping that low between your boobs."

"True. I do have good breasts." Flo turned this way and that. "I still can't believe I can see myself. This is amazing." She turned to me. "How about you, Glory? Don't you love it?"

"Not so much. Because I know with demons, there's always payback." I jumped when Caryon and Spyte suddenly appeared in front of me.

"So glad you brought that up, Glory." Cary waved his hand and Flo's reflection vanished. "Playtime is over, pay time is here."

"What? No!" Flo ran up to the mirror and patted it, finally pressing her nose against the glass. "What have you done?" She whirled and glared at the demons. "Get out of here. If my husband smells demons in this house, he will get out his holy water."

"She's right." I frowned at Spyte, who was picking through Flo's blouse collection and had settled on a bright yellow one with green trim. "And Richard's is the real deal. It really hurt Alesa. What would Lucifer say if you were sent back in a steaming pile and landed right in his lap?"

"Don't think you want Richard interfering, do you, Florence?" Cary strolled up to her and plucked at her dress with a black claw. "You'd never see your reflection again."

"What do you want?" Flo glanced at Spyte. "Get away from my clothes."

"You have exquisite taste. Lucifer would love you." Spyte giggled as he threw her blouse up in the air, then ripped it apart with his claws. "I do so hope you do the right thing."

"I told you to leave my friends alone!" I started to jump up but, wouldn't you know, Cary waved his hand in my direction and I was stuck on the bench, solid as a rock. When I tried to scream, my mouth was sealed shut. Oh, man, did I hate this. Now I was going to have to just sit and pray that Flo had the will to resist what these demons had to offer.

"Ignore Glory, Florence." Cary pulled an envelope out of his pocket. "Now, here's all you have to do to keep that reflection you're so fond of." He pulled out a piece of expensive paper and the envelope disappeared while a red pen appeared in his other hand.

"What is it?" Flo glanced back behind her, to make sure her reflection was still gone. Her hands were trembling and not just because Spyte had moved on to her dresses and was humming "Come on, Baby, Light my Fire" as he pulled out a red number. He held it up, then shook his head. In seconds it was full of blackened holes and lying on the floor with wisps of smoke curling up from it.

"Just sign this little contract giving your soul to Lucifer and your reflection will be restored." Caryon smiled, showing all his fangs this time. "No biggie. You're immortal. What difference does it make where you go when you die? *If* you ever do. Hmmm?"

"I, I can't. My Ricardo. He would never forgive me." Flo cringed when Spyte pulled open a drawer and began ripping his way through silk panties. "Make him stop. Why is he doing that?"

"Spyte, bad boy. You're upsetting our Florence. And she's on the verge—"

"Out of my house!" The roar made the crystal chandelier in the center of the closet rattle. Richard held his Bible in front of him and wore a crucifix around his neck.

"Spoilsport." Cary whirled and let his true and hideous scaly snout show. "I'd refuse but I have other business elsewhere and this was getting boring. Come, Spyte."

"Aw, I was having fun." Spyte blinked. "Here's a parting gift, Florence, to keep us in your heart." He grinned, then disappeared along with Cary. Suddenly the air was filled with flying insects.

"Moths! *Mio Dio!* They will devour my silks, my wools! Ricardo, do something!" Flo collapsed in his arms, tears running down her face.

I leaned over, feeling sick, like maybe I could throw up.

"Glory, are you okay?" Jerry sat beside me and put his arm around me.

"No, I did this. Got them interested in Flo."

"Yes, you did. You'd better leave." Richard still held Flo but he was staring at me. "Darling, calm down. I'll call an exterminator. Surely they can't do that much damage."

Flo jerked away from him, grabbed a leather bag and started swatting at the hundreds of moths. This just made them dive into her clothes to hide. "This is too cruel. I can't bear to watch." She threw herself on Richard again and buried her face in his shirt, sobbing.

"I'm sorry. I didn't mean . . ." I wiped the tears off my cheeks.

"Glory!" Flo pulled away from Richard and held out her hands to me. "I don't blame you. I am weak. I never should have listened for even a minute."

"They're clever, Flo. And Richard is right, I got you noticed." I stood, my legs rubbery, and leaned against Jerry. "We're going. I'm sorry for this . . ." I waved my hand, batting at the moths that had ventured out again. I felt some on my hair and brushed them away.

"Not your fault, *amiga*." Flo frowned when he tried to stop her and finally stepped away from Richard to hug me. "I will call you tomorrow."

"I won't hold you to that. Just save your clothes. I'm so, so sorry." I noticed Richard didn't say anything. Jerry was quiet too as he led me out of the house and to his SUV. It wasn't until we were driving back down the hills and toward his house that he finally spoke.

"What did we walk in on?"

"The demons were trying to get Flo to sign away her soul." I took a shaky breath. "I swear, if you two hadn't intervened, I was afraid she was going to go for it."

"This demon shit has got to end, Glory." Jerry reached over and took my hand.

"You think I don't want it to?" I sighed.

"This all goes back to Valdez." Jerry squeezed my hand.

"I'm still helping him, Jer. Besides, I don't think they'd let me back out now anyway. They seem to be having too much fun at my expense." I sighed and looked out the window at the dark night. "Take me home. I need to make sure Penny gets in all right."

"Fine." He took his hand back to the steering wheel.

I decided that it was past time for me to make some things clear with Jerry and this was one of them. Yes, I hated the demon thing, but I was going to have to resolve it myself. End of story. I just hoped none of my friends ended up as collateral damage.

Fifteen

"We need to talk." This time I said it and Jerry was the one making the face like "Here it comes."

"Fine. What do you want to talk about?" He brought me a bottle of synthetic and settled me on the couch. "I know you're still upset about what happened with Florence. So am I."

"Yes. The demons are out of control. I'm surprised they haven't approached *you*." I took a sip of the cold drink but it didn't help. My insides were still Jell-O.

"I think they sense that it would do them no good. They obviously poke about for vulnerabilities. I've learned to hide mine pretty well over the years." He sat beside me, his arm along the back of the couch.

"But you have some." I studied him in the dim light from the kitchen, the only light we'd turned on. Penny wasn't home yet, but I really didn't expect her until right before dawn. She still had two more hours.

"You, of course. And my family. I have that need to protect what I consider mine, you know." He met my gaze, his dark eyes serious. "I know you hate when I say that. The 'mine' thing."

"Yes, I do. I don't belong to anyone but myself." I sighed. "And you see that as me being difficult."

"Gloriana, I made you vampire. To me it's simple. I'm responsible for you. It's been bred into me not to shirk my responsibilities." He touched my cheek. "And then there's the fact that I love you. So I want to keep you safe. It's a strong need that I can't seem to deny. No matter how many road-blocks you throw in my path."

"I guess most women would be honored, would let you have at it." I sighed at the touch of his hand. "I just wish we could be together without complications."

"What you see as complications, I see as simply the way things should be." He tugged me closer. "You are so damned stubborn about this. Is it because of Valdez?"

"Don't put this on him. It's all about me. Because I have to be free to choose my own way. To fight demons by his side. Or make love with you." I threw out my hands. "Or even spend time with Ray if I wish."

"You ask a lot, Gloriana." Jerry withdrew his arm and stood. "I don't know if it's in me to share you like that."

"I know." I didn't cry, my eyes suddenly very dry as I felt that truth down to my toes. "I've always known, Jerry. But I don't want to lose you. So my wish is that you'll work on being less, uh, I hate this word, but *controlling*."

"That *is* a harsh word." He ran his fingers through his hair and walked around the coffee table to pace the length of the room. "But I learned to do it at an early age. It's what a commander must do to his troops."

"I'm not a troop." I leaned back, glad we could talk calmly about this.

"Of course not." He stopped, his back to the TV. "I'm trying to explain where my attitude came from. Da taught it to me as a boy. Along with the way the men in my family have always treated their women."

"Oh, yes. Don't get me started on that." I leaned forward. "You know your father isn't exactly a good role model for you. Your parents have been separated for more decades than they've been together. And when they're together, it's like being in the middle of a battlefield."

"True enough." Jerry started pacing again. "'Tis the fate of the Campbell men to love strong women, it seems. Bloody hell, but I can't just talk this out and suddenly be a different man for you, Gloriana, much as I'd like to be."

"Obviously. Or I think you would have done it long ago. You've always seemed motivated." I stood and walked over to him. "I'm just asking for an end to this constant jealousy. To this feeling I get that I have to hide things from you, tiptoe around you or you'll go off."

"You are hiding things from me?" He grabbed my shoulders.

"See? That's all you heard." I stepped back. "Stop it. Don't do this again. No, I'm not hiding anything. Or I don't think I am." I put my hand to my head. What I'd told Jerry or what I hadn't seemed impossible to keep straight right now and I wasn't sure I had it in me to even try.

"Come here. Let me hold you." He pulled me into his arms, which felt way too much like a safe haven.

Oh, but it was seductive. I was feeling much too vulnerable after that whole demon incident with Flo. It was tempting to just take the easy way here. My head hurt, my stomach still rolled and Jerry's broad shoulders could take on everything, even demons.

And those evil slimes were always watching, apparently, just waiting for a chance to swoop in and try their luck with anyone I came in contact with. It was enough to make me want to put my head down on Jerry's strong chest and weep. Who would they try for next? Ray? Another "easy takedown" as Spyte had said.

"Gloriana, sweetheart. You're shaking. I don't know what those bastards are doing to you, but please let me help." Jerry picked me up and carried me to my bedroom. He laid me on the bed and knelt beside it. "Let me get Richard involved. He helped before, didn't he?"

"He's furious with me. He won't let Flo within miles of

me now." I stared at the ceiling. "Not that it will do any good to keep her away from me. Now that they've started in on her, I don't have to be around for them to do their seduction routine. This was just their first pass."

"You're not responsible for Florence's soul. If she's weak, that's her fault." Jerry held my hand. "And anyone else who gives in to their offers, it's on their heads, not yours."

I looked at him. "So why can't you say that about Rafe? He isn't making these demons do anything. They promised they'd be satisfied with Simon and the Energy Vampires. That, if we get them, they'll leave us alone."

"And you believe them?" Jerry shook his head. "Haven't you learned anything from this latest incident?"

"You're right." I sat up. "We've got to make sure the demons know that after this they're never welcome in Austin again."

"That would be quite a trick." Jerry got up off the floor to sit on the bed beside me. "How on earth could we do that?"

"We? So you're in? You think you could work with Rafe and me to do this?" I grabbed his hands. "Without getting into a fight over it?"

"I'll do whatever it takes to make you safe. And if it means giving up jealousy." He winced. "Well, I'll be working on that. Maybe there's a twelve-step program I can join."

I hugged him. "There is! I'll get online and find a meeting for you here in town."

"Seriously?" Jerry had obviously been bluffing and I'd just called him on it.

"Seriously. Bottom line, either you trust me or you don't. I've told Rafe we're done. Do you think I'm so weak I can't resist him?" I leaned back and gave him a look that meant business.

"No. You've proved time and again that you aren't weak, my girl. You're getting stronger all the time and I love that about you." He leaned down and kissed me. "So the fault here is mine. I'll go to the bloody meetings and do whatever it takes to prove I want us to work."

"Thank you, Jerry. And I take blame too. I betrayed you. You have reason to wonder about Rafe, I know that." I kissed *him* this time, showing him how much I loved him.

"Now all we need to do is survive." Jerry held me close. "I'm talking to Richard. He can't guard Florence twenty-four-seven. He'll want to help us send these demons back to hell and he's something of an expert with these matters. Am I right?"

"Yes, you are." I actually began to feel hopeful. Which was Jerry's power. His confidence that he could always put things right.

Jerry brushed my hair back from my face. "You look like you're feeling better."

"I am. Talking isn't such a bad thing, you know. We needed to clear the air." I pulled Jerry down to the bed. "Now I bet we have an hour before Penny gets home. How about we seal the deal on this promise you just made. One of the twelve steps is making amends. I'll lie here while you show me how sorry you are that you ever acted jealous of my men."

"Oh, I am very sorry." Jerry came down on top of me. "And I may have twelve different ways of showing you that, my love."

Jerry decided to leave just as Penny and Trey hit the door a few minutes before dawn. I was relaxed and naked in my bed and didn't bother to get up. But I could hear well enough as Jerry and Penny made plans to drive to San Antonio with the rats the next evening.

I made my own plans. I was going to church the next night. I'd been with the demons enough to feel positively filthy with evil. An evening of joyful music and the positive message from Pastor John at the Moonlight Church of Eternal Life and Joy would go a long way to restoring my soul.

When I woke up, I waited until Penny had showered, then listened to her excited chatter about her date and her meeting with Jenny the night before.

"I did what you said. Kept my cool and wasn't alone with her at all. We squeezed them in at the bar and Jenny tried to get me to go to the bathroom with her so we could gossip, but I wouldn't do it." Penny laughed. "Totally blew her mind. But I just kept going to hang out with Trey who had door duty and left her with her date. That solved the problem." Penny flushed. "She thought Trey was cute too. Was totally jealous. I read her mind."

"Why not? Anything else good in there?" I sat in my robe, thinking about trying to call Flo to see if my friend might go to church with me. Would she pick up if she saw on the caller ID that it was me? Sure she'd been all BFF last night, but Richard had probably been giving her an earful since then about my bad influence. And I couldn't blame him.

"She wasn't too happy with her date. Thought he was immature compared to Trey. Didn't help that his fake ID didn't pass at the bar. That embarrassed her." Penny had a really wide grin. "Can you believe she was jealous of me? Even liked my skirt!"

"Well, there you go." I patted her knee, then nodded toward the door. "Jerry's coming up the stairs. Get the door."

"Oh, yeah. We're taking the rats to a guy in San Antonio who has some homes lined up for them." Penny got up and unlocked the dead bolts. "Hi, Mr. Blade. I'll start bringing out the cages."

"Good evening, Penny." Jerry walked over and dropped a kiss on my lips. "Gloriana." He noticed Penny had disappeared down the hall and ran a hand inside my robe. "Mmm. Sorry you're not going with us. I assume you're not, since you aren't dressed yet."

"Nope. The idea of an hour in the car with fifty-three rats doesn't sound like my idea of fun." I swatted at his hand. "Don't start something you can't finish, big guy."

"Later." He leaned down and kissed me again, a wonderfully thorough job this time.

"Mmm. I'll keep that in mind." I pushed him back.

"It's up to sixty-seven rats now. They were supposed to be

segregated in the lab but obviously somebody messed up."
Penny carried in two crates. "Anyway, we've had some developments, so they are really crowded."

"I'll get the other crates." Jerry charged off down the hall.
"Gloriana, you might want to air the place out while we're gone."

"Sure, after I get back from church." I got up to take my empty bottle to the kitchen.

"You're going to church?" Penny stopped in the open doorway.

"I told you I went. I thought I'd already proved to you that I'm not the fanged monster the comic books or movies portray, Penny. I pray, sing hymns, and there's a church that has night services. Maybe next Sunday, you can go with me."
I went to the kitchen sink and rinsed out my bottle, then dumped it in the recycle bin.

"Yes, I'd like that. And it would make my folks feel good if I could tell them we go to church together." She glanced down at the rats. "If I didn't have to take these tonight, I'd go with you. Definitely."

"Fine, we'll do it. But the rats have to leave. I'll get started on your bedroom when I get back. Keep your window open now and the fan going. Spray air freshener." I smiled as Jerry came out bearing the last of the crates. "Anything else left in there rat-related?"

"Just some food and things that we'll stick in the car and take to the rescue people along with these creatures. Go ahead and take your shower." Jerry followed Penny to the door. "I'll get her settled in the car and come back up for one last load. Leave the bathroom door unlocked." He winked. "She can wait for a few minutes."

"Bad man." I smiled and strutted toward the bathroom.
Why not? I had printed out a short list of places he could go to start work on that jealousy issue. So maybe a little advanced reward was in order.

I got the water temperature adjusted, jumped in and

started shampooing my hair. I'd just done the second rinse when I felt a hand on my backside.

"Now who could that be?" I sighed as it stroked down to insinuate itself between my legs. "And such curious fingers." I gasped and leaned against the tile wall as he plunged first one, then two fingers inside me.

"Face the wall. Don't turn around. This is your lover, come to take his due." His voice was rough, not like him. But I forgot that as his body rubbed against me and I felt how hard and ready he was. His other hand snaked around me to grasp one of my breasts and he squeezed my nipple, a little too tightly.

"But I want to see—"

"No!" He pressed his cock into the crease of my buttocks and slid it up and down, up and down, the water making the passage slippery and entirely sensual. His fingers swirled inside me, finding that tender center that screamed for him to play with it, to press against it. He pinched it between his fingers, then released. Over and over again until I shook, my head falling to my chest.

"What do you want me to do?" I panted as I bent over and widened my legs, trying to bring him inside me, needing for him to fill me. But only his fingers worked me, teasing me and making me writhe against him.

"Open for me, wider." His other hand slid from my breast and he grabbed the showerhead, pulling the detachable piece loose and aiming it at my exposed center.

"Oh, my God. Oh, my God."

"Quiet." The harsh command made me bite my lip, but I jerked at the pressure of the water on my sensitive flesh and I was willing to do whatever he said as long as the pleasure lasted. This was Jerry's game and clearly he was making up the rules as we went along.

Jerry's game. I inhaled and reached a trembling hand for the shower gel as my knees wobbled. At the same time he released me to turn the knob on the showerhead to pulse, teasing me with the firmer stream until I screamed and jerked the hose from his hands. I whirled, the gel in my hands, and aimed for his eyes, squeezing the bottle as hard as I could.

"Son of a bitch!" He threw up his hands and fell back against the tile wall.

"Out!" I dropped the bottle to shove him away from me. "God! God! God! Get away from me!"

Lucifer grabbed a washcloth and wiped his red and streaming eyes. "Not a problem." He looked me over. "What was I thinking? Your kind doesn't belong in hell. He can have you." With that he vanished. A simple now you see him, now you don't.

I reached back and found the spigots, managing to turn off the water before I collapsed into the bottom of the tub. I leaned my head on my knees. The bathroom reeked of the expensive lavender gel I'd bought as a treat for myself at the mall. Not a problem that several dollars' worth decorated the tile wall and had gone down the drain. Not a problem that the Devil himself had touched me intimately and almost . . . I shuddered and knew my legs wouldn't support me if I tried to stand. My center still quivered and, if I'd dared touch myself, I knew I'd go off. I hated that, hated that I'd responded to that creep. I trembled, disgusted and nauseated.

I pushed my wet hair out of my eyes when I heard the bathroom door open.

"Glory, not finished already, are you, sweetheart?" Jerry pulled aside the shower curtain. "Why didn't you wait for me?"

I started sobbing and couldn't stop.

"Glory? What in God's name is wrong with you?" Jerry tried to pull me into his arms but I shook my head and pointed at the fogged up mirror.

Written in the steam was a smiley face and one letter— "L." I couldn't speak.

"Lucifer? By God, are you telling me Lucifer was in here?" Jerry crawled into the tub with me and wrapped his arms around me. "Did he . . . ?"

I shook my head. "He, he came up behind me." I felt Jerry's arms tighten around me. "But somehow I, I knew." I turned to look at him. "He didn't smell right." I leaned my face into Jerry's neck and breathed in his essence. "I've been with you so long. He could have made himself look like you, I guess. But your smell." I kissed the side of his neck, my shaking finally gone. "I stopped him before . . ."

"How?" Jerry brushed my wet hair back from my face. "This is the king of hell we're talking about. He's so powerful."

"Surprised him." I reached for that bottle of gel that lay next to the drain and capped it, carefully setting it on the rim of the tub. "He thought he had me. Stayed behind me so, so I couldn't see." I buried my face in Jerry's neck. "Take me out of here. Please?"

"What was I thinking?" Jerry stood, grabbed a towel to wrap me in, then carried me to the bed. There he piled blankets on top of me. "Better?"

"A little. Don't, don't leave me." I felt raw, vulnerable. No matter what Lucifer said, he could come back, decide to finish what he'd started. I didn't say it, tried to be brave about it. But Jerry sat on the side of the bed and kept one hand on mine.

"I won't." He pulled out his phone and I heard him tell Penny to come upstairs. Then she was there, staring at me from the doorway. He issued orders like the commander he'd once been, telling her to clear out the rest of the rat paraphernalia and drive his car to San Antonio. That the destination was already programmed into his GPS.

"But what's wrong with Glory?" Penny hadn't moved out of the doorway yet. I was aware of her, but didn't look at her directly. I couldn't seem to quit doing an instant replay of the shower scene. Why hadn't I known immediately that it wasn't Jerry behind me? I'd let it go too far. I should have . . . It was an endless tape of what ifs and if onlys that made me crazy.

"She slipped and fell in the bathtub. She'll be all right but I don't want to leave her alone right now. Just go. I'll take

care of her." Jerry's voice was calm, but I knew him well
enough to sense the rage he was barely holding inside. Apparently the idea that Lucifer had tried to rape me, and that's
what I was calling it, made him as crazy as it was making me.

Moments passed as I counted spots on the ceiling and
tried to make my mind blank. Didn't work of course. By the
time I heard the hall door close and Jerry was back beside
me, I had tears running down my cheeks again.

"Gloriana, love." He pulled me into his arms and held me
close. His warmth soothed me and I knew I was safe. But for
how long?

I opened my mind to him and let him see exactly what
had happened. No secrets. He stiffened and bit back a curse,
then laid me carefully on the bed.

"I'll be right back." He stood and pulled out his cell
phone.

"Jerry, what are you going to do?"

"Don't worry, I'm not going to kill anyone." He took my
hand while he used his thumb to page through his numbers,
then hit speed dial for someone. "Get over here. Gloriana
needs you." He was silent for a moment. "Her place." He
ended the call.

I sat up. "Jerry, quit blocking your thoughts. I can't—"

"I am only doing what you asked me to do. Putting aside
my personal feelings and letting you have your life. I called
a friend for you. Someone who can help." He sat beside me
on the bed. His eyes were hot, his fists kept clenching and
unclenching like he ached for a broadsword. Yet how could
he fight the king of the Underworld? How could *we*?

I put my hands to my head. That question seemed to roll
inside my brain endlessly. How do you fight a being so powerful, so impossibly evil? Just by being good? I could almost
hear Lucifer's mocking laughter in my head at the thought.

The hall door opened and Jerry jumped to his feet. He
strode to the living room and low voices kept me from hearing what he said. Then there was a crash.

I jumped up and wrapped one of the blankets around me.

I staggered to the doorway and saw Rafe, his fist bleeding as he pulled it from a hole in the Sheetrock next to the hall door. He looked at me with bleak eyes.

"I thought . . ." I took a shaky breath.

"That we'd got into it again?" Rafe glanced at Jerry. "No, we have a common enemy now." He had a sheen of tears in his eyes as he walked toward me. "Damn me, but I'd have done anything to spare you this."

"I know, Rafe. Please don't blame yourself." I fell into his arms but kept my eyes on Jerry, sending him a message, thanking him. "Shit happens. Am I right?"

"Not this kind of shit." He said it into my wet hair and I felt a shudder go through him. "I will carry this guilt with me for the rest of my life."

I saw Jerry nod, as if this was right and proper. I couldn't get into that. Who understood the workings of hell or demons? But I knew now why Jerry had called a man he would rather I never touched again. I eased out of Rafe's arms.

"Give me some credit here. I actually stopped that creep from crossing the finish line and I bet all of hell has a nice lavender scent now. If they weren't afraid of getting sent down to test the latest torture device, the demons would probably be laughing it up at Luc's expense."

"Not much laughter down there, Glory. And you can't fool me." Rafe didn't crack a smile. "You're reeling. He invaded your privacy. Not crossing the finish line is a technicality. Blade and I figure the asshole's gone way too far. Way too far. This is war, baby, and we'll do whatever it takes to see that something like this never happens again."

"Now, Rafe, don't make me worry about you. Calm down. Let me get dressed. I need to call Simon and get moving on our plan. I've been stalling. Maybe we need more information." I managed a smile for both of them, though I was sure it was a poor effort. "Rafe, you must know something about Lucifer and the workings of that world. As Jerry would say, we need to know the enemy to defeat it."

"Exactly." Jerry stared at the hole in the Sheetrock. "Need

to get someone to repair the wall. Gloriana's supposed to have company tomorrow night, Penny's parents." He glanced at me. "Unless you plan to cancel."

"No, got to do that." I sighed. "Business as usual. I can't let Lucifer think he got to me. And—" I looked down at the hardwood floor. "If you're listening, asshole, you're pathetic, needing to sneak up on women who don't want you." I shook my head, tears coming and not wanting the guys to see them. "Forget it. Taunting him is probably stupid. Am I right, Rafe?"

"Afraid so, Glo." He glanced at Jerry. "Go, blow your hair dry. Do something to make yourself look pretty. We can wait."

"Yeah, I'll do that." I smiled at Jerry, meaning it this time. "Good call, Jer. I like seeing you two work together." I gestured toward a black-and-white photo of Ray that hung in my shrine to him near my CD player. I'd set it up long before I'd met him, a total fangirl. Since it bugged Jerry and Rafe, it had stayed. "Move that over and cover up the hole while I'm getting dressed. It'll do for now." I staggered off to my room.

Once there I shut the door, then collapsed on the foot of the bed and just stared at my reflection. Yep, still had it. I was tempted to throw something at it and shatter the mirror. Anything that reminded me of hell right now left a bitter taste in my mouth. But Glory St. Clair is a survivor. And if I moped around, cried bitter tears or railed against fate, it would only please Lucifer and make him think he'd won points in some kind of sick game.

So I got up and attacked my drying hair. When I was made up and dressed in jeans and a loose black tee, I walked back out to join the men. They jumped up, both of them with the light of battle in their eyes.

"Any conclusions?" I walked over and got another bottle of synthetic out of the fridge. I needed something to get me pumped up. Sure I was a survivor, but that didn't mean I still wasn't an inch away from crawling back into bed, pulling the covers over my head and staying there, permanently.

"Like you say, we need more information. I want to know about Lucifer's powers. How hell is set up." Jerry patted the seat next to him on the couch.

"The demons told you it's like intramural sports down there. With each of the gods and goddesses of the Underworld having their own turf. That Lucifer has his section and there's this competition going?" Rafe had pulled out a beer and took a swig. "They made it sound like it's all in fun, everything even Steven. But, trust me, Lucifer is actually the big boss. The head of the whole shooting match. His power is off the charts."

"Surely he has a vulnerability." Jerry's arm tightened around me.

Rafe shook his head. "Don't know of one. And of course cheating's expected, even applauded."

"I bet rules mean nothing in hell." I wondered how on earth you fought against an enemy like that. Especially one who thought anyone with honor was weak and stupid.

"They mean nothing in hell, but, when the demons are here on earth, they do have a few rules they have to abide by. The man upstairs takes exception to some of their dirty tricks. They aren't allowed to bug a good person indefinitely and I have a feeling they're about to wear out their welcome with you, Glory. God's bound to take notice and put the hammer down." Rafe met my gaze. "Not sure how much control He has over Lucifer, but what really blows my mind here, Glory, is that Lucifer's even bothered taking a personal interest in you." His mouth twisted in a bitter smile. "Sorry, sweet thing, but you're absolutely a tiny blip on his radar."

"Sure, I can see that. He'd usually be all about immoral dictators or instigating horrible things like genocide or a famine. Focusing on the big picture." I snuggled up to Jerry and wished for a blanket. I felt chilled as I thought of all the evil in the world. Jer read my thoughts and grabbed a throw from a basket next the couch and draped it over my lap.

"Seems like time might be on our side then," Jerry said.

Rafe set his bottle on my magazine. "From what Blade told me, Glory, you pretty well let Lucifer have it tonight. I doubt he'll bother you again."

"I can hope. Seems like his male ego wouldn't stand for him making another try. He did seem pretty disgusted with me." I held the throw around me. "But maybe his male ego doesn't let a rejection stand without payback either."

"Like I said, you're not that important. Let's just concentrate on getting this deal with Simon done." Rafe picked up his beer again. "Call him. See if he'll agree to meet."

"In a minute." I frowned at him. "Got to say, Rafael, you need a twelve-step program for anger management. Forget hitting the wall. The worst was using your demonic powers just because you had a disappointment. Look at the serious fallout it's caused." I shook my finger at him. "You really don't want this to happen again, do you?"

Jerry choked out a laugh. "You're right, Gloriana. Sign him up. I saw the list you left for me on the coffee table." He actually gave Rafe a sympathetic look, man to man. "Our girl is big on twelve-step programs. Next thing you know you'll be going to meetings in church basements."

"Don't mock. That kind of program got me through a terrible time." I still didn't use a credit card. Had a debit card and that was it. "Now be quiet while I make this call." I hit speed dial for Simon. Yes, I had his number programmed. Don't ask.

"Gloriana. How interesting to hear from you. What could you want?" Simon's deep voice really didn't go with his usual weasel face.

"To talk. Freddy told me you aren't allowed to have a female Energy Vampire. And I was all primed."

"Really?" Simon cleared his throat. "Doubt it. Rumor has it you lost any special abilities when you lost your demon visitor. Bet you didn't think I knew about that, did you?"

"Nothing you know surprises me, Simon." I frowned though. Did Simon still have video cameras hidden in my shop somewhere? I hated the way he sneaked around. "But seems like Honoria really enjoys pulling your chain."

"It's the price I pay for power." Simon chuckled. "Nothing for you to worry about."

"But it's costing you your son. How does that feel?" I waited as silence stretched. "Freddy's pretty torn up about it. He moved to Texas to get to know his father, but he just can't deal with the whole Energy Vampire thing. Bet that was a major disappointment to you."

"What is this? A therapy session?" Simon's voice hardened. "I don't need it."

"Don't hang up. I get that you probably can't talk out there. Not about this. But I may be able to help you shake loose of you-know-who. I have some connections. Because of my recent demonic possession. Meet me in my shop and we can discuss things. If you really want to see Freddy again." I said this in a rush, pretty sure Simon had been close to ending the connection.

"When?"

I did a gut check. "Tuesday night. Back room of my shop. Nine o'clock. Can you make it?"

"Be alone. I don't want to deal with your friends." He ended the call.

"Good job, Glory. He actually bit." Rafe gave me a high five.

Jerry squeezed my shoulders. "I know why you couldn't meet him tonight. Go rest, sweetheart. We'll talk about the actual meeting later." He looked at Rafe. "I think Penny's room needs a thorough cleaning. What do you say we prove to Gloriana that we can work together on a project, Valdez?"

"Sure. I can get behind that. And we don't need to leave Glo alone either." Rafe winked at me. "Should do you good to see Blade pushing a vacuum cleaner. Am I right?"

"That's not necessary. I can do it. Later." I struggled to my feet. Jerry kept his arm around my waist to steady me.

"No, we've got this. Take care of yourself." He settled me in bed and strode back to the living room. I heard Rafe tell him where he could find that vacuum cleaner.

I lay back and thought about calling Flo. No, it would just upset her. She was safe in Richard's hands and didn't need to be anywhere near me and my angst. Instead, I called CiCi and gave her an update about my meeting with Simon. It felt good to be proactive instead of waiting for something else to happen to me. I fell asleep to the roar of the vacuum, glad that a vampire couldn't have nightmares.

Sixteen

"Are you sure you're feeling okay, Glory?" Penny asked me for the fifth time. She still thought I'd just suffered a fall in the bathtub.

"Yes, I'm fine. Healing sleep does it every time." I wished that healing had done a job on my soul; it still felt violated. But the fact that I'd sent Lucifer away short of reaching his goal had to count for something. At least that was the positive self-talk I was using to try to get through this night.

"That's amazing. So if I broke a leg or got shot, I'd heal overnight?" Penny settled on the couch.

"Yes, as long as you'd fed well. It can take a couple of nights if you're severely hurt, but that's part of the miracle of immortality. The healing thing. You saw some of that with Ray, though his alcoholism slowed the process." I smiled. "Now I'll ask *you* for the umpteenth time. Do you need another bottle of synthetic? Are you okay to be around mortals?" I had finished my second bottle and was eyeing the vial Ian had given me. Was it worth the risk? I'd wait and see if Penny's mom's food looked tempting enough. I'd never forget the side effects from Ian's diet drug. Of course Ian had sworn I was the only vampire to ever experience those. Surely I wouldn't be that unlucky twice.

"I'm good to go. Jenny will be here any minute." Penny inhaled. "Can't believe you got rid of the rat smell. The lavender is a nice touch. And then there's my room. Spotless!"

"Thank Rafe and Jerry. They worked like maniacs. It became a contest, apparently. To see who could do the most, get things the cleanest." I laughed. "Everything between those two ends up a competition but at least no blows were exchanged. I'd like to see them go head-to-head over getting my sheets white enough."

"Yeah, but how did that hole get in the wall?" Penny lifted the picture of Ray, which I had to admit was in an odd spot. "A blow that missed?"

"No, Rafe heard something upsetting and hit the wall. Since the guy he was mad at wasn't in the room. He'll get it fixed." I adjusted the picture. "Hey, Ray looks good anywhere. You can throw his name into the conversation. Tell how it was with him here for a while. Make Jenny jealous again."

Penny grinned. "Can't say I'd hate that." Her nose twitched. "Mortal at the door. And I think I recognize my sister. I'm getting better at this sniffing thing."

"Good for you." I sat on the sofa and settled my skirt around me. I'd dressed carefully, successful businesswoman but hip and trendy in my print skirt and purple sweater. My shoes were expensive, my bridesmaid's gift from Flo. I'd picked the whole outfit just so I could wear them.

I still hadn't gotten into my bathtub again. Not sure when I'd be able to. It was sponge baths for me until I was sure Lucifer was permanently back in hell where he belonged. I'd probably have to go to Jerry's to wash my hair, but that was okay; he'd be happy to have me.

"Come in. You remember Glory." Penny showed Jenny into the living room.

"Sure. Cute place. Too bad you had to bring that monster computer, Pen. Where are we supposed to eat?" Jenny dropped her purse on the coffee table.

"We can eat on the table where you just dumped your purse or we have some TV trays." Penny frowned. "Lighten up, Jen. You know I need my computer."

"Sure, sorry." Jenny smiled at me. "Hi, Glory. Nice place, really. It's great that you took Penny in." She said this like maybe Penny had been a street person.

"Penny's a cool roommate. We have a lot of fun." I smiled back. "Show her your room, Penny." I reached for my copy of *InStyle*. "Nice shoes. Last year?"

"Oh, yes." She noticed mine when I crossed my legs but didn't comment. Hah. I knew jealousy when I saw it. "Come on, Pen. Let's see how bad you've trashed your crib."

Penny headed down the hall. "Not trashed at all. Who has time to mess up when I'm so busy dating?"

I heard Jenny snort. Interesting. She had to know Penny wasn't lying. So what was that about? I just stayed on the couch and flipped through my magazine, perfectly able to hear their conversation.

"You've had quite a run lately. What about your research?" Way to bring Penny down, Jenny.

"Oh, luckily I'd turned in the important part of my grant work before the break-in. Now I'm thinking of going in a new direction since the ongoing experiments were trashed. No use crying over what can't be fixed. I talked to the department chair. I'm not using animals for research again." Penny's voice was muffled. "What do you think of this blouse? Glory found it for me. She's a genius bargain hunter."

"Cute and on sale. Of course they wouldn't have anything in my size in *that* store." Oh, could Jenny poke the knife any deeper?

"Quit being a bitch, Jen. What's got you so bummed?" I heard the mattress squeak, Penny sitting on her bed. "Tell me all about it."

"Okay, smarty-pants. Here it is." Jenny sighed. "My grades are gonna suck this time. If I don't ace my finals, I may not be able to do the cheerleading next year." Big sniffs from Jenny. "They have grade-point standards. So does the sorority.

And I was supposed to be in charge of rush next fall." More sniffles.

"I'm sorry. What happened? This isn't like you." Penny must have pulled out tissues because I heard Jenny blow her nose.

"Some of this is your fault. We usually met in the mornings. You checked my homework, finished a few problems for me. It's our thing. What happened to that?" Jenny's voice was hitting high C. "Huh?"

"Mornings don't work for me now. And was that all our meets were for? To get some free answers?" Penny's voice wobbled.

"Chill, Pen. I admit I got caught up in the college thing. Having fun. Partying. Not anything *you'd* understand." Seems the bitch was back. "Damn it. I wish we looked more alike. You could go in there and ace those tests. But . . ." A long pause. "Maybe if you could tutor me? Just this week? The math and science. Stuff you could do in your sleep."

Nice. Treat your sister like dirt, then ask for a favor. If Penny said yes, I was going to shake her till her new fangs rattled.

"Sorry. No can do." Yes! I wanted to hug Penny and see Jenny's face.

"But, Pen . . ." Bet Jen was getting ready to try some serious tears. Or a guilt trip. Penny must have seen it coming.

"Don't even. I'm starting a new job, might even get to go to California. I was going to tell the family tonight after dinner. It's a chance to do cutting-edge research in a new field." Penny kept going, throwing out technical words that I'm sure Jenny understood about as well as I did. "Bottom line: I'm not missing this opportunity. Certainly not because you spent more time having fun than hitting the books."

"Thanks for nothing. As usual, it's all about you. The big brain. Doing something important. Forget me. I'll just stay here and fall into the abyss." The way Jenny's voice cracked on that last word was pure drama.

"You want to talk about an abyss?" Penny's voice rose and

I jumped up. Oh, she was not going there. "Let me show you an abyss."

Jenny shrieked. "What the hell is that?"

I got to Penny's door in time to see my fledgling giving her sister the full-fang treatment. I shook my head but Penny ignored me.

"It's my fangs, sister dear. I'm a vampire, a bloodsucker. I'll never see daylight again thanks to Josh and his Ugly Chick caper."

"No, I don't believe you. Get rid of them. You're creeping me out with your stupid Halloween teeth." Jenny backed up and bumped into me. "Glory, what's the matter with my sister?"

"Penny, quit playing games now. Can't you see how upset Jenny is?" I gave Penny a stern look.

"Yeah? Funny thing. Since I can read her mind, I'm not so sad that she's 'upset.'" Penny marched closer, until she was nose to nose with Jenny. "Why do you hate me? I'm the fat sister, the one who never got to be cheerleader. Who went to her senior prom with cousin Ollie, who spent the whole time in the men's room smoking weed. Weed he bought with the money Daddy paid him to take me there."

"Boo hoo. You went to that prom at twelve. Didn't even have boobs yet. You made me look like the village idiot since I could only do what normal kids could do." Jenny put a hand in the middle of Penny's chest and shoved. It didn't do any good. Penny had vamp strength and didn't budge. "Lose the pointy teeth, pinhead. Hate to tell you, but they don't make you look any thinner."

I kept my mouth shut. I had a feeling this showdown was long overdue. And if Jenny didn't believe Penny about the vampire thing, we were still okay here. Of course Mom and Dad could arrive any minute. Not cool if they landed in the middle of a catfight. Or had this happened before? Penny glanced at me.

"No, Glory, we've never had this out. And, yes, I peeked under your bangs for that thought. Sorry." She didn't look sorry. "Okay, Jen, so I'm smart. I never rubbed your nose in it. Even helped you whenever you asked for those free answers. But did you help me? Not on your life. Glory here has acted more like a sister in the week I've known her than you have in nineteen years."

"How was I supposed to help you? All you did was sit on your lumpy ass in front of a computer all the time. You never wanted to do anything I liked. Play sports and games like a *normal* person. Or even look like a normal person. Hell, your brain is totally warped." Jenny turned and flounced out of the room. She stopped next to the coffee table and picked up my magazine. "Look at this. I showed you my copy once and all you said was something about the number of trees per subscriber per year it took to support such a frivolous waste of paper."

I narrowed my gaze on Penny. "You didn't!"

"Maybe. Who remembers? I told you I don't pay attention to details. Not when I'm thinking."

"You were *always* thinking, but not about your family. Just about weird stuff." Jenny threw the magazine at Penny. "I said lose the stupid fangs!"

Penny shut her mouth. "Okay, I will." She looked at me. "Not a good time. I smell pot roast."

"Mom and Dad?" Jenny picked up her purse and pulled out her compact. She began to dab powder on her shiny nose. "They hate for us to fight."

"We never fight." Penny sighed and picked up the magazine, laying it carefully on the coffee table.

"Because they'd hate it. We're supposed to be the perfect family. The beauty and the brain. Gag me." Jenny glanced at me. "Sorry, Glory. Please try to forget all that. I guess stress is getting to me. I usually have things more under control." She sniffed. "You sure you smelled pot roast? I don't smell a thing."

I smiled. "Oh, I do too." I walked to the door. "And it smells delicious." There was a knock on the door. "Penny, you must have given your parents the code for downstairs."

"Yes, I did. Was that a bad idea?" She glanced significantly at Jenny. "I gave it to Jen too. But no keys to anyone."

"That's fine then. I'm sorry, but I have my reasons for the tight security, Jenny. Women living alone. I'm sure you get it. Can't have keys just floating around." I shrugged, pasted on a smile, then opened the door. An attractive middle-aged couple stood there. The woman held a casserole in her hands, the man was weighed down with two sacks. The smells coming from their packages made my mouth water. I was definitely trying Ian's potion.

Penny and Jenny ran forward to help their parents, make introductions and carry in the meal. Neither of them let on that they'd just had a fight and we were soon setting out the food in the kitchen. I'd had a challenge figuring out how to make my space there mortal friendly. Penny had explained that her own kitchen was usually almost empty. So we'd hidden the synthetics in a cabinet, put Rafe's snacks front and center and figured that would have to do. Of course Mrs. Patterson, who insisted I call her Melissa, exclaimed at the sight of all the junk food.

"Penny, you told me you and Glory were on a special diet. What kind of diet calls for Twinkies, Cheetos"—she opened the refrigerator—"and beer?"

"Uh, I'm over twenty-one, Melissa." I pointed to the bottles of designer water I'd brought up from the shop. "Those are Penny's. And we've been trying to resist the snack food. Seriously."

Jenny snorted. I was seeing that as a really unattractive habit of hers. "Yeah, I just bet you have." She looked Penny up and down.

"We eat out a lot, Mom. Or call for delivery. There's a great place that brings us healthful salads." Penny pulled out a bottle of water and handed it to her dad. "Come check out my computer setup. Glory's been cool, letting me take over her dining area."

Mark followed her while I lifted the lid on the pot roast. It was still warm and swimming in brown gravy, with carrots, onions and potatoes nestled alongside it. I'd already slipped into my bedroom and taken the potion and my stomach rumbled.

"Someone's hungry." Melissa laughed. "It won't be long. I'm going to just pop some rolls in the oven." She pulled out a bag of frozen rolls and set them on a cookie sheet she'd brought with her. "Why look at this oven. I don't think it's ever been used."

"No, uh, well. I really don't cook."

"Where'd the hole in the wall come from?" Jenny came into the kitchen carrying my picture of Ray. "It was behind Israel Caine's picture. Mom, look. Autographed. I told you Glory dates him."

Melissa smiled at me. "Wow. He's so hot."

"Mom!" Jenny and Penny, who'd followed her in from the dining room, for once were in sync.

"I may be married, but I can still appreciate a good-looking man. And talent. I love his music." Melissa licked her lips. "Glory, I'd like to hear about Israel after dinner. I dragged Mark to that concert at Zilker Park where he fell off the stage." She grabbed my arm. "How is he? Can he still sing?"

"He's fine, Mom. Glory brought him back here to recover." Penny squeaked when her mother grabbed her arm next. "Wow, get a grip. Just not on me."

"He stayed here. With you?"

"Don't like the sound of that." Mark walked in behind Penny. "And where did that hole in the wall come from?"

"It's the twenty-first century, Mark. Of course Israel can stay here if Glory wants him here." Melissa was gazing at Ray's picture.

"I put the hole there, Dad. One of my spaced-out moments. I wouldn't let one of the movers touch my computer tower and backed into the wall. The corner knocked a chunk out of the wall." Penny sighed. "Not paying attention again."

"Don't worry about it, Penny. I told you, I have a friend who will fix it. No big deal." I sniffed the air. "Those rolls smell delicious."

"And they should be ready. Let's eat." Melissa started handing out plates. "Help yourself, girls. I don't want to hear about a diet tonight. I know you never get a home-cooked meal."

I heard Jenny mutter something that sounded like "Thank goodness." I gave Penny an inquiring look.

"Mom, the rolls!" Penny bent over and opened the oven. Sure enough, they were a little on the well-done side, the bottoms charred. "I think you should have checked the temperature setting."

Jenny just rolled her eyes.

"Never mind, honey. We'll just eat the tops." Mark began to dish up generous portions for everyone except Jenny, who got a plate of macaroni and cheese. "Roast looks good. Jenny, you should rethink this vegetarian thing. It makes extra work for your mother."

"Just opened a box and followed directions. No trouble at all." Melissa put a spoonful on my plate too. "Try some, Glory."

"Everything looks great." I took my plate to the living room and sat on the floor. My hand shook as I lifted my fork. I waited until everyone was served, then carefully put a bite of roast in my mouth. I saw Penny watching me. I knew she was remembering her drink of soda at the movies. Not fun.

I savored the taste of rich gravy, then carefully chewed and chewed and chewed. Okay, I knew it had been hundreds of years since I'd had roast beef, but surely it should eventually get smaller, not larger in my mouth. I fought my fangs, trying not to notice the mortals surrounding me. The parents were on the sofa, squeezed in with Jenny. And Penny sat in the chair, her plate on her lap.

I finally gave in, hesitated, then swallowed the enormous bite. When it stayed down, I looked at Penny and smiled. Only then did she attack her potatoes. I noticed that she cut her beef into tiny pieces. Okay, obviously that was the secret here. Because this was the toughest piece of meat ever. The carrots were strangely crunchy too. The first one flew off my plate and I heard Jenny snicker.

"Glory, don't worry about it. I'm sorry, I always forget to put the carrots in early." Melissa shook her head. "I'm not much of a cook."

Mark was busy chewing but patted her back. No one else bothered to contradict her.

"No, please. I can honestly say this is the best meal I've had in years." I smiled and calmly picked up my carrot from the floor. I realized Boogie had taken up a position under the coffee table and I offered it to him. He wasn't interested.

"Try the green beans. From a can, but I added a few things to make them interesting." Melissa smiled.

"They're good, Mom. Is that, uh, sugar in there?" Penny forked up a big serving.

"Yes, it was a new recipe from one of those newsstand magazines." Melissa took a taste. "Yummy. But more like dessert, I guess. Of course you always were my dessert girl."

"You can say that again." Jenny pushed her food around on her plate and actually ate very little. "Penny may be going to California. Big new job."

"What?" Mark and Melissa stared at Penny like she'd just proposed taking the space shuttle to Mars.

"Thanks, Jenny. Yes, I have a wonderful opportunity. I've got a chance to work on cutting-edge research with a scientist who has a lab outside of Los Angeles. Glory arranged an introduction."

Now eyes were on me and I was the snake in the Garden of Eden. "Uh, Ian MacDonald does great things. And he has a fabulous setup, right on the Pacific Ocean in Malibu."

"Are you kidding me?" Jenny was totally envying.

Melissa's eyes narrowed. "You realize that area is just one earthquake away from sliding into the ocean, don't you?"

"And there are forest fires, not to mention mud slides." Mark leaned forward. "Have you researched this guy's background? What kind of money are we talking here? You have any idea how expensive it is to live in California?"

"Daddy, Mom, calm down." Penny got up and took her plate to the kitchen. "Chocolate cake, Glory?"

"Are you kidding me? I'd kill for chocolate cake." I smiled. "Not literally you understand." Blank stares from the family.

"Don't worry. She buys this from a local German bakery. Delicious," Penny whispered as she got busy cutting big slices.

"None for me, Penny. I've got to leave soon and hit the books." Jenny came to stand in the kitchen doorway and made sure to put a sad note in there.

"I'm going to pay for you to get a tutor." Penny sighed. "It'll be our secret."

"Seriously?" Jenny grinned and hugged her sister. "I knew you wouldn't let me down. Now I'll go talk up California. You should hear Mom and Daddy whispering about it. You'd think you were going straight to hell." She giggled and gave Penny the once-over. "As if you'd get so lucky."

I turned to Penny as soon as Jenny disappeared. Penny held up her hand.

"Don't say it. She's my twin. And I usually do help her."

"Not saying a word." I took a plate with a huge slice of cake and picked up a fork. "You do whatever you want. Me? I'd let her sink like a rock. But then I'm not related to her." I took a bite and felt the bliss of rich chocolate hit my mouth and tongue. "Oh, God, but that's good."

"Better than." Penny handed me another plate. "Now please help me with the folks. If I get the chance, I'm going to California. Tell them great things about Ian. Make stuff up if you have to."

"Not necessary. He's brilliant and I know this could be a fantastic opportunity for you. It's an easy sell." I carried a plate to Melissa and started in with a glowing recommendation of Ian. I described his advanced degrees and first-class setup. Of course I left out that he charged megabucks for whatever he invented so only rich vampires benefited. Hooking up my fledgling with Ian felt right.

What didn't feel right was my tummy. I felt a gurgle first and looked around, hoping no one had noticed. Not a chance, they were too busy shouting about how Penny should stay at the University of Texas.

"Actually Ian is thinking of opening a lab here in Austin. That's why he was visiting Ray, Israel Caine. They're friends and Ray had told him about our cheap land here, compared to L.A. anyway. Ian's other interest is real estate and he knows a good deal when he sees it. I think there's a good chance Penny could stay here in Austin and never go to California at all." I barely got this out before my stomach rumbled again. I rattled my fork against my empty plate to try to cover the noise.

Not necessary. Penny jumped in with another reason why she was done with the grant program here and the shouting started again. I tuned out. I'd finished my second piece of chocolate cake but that last bite had pushed me past full to miserable. Now, when I looked down, I noticed a bulge under my skirt. Swollen stomach? Wait a minute. This wasn't a tiny bulge. It was like everything I'd just eaten had decided to stage a sit-in. Like back in the hippie era.

I glanced around, glad Penny was the one in the hot seat, then pulled down my sweater. The stupid thing slid right back up again. That did it. I had to get out of here. But, when I struggled to my feet, I heard a pop.

"Glory, I think you just lost a button." Jenny giggled. "Was that off your skirt?" She rolled her eyes. "Careful, Penny. If you two eat like this all the time, you'll soon be giving the blimp a run for its money."

"Jennifer Louise!" Melissa gave Jenny a stern look. "Pay no attention to her, Glory. I just love to see someone appreciate food."

"Oh, I appreciated it all right." I heard my stomach rumble again. "Excuse me." I headed to the bathroom, where I shut the door and sat on the lid of the closed toilet. What was going on? My stomach was growing, and the noises! I heard a knock on the door.

"Glory? You all right?" It was Penny.

"Get in here." I unlocked the door and dragged her inside. "How are you feeling? Did you take Ian's potion?"

"Of course I did. I ate, didn't I?" She stared at my stomach. "It's moving. I need to get my notebook. Damn, I wish I had a stethoscope. I can hear the strange sounds from here." She leaned down like she wanted to press her ear to my stomach. "Gurgles and—whoa!—I think it's calling for help."

"Not funny." I popped her on the arm. "I'm making a run to my room. Can you make my excuses to your folks? Keep your fangs out of sight?"

"Sure, that's no problem." She pressed her hands to her own stomach, which had no unusual bulges. "And my tummy is quiet. Nothing going on there." She stretched out her hand. "Seriously. Are you in pain? Maybe I should get Ian over here."

I felt a lightning bolt shoot through my midriff. Power of suggestion?

"Oh, ow! Thanks a heap. Didn't hurt till you mentioned it. I'll call Ray, he can send Ian over. Just get rid of your parents. Please?" I burped what sounded like the mating call of a lonely foghorn, then clapped my hand over my mouth.

"Another symptom. I ate as much as you did. I wonder why nothing's hit me." Penny's eyes gleamed and I had a feeling she was going straight for her notebook when she left me. "Go lie down. It's not unusual for people to have digestive issues the first time they eat Mom's food. Maybe it's nothing to do with Ian's stuff." She grinned, then clapped her hand over her mouth.

"You couldn't have warned me?" I managed to gasp. "We could have saved that potion for steak at a fabulous restaurant, you know." I moaned when another pain hit.

"You're right. But, if I get this job, you can have more of the formula, all you want." Penny wasn't smiling now. "I know I should have admitted that Mom's not the greatest cook in the world. That's why I told her we were on a diet. Tried to keep her from bringing dinner in the first place, nothing to do with the vampire thing at all. Honestly, it would have been easier chewing a rubber band than that pot roast." She patted my shoulder. "But the cake was stellar, you have to admit that."

"Oh, yes. Two pieces of heaven." I gasped as agony ripped through me. "You sure you're okay?"

Penny frowned, checking herself, then shook her head. "Not an ache, not a twinge. Ian's formula worked perfectly on me."

"Great, just great." I kept my head on my knees, nausea now an extra added attraction.

"Try to relax, Glory. I'll get rid of Mom, Dad and Jenny. No worries." Penny patted my back, then closed the bathroom door.

No worries? I breathed through the nausea, held on to the wall to stand, and made a run for my bedroom. There I eased my door shut before I collapsed on the bed. I fumbled for my purse on the floor and pulled out my cell phone, barely managing to hit Ray's number before my stomach rumbled again and made me double over. I shoved my purse away and grabbed my trash can, just in case. Thank God, I didn't throw up but it was close.

I listened to the phone ring with my eyes closed. This had to be way more than a simple case of gluttony that a Tums could cure.

Seventeen

"**Glory?** How's it going? Isn't this the night you were having Penny's folks over for dinner?" Ray's voice sounded wonderful, not slurred. He was sober and cheerful. I was so . . . not. I could barely talk as my stomach did a bob and weave. Shapes moved under my skirt. Like a boa trying to make an escape.

"Not great. Tell Ian I'm having one of my weird reactions to his stuff." I gasped. "Pain."

"We'll be right there. Hang in, babe."

I tossed the phone aside and grabbed my middle. Skirt. Even without the button it was too tight. I managed to get the zipper down and wiggled out of it, then kicked it to the floor. I slid under the sheet and coverlet, shaking as another pain hit me. I'd been a pig and this was what I got.

But Penny was right. She'd eaten just as much and she hadn't looked like she'd swallowed a water balloon. I huddled under the covers and curled onto my side, my knees pulled up toward my chest. Even my black silk panties felt tight, but I wasn't about to shuck those. Why couldn't anything ever be simple for me? I don't know how long I lay there before Penny opened the bedroom door.

"They're gone. They left a bunch of leftovers in the fridge. I figure Trey or Rafe would enjoy them later. Or not." Penny had a pen and notebook in her hands. "Let me take your temperature." She stopped by the bed. "Do you have a thermometer in the bathroom?"

"Uh, that would be a no. Vampires don't worry about stuff like that." I groaned and rolled over. "Ian's on his way. Look at my stomach." I pulled down the covers. "It's like it's alive."

"Damn. And I always said Mom's roast beef was cooked to death." Penny poked my swollen skin. "You may be right; something's trying to get out of there."

"Answer the door. They must have shifted to get here so fast." I recognized Ray's scent.

"No kidding." She turned and ran to the front door. I heard her greet Ian and Ray. She was busy answering questions about when we'd taken the drug and what we'd eaten when Ray came to stand next to my bed.

"What the hell, Glory?" He sat beside me and brushed back my hair.

"Don't know." I blinked and a tear rolled down my cheek. "Penny's fine. But my stomach—" I bent over and held it as pain ripped through me again. "Damn it!"

"Gloriana, breathe through it." Ian pushed Ray out of the way. He opened a doctor's bag and pulled out that stethoscope Penny had wished for. "I'm going to take a listen. See what's going on." He rubbed the metal sensor with his hand, then placed it on my chest, right inside the vee of my sweater, then he lifted that sweater to check below my breast, moving down toward my stomach.

I could see Ray watching his every move. I stretched out my hand and he took it, squeezing my fingers reassuringly. When Ian pulled down the sheet and my stomach was exposed, he hissed and Ray leaned to see over his shoulder.

"Damn, Glory. Did you eat a side of beef?" Ray gawked at my stomach.

"Very funny." I moaned as my stomach rolled. "No, but I ate two enormous pieces of cake, three rolls, or at least the tops of them, slathered with butter. And some weird but tasty sweet green beans. We both did. Right, Penny?"

"Yes. We were pigs. My mom's not a great cook, but with a chance for a vampire to eat . . ." I saw her look to Ray for sympathy and he nodded.

"Yeah, I get it, especially for my gal here. Glory's been without solid eats for way too long. But you seem to be holding up fine, Penny. Glory's stomach looks like it's about to blow open and I wish I was exaggerating." Ray pulled my hand to his lips and kissed my knuckles. "Crazy."

"There is something about you, Gloriana. This is the second of my formulas that hasn't agreed with you. It's like an allergic reaction. At least that's what I think this is." Ian pulled a hypodermic needle from his bag. "This time I hope you'll let me treat you."

"Yes. Whatever it takes to stop this. Surely this tummy bulge won't be permanent." I looked like I'd swallowed a small watermelon.

"You mind if Penny listens to your stomach before I give you the shot? This is a chance for her to learn something." Ian took off his stethoscope.

I glanced at Penny's eager face. "Sure, go ahead. But hurry."

She took the stethoscope and carefully placed the earpieces, then leaned over. "Wow, fascinating." She and Ian said a few things that I ignored. It was technical jargon and I had a feeling my fledgling was going to end up in medical school after all. Maybe I could plant the idea in her parents' minds that time spent with Ian would make that happen. Surely that would make them happier about her possible trip to Sodom and Gomorrah, otherwise known as California.

"Okay, I think I've suffered enough for science. Give me the damned shot." I offered my arm.

"Wait. What is it?" Ray blocked Ian. "Yeah, yeah, I'm a sap, but this is what Blade would want to know."

"Hello? In pain here." I didn't care what Ian gave me, just wanted the next lightning strike headed off before it hit ground zero.

"No, Ray's right." Ian smiled at me. "It's a cocktail of a common antihistamine and a muscle relaxant." He glanced at Penny. "Your fledgling saw me fill the syringe out in the living room after she described your symptoms."

"That's right, I did. You want me to read the labels on the vials? Look the stuff up on the Internet?" Penny didn't know much about Ian's history with Jerry, but she had a lot of respect for Mr. Blade.

"No, just shoot me." I looked at Ray and Penny. "I appreciate the protective bit, but Ian is just trying to help. And if this kills me? He won't live to see another sunset. Jerry will see to that." I handed Ian my arm again. "Now get after it."

"Sorry, Glory, but this goes in the bum. Like I said, these are common meds, but pretty strong doses. They'll make you drowsy, but should take care of this reaction." Ian frowned. "As for the swelling? Well, we'll just have to wait and see if it goes down." He gently rolled me over until he could see my hip, slid down my panty and injected the medicine before I could object to the familiarity. To tell the truth, I was in too much pain to care.

"Penny, why don't you come into the other room and we'll go through the symptoms you noticed as Gloriana presented them. She needs to rest." Ian closed up his bag and led her toward the living room. "Ray, you'll let me know if she shows any new signs of distress?"

"What? Any new signs?" Ray's eyebrows went up. "I thought what you just did was supposed to fix her up."

"So it was. But Gloriana never responds to any treatment as I expect, so I'll trust you to keep a close eye on her." Ian smiled at me. "Feeling any better yet?"

I smiled, surprised to realize I was. "Hmm. Yes, I think, um, well, maybe." I looked over at Ray. "Come lie next to me. I'm worn-out and cold. Will you hold me?"

"Sure, babe. Whatever you want." He kicked off his shoes and climbed in under the covers. "How's the stomach?" He laid his hand over my tummy. "Still swollen, isn't it?"

"Stupid me. Can't anything be easy?" I sighed as he

pulled me against him. "But chocolate cake, Ray. It was delicious." I ran my hand over his cotton shirt. "You feel delicious too. Whatcha been doin'?"

"Are you okay?" He looked down at me. "You sound drunk. And I should know."

"Just relaxed. Ian's medicine is pretty good. Took the pain right away." I slid my leg over Ray's. "Now talk to me while I'm waiting for my tummy to shrink. Tell me what's up. Besides Little Ray here." I discovered the bulge behind Ray's zipper. "Shame on you. I'm a sick woman."

"I'm not the one making moves. And it's Big Ray who's happy to see you, nothing little about him." Ray picked up my hand. "Lie still, woman. You should know a guy can't always control his body."

"Liar, liar, pants on fire." I put my hand over my mouth. "Oops. Not mentioning fire or hell or any of that stuff. Don't want the demons bugging me now." I blinked when the room blurred. "Last night was a bad night, Ray." I buried my face in his shirt and sobbed.

"What? What happened, Glory?" Ray stroked my hair.

"Lucifer tried to do something horrible to me. In, in the shower." I couldn't seem to stop crying as I poured out what happened. Why now? Why to Ray? Some part of me realized it was the medication working on me, loosening my inhibitions. But another part of me realized I needed to get this out and Ray had always been easy to talk to. I could trust him to get me and not judge. Or rush to take over and try to fix things.

I finally came to the end, cried out and drained. Ray rocked me against him, humming a sweet song in my ear that soothed me and lulled me into a calm I hadn't felt since I'd fallen to the bottom of that bathtub. My own abyss.

"I'm sorry, Ray." I lifted my head and looked at him.

"Sorry for what?" He kissed my damp cheeks. "Glory, Glory, Glory. I can't believe you kicked Lucifer's butt. Damn, girl."

I smiled. "Yeah, I did, didn't I?"

"Hell, yeah. I'd like to hear what he said to the guys down under when he came back smelling like he'd been dropped on his head in that girly shit." He kissed my forehead, then pulled me close. He was putting a light spin on this, but I'd seen that this had hurt him, that he hurt *for* me. And easygoing Ray was struggling with the same rage that Jerry and Rafe felt. If we were fighting against normal men, the demons and Lucifer wouldn't have stood a chance.

"I was lucky he decided I wasn't worth his time after that." I shuddered. "But I'm feeling better now. I needed to unload, I guess. If I fall apart with Jerry and Rafe, they . . ."

"I get it. They go all warrior on you, start looking for the nearest battlefield. Beating their chests and putting you behind them like you're the helpless female." Ray breathed into my hair. "Shit, right now I can relate. Would do me some good to hand that bastard a big dose of whoop-ass. Creeping into your shower, invading your privacy . . ."

"Yes, well, it's over. Moving on." I yawned.

"How is she?" Ian spoke from the doorway. "Any change?"

"Well, she's woozy. I guess that's from the shot. Pain's gone." Ray rubbed my back. "Still is, right?"

"All gone." I lifted the sheet and looked down. "But my damned tummy is still poking out." I sat up but the room spun so I fell back. "Ian, this is unacceptable. My stomach had better be flat, er, flatter, anyway, when I wake up tomorrow night or I'm suing! This has malpractice written all over it."

I saw Penny's eyes widen. "But I took the same thing, Glory, and I didn't have any problems."

"Yes. But you don't have a boyfriend named Campbell. Truth now, Ian. Did you put something extra in my vial that you didn't put in Penny's?" I used Ray's shoulder as I struggled to sit up again. Maybe paranoia was contagious or I'd been around Jerry too long.

"You know, somehow I knew this question might arise. So I took precautions." Ian turned to Penny. "When I gave you the formula, Penny, how did you select the vials?"

"You had a bagful of samples. You told me to help myself. To take two, one for me and one for Glory. Any two I wanted. It was totally random." Penny smiled at me. "So he couldn't have rigged yours, Glory. No conspiracy possible."

"Well, that's a relief. Would hate to see that old feud start up again. Campbell versus MacDonald." I leaned against Ray and he squeezed my shoulders. I'm sure he'd just loved hearing me call Jerry my boyfriend. "But you're not off the hook. This is the second time you've made me sick, Ian, instead of delivering the benefit you promised."

"Did you enjoy your meal, Gloriana?" Ian strode over to the bedside.

"Yes." I looked up at him. "Well, as much as I could considering the beef was rubbery and the carrots were underdone. Not your fault." I smiled at Penny. "Your mom doesn't teach home ec, does she?"

"Are you kidding? The school board wouldn't inflict her on future homemakers. Now come on, Glory, you know what Ian is asking." Clearly Penny had a new idol and it wasn't me.

"Fine. To tell the truth? If you could just perfect that damned formula, Ian, it would be worth its weight in gold." I sagged against Ray. "Chocolate cake. Roast beef done right? Oh my God! And live forever too? Now there's a vampire's dream."

"Don't forget living in daylight." Ray kissed my cheek.

"Right. You're right, Ray. Keep working on that too, Ian." I reached back to pat Ray's cheek. I was definitely feeling drunk. But it was a happy drunk and I didn't have it in me to be mad at Ian. Not now, anyway.

"Then give me a blood sample and I'll try to figure out why my formulas give you problems. I promise to work on the food one first. Maybe I can get the kinks worked out and you can give it another shot." Ian opened his bag again.

"Not a good idea, Ian. I think Glory's been through enough." Ray eased me back on the bed. "You don't even know if your stomach will go down yet, Glory. You really want to try this again?"

"In the interest of science?" I glanced at Penny and she nodded. "I *would* like to know why I reacted weirdly and Penny didn't. But I get freebies if you get answers, Ian, and you fix this so it'll work on me without side effects." I threw my arm out where Ian could reach it.

"Of course. And this should be the first project Penny works on if she comes on board as my assistant. Would that make you feel better, Gloriana? Ray?"

"It might. What do you say, Glory?"

I watched Ian take blood from the vein in my arm and I was suddenly thirsty. "Huh? I say someone get me something to drink." I looked at Ray with a smile. "Ray? Come here, honey. You've got some rich and delicious blood wrapped in a pretty package."

"Uh, I think I've got places to go, people to meet." Penny backed out of the room.

"Me as well." Ian closed his bag with a snap. "I'll let you know the results, Gloriana. And Penny will let me know tomorrow if your stomach benefited from a day's sleep."

I glanced down at my swollen stomach. "Oh, yeah. Full report. Thanks for the shot. Definitely feeling no pain. Bye." I reached for Ray and dragged him to me.

"You know you're not going to do this." Ray laughed as I fell on top of him. We both heard the hall door close and I realized we were alone. My fuzzy thinking might be from the drug Ian had injected in me, but there was nothing fuzzy about my raging thirst.

"Why not?" I slid my fangs along the front of his shirt, popping buttons as I went. I was headed to his jugular. I ran my hands over his smooth chest, not so drunk I didn't appreciate the view. "You really don't mind, do you?"

"Not at all. Go ahead. Have at it. You've been generous enough with me. But I've got to warn you, my self-control is slipping. You are much too tempting in your silk panties and bare legs. And then I saw Ian push up your sweater to listen to your heart. Leopard-print bra. Don't you know what that does to a man, Glory?"

"Good eye, Caine." I grinned and lifted my sweater. "Wasn't baiting a trap. Last one clean. I really need to do laundry."

Ray groaned, rolled me off him and eased out of bed. "No, not happening. I'm getting you a bottle of synthetic and then I'm calling Blade."

"What?" I managed to sit up on my own.

"You're high. That shot of Ian's did this to you and I seem to have found some sort of moral high ground since I got sober. It's a bitch, but there it is."

"Well, that's a hell of a note." I pulled down my sweater and covered my panties with the sheet.

"You said Blade was your boyfriend. *He* should be here taking care of you. So I'll call him." Ray picked up my cell from the nightstand. "Yep, he's your number one. Enough said."

"You're being awfully noble, Ray. Can't say it suits you. Where's the bad boy when I need him?" I tried for a pout, but didn't have the energy for it. Muscle relaxant. Sitting was too much and I fell back again.

"Well, maybe I'll kick myself all the way home. But I know you, Glory girl, and you sure don't want to wake up tomorrow night smelling of sex with me and not remember it." Ray's smile was wry, like maybe he was already wondering if he'd made the wrong call.

"No! That would be the worst. If, when, we ever . . . Well, I'd want to remember every second." I couldn't look away from his gleaming blue eyes.

"You just made my point. And I'm here to tell you that you'll conk out soon and probably not remember much of what you did or said after Ian gave you that shot." Ray hit speed dial on my phone. "Now lie back and close your eyes. Dream of me, if you want. But that's all you're getting."

I didn't dream. Didn't wake up at all till the next night. My stomach was still swollen, damn it. Not as big as it had been right after my binge, but definitely showing the effects.

Penny couldn't wait to fill Ian in. I was wishing for a vamp Yellow Pages so I could find that malpractice lawyer. At least my tummy stayed quiet.

Jerry had slept the day away beside me but I let him know I needed to work and that I felt well enough to keep my appointment with Simon. Of course he'd wanted to be in on it. I knew Simon would take one whiff of a second vampire and never even knock on my back door. Jerry had to see that logic and gave in, reluctantly. So I headed down to the shop alone.

"Glory, did you forget that today is payday? Lacy said to tell you she'd call and see if her check might be ready later tonight." Erin greeted me at the door. "I know you've been busy, with your new roommate and all, but, uh, I have to eat and pay rent, you know."

I held up my hand. "I'll get right on it, Erin. So I'll be in the back room, taking care of it." I headed straight there. I'd spoiled my clerks. Doing my bookkeeping on my day off, Monday, so that their weekly checks were waiting for them on Tuesday. Now I had to sit with time cards and payroll. Some fun. Somehow business hadn't entered my mind after the hell-storm of the weekend.

I pulled out my records and sat with my laptop on the worktable, ready to knock this out. I only had five employees, two full-timers and three students who worked part-time. They were on the honor system and left their time cards in the back room for me. Lacy managed the day, Erin the night crew. I hired paranormals exclusively. It was the way we helped each other. I'd just signed the last check when I felt a presence on one of my shoulders.

"Finally. We didn't want to interrupt you." Emmie Lou sighed in my ear. "Figured it was good for you to get your work done."

"Thanks. Let me run these out to Erin and then we can talk." I stood as soon as Emmie flew up to join Harvey on his perch at the top of the shelving unit. I slipped the checks into envelopes, wrote the names on the fronts and then sealed them. I took them out to a busy Erin, then actually took the time to glance around the shop.

It looked pretty good. Stock was straight, though it was still on the skimpy side. There were several customers with clothing on their arms, obviously getting ready to try them on. And the vintage books were getting some interest from a pair of professor types. Best of all, no sign of Caryon or Spyte. That cheered me.

Because I still had these waves of depression, I'd guess you'd call it. One would hit every time I remembered how Lucifer had attacked me when I was naked and vulnerable. Damn him. Ha. Like that weak word was anything but a compliment to the creep.

Then to top things off, I'd had that stupid reaction to Ian's potion. You can bet Jerry had been upset about that. Of course that had gotten me a lecture. Not a long one. Jerry figured out pretty fast that I was in no mood to hear how wrongheaded I'd been to try anything a MacDonald gave me. And he'd clearly still been reeling from the Lucifer invasion himself, treating me like I was made of glass. I took a breath, then finally walked back into the workroom.

"What's up, guys? Any demon sightings?" I tried to sound flip, but felt anything but.

"They'd better not come in here." Harvey flew down to land on the table in front of me. "I tell you, little gal, their boss has gone too far."

"Yep, Harvey's right. Too far. And someone higher up is not goin' to stand for it." Emmie Lou settled beside her husband.

I sat on the chair. "What could anyone higher up do about it besides send you two here? Lucifer is the head honcho in hell and he does what he damn well pleases." I shuddered. "I had a demo of that." And the idea that these two gentle souls somehow knew? I blinked back tears.

"Now, now. Don't go fretting about anything we know or don't know. I'm just telling you that we got word this evening that the Master is keeping a special eye on you. He knows you're good through and through and he doesn't like seeing decent people pushed around." Harvey popped his suspenders, his face red. "Trust me, there ain't no bullies sitting at the banquet table up where *we've* been."

"You've got that right, honey bun." Emmie patted Harvey's knee. "Those black-hearted good-for-nothings need to stay down below where they belong." She gave me a sad smile. "So we're gonna try to even things up a bit. Got some special stuff to help you. As long as you're in this back room."

"What kind of special stuff?" I leaned forward. Help. It was almost too good to be true. Sure I had my three guys who would literally face hell for me, but I was afraid it was all good intentions. They'd be turned into stone warriors at the first sign of trouble and I'd be at Lucifer's mercy again. And there are only so many times you can pull the shower gel trick.

"First, you'll love this. I got it from *Get Smart*. I watched the original show on TV, might even have been in black-and-white. I can't remember. You're old enough, Glory, you might have watched it then too, but youngsters just know that new movie." Harvey winced and glared at Emmie. "You pinched me!"

"Quit carrying on and get to the point." Emmie smiled at me. "He has endless cable up in Heaven, every channel they put on. His own remote and a top-of-the-line La-Z-Boy. It's a wonder he stirred himself to come help you."

"Now who's off the point?" Harvey poked Emmie with an elbow. "I'll *always* stir myself for our Glory. Now, as I was saying, that show had what they called a 'Cone of Silence' and that's what the Big Guy upstairs has given us here." He chuckled. "I just love technology."

"Huh. To you technology is the icemaker in the door of the Frigidaire." Emmie huffed.

"Anyway . . ." Harvey ignored his wife who was muttering. "When you're in here, Glory, those demons and suchlike can't hear you. You can make your plans, figure out your moves, and they won't be able to hear a thing. This back room is your Cone of Silence."

"Seriously?" I jumped up. "That's amazing! And just what I need for later tonight."

"And if them demons try to get in here?" Emmie pulled a bottle out of her apron pocket. Tonight she wore a blue print shirtwaist, circa 1950, with a frilly white eyelet apron. "We've got this."

"What is it?" I saw a clear liquid sloshing in the bottle.

"It's water from a lake up there." Emmie grinned. "It's beyond holy. It's sacred. Burns like acid on a demon's skin. Even Lucifer would squawk like a scorched chicken if this hit him."

"Hot diggity dog. I hope those bad boys do make a run at us." Harvey popped his suspenders again. "I'd like to make 'em squeal. Chase 'em straight back to hell, I will."

"I can't believe this." I really wanted to hug them, but they were just too tiny. "You mean someone up there thinks I deserve all this?" I sank down on the chair again. "Sometimes I'm really not so sure."

"Now, now, don't you be downing yourself, little gal." Harvey fluttered over to sit on my shoulder. Emmie landed on my other one. "You take our word for it. You've been around an awful long time and your good deeds have piled up pretty durn high."

"That's right, Glory. You surely do deserve our help. Now suck it up and fight off these critters. Win the night!" Emmie flew back to the table. Harvey joined her.

"Are you allowed to tell me any more about Heaven? Is it all cable TV and easy chairs?" I could tell by looking at them how happy they were. They glowed with it.

"La, no! I sure don't sit around all the livelong day watching no box." Emmie laughed. "Honey, Heaven is what you want it to be." Her eyes glittered. "Up there I've got the children I never could have, the grandbabies I always wanted. It's, it's wonderful. Glorious."

"Yep. And my old dog, Traveler, is there at my feet when

I feel like watching sports. Or we go out to a real game. Sometimes I play quarterback like I always wanted to, in the NFL." Harvey laughed. "Lot tougher than it looks on TV."

"You two are together. Obviously. What if, what if you love more than one person in your life?" I twisted my fingers in my lap.

"Like three, honey?" Emmie smiled. "I'm here to tell you, it's common as all get-out in Heaven. Think of all the widows who lost number one. Some in a war, some with heart trouble or whatever. Then they fell in love again, maybe even a third time if they outlasted number two." She sighed and looked at Harvey. "My guy never moved on, but he could have. I wouldn't have minded."

"Just never got struck by Cupid's arrow again, honey bunch, and that's a fact. Though the Widow March gave me a run for my money." Harvey winked at me.

"Oh, you!" Emmie patted his knee. "Anyway, these women who loved more than one man just spend time with each of them as they feel the urge. There's no jealousy there. The men don't bump into each other and they stay busy doing whatever they dreamed of on earth. Maybe lying back in front of a TV like Harvey, though the golf course gets a lot of play."

"Yeah, never did cotton to that game." Harvey leaned against Emmie. "Glad I don't have to share you, though, hon."

"As far as you know." This time Emmie winked at me. "Anyway, the ladies see who they want as long as they want, then move on. As I said, Heaven is how you want it to be." She grabbed Harvey's hand and squeezed it. "Calm down. You know you're my one and only." She kissed his flushed cheek.

"Sounds perfect." I sighed.

"There you go." Harvey cleared his throat. "But no need for you to rush to get there. You got a good many years left on this earth. I got that on good authority." He flew close and brushed my cheek with his wings. It felt like a gentle tickle.

"Hush, now, Harvey. We got rules, you know." Emmie sounded hoarse, like maybe she was choking back tears.

"Can I ask you one more question?" I was pretty choked up myself.

"Not sure we can answer it, but shoot." Emmie smiled as Harvey kept flying in circles. "Ignore him, he just loves those wings."

"Why did you come back so tiny?" I reached out my hand and Emmie flew into it. I knew if I closed my fist, I'd crush her. Of course I couldn't imagine doing such a thing.

"Simple, Glory. Just provin' a point. Size don't really matter in the long run. It's how you live and what's inside that counts." Emmie took off then, fluttering past my cheek like Harvey had.

"Just keep fightin', Glory, and let your good heart guide you." Harvey flew a circle around the room. "Rules. Bet those demons don't abide by no rules."

"Bet they do. Now let's go patrol the shop. Head out, Harvey." Emmie buzzed close to my ear. "Our money's on you, Glory. Have faith." Then they both disappeared through the closed door.

I sagged back in my chair. Heaven or hell? No contest. And I sure wanted to meet everyone I knew and loved there someday. So the challenge ahead meant everything to me. This Cone of Silence thing was fantastic and I was putting it to work immediately as I heard a knock on the back door and recognized the reek of Simon Destiny.

I hurried to open it and let him in. Simon stood there for a moment and sniffed the air, then just stared at me. Simon pulled out a handkerchief. It went with the black suit he wore, old-fashioned but clearly custom-tailored and very expensive. Savile Row, if I knew my menswear, and I did. His white shirt had the same look and his tie was a school tie, the kind English gentlemen wore to proclaim their status. That was a laugh. As if Simon had any status outside his ghoulish boys' club of vampires.

"You're alone." He seemed surprised.

"So are you." I wasn't surprised. Simon wouldn't doubt he could take me in a fight. I was no match for an Energy Vampire, never had been. "Come in."

He stepped inside and nodded when I gestured that he could take the chair. He sat, then waited for me to plop down on the table. I really needed to haul in another chair.

"You mentioned a way for me to get to know my son. He gave me an ultimatum. I assume he told you about it." Simon didn't smile and obviously wasn't going to waste time with small talk.

"Yes. Freddy would like to get to know you. Apparently it's a son-father thing. But can't get past the whole EV hoopla. Guess you know what I'm talking about." I sighed. I couldn't do this sitting on a table swinging my legs. I jumped down and began to pace. "You serve one of hell's goddesses. She scares Fred. Scares anyone with good sense. And of course you use that fear to your advantage, Simon."

"Of course." He nodded, looking thoughtful. "I've had centuries to think about this. But I am tied to Honoria. You don't just tender a resignation. She expects a lifetime of service."

"Is there any way to, um, destroy her?" I held my breath. This was the big gamble. If Simon didn't trust me to do this and not take him out too, it was all over. "I'm asking you because I've got an alternative for you. Lucifer has sent a couple of demons here to bug me. They've threatened Rafe Valdez and the only way I can get them off his back is to deliver a major soul or dozen to Luc's team."

"Hell's politics. I get an earful of that every time I visit my goddess." Simon made a face. "So?"

"So if you will agree to transfer your allegiance to Luc's team and take your followers with you, Rafe will be off the hook."

"You know I don't give a damn about your dog." Simon examined his nails.

"But you do about your son. I'm just showing you why I have an interest in helping you get rid of your goddess. Tell me how to take her out and I'll do it. Rafe and Blade are in it with me. We will blow her to bits or whatever it takes to free you if you will sign on with Lucifer. You know you're hell-bound anyway, and Freddy won't mind getting involved with you once Honoria is out of the picture. It's the EV thing he objects to."

"How do you know that?" Simon looked up, his eyes gleaming. I knew he was reading my mind and he saw that I was uncertain.

"Guess you could make that part of your terms with Lucifer. And you're clever enough to play the game, act like you've come to your senses and want to start over. Play the good guy." I rolled my eyes. "Why am I bothering to tell you anything? Manipulate. It's your stock-in-trade." The fact that my good friend Freddy would be on the receiving end of that gave me chills. No. I'd warn him. He was smart enough to figure things out himself. And I was smart enough to stop thinking about this because Simon could read my every thought. Argh.

"What makes you think I'd be interested?" Simon lifted his chin. "I have everything I ever wanted. Money, power and the respect being the king of the Energy Vampires brings me."

"Do you have your heart's desire?" I blurted it out.

Simon swallowed. "What do you know about that?"

Wow. For a moment I could just stare. I'd hit a nerve. Go figure. "Lucifer can offer you that. Promise your soul to him and he can deliver anything, anything you've always wanted but might have eluded you." I ran my hands down my body. "He even said he could make me a size six." I laughed. "Stupid, but he did a demo. It works." I grabbed Simon's hand and pulled him into the bathroom. "Look, I have my reflection. As a sign of good faith or to torment me, depending on how you look at it."

Simon stood behind me and examined the evidence. "So I see. Are you telling me you sold your own soul?" Simon's eyes widened. "Bravo. I didn't think you had it in you."

"You're right. I didn't do it. I'm not going to hell. At

least not on Lucifer's account. But since you're doomed already, thanks to your work with Honoria, why not play for a new team? Broker a new deal." I pushed past him, already regretting the close quarters of the bathroom. Maybe I was seeing him more as a man, though, because we'd been talking for a while now and he hadn't knocked me down or frozen me. Hey, it had been almost civilized.

"That's impossible, Gloriana. I am never getting away from my goddess. She wouldn't stand for it." Simon stalked to the door. "I'd not live to make any such deal, no matter how much I wanted it."

"What *is* your heart's desire, Simon?" I was grasping at straws. Thought maybe if I got him to say it, I could somehow work something out, tempt him past logic.

Simon stared at me, obviously thinking about whether he should share something so private with me. "All right. I'll tell you. Not that it will do any good. But I always regretted leaving Cecilia and our child. I wanted . . . a family." His smile was wry. "How plebeian of me. I realize that. But I loved Cecilia. Still do. I doubt that Lucifer could make her love me again. Too much water under that bridge."

I swallowed. My dear friend CiCi with Simon? How was that for a hellish bargain? "I figure with Lucifer, anything's possible. Hammer out a deal. Ask for what you want from him. Or the demons he sends." I let Simon see that I was being honest.

"You're assuming Honoria can be killed." Simon sighed. "Fact is, she's always surrounded by her army of loyal followers. No one gets past us." Simon smiled now. "The Energy Vampires not only feed her, we are sworn to protect her. Killing her?" He shrugged. "Difficult, but not impossible."

I stopped in my tracks. He was actually interested. "Tell me."

"First, you'd have to lull her to sleep. That means depriving her of as much energy as you can. I can take most of my men away from the compound on some pretext, but I always have to leave at least ten there as an energy source. Sleeping, they don't give her much energy. That would make her fairly listless. That would be the best time to approach her."

"Okay, maybe I can find a way to knock them out temporarily." Ian might have something for that. "So then what? She's taking a siesta. I heard she's down underground."

"Yes, you walk down a steep trail into the bowels of the earth. It's not pleasant, like walking into hell until you get into her chamber. You'll have to sneak up on her, try not to wake her and then cut off her heads."

"Heads?" My voice was a squeak. "How many are we talking about?"

Simon managed a smile. "Three, Gloriana. Three of the ugliest visages you'd never hope to see. As you can imagine, I would gladly take what Lucifer's offering to get away from an afterlife of sex with that creature. Kill her and you'll not only give me my son, you'll free me from that." He stood. "I'll owe you. And I don't say that lightly."

"Wow." I closed my gaping mouth. "We've got to do this soon, Simon. Give me a night to work this out." I glanced at my watch. It wasn't even ten o'clock yet. I'd have to call Jerry and Rafe. Of course they were champing at the bit, not happy that I'd insisted on this meeting without them.

"Tomorrow night I'd planned to take a large contingent of men to a meeting in Houston. If you could do it then, you would have only a small force to deal with. I could put something in their blood supply to slow them down but I don't dare drug them and knock them out completely. It would be too suspicious. Honoria would know if all her energy suddenly disappeared. She can cause quite a disturbance if that happens." Simon ran his hand over his thinning hair.

I swallowed. Tomorrow night. So soon. But we'd waited long enough. I wanted the demons gone. And couldn't risk Lucifer showing up again either.

"Fine." I held out my hand, something I rarely did to Simon. "You promise to sign with Lucifer once this is done?"

"I give you my word." Simon looked me directly in the eyes and took my hand. "You've made it sound like the thing to do."

I felt the shock of his power and suddenly knew the truth of that promise. "All right then."

"I will know when it is done. Many of my powers will be gone." Simon released my hand. "Fortunately, Lucifer can restore them. So you can relax and know I will follow through on this thing to save your Valdez." He stalked to the door and threw it open. "Good luck, Gloriana. You'll need it. And, Gloriana."

"Yes?" I braced myself. Something in his eyes told me the worst was yet to come.

"If she wakes up, don't be fooled by her. She has many tricks. The men with you . . ." Simon shook his head. "They will be dazzled. She doesn't always look like the monster she really is. That is one of her powers. Be on guard." He stared into my eyes for a moment, then quietly closed the door.

"Damn." I leaned against the door and pressed my hand against my heart, which was pounding pretty hard for an undead vampire. Had I lost my mind making a deal with Simon Destiny? Some of my friends would be shocked if they found out. Shocked? They'd haul me off to the vampire equivalent of a funny farm. Not a cool place. Think coffins in basements with keepers who carried stakes in holsters.

I heard a commotion at the door into the shop and ran to open it.

"There you are." Caryon pushed past me into the back room. "I'm getting the strangest vibe tonight. And no sense of where you were. We don't like to lose touch. Progress report."

I decided the less said about my plans the better. Good thing since Spyte was right behind him.

"I told you she had to be here." Spyte swatted at the air around his head. "What *is* that?" He shoved Cary into the room, slamming the door behind him.

"Hah! Now we can get to work! They've been trying to

steal souls in your shop, Glory. Propositioned some of your best customers." Harvey buzzed past Cary, dousing him with his special water, a heavy stream that was way more than his tiny bottle could logically have held. Heavenly magic, of course.

"Son of a—" Cary stared in horror at his gray suit, which now had steaming holes in it. "Ow! Shit! It's seeping through to my skin! What the hell *is* that?"

"Our secret weapon, lowlife loser. And there's more where that came from." Emmie threw the contents of her bottle in Spyte's face. "Take that, you sugary-smelling sack of horse manure. You've been tormenting her friends. No more of that, you hear me?"

"My eyes! You burned my eyes!" Spyte clapped his hands over them and screeched, bumping into the table and knocking over my chair.

"You tried to get souls here? That is beyond creepy." I moved my chair so it wouldn't be broken.

"They propositioned that sweet clerk of yours. Almost had her too. Had to throw three purses and a blouse to get him to stop." Emmie grabbed Spyte's hair and pulled him toward the door.

"Bastards!" I pressed myself against the wall and tried to stay out of the way. I loved that the demons were getting what they deserved. "Get them out of here, gang!"

"You got it, Glory. Out! Shoo!" Harvey somehow managed to toss the extra rolls of paper towels and toilet paper from my storage closet at Cary. More angel magic. "Leave our Glory and all her people alone!"

"Angels? You've got angels on your side now?" Cary dodged a can of air freshener. "Gag me. You must be disgustingly good." He picked at the hole in his suit and tears came to his eyes. "Premium Italian silk. Ruined."

"Better listen to him, Cary. He's going for the toilet bowl cleaner. Bet that just kills silk." I didn't bother to hide my smile as I threw open the back door. "This way's faster. Scram. Don't ever come in my shop again."

"Lead me out of here, Cary. I'm blind!" Spyte tripped over a roll of toilet paper and now trailed a streamer on one foot.

"We're going. But, listen to this, Glory. You think this is funny? Well, let's see if you're laughing when we haul your buddy Rafael's ass down to hell with us." Cary swatted Spyte's flailing hand away. "'Cause that's the way this is going to be if you don't pony up soon. Clock's ticking. Forty-eight hours and he's gone." He kicked paper towels out of his way. "Oh, not smiling now, are you?"

"Leave Rafe alone!" I got in front of Cary. Maybe I was crazy, but I knew Harvey and Emmie had my back.

"Not possible." Cary smirked. "You? You're off our radar now." He glared at Emmie, who'd landed on my shoulder again. "We wouldn't have you polluting hell on a bet. But that half-demon Rafe? He'll be toast, and I do mean toast, scorched and blackened, if we don't get damned important souls from you in two days' time." Cary screeched as Emmie sprayed him again with her water. Guess instant refills were part of the package.

"Cary! Please! I have to wash out my eyes!" Spyte managed to grab his hand and tugged at it.

"Shut up!" Cary dragged Spyte toward the back door. "You'll be sorry for this, Glory St. Clair."

"Bastard." I stepped out of the way, reached into the storage closet and grabbed the first thing I could find. I glanced at Harvey, who nodded, then just let it fly. A can of Drano hit Cary's back, burst open and sprayed him with white crystals. Caryon paused for a moment, his body trembling with rage.

Spyte whimpered. "What's that smell? I need air. Cary? Are we outside yet?"

"Shut. Up." The two demons vanished.

"We won. I think." Emmie Lou buzzed around, clucking at the paper rolls and the crystals littering the floor.

"Did we?" I picked up the chair and collapsed in it. Cary's taunts left me feeling sick. I leaned back and shut my eyes, not surprised when my stomach decided to growl and make a statement of its own. I put my hand over that damned new bulge and tried not to think about how I was going to trek down to the bowels of hell and face off with a three-headed monster. And, trust me, if Simon thought she was hideous, she was hurt-your-eyes ugly. Time for a miracle. But I had a feeling the two angels buzzing around overhead were all the miracle I was going to get.

Eighteen

Jerry and Rafe hated everything about my plan.

"We're supposed to kill a three-headed monster." Jerry had brought his broadsword, of course. He'd also carried in a sword for me, griping about it endlessly.

"Simon says we have to cut off her heads." I was getting dizzy watching him pace one way and Rafe another.

"Glory, Blade is right. This is insane. And we're sure not taking you with us. Let me call in one of my shifter friends." Rafe stopped and put his hands on my shoulders. "You're staying here."

"No, I'm not. I can go with you or I can follow you, but I'm going. Best way is that we go as a team. And I've got a secret weapon." I pulled a spray bottle out of a bag on the floor. "Penny got these for me. I have three of them. Ian made this formula. If we spray this in a vampire's or mortal's face, it will put him out for thirty minutes. Time enough to get down there and get the job done."

"More madness. You're trusting MacDonald's word that this works."

"No, she's not." Ray stepped into the room from the shop. "I tested it myself. On one of my bodyguards. Worked like a charm." He grinned. "Not that he didn't bitch about it after he woke up. And ask for some for himself." Ray slung his arm around me. "I'm going with you guys. I've got my own spray bottle and a machete. Can't hurt to have an extra pair of hands."

"Are you sure, Ray? How are you feeling?" I looked into his eyes. He looked good, clean and sober. But he could fake his way through a lot.

"I'm fine. And I'm going. I can be just as stubborn as you, Glory girl." He grinned. "And, Blade, quit looking at me like I'm useless. I did a few martial arts lessons. Got some moves I never showed you. Want a demo? This room's a little small, but we can take it out to the alley. The paparazzi would love a shot of that."

"Great. I should have figured they'd show up." I stuffed my spray bottle in my small backpack. We were shifting out there anyway. Now we'd have to go from the roof.

"No, I'm glad for more men." Blade shook his head. "Sorry, Gloriana. But I'm sure you realize men do have more upper-body strength. Not sure you have the power you need to take off a head."

"I admit I've never had to test myself." I wore all black: pants, boots, long-sleeve T-shirt. I'd even tied my hair up with a black scarf. The men were in black too. We were the vamp equivalent of a black ops team. Except without the training on my part. I was nervous, would have bitten off my fingernails if I had any left.

"Ian gave me something else for tonight." Ray patted his own backpack. "Explosives. He's been doing research. Kind of getting off on what we're doing." He gave me an apologetic look. "Sorry, but Penny's there and all over this. She knows what we're up to now. Not happy and worried sick. I promised we'd phone as soon as we were clear."

"We will." I hated that she had to know about this. My stomach rumbled. I had to live through tonight, if only to get back out to see Ian and have him fix the swelling, which still resembled bread dough. I tugged down my T-shirt.

"So why explosives? Won't taking her heads do it?" Rafe was antsy and eager to get started.

"Ian thinks closing the hole is a good idea. Just to be on the safe side. And I agree. Why not? You've seen the place. Glory says they even took energy withdrawals from you there. Wouldn't you like to see that gold dome go sky-high?"

"Simon won't like that." I knew he'd be furious.

"I don't give a damn what Simon likes or doesn't like." Jerry pulled me to his side. "I think it's an excellent idea. A reminder to Destiny that we didn't do this for him. But for Glory and Valdez here."

"Yeah. Thanks, all of you." Rafe looked like he wanted to say more but couldn't figure out what.

"Let's go. I want this over with." I led the way out of the shop, wishing we didn't have to go through the gauntlet of photographers. Ray stopped and said something about a music video to explain our costumes before we ran inside the apartment part of the building and up the stairs to the roof.

"Good explanation." I smiled at him as we strapped on everything we needed before we shifted.

"Seemed as good an excuse as any for the ninja look." Ray squeezed my hand. "Last chance, Glory. Stay here. Let us deal with this."

"Not happening." I swallowed my fear, then shifted. We were large black birds because of our equipment, flying off toward the EV compound. We soared into the night, four dark shapes headed into the hills where the isolated headquarters were. In about thirty minutes we saw that gold dome through the trees and were careful to land a few yards outside the cleared area, where we could see a pair of guards patrolling.

Jerry and Rafe pulled out spray bottles and sneaked up to take care of those two, then gestured for Ray and me to come closer. We eased inside the buildings, one at a time, surprising EVs watching TV or reading and even enjoying their famous sunlight room. That one made Ray sigh.

"Man, I wish this was available."

"Maybe it will be once this goddess is history. Simon will owe you." I patted his shoulder.

"Good point. I'll be sure to remind him." Ray tucked his spray bottle in his belt.

"I think there's a mortal here." I nodded toward a bungalow near the back of the compound.

"Yeah, and I hear noises that mean she's having sex with one of our EVs." Ray grinned.

"Great." I made a face. "You take him. I'll take her." We approached the door, stopping to glance inside the window that was open to the cool spring night air.

"Ooo, baby, yes, do that again."

I recognized the vampire. Greg was a jerk who'd once been my boyfriend, pre–EV days. It would be a pleasure to spray him. Too bad I'd given Ray the honors. The woman on her knees in front of him had blond hair that he held in his fist. I don't think she had much choice in the "do that again" thing.

I threw open the door and grabbed the girl, spraying her as she hit the floor. Ray knocked Greg down, but his spray missed.

"Glory, what the hell?" Greg struggled with Ray. "Why'd you Windex my lady?"

"Windex?" I laughed, then aimed my spray at him. I was happy when it put him out. "Let's go, Ray."

We ran outside, meeting Jerry and Rafe in front of the dome.

"We've got them all. Ready?" Rafe pulled out his own machete. Guess he and Ray had the same taste in weapons.

"No, but let's do it. We've got less than thirty minutes of quiet time." I took the sword Jerry reluctantly handed me.

"Gloriana, please let us do this. Stay behind us and only come forward if it looks like one of us is in trouble."

Now I may be all for women's lib, but I know when to be smart. "Fine. I'll be your backup. But, all of you, don't take chances. If she's too much for us to handle, just take off and we'll throw the explosives down the cavern and hope that's enough."

"You said that Simon—" Rafe was very serious as he led the way inside the dome.

"I know. Got to take her heads. We intend to. I'm just saying we can't sacrifice our lives at this point, Rafe. Then where would we be?"

"I get it." Rafe turned and stared at each of us in turn. "Comes to that. I can take my medicine. I mean it. Run like hell. I can stay down here and face whatever. Glory, I don't deserve this." He pulled me to him for a quick kiss. "Sorry, Blade. Had to do that. Now let's go."

Jerry just pushed me behind him and followed Rafe down the path cut into the rocky hole that had obviously been drilled into the floor of the building. I swear I could hear the screams of damned souls as we stumbled down the crudely hewn steps. Rocks broke away and I held on to Ray, who'd managed to get in front of me until I was last in line.

We didn't speak, afraid we'd wake the sleeping goddess. Not that she was quiet. That horrible groaning, sucking sound that I'd heard before when I'd been out at the compound echoed off the walls of the cavern, which got wider the deeper we climbed. It also got hotter. It had been warm near the surface with a breeze that soon turned into a windstorm that tore at our clothes and made sweat pop out on my forehead. I wished I could tear off my scarf and wipe it away, but I was too busy hurrying to keep up with the long strides of the men.

Suddenly Ray stopped and I bumped into his damp back. I realized he must have left his pack at the top of the hole just as I had.

"What?" I whispered but it carried in the chamber, as loud as a shout.

"The wind stopped and look at that glow. I think we're here." Ray turned and I saw fear in his eyes. "Stay. Don't freakin' move."

There was a red glow that made it difficult but not impossible to see, and it was coming from a huge cavern that had opened at the bottom of the steps. We crept across the floor toward a golden platform with a wide set of stairs leading up to it. Jerry stopped at the bottom and glanced back at us. He used hand signals to get the men to spread out, shoulder to shoulder. Ray kept me behind him.

We were on the third step when a sigh and movement on the top of the platform froze us in place.

"Ah, what have we here? Dinner?" Suddenly a beautiful woman stood at the top of the steps, her body wrapped in a sheer golden robe. And what a body. It was perfection. She tossed a mass of flame red hair back over her shoulders and put one sandaled foot on the step as if to come toward us.

"Where's Simon? I am starving." She held out a hand covered in glittering jewels. "I think you are here with bad intentions. Naughty boys." She smiled and there was the glimpse of evil I'd braced myself for. "Mmm. I do so love a vampire threesome." She wrinkled her perfect nose. "I'll have the shifter for dessert." She waved her hand and I realized she'd frozen Jerry, Rafe and Ray in place. Simon's trick. She yawned, though, as if the effort took a lot out of her. So we *had* depleted her energy.

"No! Please." I heard my plea echo around the huge chamber.

"So *you* are the infamous Gloriana St. Clair. The one Lucifer has been so interested in." She laughed and my body trembled and quaked. It was all I could do to stay on my feet. "Oh, yes, hell is all abuzz about his latest intrigue."

"I am no one. Nothing." I moved around my men, touching Jerry. His eyes were the only things he could move.

"So I thought." She looked me over. "But Lucifer doesn't waste time on nothing, does he? It makes me wonder." She moved closer and raked my face with a golden nail, lifting it to her nose to sniff the blood she'd drawn. "Hmm. Interesting. I'd never have suspected." She staggered back toward her platform.

"What? What is special about me? I'm just an ordinary woman from London, turned vampire." I swung my sword at her head. "Here to kill you." It moved through air, hitting nothing.

Suddenly the beautiful woman was gone and there was only a moving mass against the far wall. Groans filled the chamber and I felt a pull, like I was being drawn toward that wiggling, writhing creature.

"Never ordinary, Gloriana. But it is not my job to answer that question. Kill me? How amusing." Suddenly the three-headed monster Simon had described reared her hideous heads and hissed.

I backed away, bumping into Jerry, who was suddenly no longer paralyzed; none of the men were. Had she decided to play with us? Enjoy the sport of taking them down one at a time?

Jerry shoved me behind him, then moved right, Rafe left, exchanging hand signals. Ray took the center. All of them were straining as the thing must be sucking at them too. Suddenly Ray went down to his knees, skidding toward the awful blob that rose up and had not one but three faces. One of them smiled and opened a mouth large enough to take Ray in whole.

"No!" I ran forward and slashed at it with my sword, drawing blood as I braced myself between Ray and the beast. Jerry and Rafe were by my side and held on to me when we were sprayed with a sickening sludge that stank of hell and worse.

"Duck, Glory." Jerry used his broadsword and the head that had pulled at Ray dropped to the rock floor.

"One down. We stay together. Go right." Rafe held on to me. Ray was on his feet now and the four of us linked arms to resist that insistent sucking determined to drag us in. Jerry's broadsword proved to be the only thing sharp and strong enough to take a head. The monster shuddered and screamed its outrage, slashing at us with teeth the size of my arm. We all fell back, but Jerry managed to get his sword under its neck and struck the killing blow again. Head two was on the floor.

"Now left." Jerry gripped the sword in both hands and I kept my arms around his waist as we slid toward the left and that last horrific head. This one seemed to gain strength as it did the work of its fallen sisters. It grew in size, doubling before our eyes. Its teeth were even bigger now; my legs weren't so long. And slits for eyes gleamed with the fires of hell itself. We couldn't even pretend to breathe in the fumes from the blood and haze of the miasma that had come out of the awful creature. *Goddess.* What a flattering word for such an abomination.

"Take her now, Blade." Rafe suddenly let go of our human chain and danced close to her as if to offer himself like a tasty treat. "Honoria! Like what you see?"

"Rafe, no!" I screamed and tried to get to him. "Don't let him do this!"

"Right!" Jerry ordered, then slashed with the sword as the thing took the bait, making a swipe at Rafe and getting a bite of his arm.

Rafe jerked loose and fell to the right, the head barely missing him as it fell to the floor with a noisy plop. Suddenly it was quiet in the cavern except for the sound of Rafe's labored breathing and my own moan at the sight of Rafe's bloody arm.

"Rafe!" I jerked free of Ray's grasp and slipped my way over to check on him.

"I'm okay, let's get the hell out of here. I think she's dead, but there are Energy Vampires up above scheduled to wake up and they won't be happy once they realize their powers just took a nosedive."

"No kidding." I helped him to his feet and turned to Jerry. "You were amazing." I looked at Ray. "All of you. Now let's get going. I may never feel clean again."

"Yeah, this was a hell of a job." Ray wiped his hand on his jeans.

"Ha. Ha." Rafe pulled off his shirt and wrapped it around

his bleeding arm. "I mean it, let's hurry. And I do want to blow this place up. We can throw those explosives down the hole. Just to be on the safe side."

"Right you are." Jerry helped me get up the stairs, which seemed way steeper going up than they had coming down.

When we got to the top, Ray pulled out his package of explosives and a timer. "Ian said this has a ten-second delay. So I'm setting it now. Ready?" He looked around and we all nodded. "Go!"

We all ran outside, relieved that apparently we'd beat the clock as far as the EVs waking up, and shifted out of there. When we got safely into the woods, we landed under a tree and waited until we heard the explosion. The dome collapsed but the outbuildings were unharmed.

"Excellent planning. I guess Ian didn't want to blow up the entire countryside." I glanced at Jerry.

"It was wise of him. This way Destiny will still have his headquarters if he chooses to use them and there wasn't enough of a disturbance to alert authorities." Jerry nodded at Ray.

"I'm telling you, Blade. Ian's all right. He's going to be here awhile, so get used to him." Ray frowned down at his filthy clothes. "I'm going straight home to burn these. You okay now, Glory?"

"Yes, fine. Thanks, Ray." I kissed his cheek. "You were a champ down there."

"Not so much, but I didn't wimp out, did I?" He grinned and nodded to Jerry. "I'd say you kicked some goddess ass, Blade. Good job." He and Jerry bumped fists. Guess Ray had taught him that. "Valdez, hope this is the last of the rescues, my man. My heart can't take much more of this."

"You got it. My demon side is staying down from now on." Rafe gave me an apologetic look. "I'll never forgive myself for putting Glory in harm's way like this."

"There you go. See ya, Glory." Ray shifted back into bird form and took off.

"Great idea. I'm going home to my own bath. We'll talk

later." Rafe saluted me and put his hand out to Jerry. It was the one on his injured arm, but he didn't even wince. "Wouldn't blame you if you refused to take it, but you were quite a sight down there tonight, Blade. I owe you everything."

"I'll shake your hand. Got to start being civilized. Gloriana is right about that. And you acquitted yourself well. Let's not do this again, shall we?" He shook hands with Rafe, then put his arm around me.

"No problem. Good night." Rafe shifted and was gone.

"Well I have to agree with both of them. You were amazing, Jerry." I kept my arm around his waist. "I have never seen you in battle before. It was quite a turn-on."

"Oh?" Jerry grinned. "Shall we go to my house and try out my Jacuzzi tub, then you can show me how turned on you are?"

"Sounds like a plan to me." I kissed his lips. One more thing to do and I was free of all my demons. I felt like celebrating.

"CiCi's having a birthday party for Freddy later. First, Simon will meet us at the club and get his deal with the demons set up." I paced the back room. It was deadline night.

"I hope this is the last of your work with stuff from hell." Penny sat on the table. She was supposed to report to Ian in a few minutes. They were scouting lab sites tonight.

"So do I. Have you thought any more about what to do about Jenny?" I was still haunted by what Honoria had said about my blood. Of course I was ordinary Glory St. Clair. That had been typical goddess stuff, messing with my head. A distraction. I had to forget about it or it would drive me crazy.

"Yes, I'm not telling her now. Maybe after she graduates from school." Penny sighed. "She's got a full plate. Studying for finals. Boyfriend trouble. And now she's going home for the summer to work with Mom. Cheerleading camp."

"I'm proud of you." I put my arm around her. "That's a

mature decision. Let her enjoy college life. You can keep doing what you've been doing. Meet her after dark, get to understand your new life. Help her if you want to. Guess the mind reading has given you a new perspective on your relationship."

"No kidding. I never realized what my 'gifts,' if you want to call them that, did to her." Penny made a face. "I was always jealous of Jen's popularity, the way she fit in everywhere. I had no idea she hated the way I got my parents' attention with my scholarships and school successes."

"You each have gifts. Now you are extra special, working for Ian." I rubbed my tummy, which still looked a little lumpy. "Any progress on my blood analysis? Figuring out why I'm the lucky one in a million who has a freaky reaction to the genius's drugs?" And could this be related to whatever the goddess had smelled or pretended to smell in my blood?

"Ian's onto something but won't tell me about it. I think he's waiting until he gets back a certain test result." Penny leaned against me. "Obviously you're the one who's special. You got me this gig and it's given me a new purpose. Introduced me to Trey too. We're really getting along."

I knew that. She was on the phone to the shifter or making plans to meet him every time I turned around.

"Good. Now I've got to go. Jerry's meeting me at the club for this last deal and the party." I jumped off the table and picked up a wrapped package. "Once this demon stuff is over, I'll make sure you get introduced to my friend CiCi, her son and his partner. Are you going to be at N-V later?"

"After Ian and I are through. Maybe I'll see you there." Penny hopped off the table too and gave me a hug. "Seriously, thanks for taking me in. I owe you for your patience. I realize I didn't make it easy. And I'll be so glad when you're free of the demon thing. I've been praying for you."

"Good. I appreciate it." I hugged her back. "And you've been coming along faster than most fledglings would have. Meeting Ian here?"

"Yep. I'll hang around and pick out a few things." She laughed. "I know. No horizontal stripes."

"Excellent. You really do learn fast." I walked with her through the shop, then fought the paparazzi horde as I headed down the sidewalk to N-V. I'd agreed to meet the crew there rather than be bombarded with questions from the photographers about Jerry or Ray.

Rafe's club was jumping as usual. Trey met me at the door and pointed me toward the bar. Rafe waved and downed a glass of Jack Daniel's.

"I'll be glad when this night is over." He lifted his glass in a mock toast, then drained it.

"Man, way to shove it in my face." Ray came up behind me and signaled the bartender. "Give me some of your vamp special, without the alcohol." He smiled at me. "I'm staying on the wagon."

I turned and smiled back at him. "Love to hear it's still holding. What are you doing here?"

"Got to see this all the way through. Am I right?" He glanced at Jerry, who'd come up on my other side. In true Ray-style, Ray slung an arm around me and drew me close. "You want something stronger?"

"Why not?" Jerry smiled grimly. "Glory?"

"As you say, why not?" I was proud of Jerry for not doing his usual jealousy thing, trying to wedge himself between Ray and me. Not even a growl. I kept things cool myself, easing away from Ray. But I had to go to Rafe and check in with him.

"How are you doing?" I bumped him with my shoulder.

"I'm still wondering if this will all go down like it's supposed to. You can't trust a demon to keep his word. Or Simon. Bet the fact that we demoed his golden dome didn't sit well." He gazed around the crowded club. "Man, just when things were going great. Isn't that always the way?"

"Think positive. We did what we set out to do." I dredged up a smile.

"Yes, we did. Let's go." Rafe took a fresh drink that I hadn't even seen him signal for and tossed it back. He pushed away from the bar. "Clock's ticking." He nodded toward

Jerry and Ray. "Maybe I should do this alone. In case things go bad."

"No, no way!" I grabbed his arm and looked back at Jerry and Ray.

"We're coming. I didn't dirty my broadsword to sit out the finale." Jerry grabbed his drink and mine, Ray right behind him as we headed for the stairs.

The music was loud and a recent hit. It was about having it all. Yes, that's what I dreamed of—having everything, these three men who were so important to me, my friends and security with my business. Why couldn't I ever get it all together? Rafe was right. The timing here sucked.

We got to the deserted balcony, which Rafe had had roped off with a Closed sign at the bottom of the stairs and looked around. It didn't take long for the telltale sweet smell to fill the area.

"Ah, what have we here? The gag-me gang and the demon child." Caryon materialized next to a round table, Spyte right beside him. They were both dressed in their disco best, as if they'd been back in the seventies. Cary had on the full bell-bottomed pants and matching vest in white with a red and gold print shirt with full sleeves. He could have been Travolta in *Saturday Night Fever*. Spyte had done a white suit with an open-collared red shirt.

"Look at you two. Did you forget to check a calendar?" I couldn't help taunting them. I hated them so much I wanted to spit, then kick them with my pointed-toe shoes if it wouldn't have damaged the leather.

"It's a dance club. We got into the spirit. And this is an homage to you, Glory. You do love the vintage look." Cary grinned at me with fangs showing.

"Spyte? Not saying much. How are your eyes?" I felt Jerry's hand squeeze my shoulder. I'd told him about the confrontation in the back room. Guess he thought I was pressing my luck now.

"I can see, no thanks to your chubby cherubs." Spyte cackled. "Oh, I love that. Chubby like your chunky self, eh,

Glory? Now you'll never be a size six. We've got orders from Lucifer himself. You are on our no-fly list."

"Good to know." I smiled. "Now why don't you two give up and go home. I'm sure there's a torture chamber down there calling your names."

"Gladly. Come here, Rafael." Cary crooked his black claw. "Unless you have a surprise for us, Glory?"

"You can't have him." Jerry stepped in front of Rafe.

"Right. You have to go through us." Ray was suddenly shoulder to shoulder with Jerry.

"Give it up, guys." Rafe put his hands on their shoulders. "You can't fight this."

"How do you know? Have you tried?" Jerry glared at Caryon. "Concentrate. All of you. I've had centuries to build my power of mind control. I think I can make these assholes change their minds."

I gasped. To try to manipulate the minds of demons? Was it possible? I focused on Spyte. He and Cary looked bemused, like maybe this was something new to them.

"Rafe, you too. Focus on them and make them think they are going to head home empty-handed." Jerry was in his element, commanding the troops. I didn't mind. I just prayed it worked. But then I looked around. Ray was stone. And those were the last words Jerry uttered. Because he was now a statue too.

"No! Please, can't I do something to make you stop this?" I pressed my back against Rafe, trying to stop him as he walked around Jerry and toward the demons, a zombie and not his usual warm and caring self.

"Sure, there is, Glory. Deliver those souls you promised. Then we'll leave Rafael alone. Forever. Done deal." Spyte shed his disco garb for his clown suit. "Either way, we're taking someone or a signed contract home with us. Time is up."

"I'll do it."

I turned toward the top of the stairs. "Simon?" Leave it to the EV king to wait until I felt like I was on the ropes to make his grand entrance.

"My heart's desire. Gloriana assured me that you could deliver." Simon walked around my statue men and Rafe stopped, now a statue himself.

"Yes, of course. You must be Simon Destiny, king of the Energy Vampires." Caryon grinned. "So deliciously evil. I can smell it from here. Delighted to meet you." Cary waved a hand and a document and red pen appeared. "Let's talk business. I heard Honoria met with a little, um, accident." Cary looked at me. "Unfortunate. It left so many souls adrift."

"Yes, it did. Souls I now have under my control." Simon smiled. "I believe you might be interested?"

"We might. Well, Lucifer might. What do you want, Destiny?" Caryon got right down to details. I could see him quivering with excitement. This was a major coup.

"First, I need clarification." Simon glanced at me. "As I told Gloriana, I want to make sure Honoria is actually gone. I saw some"—he cleared his throat and glared at me and my guys—"wreckage. But I want to be sure she can't be resurrected. The creature was immortal. She would punish me for deserting her."

"Ah, you want protection." Cary nodded. "Consider it done. As far as we know, she's deader than Glory's chances of ever being a size six. But if she does happen to find a second wind . . ." Cary shuddered. "Well, Lucifer is actually a level above that three-headed thing. He can command her to leave you alone. But you will still be stripped of your special powers as an Energy Vampire. Can you live with that?"

Simon took a breath. "As long as you deliver on the promise that I will receive my heart's desire as well. I believe you can see into my soul. I don't want to spell it out here in front of *these* people." He said that as if Jerry and the other men were inferiors he didn't care to recognize. Simon was nothing if not arrogant.

"Oh, yes. Yes indeed. We can take care of everything. In ways you can't imagine." Spyte capered about the balcony, knocking over chairs and ruffling Rafe's hair. "Who would have thought a man such as yourself would have . . ." He caught a hard look from Cary. "Never mind. Your secret's safe with us." He crossed his heart. "We always deliver. Quickly too. Just wait and see."

"I want it in writing." Simon blinked and I wondered if those had been tears in his eyes. No way.

"Of course." Cary waved his hand. "Now, it's all there. Look it over before you sign. I even threw in a power or two for you, to sweeten the deal. Lucifer takes care of his own." He handed Simon the paper and pen, then turned to me with a fangy grin. "Well, Gloriana, seems you've been a busy girl after all. Well done."

"My cherubs, as Spyte called them, arranged some alone time for me and I used it to talk to Simon and plan." I saw him reading through the document carefully. "I never had a doubt. When Simon signs this, Rafe's off the hook. Right?" I felt my stomach twist. Did this mean Simon planned to get back with my friend CiCi? And intended to act like a real father to Freddy? I hated the idea. But this Rafe situation was urgent. Besides, CiCi and Freddy were intelligent people, capable of making their own judgments about Simon. Just because Simon wanted them, didn't mean they had to accept him into their lives.

"That was the deal. He signs, Rafael's fine. Ooh, a rhyme. Almost. And just under the wire too." Spyte did a cartwheel while Cary kept a close eye on Simon, a little more restrained in his excitement.

"It's fine." Simon signed it with a flourish. "Now how soon . . . ?"

"Simon?" CiCi appeared at the top of the stairs. "What did you just do?"

"My dear." Simon turned and walked toward her. "I gave up the Energy Vampires."

"Why? I thought that was your dream." CiCi took his hands and I glanced back at Cary. Oops. He was gone, along with Spyte.

"Dreams can change. And there was no way that I could

drag my son into that whole scene and not hate myself."
Simon glanced at me. "Gloriana helped me see that it wasn't
the best thing for Frederick."

"Wow. I, just wow." I jumped when a hand slid around
my waist. Jerry, finally able to move. Rafe and Ray were
mobile too. "CiCi, you weren't supposed to come yet. The
demons . . ."

"Why, it's almost time for the birthday party. The caterer
will be here soon. And then something told me I had to
come now. That you needed me. Or someone did anyway. No
matter how scared I was of those . . . things." CiCi couldn't
seem to look away from Simon. "I just got in the car and
drove as fast as I could. Ran a red light, I think." She shook
her head. "I don't see any demons here."

"No, they're gone. For good, we hope." I wanted to jerk
her hands from Simon's but I could see that wouldn't go over
well. This was hell pulling the strings now, part of making
Simon's dream come true. I could only hope he wouldn't
hurt her to make it happen.

Rafe shook his head. "Simon? You just signed over your
soul to Lucifer?"

Simon shrugged. "No big deal. I've been on the fast
track to hell for centuries. And this arrangement frees me to
pursue"—he met CiCi's gaze—"other interests."

"So Rafe is seriously off the hook? Not going to be sucked
down under?" Ray smiled at CiCi, who is very attractive and
doesn't look a day over thirty.

"No, Rafe's fine. We made it in time." I sagged with relief.
Ray moved closer to CiCi. "Israel Caine. Have we met?"

"No, I don't believe we have. Though I saw you at Florence's wedding and heard you sing. It was wonderful and I
know Gloriana arranged it." CiCi finally stepped away from
Simon. "Cecilia von Repsdorf. My friends call me CiCi."

"Thanks, CiCi. It's a pleasure to meet you." Ray shook
hands with her, then looked at me. "Now, sorry, but I'm more
than ready to split. This has been one freaky night. Are we
done here? Are you in the clear too, Glory?"

"Guess so." I made myself approach Simon. "What are your plans, Simon?"

"No reason not to keep my crew together. They need a leader now that our powers are diminished. And we have our product line to sell. I still have all the formulas." He shook his head as CiCi moved to the stairs to direct a man carrying in a birthday cake. "I know the goddess is gone, but I had to cover my back with that clause about reprisals. You have no idea how tricky those bitches can be."

"I imagine. You'll need another name for the group now. And to convince Freddy that you're not in charge of the evil empire anymore."

"Yes, there is that." Simon kept his eyes on CiCi, who was talking to Ray again. "I definitely plan to stay in town and get to know my son better."

"Right. Bond with him." I kept my face neutral though I still didn't like the idea of Simon anywhere near Freddy or CiCi. "They're my friends, Simon. I hope you'll be careful. I don't want to see either Freddy or CiCi hurt."

"Everything will work out for us. No one will get hurt." Simon smiled as CiCi drifted over to his side again. "I have a guarantee that things will work in my favor."

"And you trust the word of those demons?" Jerry stood close beside me.

"Why not?" Simon patted his breast pocket in the dark suit he wore where he'd stashed his copy of the agreement. "I'm very well acquainted with how hell works. This deal will stand. Otherwise . . ." He glanced at Rafe. "Well, let's just say there's honor among thieves and leave it at that."

"Yeah, let's leave it. All of it. I swear, if I didn't know I was sober, I'd think I'd been hallucinating this whole freakin' week." Ray gave me a crooked smile. "Glory, I've suddenly got a song in my head dying to get out. Mind if I take off?"

I kissed his cheek. "Not at all. Thanks for coming. Your support meant everything to me."

"Babe, you know I'll always be there for you. And any way you want me." He slid his hand down my back to pat my backside. "Just had to do that. Love to see Blade's eyes throw one of his mental knives."

"Always the bad boy." I pulled him down for a kiss on the lips. "And don't I love that."

"Yes, you do." He grinned and headed down the stairs.

"Freddy and Derek should be here soon. And our other guests." CiCi smiled. "I'm so glad Simon has come to his senses at last. Now maybe Frederick can have a father to be proud of."

"Uh, CiCi, Simon just made a deal with the Devil. Please be careful." I felt Simon's stare on me, but ignored him.

CiCi waved an elegant hand. "Of course, *cheri*. I have to admit, though, the worst of his evil was with those terrible Energy Vampires. To have given them up . . ." She gave him a serious look. "And for his son. Well, that is something for me to think about."

"I appreciate your openmindedness, my dear." Simon pulled her hand to his lips and she let him. "I would never cause harm to come to you or our son."

"We will see. This time I am not so young and naïve." CiCi eased her hand from his grasp. "We will move slowly."

"Keep your eyes open, CiCi." Jerry gave Simon a hard stare.

"Deal be damned. You aren't suddenly a saint, Destiny. I'll be watching you. So will Glory." Rafe took a step toward Simon.

"Go ahead. All you'll see is a man working to reunite his family, nothing more. Shall we go get a drink at the bar while we wait for our son?" Simon escorted CiCi with a solicitous hand at her elbow down the stairs.

"I feel like I just threw a good friend to a wolf. No, to a hellhound." I sat at a table and picked up my neglected drink.

"No kidding. And he'll do whatever it takes to get what he wants." Rafe glanced over the railing. "Oops, got something going downstairs that needs my attention." He turned to me. "Thanks, you two. Damn that sounds inadequate. Guess I'm officially off the hook."

"For now. I'm serious about that twelve-step program, Rafe. Get the anger under control. You can't afford to draw attention like that from hell again." I sighed as I sipped my drink. Jerry sat across from me and gulped his own synthetic.

"I get it. I'm serious. I need more self-control. No more outbursts. E-mail me some meeting places." He leaned down and kissed my cheek. "I'll send a guy over to fix your Sheetrock. Sorry about the hole in your wall."

"Yes, well. I understood." I rubbed his cheek with my thumb. "You care. I get that. And I love you for it. Now take care of business." I realized the band was taking a break. "Sounds like you need to get the DJ going."

"You're right." He turned and extended his hand to Jerry. "That was a stand-up thing you did for me. Putting yourself between me and the demons. Might have ended really badly. Thanks."

Jerry shook his hand. "Did it for Glory. She seems to love you, though I don't have a clue why. Guess she's drawn to all types. Me, you, Caine."

"Yes, I am." I smiled, really liking that bit of wisdom from my guy. "Now hold that pose while I take a picture with my phone. This may be a once-in-a-lifetime opportunity. I wish I'd done it when Ray was still here. All three of you together. That would look great on my wall."

Jerry and Rafe immediately pulled apart, both of them horrified, and Rafe shook his head. "No frickin' way. Evidence like that could get me drummed out of the shifter community."

I just laughed as Rafe ran down the stairs. Then I turned to Jerry. "Well, he said it, but I have to agree. That was one extraordinary thing you did tonight. Putting yourself in danger for him."

Jerry reached across the table and took my hand. "No, I put myself in danger for *you*. Always will. Now, drink up. I'm going to dance with you, then take you back to your empty apartment and take advantage of this gratitude you're glowing with."

"Sounds like a plan, Jer. Sounds like a plan." We danced until Flo and Richard arrived and let them know that the demons were gone and there would be no more problems from that quarter. I was relieved to see that Flo had never held a grudge, though it was tougher for Richard to forgive my part in drawing the demons to his "beloved." We were all good by the time Damian showed up. He was glad to report that the council had forgiven me too. Penny's progress had been duly noted and her job with Ian seen as an excellent move. I was given credit for all of it. Who knew that Ian MacDonald was acquainted with most of the movers and shakers of the vampire community in Austin? And he'd vouched for me. Jerry wasn't happy that Ian's word had held more sway than his in making the council forgive me.

Hours later, with dawn a few minutes away, I lay in Jerry's arms, drowsy and, for once, feeling like everything was right in my world. I eased out of bed, determined to brush my teeth so I wouldn't wake up with dragon breath. We'd left the bathroom light on and I squeezed toothpaste on my toothbrush before I remembered to look up.

I still had my reflection. Why? Why would the demons leave me with such a gift when I knew they despised me? Then I saw something shift in the mirror behind me and whirled, my heart dropping to my toes.

"Lucifer!" I backed against the sink, my toothbrush a sad excuse for a weapon. I smelled lavender and breathed through the urge to gag.

"Relax, Gloriana. You asked why the reflection?" He smiled, his perfect teeth gleaming in the light. How could something so evil be so beautiful?

"Yes, why?" I felt the cold porcelain sink against my thighs and wished I wore more than my black silk teddy.

Lucifer's bright eyes gleamed but he didn't come closer. "I want you to remember, Gloriana, every time you see yourself, what you could have had if you'd just been a little more, um, cooperative." He flicked his gaze over me, stripping me no doubt. "Yes, those thighs could be trim, that waist tiny. But you won't see a size six now, will you?"

I shook my head. "Go away! I will never be interested in anything you have to offer or anything from hell, period."

Lucifer's laugh sent chill bumps racing across my skin. "Really? We'll see. Oh, yes, we'll just see about that."

As soon as he vanished, I threw my toothbrush into the sink and ran back to the bedroom, where I slid in beside Jerry.

"Gloriana? You okay? You're shaking."

"Just cold. Hold me?"

"Always, my love. Always." He pulled me close, his arms around me, his legs entwined with mine.

I sighed and snuggled in, closing my eyes. A bad dream, surely that was all it had been. I was safe with the man I loved. A happy ending.

Read on for a special preview of
Gerry Bartlett's next novel

Real Vampires Hate Skinny Jeans

Available April 2012 from Berkley Books!

"*Knock. Knock.*"

"Who's there?" I said it without thinking, then realized there was someone inside my head, playing the old joke on me. I jumped up just as the dead bolts flipped and the door to my apartment crashed open.

"Your favorite nightmare, Glory St. Clair." Alesa, a demon who could look gorgeous when she wasn't showing her true nature leaned against the doorjamb, a grin on her face. Tonight, she wasn't bothering to hide a thing and I shuddered.

"You're not my favorite anything. Go back to hell where you belong." I frantically glanced around for a weapon. I was at a serious disadvantage with wet polish on my toenails and a deep conditioner on my hair under a towel turban.

"I wouldn't toss that polish remover if I were you. It won't hurt me and it'll do a real number on your hardwood floor." Alesa sauntered into the room, morphing into her human form, which was a huge relief. Not that it meant she'd *act* human, but at least I didn't have to stare at razor-sharp fangs or scaly snout and skin anymore. Total freak-out.

"What do you want?" I grabbed a nail file with a sharp pointy end. At least I could make her bleed. Oh, wait.

Demon blood, black and oily. Infectious. Not a good idea. I'd learned that the hard way.

"That's right, sugarplum. Don't want to get my blood in you again, do you?" She smiled, reminding me that she could read my thoughts without breaking a sweat. She was still sporting those evil teeth. "Last time I got inside you, we did some serious partying." She glanced down and patted her tummy. "Guess what? I got what I wanted out of it."

I gawked. Oh, no. It couldn't be. "Is that what I think it is? Say it isn't—"

"A baby bump?" Alesa came closer and I could smell her sickeningly sweet scent, the burnt-sugar candy smell of hell gone terribly wrong. "Oh, yes. When you and Rafe made it, Gloriana, you *made* it, if you get my drift."

"No, that's impossible. I'm a vampire. I can't have children. My equipment died when I died. When Jerry turned me." I sank down on the couch, my hand over my own stomach. It had been one of those unforeseen consequences I hadn't thought through at the time. I'd been young and so hopelessly in love with Jeremiah Campbell back in 1604 I hadn't cared what I'd lose as long as I could live forever with him. Only later, when the lust had burned off a little had I realized my hope for children had disappeared along with my mortality. Tears blurred the room.

"Aw, dry up, kiddo. This is great news. In a way, this baby is part yours, you know. You were my hostess with the mostess while I got Rafe to give me what I wanted. I told him when I arrived here in Austin that I wanted his baby." Alesa sank down on the couch next to me and I gagged at the smell this close. "And I got it." She looked at me critically. "Quit breathing, dumbass. Vamps don't have to inhale, you know. Geez, who has morning sickness here, anyway?"

"Sorry, I guess it was just . . ." I took a last shuddery breath. What was Rafe going to do? He hated Alesa and sure didn't want a child by her. A demon child. Sure, he had some demon blood, but he didn't want to perpetuate that. "I've got to call Rafe."

"Sure you do. Call the man and give him the good news." Alesa leaned back and rubbed her swollen stomach again. "Get him to bring in some food. I know better than to expect you to have anything here. Burgers, fries . . ." She glanced down. "Chocolate milk shakes for the little nipper."

I began doing some mental calculations. It had been a tense spring, but a peaceful summer since I'd rid myself of Alesa. That bump was significant. "How far along are you?"

"Do the math, Glory. Six months. And I'm planning to stay right here until the little demon pops out. Won't that be fun? We can be roomies." She looked around, spotting my current roommate's computer on the kitchen table. "You are living alone, aren't you?"

"No, I'm not. This won't work, Alesa. I have a fledgling vampire living here with me. And I really don't want her around you. She's already met two of your cohorts from hell. That was two too many." I grabbed my cell phone. I did need to call Rafe but I dreaded it. He was doing well with his new club. We'd settled into a nice friendship, though it was still a bit tense since I'd gone back to Jerry, my sire, my always lover. Oh, God, what would Jerry think of this situation? Nothing like reminding him that I'd slept with Rafe while Alesa possessed me.

I stopped with the phone in my hand and gave Alesa a narrow-eyed look. "Are you sure that's how you got pregnant? While you were inside me? That really doesn't make sense."

"Sense? What world are you living in, vampire?" Alesa put her feet on my beautiful black lacquered coffee table. Nobody put their feet on that, especially not while wearing high heels, even if they were this season's Prada.

I stalked over and lifted them off and pushed them over to my tired thrift-store sofa. I had a few pieces of nice, new furniture, courtesy of a fight Jerry and Rafe had had in my living room. They'd replaced the stuff they'd demolished and I was trying to keep the quality pieces in good shape. The sofa? I was saving up for a new one. Prada was actually an upgrade.

"Look. I'm not buying your story. I think you got yourself knocked up by someone else. Either after you left Austin or before you got here. Now head out. Take your tale to the real daddy. Or let Lucifer take care of you."

Her lips trembled and her eyes filled with tears. "Lucifer? Are you kidding me? He won't help. He's furious with me. Because I came back to hell pregnant. He didn't want me to ruin my figure. Doesn't want brats running around down there either. It's an adult playground, he says. Babies spoil the mood." She wiped her wet cheeks. "Bastard. He couldn't care less about *my* needs."

"Yes, well, he's the Devil, Alesa. What do you expect?" I almost felt sorry for her. Except she was such an evil person herself. What kind of mother would she be? And what kind of mother would want to bring up a child in hell anyway? I shuddered. "Who's the real father, Alesa?"

"I told you, it's Rafael. I'm thrilled. He'll be a wonderful father." She sighed and leaned back on throw pillows. "This is a miracle. A dream come true."

"No, it's not. But I'm calling him anyway. He can help me get the truth out of you." I hit speed dial for him. When he answered, I was suddenly speechless.

"Glory? What's up?" His voice was calm and I could hear music in the background. I glanced at the clock. It was still early and the club wouldn't be too busy yet.

"Can you come over, Rafe? I have sort of an emergency here." I turned my back on Alesa's grin. Oh, but she was loving this, that she'd get Rafe involved with her again and that I was the one putting them together.

"Food," she whispered.

"Sure. Can you give me a hint? What kind of emergency? Life and death? Or just one of your mini-crises. If it's one of those, call Blade." Rafe was all business. Which was the way he'd been treating me lately. It broke my heart.

"Work with me, please. This isn't a Blade problem. I need you. I have company. Someone only you can help me with. Could you stop and pick up a sack of burgers and fries on your way? Oh, and a chocolate shake?" I was getting mental messages for dessert but ignored them. The baby was probably already going to be born reeking of sugar. Who knew what pouring more inside it would do. Bad enough that it had Alesa for its mother.

"You sure you didn't take one of those drugs again? That lets you eat? You remember what happened last time."

"No, I learned my lesson." I put my hand on my tummy that could have passed for a minor baby bump itself. "Please hurry. This is someone you need to see."

"From the amount of food, sounds like you have more than one person there." The noise around Rafe stopped, so he must have stepped into his office. "You okay?"

"For now, but I'll feel better when you get here. See you soon?" I gripped the phone tightly, wishing we were back to our old easy friendship.

"On my way." He ended the call.

I turned to Alesa. "I swear." I cleared my throat. "I swear that if you hurt my friend I will make sure there aren't enough pieces of you left to go back to hell for Lucifer to fry. Are we clear?"

"Wow, Glory, get radical, why don't you?" Alesa widened her eyes. "And, remember, I'm going to be a mommy. Think of my baby."

"I am. The biggest favor I could do that child is to make sure he or she never sets eyes on you." I stomped into the kitchen and plucked a bottle of supercharged synthetic blood out of the refrigerator. I twisted off the top and took a gulp. It wasn't as good as fresh, but took the edge off. Then I hit speed dial and called my fledgling.

"Penny, are you working all night?" I'd seen her off to her job at a lab just an hour before Alesa had arrived.

"Supposed to. Though Ian's talking about letting me off early. Trey and I may hook up later."

"Great. Can you stay with him? I've got some company. An old, uh, friend." I hated calling Alesa that, but didn't want Penny to worry. My fledgling had a relationship with

Trey, the shifter who worked for Rafe at his club, and had been spending a lot of time with him lately. I wasn't going to feel guilty now suggesting she stay with him for her death sleep. She'd done it before and was basically an adult. We'd recently celebrated her twentieth birthday.

"No problem. You sound funny. You sure you're okay?"

I sighed. Penny Patterson is a genius. No kidding. A prodigy with a doctorate and a bunch of other degrees at her young age. Of course she'd picked up on my stress.

"Not okay, but Rafe is on his way over to help me with this person who isn't actually much of a friend. We'll manage but thanks for asking. Just stick with Trey so I don't have to worry about you too, okay? I don't want you to meet this character. We have a bad history." So much for not worrying Penny. But I really didn't want her popping in, not even for a change of clothes. "Seriously, don't drop by. I mean it."

"Whatever you want, Glory." Penny sighed. "But I could help, you know. Don't underestimate me in a fight. Ian's been working with me. He's got some amazing weapons here."

"I just bet he does. Thanks, but not this time." I hung up. Penny worked for Ian MacDonald. The vampire was another genius and had probably come up with some stuff I could use against a demon. But a pregnant one? That had to give me pause.

"Glory, you know I can read your thoughts and hear your conversations, don't you?" Alesa stood in the doorway. "Come back to the living room and tell me what you've been up to lately. Who is this Penny?"

"Like I'd confide in you? Forget Penny. Sit on the sofa and wait for your food." I finished my synthetic and rinsed out the bottle for the recycle bin. Good thing I didn't need to inhale, because the sweet stench of hell would have put me off my drink completely. When I heard the knock on the door, I realized I still had a turban on my head and no makeup. Swell. The only upside of this is that Alesa's news was bound to take my looks completely off Rafe's radar.

At least my jeans were clean and hugged my butt and my T-shirt was a flattering red color.

I walked to the door, aware of Alesa's eyes following me. She had a smirk on her face that made me want to slap her. My stomach knotted as I threw the dead bolts.

"I could smell demon from the bottom of the stairs, Gloriana. What the hell is going on here?" Jeremy Blade, my lover and my maker strode into the room. He stopped at the foot of the couch and stared at Alesa, who stretched as if to show off her plump breasts in her low-cut violet sweater. He didn't seem to notice, busy pulling one of his knives out of his boot.

"Jerry, stop. You know you can't kill a demon with a knife." I put my hand on his arm. I wasn't sure what it took to kill a demon. Everything we'd tried had failed. They seemed indestructible. The most you could hope to do in a fight was to send them back to hell and it took a priest or other type of holy man and some other powerful stuff for that.

"Maybe not, but I could enjoy trying." Jerry wasn't about to put his knife away. "What's this bitch doing here?"

"Causing trouble, what else?" I pulled Jerry toward the kitchen. "Alesa, don't say a word. Please. Let me handle this." I gave her a look that she actually heeded. She just sat back with a smile and a wave.

"Handle what? Me?" Jerry looked down at my hand on his arm. "I thought we were finally done with demons."

"So did I." I sighed and leaned against him once I had him in the kitchen. Jerry and I had been through some really rough times. He'd managed to forgive me for betraying him with Rafe, who was part demon. I'd blamed my infidelity on Alesa being inside me. Demon tricks. Then other demons had come back and made more mischief in our lives. Through it all, Jerry had been there for me.

I held on to him. He'd positively hate this latest development, but he'd see this as nothing to do with us. That Rafe had a problem, end of story. So I knew I was going to have a fight on my hands if I wanted to help see Rafe through this. And I was determined to do just that.

"She's pregnant, Jer." I looked up when I said this. To gauge Jerry's reaction.

"The hell you say." He slid his knife back into his boot. "Why'd she show up here?"

"She claims it's Rafe's child. Made while she was inside me."

"That's a cock-and-bull story if I ever heard one." Jerry shook his head. "She wasn't corporeal. And you . . ." He hugged me. "Sorry, lass, but you've got to know you can't conceive a child."

"I know that. I said the same thing to her. But here she is, stomach swollen, claiming Lucifer kicked her out for being pregnant and saying it's Rafe's." I pushed back. "He's on his way."

"Let them hash this out, demon to demon." Jerry watched me with narrowed eyes.

"You know I can't do that." I sighed. Now it started. Jerry would never understand the depth of my attachment to Rafe, the man who had guarded me for five long years. He'd risked his life for me and shared secrets that I'd told no one else. I loved Rafe. Just as I loved Jerry. Well, maybe not just as. Jerry and I had a long and turbulent history, four hundred years' worth. Rafe and I were friends, briefly lovers and equals in a way Jer and I could never be.

"You *could* leave them to it, but you won't." Jerry turned his back on me. "I see no way for this to be resolved without you getting hurt. Demons play dirty, you know that. Alesa will make sure you have naught to do with Rafael if she wants him for her babe's father."

"You're right. Yet here she is. At my home, asking for my help." I bit my lip. Was I being set up? Alesa hated me. I'd humiliated her in her world, keeping her trapped in my body far longer than most hosts would have managed, according to the other demons I'd met. And Lucifer wasn't crazy about me either. Had he sent her here to get even with me? I'd managed to best him the last time we'd met. I knew he'd been pissed off about that. And when you pissed off the Devil . . .

"Tell her to leave. To take her brat and deal with Valdez elsewhere." Jerry grabbed my shoulders. "It's the only way you'll be safe."

We both turned at the knock on the door. I really needed to breathe. I'd missed the smell warning of Jerry's arrival and now Rafe had managed to sneak up on me.

"Well, he's here now. Let's see how this plays out." I touched Jerry's cheek. "No matter what, please don't pull out a knife. That will only make things worse."

"You've got a pregnant demon on your couch and another demon at your door. How could it get worse, Gloriana?" Jerry strode toward the door.

Good question. But it certainly could and did.